Rhiannon

Jarreth and Daemon
By Katie Ebensteiner

Rhiannon

Evangelynn Stratton

Writers Club Press
San Jose New York Lincoln Shanghai

Rhiannon

All Rights Reserved © 2001 by Evangelynn Stratton
http://knightimes.com

No part of this book may be reproduced or transmitted in any form or by any means, graphic, electronic, or mechanical, including photocopying, recording, taping, or by any information storage retrieval system, without the permission in writing from the publisher.

Writers Club Press
an imprint of iUniverse.com, Inc.

For information address:
iUniverse.com, Inc.
5220 S 16th, Ste. 200
Lincoln, NE 68512
www.iuniverse.com

Designed and edited by StormKatt Productions
PO Box 88799, Seattle WA 98138
http://stormkatt.com

Although the historical references are factually based, all character representations are fictional and any resemblance to any persons living or dead is strictly coincidental

ISBN: 0-595-19272-6

Printed in the United States of America

OTHER BOOKS BY EVANGELYNN STRATTON

𝔏𝔞𝔡𝔶 𝔎𝔫𝔦𝔤𝔥𝔱

The book that started it all! Can a lady warrior revenge her family and escape the romantic advances of Matthew Cameron?

𝔏𝔞𝔡𝔶 𝔖𝔢𝔢𝔯

The dramatic second book in the series. Luke Cameron and a girl with incredible powers must fight her only relative, who wants her dead.

𝔏𝔞𝔡𝔶 𝔅𝔩𝔲𝔢

The hilarious third and final book in the series. Paul Cameron plans to sail the seas to flee unrequited love. Then he meets Willow, and his life takes a different turn.

Available now at all Barnes and Noble bookstores, or online at barnesandnoble.com, amazon.com, or booksamillion.com. (Go to knightimes.com for more details)

Artwork by:
Brandye Guiler, front cover
Katie Ebensteiner, inside illustration
Dorsey Marx, back cover lion

Formatted by:
StormKatt Productions
http://stormkatt.com

For my daughter Felicity

Acknowledgments

I wish to thank:

The wonderful team effort that went into producing this book; My daughter Mélanie, for designing the front and back covers, Brandye Guiler for the fabulous cover art 'Lady in the Lake' drawing, My daughter Felicity, for allowing her face to be portrayed on the 'Lady in the Lake' drawing, Katie Ebensteiner, who supplied the fantastic artwork for the inside illustration, Dorsey Marx for the incredible back cover lion drawing, and the group at iUniverse, who offered both advice and support.

A LITTLE BACKGROUND HISTORY

Unlike my first trilogy, (Lady Knight, Lady Seer, Lady Blue) this book takes place DURING the War of the Roses. This war can be traced back to 1377, when Edward III died and left no direct heir to the throne of England. The king's eldest son had died a few years earlier. It was decided that the late king's grandson, Richard II, would inherit the crown. This enraged Henry, Duke of Lancaster, the late king's second son, who felt he was the rightful heir. He spent his life in pursuit of the kingdom, never reaching his goal, but leaving his son, Henry Bolingbroke, to carry on the quest for the crown.

The battle for the crown bounced back and forth between the two houses. Henry Bolingbroke seized the throne from Richard II and declared himself King Henry IV. His son, Henry the V, was the next king. He died suddenly in 1422, leaving his one-year-old son Prince Henry as heir. Ruled by advisors, he became a very unpopular king, and finally angered Richard, Duke of York. Richard was banished to Ireland because he was seen as a threat to the crown. It was then that the Wars of the Roses truly started, with Richard seeking the crown for himself. He never gained it. However, his son, Edward IV, took the kingdom from Henry in 1471.

Rhiannon

A few months after being crowned, Henry once more regained the throne. He held it for only a few months, whereupon Edward captured Henry and seized power for himself again.

All was quiet for eleven years, until 1483 when Edward IV died. He left his two young sons, Edward and Richard, in the care of their uncle, Richard of York. Both boys vanished, presumed killed in the tower of London by Richard, who then pronounced himself king.

This is when my story takes place. My Character Jarreth unwillingly becomes involved in a battle he had no intention of fighting.

"Death cannot stop true love…all it can do is delay it for a while."
The Princess Bride

Prologue

England, summer 1483

Earl Hilton Stanwyck of Suffolk lounged back in his chair as he gazed upon his nephew, Viscount Jarreth Stanwyck. The younger man sat sprawled, his long legs reaching far in front of him as he leaned to one side on one elbow, making no attempt to hide an apathetic expression to match the equally monotonous news.

"So, to whom have you betrothed me this time, Uncle?" he was saying. "Is she as exciting as the last one, with buckteeth and the girth to match my horse? Or the one before, that Alma somebody, who had already serviced half the knights in her household and tried to seduce me within minutes of meeting." He shuddered. "That one was scary. And let us not forget last year's fiasco. That woman had a voice so shrill, my ears are still ringing."

The Dark Count, as he was infamously known, looked at his despondent nephew as a sly smile formed. "This time is different. While in London, I met a man with a beautiful daughter who is as loathe to marry as you are. You should make a good couple."

"May I ask why she is so reluctant?"

"I never inquired as to the particulars, I only know her father was most anxious to make an arrangement."

Rhiannon

"An anxious father means a homely bride."

"I was assured most unequivocally that the girl is gorgeous, just a bit…*undisciplined*. I am sure you shall have no problem taming her."

"Wonderful…not only must I marry her, now I must tame her."

"Have you not always said you wanted a girl with spirit? Well, from what I understand from her father, she certainly will not disappoint you."

Jarreth sighed deeply. "Very well. When do I meet her?"

"You are to leave immediately. Of course, you have the last word on this. If you truly do not think a union is possible, you can refuse to sign the papers…*again*. But I remind you, Jarreth, as my only heir, I shall like to see you married and blessed with children before I die."

"You are not even close to dying, uncle."

"Well, I am not getting any younger. And, may I add, neither are you. Here are the directions. Bring back a bride this time, Jarreth."

The darkly handsome viscount sat up and took the parchment. "Does she know you are my uncle? That could make a difference; your reputation is not exactly sterling."

"The father knows of me, and is aware that my reputation is founded mostly on rumors. We had a good visit before the subject of marriage arose and we matched you two up. Now go! Your bride awaits."

Jarreth looked at the map, stood up and cast his uncle a sour look. "Yorkshire? She better be very special, uncle. This is a long ride for yet just another homely face."

Chapter One

Yorkshire, England

Rhiannon was in the garden attempting to prune a rosebush when she saw Kady running from the castle, waving her hands in the air and shrieking something inaudible. As she got closer the intonations began to form words. Rhiannon thankfully put down the pruning shears, since all she had accomplished so far was crippling the plant down to one long stalk and two spindly stems without buds. She concluded she had no talent for gardening. Kady finally arrived, her dark hair matted to her forehead in sweaty ringlets, and her rotund face red as she gasped for breath.

"The master…your father…he is back."

Rhiannon smiled widely. "I shall race you there!" She took off running, holding her skirts high as she sprinted down the garden path, leaving Kady far behind.

"Not fair," the weary servant yelled in protest. "I am already tired!"

Rhiannon

"Then I shall win handsomely!" Rhiannon grinned as she quickened her pace, knowing the older, plumper Kady would never be able to catch her now. Ignoring the bridge, she leaped over the small stream and ran up the gradual incline between pinkish-white blooming cherry trees that led to the castle. Busy servants bustled about nervously as she burst in the door, for the master had not been due home for another week. Rhiannon, of course, was not in the same predicament as the servants, and was delighted her father, Baron Cedric Harrison of Yorkshire, had come home early. She skipped down the corridor, and upon seeing her father took a running leap and threw herself into his arms.

The baron swung the laughing girl around a few times, then dropped her to her feet and gave her a large hug. He gazed lovingly at his beautiful only child, whose presence had lit up his lonely life since his beloved wife died when Rhiannon was just a baby.

"Here, let me look at you!"

She stood up straight at attention as he did a mock inspection of her, a little game they had played since her childhood.

"Hmmm…I do believe you have grown another inch during my absence."

She snickered in delight as her dancing blue eyes glistened with exuberance. She tossed her head, causing her long golden hair to spill over her shoulders and down her back.

"Really, father. I quit growing years ago!"

"Aye, that is true. I should have grandchildren by now."

Her face sobered; he had touched a sore subject with her. He had tried for years to marry her off to numerous rich and successful barons, lords, even an occasional count, but she was always able to discourage the arrangement. Now at the advancing age of seventeen, he feared his only child would die an old maid, which seemed fine with her.

"Speaking of which," he continued, "I met an interesting man on my trip."

Rhiannon drew herself up and held her breath. All the horrid, failed betrothals always began with *'I met an interesting man.'* She smiled lamely. "You did?"

"Aye, and this time I am not telling you anything. You shall not scare this one off like all the others."

Her face fell in disbelief. "Oh, father! You did not make another arrangement!"

"Aye, that I did, one you shall be happy with. He is on his way as we speak."

"What! You did not even consult me?"

"Rhiannon, you are not getting any younger. I guarantee this betrothal shall be successful. I have already signed the agreement. 'Tis contingent on his acceptance."

Tears welled in the center of her eyes as she took a backward step. "How could you?" Turning abruptly, she ran down the hall and up the stairs.

Her father watched her go with trepidation. Perhaps he should have consulted her, but an opportunity presented itself, and he couldn't pass it up. The young viscount needed a wife, and Rhiannon needed a husband. What could be more convenient? He hoped the Dark Count got a better reaction from his nephew than he just got from his daughter.

Up in her room, Rhiannon plopped face down on her bed and pounded it with her fists.

After pouting for a while, she sat up with her jaw set in determination. She was always able to chase off the dreadful men her father sent to marry her, why should this one be any different? But she needed help. She needed a spy.

Kady opened the door and peered in. "Milady? Are you all right?"

"Come in, Kady, and close the door. I need your help."

Kady rolled her green eyes in dismay. "Do not tell me he did it again?"

Rhiannon

"Aye, and this time he is divulging no information." Rhiannon's eyes flashed mischievously. "But that is not going to stop us."

"Us?"

"Kady, you are going to have to eavesdrop on my father until you hear something."

Kady's eyes widened until the whites showed all around. "Me? You want me to spy on the master?"

"Aye, you! Who else do I have?"

"But…"

"Kady, I am sure this one is just as bad as the rest. We must find out who he is so I can start planning."

"But, what if I hear nothing?"

"That is not an option. Talk to all the servants who serve my father. You are friendly with his knights…ask them. All of them. Somebody has to know *something*. Just find out who my betrothed is!"

Kady made a face, and then slowly smiled as she ran her fingers through her disheveled brown hair that had started the day in a graceful upsweep.

"All the knights? This might be fun…very well, I shall do it."

"Wonderful! Just do not let my father catch you."

"I will try." She sighed. "Why is this always happening to you?"

"My father is determined to marry me off so I will give up my notion of going to Africa."

"Africa?"

Rhiannon bounced on the bed as her face took on an excited expression. "Aye, Africa! I heard all about it from one of father's guests. It sounds so… so…"

"Dangerous."

"Aye, that too, but I was thinking exhilarating! Imagine, coming face to face with a wild beast that could pounce on you and eat you alive! Does that not sound fantastic?"

"Very."

"Now, help me look my best for dinner. I shall play the part of the demure little daughter to throw my father off guard. Perhaps he will give in to me."

The baron sipped his wine as he suspiciously observed his daughter. He expected her to sulk and not speak to him for days, but here she was, smiling and being charming as if nothing had occurred between them. She had even taken pains to look extremely presentable, and his guests were taking full advantage of gazing on her beauty. Her actions made him nervous, as it was not like Rhiannon to give in so easily. She was conversing with his steward, Lord Walton, a horribly thin and single man who owned his own land but ran the castle in the baron's absence. He was not even aware that she could tolerate the man before; why was she being so appealing now? She was offering him suggestions for the meal, and he was lapping it up like a thirsty dog.

"Try the oysters, Lord Walton, they are simply divine."

"Thank you, I shall." The homely older man heaped oysters on his plate until there was room for little else.

"The pheasant is also moist and tender." She picked up a small piece and held it to the besieged man's mouth; he practically bit her fingers as he snagged the tasty tidbit with his large buckteeth.

Rhiannon felt like gagging, but kept the sweet smile plastered on her face. Her father discussed everything with his steward; he might be useful for some information later on.

She turned her attack on her father, who had remained quiet for the most part while all his other usual guests competed for the attentions of his lovely daughter.

"So father, aside from managing to once again betroth me to an unknown horror, what else transpired on your trip?"

Rhiannon

The baron smiled; this was more like it. She was hiding behind her deceptive smile and fishing for details. This he could deal with.

"Naught that you would be interested in, my precious daughter. And he is not a 'horror'. This time you shall be pleasantly surprised."

She furrowed her eyebrows and grimaced. "I can imagine." He obviously was holding to his threat of telling her nothing. Her face brightened as she thought of another tactic. "Shall you at least tell me his name, so I may mention him in my nightly prayers?"

"More like curse him to an early grave. Nay, this time you shall know naught until he walks in the door to claim your hand."

She contrived a syrupy smile, and innocently batted her eyes. "Are you so sure I shall please him? He may take one look, and…"

"Oh, nay, Rhiannon. When his arrival is imminent, you will be dressed in your finest clothes and closely guarded. There shall be no rolling in mud this time."

"'Twas not mud, 'twas pig swill. It worked most effectively; that ugly lord took one whiff and ran." She snickered at the success of her latest deterrent to marriage.

"He is probably running still. You stunk up the entire castle. And that 'ugly lord' was very rich, and would have provided for you most graciously."

"He had the face of a donkey. Really father, do you want your grandchildren to be born with foot-long ears? Does this new prospect also resemble a beast of burden?"

"Enough! You can talk yourself blue, you shall learn nothing more from me."

She closed her mouth and glowered, hoping that Kady was having more success than she was.

Later in her room, Rhiannon waited impatiently for Kady to report her findings. When the servant girl finally did appear, Rhiannon knew instantly that Kady's mission had been a failure. She stalked in the room and threw up her hands in dismay.

"No one knows anything! The master was alone when he made his arrangement, and he has talked to no one since! 'Tis hopeless."

"Nothing is hopeless, Kady. We shall simply have to strengthen our efforts. My father is bound to extol his good fortune to someone, and you must hear every word."

"But I am *your* servant! He shall get suspicious if I follow him around."

Rhiannon puckered her face in thought. "Everyone must be put on alert, especially the kitchen staff." Her face brightened. "I have an idea! I shall feign illness tomorrow, and father shall dine with his regular guests for company. He is bound to divulge something without me there."

Kady nodded. "Aye, that might work. He would talk more freely."

"I know—you could hide! That way, you shall hear all that is said!"

"Hide? But what if I am discovered?" Kady's sudden blanched face would have made freshly laundered linen appear dull.

"You shall not be. Kady, you have to help me!" Her expression changed to desperation, as her large blue eyes blinked back tears, forcing Kady to cast her eyes to the ceiling in capitulation.

"Very well, do not cry. You know I cannot stand it when you cry." Even though Kady was only six years older than Rhiannon, she had been her servant for eleven years. They were more like sisters, rather than Lady/servant.

Rhiannon's smile instantly returned. "Thank you, Kady! Now, let us go to the great hall and find the ideal spot for you to hide."

Down in the deserted great hall the girls planned their strategy. Rhiannon shuffled around the lord's table with a hand on her chin as she pondered all possibilities.

"I suppose under the table is out. You might get kicked and then discovered."

Rhiannon

Kady's face showed relief at the elimination of that hiding spot, as Rhiannon continued her inspection. Suddenly her face exploded in a smile. "The curtains! They should easily conceal you." She motioned to the long drapes against the back wall behind the master table. "Go ahead, get behind it…I want to see if you are noticed."

Kady reluctantly placed herself behind the thick red velvet curtains. "'Tis hot back here."

Her muffled complaint fell on deaf ears as Rhiannon stepped back, cocking her head as she stared at the obvious jut.

"Nay, you are too large. You make a huge bulge."

Kady thankfully came out from behind the heavy, hot curtain. "Good. I would have suffocated back there."

Rhiannon sighed deeply in exasperation "There must be somewhere. Wait—I have an idea."

Kady grimaced in dread; Rhiannon was having way too many ideas for her own good.

"You shall become part of the kitchen staff and help serve the meals tomorrow. We can disguise you."

"But I do not want to be part of the kitchen staff." Kady's face fell into a pout.

"Oh Kady, 'tis only for one day." Kady's expression didn't change, and Rhiannon slyly added, "I shall give you the next two days off."

Kady raised an eyebrow. "Three."

"Oh, very well, three. But only if you find out anything. Agreed?"

"Agreed."

They exited the great hall, each thinking they had made the better deal.

The following day the baron was informed that Rhiannon was feeling poorly. Instantly suspecting a contrived scheme, he visited his daughter's room to see for himself this terrible sudden illness. He did indeed find her in bed, her face pale—due mostly to the powered chalk she patted all over it—and displaying a pained expression.

The baron narrowed his eyebrows in suspicion. "Are you ill?"

"I shall be fine, father," she said, faking a tired, sick voice. "I just need a day of rest."

"Are you sure? I could send for a healer…"

"Oh, do not bother yourself, father," she quickly jumped in, knowing a healer would find nothing wrong. "I am just tired. It is the excitement of your return, and the news of my impending betrothal, that is all."

The baron cast her a long look. It might be possible that she was just tired. Possible, not probable. But he saw no harm in letting her spend the day in bed, sick or not. He tucked her in and kissed her forehead. "Very well, you rest. I want you well and smiling when your betrothed arrives."

"Will that be soon?" Her voice reeked of innocence as she hoped to catch him unaware.

"Sooner than you think. I shall have your meals brought up to you. I do not want you weak with hunger. And you can wipe that hopeful look off your face; I am telling you nothing."

As soon as he left, she hopped out of bed and stuck her tongue out at the door. "Augh! He is being impossible!"

Kady stepped out from her hiding spot in the wardrobe. "Whew, I did not think he would ever leave."

Rhiannon sat on the edge of the bed and looked miserable. "This better work—I am stuck in my room all day, and 'tis beautiful and sunny out."

"I have already secured a food server's cap and apron," Kady said, holding out the items in front of her. "I shall keep my eyes lowered and try to keep from your father's sight." She slipped out the door, leaving Rhiannon bored but hopeful.

Rhiannon

Breakfast produced nothing. The master did not seem to even notice Kady as she brought trays of food from the kitchen and stood close by, listening to any conversation he became involved in. She reported to Rhiannon, who was not pleased, but there were still two other meals to render.

The mid-day meal was also fruitless. Rhiannon was starting to get frantic, feeling like a caged animal, pacing in her room all day while the world went on outside without her. She vowed to be extra obnoxious to this new suitor, just for the agony she was going through.

Dinnertime approached, and Kady grew more and more anxious. She had to hear something this time or the whole day was for nothing, and she had never worked so hard in all her life.

The master had his usual guests with one addition—a visiting lord from an adjoining manor, a lord Preston somebody. Kady noticed this new person was seated directly next to the baron, where Rhiannon would ordinarily sit. This meal was prepared more lavish, due to the special guest, and the great hall was merry and loud with the chattering diners. It was impossible for Kady to hear anything over the din of the crowd, and she resigned herself that her mission was a total failure.

After the meal, the baron and the visiting lord withdrew to the master's study to imbibe in a brandy or two. Kady was bringing yet another tray from the great hall past the study entrance, when an overeager maid came rushing around the corner and smacked right into her, causing the entire tray to come crashing to the floor. The young maid burst into tears, and Kady sent her to fetch some cleaning rags while she kneeled to pick up the mess of broken crockery. The baron was over-imbibing, as usual, and sat in his favorite chair with his back to the door, not noticing the two-inch crack.

"Preston," he began, "have you ever heard of the Dark Count?"

"Good Lord, aye…everyone has. Why do you bring him up?"

The baron leaned forward in his chair and motioned Lord Preston closer. "I am bursting to tell someone. Can you keep a secret?"

"Aye, of course."

In the hall, Kady stopped picking up the mess and leaned her ear closer to the door, hoping no one passed by to see her listening.

The baron smiled as he swirled his brandy in the goblet. "First of all, what do you know of the Earl of Suffolk?"

"Only that he is ruthless, cruel, and most fearsome to gaze upon. His face is scarred and gruesome. 'Tis rumored that he once had a servant hanged simply for overhearing a private conversation."

Kady's hand went to her throat and she stopped breathing.

"'Tis also rumored he has had three wives so far; when he tires of one he simply kills her and moves on. He supposedly beats his servants for the slightest mishap, and is so large he can break a man's neck with just one hand. He is the devil incarnate; sounds absolutely horrid to me."

"Aye, I have heard the same rumors." The baron chuckled. "I met him during my latest trip to London, at the king's castle. I made an arrangement with him for my daughter's hand."

Kady's eyes grew large and she slowly backed away from the door. The hapless maid returned with the rags and Kady stammered for her to clean up the mess. She then made her way directly to Rhiannon, not staying to hear the rest of the conversation.

Lord Preston's small eyes widened in disbelief. "You are marrying your lovely Rhiannon off to the Dark Count?"

"Nay, to his nephew, Viscount Stanwyck. The young lad is his only heir, and stands to inherit his entire vast fortune. And I can assure you, the rumors are mostly false. Aye, he did have a servant hanged, for raping a young maiden who afterwards threw herself off a cliff in anguish. His wives all died of totally natural causes, and he does not beat his servants anymore than I do. But he rather likes his dark reputation; it keeps people from challenging him and makes for loyal servants." He grinned with a satisfied nod. "Aye, this shall be a good match. The young lad is handsome, rich, and ripe for marriage."

Upstairs Kady didn't bother to knock, just rushed in Rhiannon's room and slammed the door behind her, leaning against it as if she expected the Dark Count himself to burst in at any moment and drag her to the gallows. Rhiannon looked up from her book, and upon seeing Kady's white face and look of horror stood and swallowed hard.

"What did you find out, Kady?"

"Oh, Rhiannon! 'Tis much worse than we thought! You are to marry the Dark Count!"

"The who?"

"The Dark Count! Oh, 'tis terrible! He is awful, and old, and ugly, and kills servants, and shall hang me!"

"Calm down Kady, now, just exactly what did you hear?"

Kady took a deep breath. "Your father has betrothed you to the Earl of Suffolk, the Dark Count. He has had three former wives, all of whom he likely killed with his bare hands, and he hangs servants for doing nothing. Oh, Rhiannon! 'Tis simply terrible!"

Rhiannon felt a sense of betrayal by her father. How could he make an arrangement with such a horrible man? "Kady, are you sure you heard correctly?"

"Aye, he said 'I have made an arrangement with him for my daughter's hand.' Those are his exact words."

Rhiannon fell back on the bed, hopelessness engulfing her for the first time. "It does not appear that anything would scare this one off. I could roll in pig swill all day, and he would probably like it."

"Aye, he would most likely join you. Milady, what are you to do?"

Rhiannon sat up and began thinking. Her father had really pushed her this time. If he thought she was just going to sit around and accept her fate, well, he had another thought coming. "Kady, I am going to leave."

"Leave? Where?"

"Remember the caves?"

"At the shore? But that is so far! Is that not a bit...*drastic*?"

"This calls for drastic measures. I shall have to disguise myself as a peasant; I need plain clothes and enough food to last me for at least a week. When this Dark Count shows up, he will find a castle void of a bride."

Kady gasped. "You are going alone? Should I not go with you?"

"Nay, that would arouse suspicion. You must pretend not to know where I am. Do not worry; I can hide in the caves quite nicely. No one knows them as well as I do."

"All right, I suppose there is no other way. But your father is most likely to be very enraged at your absence."

"It serves him right, betrothing me to such a ghastly fate. I shall leave tomorrow night. We must act totally natural until then. I am counting on you, Kady."

All the next day Rhiannon still feigned illness, while preparing for her bold adventure. Kady found her some simple peasant clothes, which Rhiannon packed along with large amounts of cheese, dried meats, and twice-baked bread. At least she wouldn't starve.

Toward late afternoon, Rhiannon slipped out of her room dressed in fine riding clothes and headed directly to the stables. The groom, suspecting nothing, saddled a horse for her to take on a short afternoon ride. She purposely chose a simple brown mare of substandard quality, to test it, she said. Her direction was stated to be the exact opposite of where she was going when she casually rode off. As soon as she was a good distance away, she found a clump of woods and changed into the peasant clothes. She hid her fine clothes—along with the expensive sidesaddle that would arouse suspicion—then jumped on the horse bareback with her sack of food. She was an excellent rider, and didn't need a saddle, anyway. A simple peasant girl riding with a bundle to deliver would be common, and no one would give her any notice.

Rhiannon

She smiled with satisfaction at her devious plan. Maybe her father would finally understand that his arrangements were intolerable, and that this time he went too far.

Chapter Two

Jarreth was hot, tired, and hungry. He had ridden for four days, camping at night, living off the land. Being in no real hurry to meet this latest prospect, he kept his pace moderate, stopping when the mood hit him as it did now. He probably could have made the trip in three days, riding hard and resting little, but saw no need in that. Why rush to what most likely was just more disappointment?

The hot August sun was particularly unyielding today. A passerby had told him of a small nearby lake, and he had full intentions of making use of it. A cool swim would be enjoyable, and would kill more time. Besides, it was almost dark, and camping by a body of water would be refreshing.

Following the directions to the lake, he finally saw the sparkling water glisten through the grove of trees. It was now past sundown, but the large, bright harvest moon made seeing easy. He dismounted, leaving his huge black warhorse to graze in a small meadow, and stripped off his doublet and shirt. Just as he reached the tree line, he heard splashing in the center of the lake.

Rhiannon

He frowned in disappointment. He was hoping for some solitude. The moon cast a blue, glistening sheen over the small lake, and he grew more and more resentful of the person who had reached the lake before him. Probably some filthy peasant taking his yearly bath. Well, he would just have to wait until he or she left. He crossed his arms, leaned up against a tree, and closed his eyes. Maybe he could catch a small nap before this rude intruder left.

The splashing grew nearer, and suddenly Jarreth heard singing. The voice was lilting, mesmerizing. He quickly opened his eyes and was instantly absorbed into the melody. As he squinted toward the lake, a head full of long blond hair suddenly surfaced. So the nighttime bather was a woman? This could get interesting.

His eyes darted to the shore for anyone in her company, but he saw only her clothes lying on the sandy shore. A lone mare was tied to a tree nearby. He didn't see a saddle, so it was most likely she was a peasant girl. His lips formed a crooked smile as he watched the bewitching sight. The girl dove, and then surfaced, shaking her long hair into a mass of swirling wet strands. Shoulder-deep in the water, her body remained a mystery, but she certainly seemed to have a fair face. Jarreth berated himself for standing there gawking at a simple peasant girl, but his body would not obey the command to move. He remained hidden behind the trees as he watched her swim back and forth, laughing and singing to herself, the greatest delight he had seen in a long time. His sour mood began to lift. He wouldn't mind sharing the lake with her.

He wasn't sure what to do. If he just boldly stepped out from the trees, she would most likely be alarmed—his size alone often had that effect on people—and he didn't want to scare her. Suddenly he blinked as the girl swam to shallow water and stood up. The mystery of her body was quickly eliminated. Her glorious body shimmering in the moonlight, he found his mouth was growing dry as he watched in silence. Waist-long streamlets of dripping, wheat-colored hair cascaded down her flawless white skin. Her ample, firm breasts were the most extraordinary he had ever seen, and he had seen quite a few. She had long, splendid legs, and a waist so small he could encompass it with his large hands. Her belly was flat and firm. No peasant girl should look like this. He felt his pulse quicken and realized he had not taken a breath for a while. Would he ever breathe again?

His eyes remained glued to her as she began wringing the water from her hair, squeezing one side, then the other.

As she stepped out of the water, she picked up a cloth lying on the shore and began drying herself. Jarreth talked himself out of any tinges of guilt as he watched her. Lord, she was magnificent. His lust began to get the better of him, and he tore his eyes away to regain his composure. The pounding between his thighs demanded the cool lake more than ever.

She was slipping a simple brown dress over her head when he brought his eyes back to gaze on her. He groaned as her body disappeared underneath the common frock. Never had he been graced with such a vision; he doubted he would ever again. His new betrothed, no matter how fair, would pale next to this simple peasant girl. Why was life so unjust?

Hoping to leave unnoticed, he made a backward step, cracking a stick under his boot. The girl instantly raised her head in his direction. Knowing his presence was revealed, he stepped out from behind the tree, and attempted to appear as if he had just arrived.

"Pardon milady, I was not aware this lake was occupied." He thought addressing her by a title higher than her standing would flatter her, but it didn't seem to faze her.

"How long have you been standing there?" Her voice seemed too indignant for a peasant girl.

He reckoned a white lie was in order. "I have only just arrived. May I share your lake?"

Rhiannon

The girl laughed, obviously put at ease at his fib. Her laugh was like music, enticing, alluring. "'Tis not my lake, I am simply borrowing it. Of course you may swim."

He began advancing closer, and it was her turn to catch her breath.

Rhiannon had been surprised when she saw a man step out from the trees that surrounded the lake. Now, as he came closer, the moonlight revealed more details. She was not aware that a man could actually look like this. He was immense; her head barely came to his chest. Long, thick sable hair flowed down to his massive shoulders; shorter errant strands fell down his high forehead, and around his youthful clean-shaven face. He was stripped to his waist, revealing a well-muscled, hard chest, huge defined arms, and a firm, slender abdomen. He had little if no chest hair, which Rhiannon instantly appreciated; she disliked hairy men like her father's smelly blacksmith who resembled an ape. His nose was long and straight, his cheekbones high, and his smile revealed straight, white teeth. When he got closer, she saw his eyes were almost as black as his hair, with an intense, piercing gaze like a hawk preparing for a kill. He looked at her with an expression of which she was not familiar, like he harbored a longing he refused to let surface.

He was not aware of her gaze as he inspected her face. It turned out to be even more interesting than her body, which a moment before he would have thought not possible. Her milky white skin was complimented by a natural glow on her cheeks. She had a small, perfect nose, full lips with a slight overbite—which he found extremely cute—and a long, slender neck he could imagine nuzzling. But it was her large eyes—the color of cornflowers framed by long, dark lashes—that captured his attention. They danced with mirth as if she were amused with life itself: mischievous, playful, and fully enticing.

She found her tongue, long before he did. "Do you intend to swim half dressed?"

He came out of his daze, and glanced downward at his fully clothed bottom half. "Er, nay. Forgive me for staring, 'tis very rude of me." He sat down on the shore, and began pulling off his boots. "'Tis just that you are a very comely lass, but I am sure you are told that daily."

She impulsively sat down beside him, bringing her knees up, and wrapping her arms around them. "Actually, nay, I am not. Although my father calls me many other things, some not repeatable."

He was surprised by her candor, and couldn't help smiling. "That is hard to believe."

"Oh, aye, he is unhappy with me much of the time. Of course, I cannot say that I do not warrant his wrath. I can be most disagreeable."

He narrowed his eyebrows in mock disbelief. "Nay!"

"Aye. This time I fear I shall be confined to my room for a year, but it shall be worth it to escape a fate worse than death."

His boots were removed, but he discovered that a swim was no longer the primary thing on his mind. "Worse than death? What horrible fate has your father threatened you with?"

She let out a deep sigh, and turned to look at him. Even though he seemed a trustworthy type, she did not know him, so a lie was forthcoming to cover her tracks. "My father is a, er, cordwainer, which as you may know, is a well-respected position but holds little wealth. He wishes to marry me off to a wealthy man, but keeps making the most horrible arrangements. I found I have had to discourage each one."

He leaned back on one elbow, amused to the core, having totally forgotten his swim. "How could anyone be discouraged by you?"

"The first one, a rich lord or something, was partial only to blondes. Since that left me at a total disadvantage, I rinsed my hair in berry juice, turning it a delightful purple. He took one look at me, and ran for the hills."

He chuckled as his dark eyes concentrated on her every move. "Purple? Howe'er did you get it out?"

Rhiannon

"It took months, believe me, but during that time my father made no more deals. I was tempted to keep my hair purple forever."

He was not able to contain his chortle. "Were there others?"

"Oh, aye, my father is not so easily discouraged. The next one, a count so and so, wished for a slender and virginal bride, both of which my father guaranteed in me. I had Kady, my serv…er, my friend, find a huge dress, that I padded with pillows and other things. When my betrothed arrived, I descended our stairs appearing very lush, and very pregnant. The hills gained another occupant."

His eyes sparkled with merriment, never had he been so entertained by such a lovely girl. "I suppose that is not all?"

"Nay, the next one was the simplest. He was some prissy baron that was a fanatic about being clean and fresh smelling. Hence, I rolled in pig swill to chase him off."

"Pig swill?" An incredulous look consumed him, and he threw back his head in laughter.

"I smelled so bad he would not even come close to me to say he was begging off. My father was angry for weeks after that one, he threatened to make me sleep with the pigs since I smelled like one, but I do not care…I remain blissfully single."

He had rolled completely over on his side, his head resting in one hand, as he stared up at her with rapture. A woman had never shown this side of herself to him before, and he hoped his reaction to her was not completely obvious.

"And this latest one is the worst…this time my father has signed an agreement with an old, ugly, horrid man who kills his servants and former wives. I could not think of anything to discourage him with, so I am running away."

Jarreth's face sobered a bit. "Running? Alone? Do you think that safe?"

She tossed her wet hair, and ran her fingers through the soggy mop. "Aye, where I am going, I shall be quite safe."

"And where would that be?"

She drew back a bit, suddenly remembering she knew nothing about this man, except he was extremely good looking, and easy to talk to. "I fear I have bored you already with my prattling tongue." She began to stand up, and he felt like someone had stabbed him in the heart.

"Do not leave!" The words came out as a command, him being used to barking orders, and having them obeyed without question. He jumped to his feet, and found he had startled her. She gazed with wide, fearful eyes, backing up away from him, her steps quickening. She turned, and ran toward her horse.

He took three long strides and caught her, spinning her around to face him. She struggled against his hold, and he instantly released her, throwing his hand up in surrender.

"Forgive me...I did not mean to frighten you. Please...keep me company a while longer?"

She cocked her head as she gazed up into his dark, unwavering eyes, and sensed there was nothing to fear from this man. "I do not even know your name."

"Then we are even, for I do not know yours."

A sly, slow smile formed on her face, developing into one more brilliant, as her eyes flashed devilishly.

"Just call me Guinevere."

"Guinevere? Ah, I understand...there is a hopeless romantic behind all your escapades. Very well, you may call me Lancelot, for I am but a poor knight on a mission for my master." He hoped the lie was convincing, as he certainly didn't want to scare her off by telling her who he really was. Most people took off screaming when they found he was related to the Dark count.

"You are a knight?" She smiled with surprise. "And what is this mission you talk of; there are no dragons here to slay."

Rhiannon

"My mission is a boring one, one that shall most likely prove fruitless." He certainly wasn't going to tell her he was on his way to meet his possible future wife.

"Well, regardless, you are correct. I am a hopeless romantic. When I marry, it shall be for true love; it shall not matter if he is neither rich nor poor. I have made a vow not to marry anyone my father arranges for me. I have had quite enough of my meddling father." She began walking along the shore as he walked beside her, both barefoot and lighthearted.

"And is there a true love in the wings, waiting for his chance to rescue the lovely Guinevere from her horrible fate?"

"Alas, nay. There is not much opportunity to meet eligible men out here. But I would rather die an old maid than match up with the awful men my father picks. That is why I am going to the caves."

"Caves?"

She stopped, lowering her sight to stare at his chest—his marvelous bare chest—and looked back up at him. "Very well, since you are a knight, I shall assume you have honor. Just east of here, at the shoreline, there are caves carved into the cliffs. I went there often as a child, and return there at least once a year. No one knows the caves like I do. It shall be difficult for someone to find me; I could hide for weeks."

"So, you are going to wait this awful, old, ugly man out, until he tires and leaves?"

"That is my plan...I have my friend Kady to tell me when he leaves. Then, and only then, shall I return to an irate father, cursing my name most horribly, I imagine."

"Aye, I would imagine."

"It shall be worth it. I would rather starve than marry this man."

He impulsively reached out to finger a strand of her golden hair, which was becoming drier and lighter in the hot summer night. She had funny, short little strands that danced around her forehead. He decided he liked them.

"'Twould be a pity to deprive the world of your beauty. I, for one, am gladdened you chose flight over death."

She tossed her head gaily as the wind caught her hair, causing it to fly randomly across her face, and spill over her shoulders in a wild, irresistible tangle of waves. "And why would that be? You are a knight on a mission, and I am a fleeing bride. Our paths are not likely to cross again."

His face grew serious at her words, as he had tried not to face the facts she just so casually cast at him. "Then, I propose we make use of this small time we do have together."

Her face also lost its joy as they stared at each other in longing, the attraction between them unmistakable yet forbidden. Finally she pulled back, and lowered her gaze to the shore.

"I should be leaving. I can find my way to the caves in the dark." She turned and began walking away; he reached out and gently grabbed her arm, pulling her back.

"Stay the night here with me." Again it came out almost a command, and he instantly realized he had misspoken by the incredulous look she gave him. He grimaced, and took a deep breath. "Allow me to rephrase that. It is not safe to travel at night, especially a pretty girl like yourself. I have freshly killed quail for our dinner, we can build a fire and talk. Since neither of us have pleasant tasks ahead, what harm could come from us enjoying a fleeting moment in each other's company?"

Her look changed to suspicion, and he quickly added, "I promise not to ravage your virtue. I shall be a gentleman simply enjoying the companionship of a beautiful woman."

Time stood still as he waited for her decision. First she puckered her face rather cutely, and then brought a hand up to her chin as she became deep in thought. Finally, after an eternity—or at least it seemed so to Jarreth—she shook her head, sending disappointment flowing through him. "Nay, I cannot."

He felt like his heart had just stopped beating. "Do you fear me?"

Rhiannon

She smiled impishly; sending shudders down his spine he hoped weren't visible. "Nay, I fear myself. If I may be so bold to say, you are the most pleasing man I have ever met. Since I do desire to remain untouched for a possible future husband, I can not put someone as tempting as you in my path." She again turned to leave; he again pulled her back.

"I give you my word, fair lady, as a knight and a gentleman, I shall not succumb to your attacks."

She giggled at his teasing, and felt blood rush to her face. "I am not quite capable of attacking, I am more inclined to douse myself in some foul stench to fend off a suitor. But, very well. I shall stay."

His heart started beating again; he was so desperate he was contemplating holding her against her will. "Come, walk with me to my horse, and I shall collect the quail."

They walked side by side through the trees to his still-grazing horse, which had not moved ten feet from the position Jarreth had left it. Rhiannon stared in awe at the huge black animal, which appeared to be twice as big as her modest little mare. As Jarreth untied the quail from his saddle, she gingerly extended a hand to pet the great beast on its nose. The horse nickered in response, and Jarreth laughed as he slapped the animal gently on the neck.

"Be polite, Daemon, she is a lady. "

Rhiannon smiled and cocked her head as she gave Jarreth an inquiring gaze. "And just how do you know what he said? Do you speak horse?"

"Nay, but I am a male, and so is he. I can well imagine his thoughts of having a vision such as yourself patting him on the nose."

"Perhaps you shall like a pat on the nose, also?" She reached out, and touched the tip of his nose as he quickly brought his hand up to grab hers. Her hand was small, soft, and sensual. He brought it to his lips and gave it a tender kiss. "Careful, fair lady. A pat could lead to greater things."

Evangelynn Stratton

She warily withdrew her hand, as his touch sent shivers throughout her body, a feeling she had never experienced. Quickly sensing a change of subject was in order, she glanced at the quail and hungrily bit her lower lip. "I hope you know how to cook them. I fear my culinary talents are quite limited."

"Never fear, my lady. I am most adept of cooking o'er a fire. Indeed, if I were not, I would have starved by now." They began walking back to the lake, the great horse following behind Jarreth like a giant puppy.

"So you travel often?"

"Aye, too damned much. I hardly remember what a real bed feels like."

"Soft, warm and inviting." Her face fell into a grimace. "Something I fear I shall not feel for a long while. The caves are cold and wet."

"These caves sound horrid. Why e'er do you go there?"

"Do you have a better idea?"

He had quite a few, actually, none that she would consider plausible. What would her father and his uncle think if he took her away to the countryside, abandoning all his responsibilities and inheritance, never to be seen again? It was a fantasy of which he could only dream.

"Nay, I do not." He felt like condemning his sense of honor to hell.

Her mood brightened when they reached the lake. "You still have not had your swim. Why do I not gather firewood while you cool off in the water?"

He hated the thought of her being out of his sight for even a second; their time together was short and he didn't want to waste it. But then, he was hot and the lake was inviting, although not as inviting as her lips.

"Very well, a short one. Take care to gather enough to last the evening; it will fend off any wild animals. I shall unpack my horse and put him with your mare."

She gave him a low, mocking curtsey, holding her plain skirt out wide with her head bowed. "Aye, milord."

Rhiannon

Although she meant it as a tease, it dismayed him that she thought herself inferior to him. He grabbed her arms and pulled her up, perhaps a bit too rough, for her demeanor changed again to mild fear. He let her go quickly, reminding himself this girl could be frightened off very easily with just his size and gender alone. His actions need not compound her anxiety.

"Do not bow before me. Tonight I am your equal."

She seriously doubted that, but was certainly not going to let on. He was convinced she was but just a poor daughter of a cordwainer, not the only offspring of a rich baron who stood to inherit her father's entire fortune.

"I am sorry, I did not mean to offend."

"You did not." Damn it, how could he have been so gruff with her? He wished he could kick himself for his stupidity. All he could do is stare at her amazing beauty, and she finally smiled again, relieving him immensely.

"Your lake awaits, Sir Lancelot. I shall gather sticks, and pray I am not carried off by wood nymphs."

"They would not dare. You would put any nymph to shame."

Again their eyes locked. It was all he could do to tear his gaze away.

After she disappeared into the woods, he stripped down naked and ran into the cool water feeling more alive than he had in years. He had the rest of the evening with this marvelous girl, who was not only beautiful, but made him laugh. As he frolicked in the water, diving and swimming without a care in the world, she appeared carrying a stack of wood so high she couldn't see over the top. He instantly assessed her load was much too heavy. He leaped out of the water to help relieve her of the load, forgetting he was totally naked. Just as he reached her, she dropped the huge bundle on the ground, practically hitting him. Her eyes focused on his feet, then very slowly rose to his bare knees, then quickly back down to his feet.

Evangelynn Stratton

"Please tell me you are wearing a loin cloth!"

Her modesty was refreshing, and he chuckled in response. "All right, I shall if you wish, but 'twould not be the truth."

She whirled around to face the other way. "Go get dressed! I do not wish to gaze upon a naked man."

"I have a better idea. Why do you not undress and join me in the water?"

He could feel her profuse blush even though she was not facing him, and he again chuckled. "Very well, my modest maiden, I shall get dressed. Keep your eyes averted if you do not wish to be embarrassed."

Rhiannon heard him walk away, and in a weak moment turned her head to watch his retreating backside. This man both frightened and thrilled her. By the saints, he had to be the most magnificent man that ever lived. His back was hard and muscled, his buttocks firm and small, his thighs large and powerful. She felt a shudder in the pit of her abdomen, a new sensation lacking in meaning for her. As he reached his clothes he started to turn, and she quickly averted her eyes again. Was she some trollop, gazing on a man like that? What was wrong with her? She left to search for more wood and to give herself a strict lecture.

Jarreth was very much aware that she had watched him; he usually had that effect on women and was very pleased she was no exception. Although, with all other women the next step was bedding them, always with their complete cooperation. Indeed, most women came to him; very seldom did he have to work to obtain a pretty maiden for a night. But this one, this Guinevere, was different. For one night with her, he would gladly give up all future encounters. He rolled his eyes at his thoughts, had this girl completely bewitched him?

When she returned with another heavy load, he quickly relieved her of the burden, this time fully dressed. He was even more formidable with clothes on, dressed all in black, looking like no other knight she

Rhiannon

had ever seen. Of course, she had no way of knowing he was the nephew of the Dark Count, and had an image to project.

He looked down at the huge pile of wood she had amassed, and could not help teasing her. "I believe we have enough wood to cook a week's worth of quail, plus half the rabbits in England."

She drew herself up and sniffed indignantly. "You said to make sure we had enough."

"I do believe you fulfilled your task. Now, sit and talk to me while I clean the quail." He motioned to a small log, and she in turn sat down as he picked up one of the quail and began gutting it. Her nose wrinkled in disgust and she cast her gaze over the still, shimmering water. The only sound was that of an occasional bullfrog.

"I love this little lake."

"Do you come here often?"

"Not often enough. My father is most stubborn about letting me leave the cas…er, the shop." She cringed at her stupid mistake, and hoped he didn't catch it.

He was too captured by her face to notice her flub. "If I were your father, I would never let you out of my sight."

"He almost does not. After this misadventure, he shall most likely tie me up and toss me in the dungeon."

"Your shop has a dungeon?"

She cringed again. "Nay, but I would not put it past him to build one, just for me." She abruptly changed the subject, vowing to watch her words more carefully. "And your mission, Sir Lancelot? Is it exciting and daring, involving true love, courage and honor?"

He finished the first bird, and chortled. "I fear your image of knights is entirely romanticized. Most missions, like this one, are boring, dull, and futile."

"But how do you know 'tis futile if you have not yet completed it?"

He wanted to tell her why, that a simple cordwainer's daughter had entirely captivated him, that no other woman would ever compare to her. But he held his tongue, not wanting to scare her off like he had almost done twice already.

"Circumstances have arisen that proves this particular mission shall not end with success. Let us leave it at that."

"Is your master mean and cruel?"

He gutted the second bird, surprised at her question. Since in essence he was his own master, he wasn't quite sure how to answer. "Some say so."

She leaned forward and sought his eyes, causing him to forget he had a knife in his hand. "Does he beat women and children, and hang servants for no reason?"

He winced as the knife sliced him, leaving a thin bloody line running down his finger. He reminded himself to pay closer attention to his task, and less on the maiden with the deep blue eyes. Her question made him ponder; she could be describing his uncle's reputation.

"Nay, of course not. Why would you ask that?"

"Because that is who my father has made an arrangement with, a man who is cruel, and shall most likely kill me if I displease him."

He was starting to immensely dislike this awful father who would condemn his beautiful, delightful daughter to a marriage with a man like she described. "You could displease no one, even if you had purple hair and smelled like a pig."

She smiled, and modestly lowered her eyes. "You flatter me, Sir Lancelot. I am just a simple maiden, with simple wants and needs."

"Who would put a queen to shame." He tossed the second bird beside the first one, and began making a spit. "Have the papers already been signed?" He hoped he said it casually enough, not with the desperation he felt in his heart.

"Aye. My father signed the agreement with this horrible man weeks ago. 'Tis most likely only breakable if he does not find me pleasing."

Rhiannon

He grimaced. "That is not likely to happen."

"It can happen if I am not there."

He put the birds on the spit, and began building the fire. He always traveled with flint, for easy fire making. His mind was reeling with dozens of thoughts, all on how to get this desperate girl out of this settlement. If an arrangement had been made, the man indeed was the only one who could break it…just as he intended to do with the most likely unworthy, ugly, Yorkshire girl his uncle had set him up with.

"Do you really think this man will just give up when he finds you are missing?"

"If he does not, I shall become a hermit, living in the caves for the rest of my life. Anything is better than marriage to him."

The fire caught, and he blew on the kindling, deep in thought. What would happen if he just didn't arrive at this Yorkshire baron's castle? He grimaced at the idea, as his uncle would most likely disown him, or worse. No, the agreement must be broken in person, which meant he had to at least make an appearance. He had no choice, which infuriated him. He suddenly knew how she felt.

She noticed his change of mood as he positioned the quail—solemn, detached, angry.

"Have I said something to displease you?"

He looked up in surprise; were his emotions that detectable? "Nay, you have done naught to displease me, indeed, I think that not possible."

She flashed him another brilliant smile, which made the fire feel hotter, at least on his side. "You only need know me longer. I am sure I would think of something to send you into a boiling rage."

He looked her over with serious, deep, dark eyes. "I would like nothing more than to know you better."

His piercing gaze made her squirm, and she decided another subject change was in order. "I have food I can share, nothing fancy, just good cheese, bread, and meats. Alas, I brought nothing to drink."

"I have wine, which shall warm us nicely, although I need only look at you to warm my spirit." He almost winced; he couldn't believe he had just said that. The flowery words just seemed to come out. What was wrong with him?

She smirked at his brashness, and stood to fetch the food from her small pack. As she approached her destination, she realized he was walking right behind her. She spun around and smacked straight into him. It was like hitting a stone wall; she practically bounced off his chest.

Taking a backward step, she attempted to stammer out an apology. "I am sorry, I did not realize you were so close."

I would like to be much closer, he thought, but left the words unspoken. "I thought you might need help."

"Nay, I am fine. You may go back and tend to your fire."

He could not resist the urge as he brought up a hand and gently brushed her cheek. She stiffened in alarm, and he brought his hand back down. Why did she fear him so? He let her leave as he went back to the fire, disconcerted to realize this girl was to be handled differently.

Rhiannon found her pack and gathered the food, her hands shaking from his touch. She didn't mean to recoil like she did, but his touch was so warm, stirring, and sensual. Not knowing how to deal with these new emotions, and being completely innocent, she reacted in the only manner she could—fear. He was so big, so overpowering, so *masculine*. He probably thought her a silly girl who jumped every time someone touched her. She desperately tried to remember everything Kady had taught her about how to act around a young, good-looking man. To her chagrin, she found she couldn't remember a single thing.

He watched with potent eyes as she walked back. Her movements were fluid, as if her feet barely touched the ground as she walked. She approached with a smile, their last encounter apparently forgotten, and to his enjoyment sat down beside him on his small log. Drawing a breath at her closeness, he simply watched as she brought out

Rhiannon

cheese, bread, and some dried meats, and carefully laid them all out on a little cloth.

"Well, 'tis not formal dining, but it shall have to do."

"I would rather dine with you, under the stars, than with the king himself. You are much prettier than the king."

She laughed, and nibbled on a piece of cheese. "So, being a handsome and brave knight, is there a Lady Lancelot?"

He smiled and shook his head. "Nay, there is no one." *Only a flaxen-haired maiden that sets my heart on fire by her mere presence.*

"And when you do marry, will it be for love or by some dumb arrangement, like it seems I am fated?"

"I have decided, just today in fact, 'twill not be by arrangement. I shall make my own mind up in the matter, if and when I marry."

"'Twould be nice to have that freedom. Being a woman certainly has its drawbacks."

None that he could see. "Do you think your father would let you out of the arrangement, if another suitor greater to this other man's status wanted you?" He watched with apprehension as she pondered the question.

She wrinkled her nose and frowned. "He would have to be very wealthy, 'tis all my father thinks about."

That was not a problem, he thought. He handed her his wine flask. "Here, have a drink."

She took a sip, carefully tasting the sweet wine, and licked her lips afterwards, sending him to a new realm of longing. "Ummm…'tis good. I have not had much wine. My father says that young maidens need not imbibe in spirits. He makes up for my lack, however." She took another drink, this one longer, as Jarreth watched on with amusement. "He says I compel him to drink to forget his problems, such a tribulation I present to him. I think that is just an excuse to over-indulge. I have often found him passed out on the floor, snoring loud enough to shake the rafters." She again took another swig. "Of course, he says my imagination has ran wild, and he most likely is right. He even gets upset by my habit of cutting my hair in front. He says a proper young lady keeps herself looking fashionable, but I cannot stand my hair in my face. I would cut it all off, if he would let me. Oh dear, I am rambling on so much you cannot get a word in edgewise. I fear this wine has loosened my tongue. Do you smell something?"

He was so enraptured in her, he completely forgot about the birds cooking—actually by now burning—over the raging fire. He sniffed the air, and quickly looked down in dismay. The birds were charred black, and still in flames. He jumped up, grabbing the spit of burning quail, and ran to the lake to extinguish the flaming mess. Rhiannon followed him, laughing uncontrollably, finally causing him to burst out in laughter also.

"How did you get so large, eating charred meat?" Her eyes danced in delight.

"Now you know my secret," he answered back as he doused the birds in the water, feeling rather stupid that he had ruined their dinner.

"I am not impressed with knightly cooking. Do you have other skills you wish to brag about?" She snickered, so cute and beautiful at the same time, and he couldn't resist the impulse any longer. He dropped the spit on the ground and took her into his arms, honor be damned.

She looked up at him in surprise, but instead of being terrified, she smiled. He gazed into her liquid, blue eyes, and realized the wine had mellowed her a little. Very slowly, he brought his lips down on hers, softly, very gently, applying pressure. She let him control the kiss, having never been kissed before. Her innocence made his desire even stronger. He tasted her lips with his tongue, begging access to her sweetness, and to his absolute euphoria she parted her lips and granted his request. His tongue probed her fragrant mouth, a mixture of wine and her own sweet essence. Her body felt fluid as he drew her close and felt her

Rhiannon

warmth next to his. He knew at that moment there could never be another girl for him.

Good Lord, this girl has managed to snare me without even setting a trap. He deepened the kiss, and found himself lost. On an impulse, he swept her up into his massive arms, still kissing her, and carried her back to the fire. She felt so light in his arms, as if she weighed nothing, almost like his heart at that moment. He relinquished her lips, and she gave him a dreamy, faraway look. A bit too dreamy, as she then blinked a few times, closed her eyes, and fell into an exhausted sleep against his shoulder.

He gazed incredulously at her, and then chuckled to himself. This was not the effect he usually had on women. But then, this one was different.

He laid her down on his own bedroll, and then sat back down on the log, watching her. Her hair lay in great cascades about her; her bosom rose gently with every shallow breath. She simply had to be the most angelic creature alive.

"Ah, my Guinevere, who are you, and what have you done to me?"

He watched her for quite some time, until his own eyelids grew heavy. Spreading out her blanket, he lay down, careful to remain far enough away to avoid temptation. He observed her for a while longer, not looking forward to the next day when they would go their separate ways. Why was life so unfair? Why would fate cross his path with a perfect woman, when he was betrothed to another, and she was running from her own betrothal? His sour mood returned, and he fell into a restless sleep.

Chapter Three

Rhiannon awoke to a slight headache, no doubt from that blasted wine that tasted so good but attacked her senses. She observed the sleeping knight a few feet away, and stood up very carefully as to not awaken him. He was magnificent even in sleep; his massive body looked ready to spring to action at a second's warning.

She went to the water's edge and knelt down, splashing the cool water on her face and neck. Then she rubbed water over her arms, and finally ran her fingers through her hair, forcing the thick mane back from her forehead. The morning sun shone down on her upturned face as she combed her hair with her fingers, getting out as many tangles as she could.

Jarreth had awakened the moment she stirred, keeping his eyes closed until she left. He silently lay watching her as she groomed herself by the lake, not wanting to move and break the spell. Envy and hate coursed through him for the man destined to become her husband. Unless the man was a complete fool, he would jump at the chance to marry her. It was highly unlikely she could remain hidden forever;

eventually she would be found. Just thinking about some bloody bastard forcing his will on her almost made him indisposed with rage.

He slowly rose up on one elbow as she walked back to the site. When she noticed he was awake, she flashed him a bright smile that set his heart beating much faster.

"Good morning! I trust you slept well?"

"Aye, I did." It was a lie. He had tossed and turned all night, knowing that today they would part company. He sat up, crossed his knees, and watched her as she began rolling up her belongings and stuffing them into the pack.

He instantly felt alarm. "What are you doing?"

"Getting ready to depart, what else? I suggest you do the same, we both have long journeys ahead of us." She looked on him with wide, innocent eyes. "Your mission, remember?"

"Ah, my blasted mission." He wished he could take his mission and send it to hell. Watching her prepare to leave was killing him. How could he let this girl just ride out of his life? Was he completely daft? He silently cursed his uncle and his persistent arrangements.

"Here, let me help." He gathered up her things and folded the blanket, then followed behind her as she walked to her waiting mare. When the horse took a limping step toward her, Rhiannon frowned and picked up the animal's foot.

Jarreth noticed her inspecting the hoof. "What is wrong?"

"I am not sure. I fear she may be stone bruised."

"Here, let me see." He took the hoof and looked at it. Indeed, the mare had bruised her frog, and would take a few days to heal. Jarreth couldn't believe this turn of good fortune—his, not the horse's.

"Your mare can not carry weight for a while. You shall have to stay here until she heals."

Rhiannon furrowed her brows in thought, and shook her head. "Nay, I shall walk her to the nearest village and sell her. Then I shall walk to the shore, 'tis not that far. Goodbye, Sir Lancelot, I wish you well on your journey. 'Twas a pleasure meeting you."

He couldn't believe it when she just casually began leading the horse away, apparently forgetting that he ever existed. "Nay, my Guinevere, I think not."

She didn't stop, forcing him to become more desperate with her every step.

"You might as well stop, as I am not letting you leave." He raised his voice. "I said, halt!"

She did, and turned around with a sour expression. "Are all knights so bossy?"

"Only when women are being stubborn." He took four long strides and caught up to her.

"I am not stubborn. I am practical. I must go to the shore, and you must go on your mission."

"I am not going to let you walk all the way to the seashore. What kind of knight would I be if I did not help a damsel in distress?" He grabbed the reins from her and walked over to his own horse. "We will lead your little mare into town, then Daemon here shall take us to the coast." He began saddling up the huge war-horse.

"But your mission!"

"Damn my mission."

Rhiannon couldn't believe he was doing this, and her emotions were rather varied from elation to stupefaction. "But…my added weight shall tire your horse."

He snorted a short laugh. "Daemon? He will not even know you are there. I have carried swords heavier than you."

"But…"

"You might as well save your excuses, I shall not abandon you as it appears everyone else has."

"I was not abandoned. I left of my own accord."

Rhiannon

"And you are quite alone. Now, get on." Without giving her a chance to respond, he put his hands around her tiny waist and effortlessly lifted her up on his horse. She looked down from the giant horse with trepidation as he mounted in the saddle behind her, wrapping one long arm around her waist. "Here—hold your mare's rope. Do not worry, I will not let you fall."

"I shall not…I am an excellent rider."

"That remains to be seen." He clicked his tongue, and the great horse surged forward.

Jarreth kept his left arm tightly wrapped around her, not for any need for safety, but simply because he liked the way she felt next to him. He was elated he would get to spend more time with her before his ill-fated journey to meet and probably reject his bride.

She was quiet; too quiet. Jarreth feared his over-bearing actions had distanced her.

"You are silent this morning."

"Aye, my head hurts."

He grinned. "I think mayhap the wine did not agree with you."

"I believe you are right. I do not even remember falling asleep."

A disappointed frown hit his face. Did she not remember his kiss? "My lovely lady, how much do you remember?" As he spoke, her golden tresses beckoned him to lean his head forward and bury it in the mass of curls.

She pretended not to notice. "I seem to remember you burning our dinner. Then everything becomes a blur. I had a strange dream, however."

"A dream? Pray, tell me of this dream."

"'Twould not interest you."

"You would be surprised what interests me."

"Still, 'tis not a dream I wish to share."

"'Twould not involve a kiss, perhaps?"

She stiffened in his arm and his smile grew wider; he was thankful she could not see it. She finally responded. "Are you telling me you kissed me?"

"Aye."

She sighed. "My first kiss, and I missed it."

"Pity, 'twas most stirring. Did you say 'twas your first?"

"Aye, unless you count a lick from my dog."

"Nay, that would not count."

"Oh well, I suppose there shall be more, eventually."

It was his turn to stiffen. "Eventually?"

"Aye, when my father finally succeeds in marrying me off to some horrid man. It seems to be my destiny. Was it good?"

"What?"

"The kiss."

"Oh, aye. You seemed to enjoy it, but then, you thought it to be a dream."

"I also dreamt a brave and noble knight carried me away to a castle with a high tower, saving me from my fate."

"I did carry you, but only to the bedroll."

"I seem to have missed a great deal last night."

"'Twould appear so."

"I apologize for my ill manners." She gave a little laugh, which in turn made him smile again. It occurred to him that he had never smiled so much before he met this girl.

"No apology is necessary, I enjoyed myself immensely."

"I am glad one of us did."

He kept his smile as they approached the village. A farmer bought the mare, being assured she would be fine in a few days, and Jarreth again lifted Rhiannon on his horse.

"There is an Inn nearby; I remember passing it when I rode in. I shall purchase us some breakfast."

Rhiannon

"I do not want you to waste your money on me. I shall pay for myself." She felt badly taking the little money a lowly knight would have, and she had the money she just made by selling the horse.

"No money spent on you would be wasted." He wanted to tell her he was rich beyond her imagining, but held his tongue. He didn't want to alienate this simple cordwainer's daughter even more.

He escorted her into the Inn and ordered great amounts of food, wanting her to be well fed when he left her at the caves. The prospect of leaving her was becoming more and more unpleasant.

He relished her company during breakfast. Her charm, wit, and beauty were unsurpassed, as he listened to her telling stories of her wild escapades.

"So, I managed to get the kitten out of the tree, but became rather stuck myself. I was forced to spend the night up there before my father found me the next morning."

Jarreth laughed heartily. "Were you not scared?"

"Nay, mostly embarrassed. My father was most distressed, however. He imagined me eaten by wolves."

"Indeed?"

"Aye, I believe 'twas too soon after the well incident."

Jarreth leaned forward and folded his hands. "Well incident?"

She gave a sheepish smile, and he swore he detected a small blush. The goat's milk suddenly became irresistible, and she gulped it down, finishing the whole cup. A little milk mustache was left, and she licked her upper lip, sending shivers down his spine.

"Are you going to tell me about the well, or not?"

"I suppose you shall badger me until I do?"

"Aye." He lifted one eyebrow in anticipation.

She cleared her throat. "I was out walking in the countryside, and got caught in a downpour. I took refuge under a tree, but the storm continued until nightfall threatened. That is when I saw the wolf."

"You do not say!"

"Oh, aye. I saw his mean, vicious eyes, and lots of fur, and well, you can imagine, I was terrified!"

"I imagine."

"So, seeing an abandoned well close by, I thought maybe if I could hide inside of it, the wolf would go away. I was further happy to find a rope left hanging from the handle."

"How convenient."

"I thought so. I lowered myself into the empty well just as the man-eating beast reached me. In my excitement the rope slipped my grasp, plunging me to the bottom."

Jarreth lost his smile. "You could have been killed."

"Nay, just a few scratches and bruises. Although, I think I would have preferred death to my father's punishment."

"He was angry?"

"Mostly frightened. Since 'twas dark, and I was tired and bored, I fell asleep. A search party was sent out, and when they shone a lantern down the well, they saw me sleeping at the bottom and thought me dead."

Jarreth mind flashed a visual picture of her still body lying at the bottom of a deep well. He would have been frantic. "Howe'er did they think to look in the well?"

She lowered her head and grimaced. "It seems I was being guarded by the wolf."

"The wolf?"

"Aye, a fluffy sheepdog, whose only threat would be to lick you to death." She displayed an impish grin, and he burst out laughing.

"You fell to the bottom of a well to escape a dog?"

"'Twas dark! It might have been a wolf!"

He studied her intently; he had never before delighted in a woman like this. "And what of your father's torturous punishment?"

Rhiannon

She drew herself up and sniffed indignantly. "He confined me to my room for a month, forcing me to do needlepoint."

"That must have killed you."

"I got even."

"I can only imagine."

"I made a fine picture, of the devil with my father's face, torturing a young maiden who looked surprisingly like me."

"You did not!"

"Oh, aye. And I presented it as a present to the Duke of Salisbury when he came through town, who liked it so much he hung it in his great hall."

Jarreth covered his mouth with his hand. "Oh, Lord!"

"My father was so distraught he had to buy it back, for sentimental reasons, of course, it being his daughter's first attempt at needlepoint."

"And, I suppose, the last?"

"Aye. I am allowed no more art projects. Should we not be leaving?"

"Huh?" He sat up and frowned, leaving was just quite possibly the last thing on his mind. "Are you in a hurry?"

She gazed at the incredible, totally magnificent man sitting across from her. "Nay, I am not, but your mission…"

"Can wait. I am enjoying your company."

"You flatter me, Sir Lancelot."

He decided to end the pretense. "My name is Jarreth."

She looked at him in surprise. "Careful, my noble knight, you shall break the spell."

"Spell?"

"Aye, the spell that brought us together for this short time. No matter what your name, you shall always be remembered as my Lancelot who came to my rescue in my hour of need."

His face grew greatly serious. "Please tell me your name."

She was tempted, but held back the truth. If her father's searchers met him on the road, he would only know her as a cordwainer's daughter named Guinevere.

"Nay, when you are older with grandchildren on your knee, I want you to remember me only as the silly girl you met by a lake and rescued from a grisly fate."

"You speak as if we are already parted." He felt a dour mood returning.

"That reality is only a few hours away."

His tongue grew thick as he looked at her; what should he say? *Excuse me, fair maiden, would you wait by for me while I tell my betrothed I am breaking our engagement?* How would she react to that? No, this girl, with a brave spirit like he had never seen, must never know his 'mission' was to get married to a woman he had never met.

She detected his mood had taken a change for the worse, and her smile also disappeared. "'Twould seem the spell is already broken." Only when she stood up did he realize his attitude had ruined the meal.

He quickly stood and took her arm. "I apologize for my sour mood. The thought of my mission has made me contrite."

She glanced at his hand circling her arm, then back at his face. "We should go. The caves are waiting."

"Aye." He escorted her outside, and lifted her back on Daemon. After he mounted, he thought desperately of some way to make her smile again. A confusing revelation struck him; he had never wanted to or cared about making a woman happy. Right then he would have given up his title to hear her laugh.

They rode in silence. Having her body so close was torturing him, and his own body let him know it. He impulsively reached up with his left hand and played with her hair, feathering the silky stands through his fingers. She seemed to relax with this bit of gentle foreplay, and leaned back against him. He rolled his eyes and moaned, how much torture could he take?

Rhiannon

"I like your hair, even if 'tis not purple."

He detected a slight giggle. Putting his hand under the masses of hair, he found her neck and began rubbing it. She in turn rolled her head to help him reach every muscle. He was finding the whole situation highly seductive, and totally on a whim brought his lips down to her neck and gently kissed it. He felt her shudder.

"What was that?"

"Nothing, I just kissed you."

"You call that nothing?" She turned around sideways to face him. He looked down at her with a steady, dark stare. He wanted her so badly he hurt, in many different places. Her eyes locked with his, and he stopped the horse.

"You are not making it easy to say good-bye."

"You are the one who kissed me."

"Then get me back by kissing me."

"I do not know how."

"Then close your eyes, and I shall show you."

"On a horse?"

"Just do it."

She tilted her face up, and closed her eyes. He brought his lips down on hers while his hands massaged her back, drawing her close, feeling her warmth. He made it a quick, tender kiss, as to not scare her off. When he drew his head back, she opened her eyes and smiled.

"I think I can do that. Now, you close your eyes."

He willingly obliged. She brought her hands up to his head, and cupped his face. His day-old beard was rough and manly, and her hands soft and gentle. He was not prepared for what her lips did to him. They were sweet, innocent and totally seductive. As she began to draw away, he took command of the kiss.

One of his hands took both of hers, and he kissed them all over. She closed her eyes and parted her lips with a small groan, not knowing what it was she was feeling, but liking it. He, on the other hand, knew exactly what he was feeling, and he knew he would die if he didn't taste her luscious mouth one more time. He brought his lips on her slightly parted mouth, and gained access to her sweetness. His tongue probed inside her, tasting her, seducing her, until she brought her own tongue on his. He moaned with wanting as their tongues played together, touching, feeling, loving. No girl had ever provoked him to desire her as much as this one.

He finally drew himself back, leaving her gasping. She opened her eyes, and flashed him a wide smile that took away what little breath he had left.

"I shall remember that one."

Good Lord, I hope so. "I am not likely to forget it, either."

She turned back around, and Jarreth kicked the horse to walk again. They rode in silence, each lost in private thoughts.

Leaned back against him, she closed her eyes and rested. Feeling him against her back, so solid, powerful, she felt protected and safe. When he brought an arm around her again she cuddled into it, much to his enjoyment. In minutes a light sleep overtook her.

As he held her, Jarreth made up his mind. He would go to this baron what's his name—it had escaped him at this moment—and release his inadequate and homely daughter from the betrothal. Then he would come directly back and redeem his Guinevere. But should he tell her? She was so young, almost still a child. Ah, but she was ready for marriage, and since meeting her he decided he was, too. He'd be damned if another man would have her, not after the way she just kissed him. The greedy cordwainer would jump at marrying her to a rich viscount, even one with an uncle like the Dark Count. Aye, it was a good plan. Of course, he had no idea how this girl could mess up plans.

All too soon he heard the ocean, and he knew they had arrived.

Rhiannon

Rhiannon stirred to life. "Turn here!" She pointed down a narrow lane. He did as he was told, and again she gave directions, taking him through a network of interwoven paths that would surely lose a newcomer. Suddenly the trees ended, and he found himself staring out over the ocean from atop a cliff. The view was breathtaking. The afternoon sun cast a shimmering glimmer over the ocean; the air was salty and brisk. A few seagulls screamed overhead as they hunted for a meal. He reined up as Daemon snorted and pawed the ground, nervous about being so close to such a long drop. Rhiannon brought her right leg up in front of her and slid off. Jarreth immediately dismounted right behind her, and watched in chagrin as she struggled to remove her pack from the saddle. She could barely reach the top of the horse.

"Here, allow me." He released the pack and handed it to her.

She smiled and walked close to the edge, looking out at the view. "Is it not beautiful?" Her hair blew wild and free in the sea breeze, whipping around her face and shoulders.

His eyes never left her. "Aye, 'tis."

"The trail down the cliff is here." She motioned to the visible path leading down the hill. "The caves are just over there." His solemn gaze touched her. "Do not worry, I shall be fine."

He simply nodded, not convinced of her safety or his sanity for leaving her.

She let out a long sigh, and shrugged. "I guess this is good-bye."

As he gazed down at her, he concluded this was going to be the hardest thing he had ever done. "I do not want to leave you here."

"But you must. Goodbye, Sir Jarreth. I shall never forget you."

Her use of his name thrilled him beyond reason, and he reached out to put his hands on her shoulders. "Again I ask you your name."

Her face grew sad, matching his heart. "There is no reason to give it, as 'tis unlikely we shall ever see each other again." She held her pack in front of her, almost as in protection from him. He took it and laid it on the ground.

"Come here, my Guinevere." He pulled her into him, holding her tightly as he nuzzled her neck and felt something entirely foreign to him—stinging tears attacking his eyes. Jarreth had never cried for anyone, certainly not a woman. He blinked the moisture away, attributing it to the sandy wind from the sea.

She pulled back, and he saw a lone tear run down her cheek. She brushed it away, then, stepping backwards, grabbed her pack and turned to leave. He started to reach out to her, but instead lowered his hand in submission. As she reached the trail, she turned and forced a brave smile.

"Do not forget me, my Lancelot." She then disappeared down the trail.

He stood at the edge and watched her bob down the trail, almost holding his breath a few times when it seemed treacherous, until she reached the bottom. She walked along the beach, a small blond figure insignificant against the backdrop of the immense ocean. Then, in a second, she disappeared into the rocks.

Jarreth never felt so empty in his entire life, not even when his parents were ravaged by sickness and he was sent to live with his uncle. He grew up under the shadow of the Dark Count, avoiding closeness to anyone, especially a woman. Who needed a clinging, demanding, hysterical female ruling his life? Certainly not him, even though he had his choice of many women, whom he always considered conquests to use at his discretion. Soon he began wondering if he were the conquest; bedding the handsome young viscount seemed to have some prestige attached to it. Lately he avoided all females, no longer interested in their silly games, until he met his Guinevere. The second he saw her rise out of that lake, he knew his life had changed forever.

The wind stung his face, and he closed his eyes in resignation.

She was gone.

Rhiannon

He took a few deep breaths, and began to walk back to his horse. Before entering the trees, he turned and gave one last sweeping look at the ocean. A girl with dancing eyes and a brave spirit had hopelessly cracked the cold shell around his heart. And he didn't even know her name.

Chapter Four

Jarreth's mood grew more surly the closer he got to Yorkshire castle. His mind could not forget the ocean, where the young girl who had stolen his heart remained. Even his horse suffered for his bad mood; the animal stumbled over a rock and received a slap on the neck and a command to pay attention. Jarreth wanted only to get his unpleasant business taken care of, then return to the girl. His lovesick mind began playing games with him as he rode morosely along. What if she didn't want him? Or, what if her betrothed absolutely refused to let her go? Many women were forced to marry men arranged by their fathers; it was just the way it was. He had never given the practice much thought before. Although fairly confident he could buy the man off, Jarreth reserved the option of running the man through if need be.

She had asked him not to forget her. He was more likely to sprout wings and fly.

By the time he reached Yorkshire castle, he was haggard, irritated and dangerous. His mood was so bad he wanted to kill the first person who spoke to him, who was a hapless groom who only asked the huge

Rhiannon

intimidating stranger if he could tend to his horse. Instead of committing murder, Jarreth just glared and wordlessly tossed him the reins.

He rubbed his two-day growth of beard as he strode up to the castle, thinking he probably looked an awful sight. Good, he wanted this hideous Yorkshire woman to take one look at him and scream. He was even prepared to offer a monetary settlement if things got ugly, like the last time he begged off. What a mess that was.

He kicked a cat that got in his way; the poor feline howled and ran for its life. A timid young servant girl answered his loud knock, looked up at the dark, angry man and took two steps backwards. He pushed past her as if he owned the place.

"Tell your master Viscount Stanwyck is here, and make it quick!"

The poor frightened girl put a hand over her gaping mouth, and took off running.

Jarreth paced in the entrance hall, growing more impatient with each passing second. The mood in the castle didn't appear to be any better than his own. Several frowning and tense servants passed by casting him worried looks. Some even shook their heads.

Finally, after what appeared to Jarreth an unreasonable amount of time, a medium-height, chubby man appeared, looking notably distressed. He took one look at the viscount, forced a smile and feigned delight.

"Viscount! How nice to see you! Forgive my delay, I did not expect you so soon."

Jarreth gave him a sour look, raising an eyebrow as he folded his arms. "Really? I am rather late, how odd you were not prepared."

The baron swallowed hard, not aware until this moment that the viscount was even more formidable than his supposed evil uncle. Great heavens, the man was huge, and every bit as daunting as the count.

"'Tis just that I am afraid the household is in a bit of a…well, never mind that. Come, follow me to my study where we can talk in private."

Jarreth followed the baron down the hall, passing even more servants who obligingly plastered themselves against the wall, unwilling to tangle with the tall, sullen man walking behind their lord. The two men entered the study, and the baron instantly went to the brandy snifter.

"Drink?" he asked Jarreth.

"No thank you, I wish to talk about my uncle's arrangement."

The baron swigged some brandy, licked his lips, and tried to calm his shaking hands. "So soon? Can we not talk, get to know each…"

"Now." His voice was harsh as he sprawled in a chair and glowered.

"Aye, very well, if you insist."

"I do. I fear my uncle spoke out of line."

"O-out of line?"

"I am sure that your daughter is just lovely, but I am not prepared to marry at this time."

The baron sat down and hung his head solemnly. "'Tis just as well. There is no bride here for you to marry."

That got Jarreth's attention. "What do you mean?"

"It seems my daughter has decided to bolt from this contract. She showed up missing two days ago."

Jarreth sat up. This was sounding a bit too familiar. "Why?"

"I am not sure. This is not how she ordinarily handles her betrothals. She is usually more, shall we say, inventive."

"Indeed?" He felt a smile begin to form.

"Aye. She has fought me on every arrangement. I fear her spirit is too much for me; she always seems to win. At this rate she shall never get married."

Jarreth folded his arms, and his smile got a little wider. "Is that so?"

"Aye. The last time, she saw fit to roll in mud."

Jarreth's smile developed into a chuckle. "Actually, 'twas pig swill."

"Aye, that is right…how did you know?"

Rhiannon

Jarreth leaned back, looked up to the ceiling, and began laughing—deep belly-wrenching laughter that filled the room. The baron was completely confused; one minute this sullen young man was breaking the engagement, the next he was lost in merriment.

"I fail to see the humor in this, Viscount."

"Aye, you probably do not." Still smiling, he felt like a grievous weight had just been lifted from his heart. "Do not distress yourself, Baron…I shall sign the agreement, right now if you so desire."

The suspicious father frowned at the viscount's sudden eagerness. "You would marry her, sight unseen?"

The image of his Guinevere, glistening as she stepped from the lake in her naked glory, shot through Jarreth's mind. "She is not exactly sight unseen."

"How do you mean?"

"It seems I met your daughter on my way here."

The baron showed a fatherly look of concern. "Is she all right?"

Jarreth nodded. "Aye, she is fine." He suddenly leaned forward, an intense look on his formerly amused face. "What is your daughter's name?"

"She did not tell you?"

"Nay, she kept her identity secret."

"Her name is Rhiannon. 'Tis Welsh for magic maiden. Her mother, God rest her soul, named her after her grandmother."

Jarreth leaned back again, staring at the ceiling with a faraway look. "Rhiannon. Aye, it fits her." He said her name over and over in his mind, liking it more each time.

Skepticism crept over the baron's face as he observed the lovelorn expression on the young viscount's face. "Are you positive 'twas my daughter? It could be some other maiden you met."

Jarreth continued to stare at the ceiling with a dreamy, silly look. "Does Rhiannon have a face that lets her get her way, masses of golden hair, and blue eyes that dance with mischief?"

"Aye, you have the mischief part right. The girl can get into more trouble than any other five people." He sighed heavily. "'Tis my fault, I coddle her too much. I never could dole out appropriate punishment for her actions."

"Do not be so sure. Forcing her to do needlepoint for a month seems to be a just punishment for someone with her spirit."

The baron's face turned white. "She told you about that?"

Jarreth chuckled. "Aye, and many other things. Tell me, did the duke deal fairly when you bought the picture back?"

A snort was his answer. "Ha! He robbed me blind! He thought the whole thing to be rather humorous."

"As do I. Your daughter is a delight, Baron. I look forward to making her my wife. Although, I am confused…she certainly has a very low opinion of her betrothed—me. Whate'er did you tell her?"

"That is the strange part. I told her nothing; I was taking no chances this time. I have no idea where she formed any opinion about you at all."

"Nevertheless, her fear was genuine. She seemed to think me an old, horrible man who would most likely kill her."

There was a slight noise at the door, and the baron's face lit up in recognition. "Ah! Perhaps Kady can shed some light?"

Jarreth sobered at Kady's name. So this was the accomplice in crime.

Kady came in meekly and gave a short curtsey, as she glanced at the ominous, disheveled man sitting next to her master, staring at her as if he knew something she didn't.

"The housekeeper said you wanted to see me, milord?"

"Aye. What do you know about Rhiannon's disappearance?"

Rhiannon

The loyal servant attempted an innocent look. "Er, disappearance, Sire?" She cast a wary look at the dark stranger and took a step closer to the baron.

"Aye, Kady...you seemed to have been missing around the same time as Rhiannon."

"Lady Rhiannon gave me some time off, Sire."

"I see. Where is she, Kady?"

The wary servant again looked at the formidable stranger. "Is he the Dark Count?" Her voice shook with fear; her eyes were wide and terrified.

Jarreth sat up, giving Kady a disbelieving look. The baron blinked in surprise.

"The Dark Count? How did you find out about him?"

Kady threw herself at the feet of the baron, and wrapped her arms around his legs. "Oh, please, Sire! Do not hang me, I meant no harm!"

The shocked baron stood up and shook her off. "For heavens sake, Kady, get up...no one is going to hang you! Where'er did you get that idea?"

She pointed to Jarreth in terror. "Him, sire! He hangs people for no reason. I heard you talking...you said you had signed an agreement with the Dark Count to marry Rhiannon."

Jarreth couldn't help himself, he threw back his head and laughed heartily. "No wonder she ran away!"

The baron was not so amused. "Kady, you told Rhiannon she was to marry the Dark, er, Count Stanwyck?"

Kady took a few backward steps. "Are you going to hang me?"

Jarreth stood up and patted his host on the shoulder, at least to Jarreth it was a pat; to the baron it was a shove. "Let her go. I think I can determine what happened."

"All right, Kady, you may leave."

As the terrified servant gladly left the company of whom she thought was the Dark Count, Jarreth sank back into the chair. His pondering smile made the anxious father nervous.

"Er, you did say you would still marry the girl?"

Jarreth's dark gaze caused the baron to shiver. "Baron, I have spent the last two days hating my life, thinking Rhiannon was engaged to a horrid man whom I anticipated killing, who turns out to be me. I have struck my horse, threatened a stable boy and kicked a cat, all because your daughter's face will not leave my mind. I dare say I would throttle you if you did not let me marry her."

The happy father quickly produced a pen and the agreement the count and he had signed. "Here, it only needs your signature."

Jarreth picked up the pen and began to sign, then paused, deep in thought. "I shall sign on one condition."

Thinking the rich viscount was beginning to have second thoughts, the baron's voice hid his apprehension. "Aye, aye, anything!"

"I shall go fetch your wayward daughter and bring her back, but you must not tell her who I truly am."

"What! Why not?"

"Rhiannon told me she would marry only for love. She has taken a vow not to marry anyone you have chosen, which unfortunately means I fall into that category."

The baron let out a knowing grunt. "I fear she can be most stubborn about this sort of thing."

Jarreth nodded. "Right now she thinks me a lowly, poor knight on a mission. I have just decided my mission is to bring her to the Dark Count for her marriage. That shall give her time to fall in love with me."

The father was torn between his love for his only child and her life-long happiness, versus her guaranteed temporary outrage at this turn of events. "She is not likely to take that news lightly, Viscount. Are you sure you wish to incur her wrath?"

Rhiannon

Jarreth hid his smile; he had a feeling her wrath could develop into something more passionate. "If she can fall in love with a penniless knight, giving up marriage to a count, I shall know she loves me and not my title or inheritance. Only after she declares her love for me will I tell her who I really am. She will be overjoyed with relief."

"This pretense is unnecessary—my Rhiannon is not the type to fall in love with a title."

"I share your misgivings, Baron. The girl is special, but her damned vow must be overcome. She already harbors strong feelings for me. We happened to share a kiss that set my loins on fire. Nay, do not worry, I shall sign. There. The girl is mine." He handed the contract back to the baron, who sighed with relief.

Jarreth felt a contentment flow through him, almost a peaceful satisfaction of being so fortunate to obtain such a prize. And what a prize! The look on his face betrayed his thoughts; the baron noticed and chuckled.

"Why, Viscount, if I did not know better, I would think that you have fallen in love with my daughter already."

Jarreth straightened his face. "Do not be ridiculous. Men do not fall in love in only two days, that is for silly girls with romantic visions."

"Son, I am her father. I can understand your not wanting to appear weak or vulnerable to your guard, and perhaps your servants, but you can admit the truth to me."

Jarreth frowned, and then gave a crooked smile. "Very well, aye… damn it, I love her." He surprised himself at hearing his words, but it couldn't be denied.

The baron's face grew somber, as deep, painful memories surfaced that brought both joy and sorrow. "I loved my wife dearly. Rhiannon reminds me so much of her. You have no idea how much it means to me that you love her. I only hope she returns your feelings."

Jarreth nodded with a smile. "It proves to be an interesting challenge, but I believe my mission shall be successful. She blessed me with a tear when we parted."

"If my Rhiannon cried, you can be assured she has strong feelings. If I may ask, what was she doing when you met?"

"Er, swimming." He quickly decided to change the subject. "If you do not mind, Baron, I am tired and hungry. I shall leave first thing in the morning to fetch Rhiannon back. She is hiding in some caves by the shore."

"The caves?" The baron's face became lined with worry. "I do not like those caves. If you are in the wrong one and the tide comes in, you could drown from no escape."

"But Rhiannon said she knows them well."

"Well enough, I suppose. Since a small child, she has played there every year."

Jarreth felt a bit of relief, but still hated the thought of her alone in cold, dark, wet caves. Why did he leave her? Had he completely lost his mind?

When Rhiannon left Jarreth, tears streaked her cheeks during her whole descent down the cliff trail. She was mindful he watched her from atop the cliff, leaving her wondering what his feelings were for her. Her self-imposed solitude would be much harder now that she knew his touch, his passion, his lips. Could she ever forget that kiss? Did she want to? Confusion muddled her reasoning as she made her way to the largest cave, deep inside the cliff. There were high ridges she could sleep on that the tide wouldn't reach. She was well aware of the dangers in the caves; many people had drowned from being in the wrong one when the tide advanced.

She climbed expertly onto a ridge and threw her pack down. She liked this particular cave, as there was an opening in the high dome that

Rhiannon

let in some light, and a small creek that ran through with fresh water. After a light meal, she laid out her blanket and tried to keep the chill away as night fell. Her dreams would surely be invaded by a black knight, who at first appeared deadly and cold, but kissed her with tenderness and warmth.

The tide began to come in. She watched safely from her perch as the water swirled down below, rising higher and higher until it came to within five feet of her. Then the rising stopped. Knowing she was safe, she lay down on the hard rock and used her pack as a pillow. She groaned as she tried to get comfortable, to no avail.

"I shall be a mass of bruises in the morning," she muttered to herself, as she tossed and turned on the hard rocky ledge. Finally she fell asleep from sheer exhaustion.

She awoke to light streaming through the ceiling hole and voices. Thinking at first that they were just exploring children, she felt no alarm; the tide had gone back out and the cave was relatively dry. When the voices got closer, however, she changed her mind. Two men, carrying a large chest, entered the huge cavern. She watched quietly as they went to a corner and threw it down.

"What the 'ell does the captain 'ave in 'ere?" one spoke in annoyance.

"'ell if I know," the second replied.

Rhiannon could tell from their dialect they were not from her providence. She kept low and still while they stashed the chest against the wall, next to other booty she had not seen when she entered the night before. There was more small talk, much too soft for her to hear, and the men finally left. Rhiannon glanced down at the loot, over at the entrance, then back to the loot. Her imagination began to run wild. Pirates! That was it, they were pirates, and this was their booty. Knowing full well she should leave and go to another cave, but also knowing she had no intentions of doing so, she slid down from her perch and advanced on the loot.

Evangelynn Stratton

She reached the chest, and to her chagrin found it was locked. Not to matter, the lock was rusty and would break off easily with a few hard hits of...what? She glanced around, and conveniently found a sword among the stuff. Lifting the heavy weapon in the air, she managed to bring a reasonable blow to the lock after first almost falling backward from the weight. It fell apart and dangled from the latch, swinging back and forth like a church bell announcing the Sabbath.

Rhiannon's eyes widened with disbelief at the jewels, gold, and silver. This was like something out of a storybook. Her mind reeled with potential. There was enough gold alone for her to live quite nicely the rest of her life, and she would never have to worry about marriage, horrid Dark Counts and handsome knights that stole her heart and then left her.

But would it be stealing? Desperate to justify her actions, she reasoned that this was all stolen property anyway, so what was wrong with stealing from the thieves? For the moment, she took just five gold coins and hid them in her pack. Then she went outside to enjoy the day.

She walked alone on the beach for hours, finding flotsam washed up from the tide. She collected sand dollars, seashells, and other worthless things. When she began to get hungry she headed back to her cave, only to discover the tide coming in, forcing her to take refuge on the hillside. The food would have to wait.

She thought about Jarreth as she watched the sea, wondering if her heart would ever again feel the joy that it did when he held her.

Not one to remain in one place for long, she decided to walk through the woods until it was safe to go back to her cave.

Jarreth rode at a hurried pace. He took the time to shave and don fresh clothes before leaving Yorkshire castle bright and early. There was a bride to collect, a winsome girl with a mischievous spirit that would

Rhiannon

certainly make his life interesting. He had a feeling he would never be bored again.

The tide went back out, and Rhiannon again gained entry to her caves. She cast a glance at the booty when she entered the large cavern, then climbed up to her perch, chewing some bread and cheese as she stared at the loot. She had to make plans. Her pack would hold a lot of the coins, although they would be heavy. Her face lit up suddenly. With just a few coins, she could walk back into that small village and buy a horse, perhaps her same one. Then she could have the horse carry the pack. Aye, that was a good plan, but she needed more coins.

She slid down from her ledge and proceeded to the chest. It was irresistible not to play in the spoils; she ran her fingers in the contents, feeling the coins and gems trickle through her fingers. A necklace beckoned and she held it up to her neck, pretending she was a princess meeting her prince. There were hundreds of rings, and she slipped one on each finger and held her hands out to admire them. She was having so much fun she didn't hear the men enter behind her.

Suddenly she was grabbed from behind and swung around. Her eyes widened in fright when she saw the same two men from that morning, leering at her with lustful expressions. They were dirty, with straggly hair, unkempt beards, and ugly faces. They reeked like she did when she rolled in the pig swill.

"Well now, what 'ave we 'ere?"

She tried to shake herself loose, but the man tightened his grip.

"Oh, I do not think so, wench. Thought you were goin' to steal our property, did you?"

Rhiannon shook her head in desperation. "Nay…I was just playing in it. Please, let me go!"

The other man, who had remained quiet until now, smiled a yellow-toothed grin, as he looked her over with eagerness. "I want 'er."

Rhiannon shook with fear. "Nay, please! My...my father and five brothers are just outside! Let—let me go!"

"I didn't see no one out there, did you Tate?"

"Nay, she's alone all right. I want 'er."

"Oh, shut up...is that you can think of? We 'ave to figure out what to do with 'er."

"Please, let me go! I meant no harm!" Rhiannon was beginning to think she had gotten herself into something she wasn't going to survive. She would rather die than be raped by these men.

Water began swirling around her feet as the men stared at her, trying to figure out what to do.

"She's seen the booty, we 'ave to kill 'er."

"Fine, kill the little wench, but I am going to have 'er first!" The yellow-toothed man shook her away from his partner, reached out to her shoulders, and ripped her dress down to her waist. She gasped in shock as he brusquely grabbed a breast in each hand, and started roughly squeezing them.

She struggled backwards, falling over some weapons that were being stored. Grabbing a sword, she tried to lift it up to defend herself, but the man knocked it out of her hand and slapped her hard across the face. As she recovered from the stinging slap, the man lifted her skirts up and began unbuckling his belt.

"Prepare yourself, darlin'." He got on his knees and leered at her, as she fought and kicked with everything she had. Water was curling around her as she struggled to fight the man.

The other man grabbed the would-be rapist and pulled him up. "Forget her, you idiot, the tide's comin' in. Let's just kill her!"

"I've got time to rape 'er, leave me be! Hand me some rope! She's a lil' wildcat, she is!"

Rhiannon

He managed to tie her hands behind her back even though she fought him, and carried her up to higher ground. The water was now several inches deep on the lowest part of the cavern.

The other man shook his head and yelled to his companion. "Tate, come on! The tide's comin' in! Let's just tie 'er to a rock and leave 'er to drown."

When the man was talking, Rhiannon used the distraction to bring both her legs up and kick her assailant directly in his manhood. He stumbled back a few steps and bent over in pain.

"Shit! You lil' whore!" He brought a hand up to strike her, when he was suddenly lifted off the ground and thrown against the wall. His head hit hard, and he fell to the cavern floor unconscious, blood streaming from his skull. Rhiannon looked up in surprise to see Jarreth standing there.

"Jarreth? Wha—what are you doing…?"

"We must hurry…the tide is coming in. Here, let me untie you."

As she turned around she noticed the other man, lying face down in the foot deep water with a dagger in his back. "Oh, my God! You killed him!"

"I killed both of them. We have to get out, Rhiannon. Come on."

With her hands untied, she grabbed Jarreth's hand and led him the other way, holding her torn dress together to cover her nudity. "There is no time…the water will be blocking the entrance further up the tunnel by the time we get there. We have to climb up to higher ground."

He didn't argue, just followed her as she scaled the wall expertly, crossing back and forth as they climbed away from the water fast filling the cavern floor. Her smaller size made it easier for her to climb, but also gave her a false sense of assurance, causing her to take chances with her footholds. Her foot suddenly hit a slippery spot, and she lost her balance.

"Jarreth!" She reached out to him, but he was too far away to get to her. He watched in panic as she plunged twenty feet below into the inky, whirling water.

Being an expert swimmer, he dove in after her with no thought of his own safety. She seemed to have disappeared. He searched frantically for her, diving and resurfacing through the cold, dark water. He shouted her name in desperation, swinging his arms through the water searching for her. Fear began to grip him; had he come this far only to lose her?

Her blond head suddenly surfaced, and he grabbed her, pulling her to him. She sputtered and gasped, while he just wanted to laugh in relief.

"Damn it, be careful!" he shouted at her. "You scared me!"

She clung to him tightly, and it was then that he saw the bloody cut on her forehead. He realized she had hit her head. "Hold on, Rhiannon. I shall get us to high ground."

She merely nodded and held her hands around his neck, thankful for his great strength. He climbed the wall, and found a ledge high enough for them to sit out the tide. When he was confident that they were safe, he cradled her in his arms and wiped her hair away from her face. She seemed to drift in and out of awareness; the blow to her head was more serious than he first anticipated. She was cold, frightfully so, and he trembled with the realization he could lose her still. His clothes were as wet and cold as her, but his body was warm. He needed to get that warmth next to her.

He stripped off his shirt and doublet, and pulled the freezing girl against him; their bodies melded together in need for heat. Stroking her back, rubbing her arms, he spoke softly to the cold and hurt girl as he attempted to warm her.

Rhiannon

"Rhiannon, how do you get yourself into these things." It was more a statement than a question. He gently kissed her cheek, and she opened her eyes and smiled.

"You came back for me."

Her smile warmed him beyond belief. "Of course I did. I am your Lancelot, remember? 'Tis my duty to rescue you from danger."

"How—how do you know my name?"

"I shall tell you later. Right now just cling to me and get warm."

He didn't have to tell her twice.

She pressed herself against him, her naked chest causing her no embarrassment as her body soaked up his heat. He closed his eyes as he held her, knowing in the part that defined him this girl was the only one he would ever give his heart to.

The night grew cold and dark. He slept little, afraid of falling over the ledge while holding his precious Rhiannon, and thought about the day. He had reached the caves mid-afternoon, but the tide was in and he couldn't investigate them. He sat on the cliff where he dropped her off and waited for the tide to leave. When he could descend the cliff trail, he began searching the caves for her, but found nothing. He was in an adjacent cave when he heard her screaming.

He determined the two men would die the second he saw them. Having killed for lessor infractions, he felt no remorse when he stuck the dagger in the first man's back. The second man's death was the result of impulse and fury. Seeing Rhiannon fighting so bravely, totally outmuscled as the man attempted to rape her, made him strong with rage. He barely felt the man's weight when he picked him up and slammed his head against the wall.

Her sleeping face was the image of an angel. She cried out several times during the night, and he spoke softly to her, cuddling her close until she drifted back to sleep.

Tomorrow he would take her back to her home. Tomorrow she would begin hating him.

He wondered if his plan would work. Posing as a poor knight was a despicable trick, but she said herself she wanted to marry for love. Could she love a lowly knight, who could offer her nothing but his protection and passion? As he gazed on her sleeping face he was sure he knew the answer. She would love him. He wouldn't give her any other choice.

Chapter Five

At The first sign of light, Jarreth carried Rhiannon out of the cave and up the hill to his waiting horse, with her loudly insisting the whole time she could walk. She still appeared weak to him, and he was taking no chances. He had brought extra clothes for her—something the baron had suggested—since she had a way of destroying clothes she wore on her little misadventures. He brought out a fresh dress from his pack, and handed to her.

"Here, put this on."

She looked at the dress with widened eyes. "This is mine! How did you…?" She took a few backward steps as her face showed sudden enlightenment. "Are you working for my father?"

Jarreth fought a smile. "Nay, but when I tell you who I do work for, you shall wish I did."

"Something is not right—you know my name, you bring me clothes, you rescue me from rapists. Who are you?"

"I told you, my name is Jarreth."

"Nay, Jarreth, who *are* you?"

He wanted to pull her into him and secure a sample of their wedding night, but fought the urge. "I am a knight on a mission, working for a man whom you fear."

Her face fell into fright as her voice searched for a sound. "W—who?"

"I believe you know him as the Dark Count."

She took another backward step. "Y—you work for the Dark Count?" Before he could make any response, she took off in a dead run through the trees.

Dumfounded, it took a few seconds for him to realize she just bolted. "Rhiannon!" He took off running after her, and discovered when he got inside the trees that there were trails all over. Which one did she take?

"Rhiannon, you cannot hide from me!" He ran down several trails, and then backtracked. He damned himself for frightening her so badly, and winced with the realization that she could indeed hide from him. She knew the trails much better than he did.

"Rhiannon! Come out and we shall talk!"

"Go away!" Her voice seemed to come from all around. "You are not going to take me to him!"

"Are you going to hide the rest of your life? You cannot run, Rhiannon. Please come out, we shall talk."

"About what?"

He followed her voice, using all the tracking skills he acquired over the years. It sounded like she was on high ground, shouting down at him. The trees muffled and camouflaged the sound, but he couldn't shake the feeling she was up high somewhere.

"About your marriage. I know your betrothed well, Rhiannon. He is not the monster you believe him to be."

"You should have left me to die back there in the caves! I hate you! Go away!"

"Rhiannon, you are hurt, angry and confused. Please come out."

"Nay!"

Rhiannon

Just then he saw the tree; a huge oak, with gnarly limbs reaching over and around one another, branches spaced just perfect for easy climbing. It was a child's dream come true, at least it would have been for him when he was a lad. He tilted his head straight up, and saw her way at the top.

"Do I have to come up there and bring you down?"

"These top branches cannot hold your weight, and I am not coming down."

"Rhiannon, you shall starve."

"Better that than marry that horrid man."

"All right, I am coming up." He smiled as he pulled himself up on the first limb; he hadn't climbed a tree in years.

Rhiannon looked down in dismay when he made the first fifteen feet in seconds. "Knights do not climb trees!"

He looked up at her, smiling. "Who made up that rule?"

"I do not know," she yelled back, "but I know they do not."

"Neither do ladies, but that did not stop you." He reached the point where the branches became thinner and weaker. She smiled triumphantly when she reasoned he would not be able to climb any further.

"Ha! I have won! Now, go away and leave me to die in peace." She jutted out her lower lip and pouted.

"You have not won." He climbed higher, until he could almost reach up and touch her feet. She quickly stood up on her branch to prepare to climb the next one; they both heard the branch crack. Jarreth flinched.

"Rhiannon, the limbs are too small. Come here, and I shall help you down."

"Nay! I would rather fall first!" She climbed to the next bough and attempted to balance on the small limb. That branch held, but the next one was not so cooperative. He watched with trepidation as it cracked, then broke, toppling her down to land at his side. Her feet were in the air and her arms were flaying wildly to grip at anything. The added weight on his bough was too much, and it also began to crack. He barely had time to grab the struggling girl as they both dropped to the next limb, her on top of him. They landed with a loud 'oomph'. This branch held.

With amused alarm he noticed all the scrapes and cuts she had acquired. He also noticed she had somehow managed to put on the dress he brought her, which was, of course, now totally ruined. Her hair was a tangled mess, her dress in tatters, her face smudged and dirty, and she was still the most beautiful girl alive. That didn't stop his anger from surfacing.

"Damn it, look at you! You could have killed yourself!"

"Better dead than married to the Dark Count."

"Your fears are ungrounded, but enough of that for now. We have to get down. You go first, and I shall follow."

She gave him a drop-dead look, wishing he would, and lowered herself down to the next limb, then the next, and the next. Jarreth suddenly concluded she was again getting away.

"Rhiannon, wait!" His added size made it more difficult for him to maneuver down the tree. He still had several branches to go when she hit the ground running.

"Damn!" He jumped the last two limbs and ran after her. She was faster than he anticipated as she bobbed and weaved through trees, but he finally got close enough to execute a flying tackle that brought her crashing to the ground.

She kicked and screamed wildly, calling him several names he never had the honor of being called before, as he rolled her over on her back and attempted to hold her still. Having no choice, he held her wrists and brought his body over on top of hers. That effectively stopped any further movement; she was totally, unequivalently trapped.

They both gasped for air as they stared at each other, she thinking him the biggest bully and most awful man alive other than the Dark Count, and he thinking her the most stirring creature that ever lived. In

Rhiannon

shame she found herself liking his weight on her. He found himself liking it even more. Neither could stop what happened next.

His face was only inches away as her expression went from contempt, confusion, then longing. When it hit longing he brought his lips down on hers, still holding her wrists. She provided no protest as she hungrily kissed him back. He released her wrists, and she brought her hands up around his neck as he cupped her face, devouring every inch, dirt and scrapes be damned.

Her mouth opened to allow his probing tongue, and time held no meaning as the kiss deepened into a desperate yearning they both craved. At that moment Jarreth was unsure if he could keep up his charade, as he wanted her so badly he was sorely tempted to make love to her then and there. Technically she was his; all that remained was for them to say their vows. As his body was screaming yes, his mind fought to take over and remind him she did not yet love him. In torture, he relinquished her lips and rolled off.

She lay still, breathing hard, her eyes closed. Finally she looked at him, unable to ignore that he was as bad off as her.

"Why did you do that?"

He was cursing his traitorous mind as he caught his breath. "Because I wanted to."

"Do you always fall prey to your whims, and do what you want?"

"Believe me, if I did, your virtue would not be intact right now."

"You admit you want me?"

"Fully."

"Yet, you take me to marry another?"

He rolled over on his side to face her. If only she would admit she loved him, he could end this right then. "I am but a lowly knight, remember? What would you have me do?"

"Let me go, Jarreth, please." Her watery eyes beseeched him with a look so sad he almost gave in.

"I cannot, Rhiannon. I have a mission. But I shall make you a promise."

"Promise?"

"Aye. If you still feel the same way after you are introduced to your betrothed, I shall make sure you are released."

"He might not be so inclined, so your promise is empty."

"Nay, he is honorable. If you truly do not want him, he shall release you." His hand stroked gently over her cheek. "Although, most reluctantly."

"Then I shall save us both a long trip. I do not want to marry him."

"Nay, my promise is contingent on you meeting him."

"I do not want to meet him."

"You must."

She sat up and folded her hands, angry he was being so impossible, and confused about his feelings for her. "Fine. Then do not kiss me again."

"I cannot make that promise."

Her eyes flashed disbelief. "You would kiss the bride of your master?"

"Would, and shall. I cannot deny my feelings."

Her face was in adamant defiance as she turned away. "Well, do not expect me to kiss you back, for I shall not. If you are so determined I am to meet this Dark Count before I reject him, I should act the part of…"

His lips silenced her. His action was so fluid, so swift, she was caught completely unaware. Her hands pushed against his chest in a feeble attempt to protest as he kissed her lips, cheeks, neck, forehead, and lips again. A moan emerged from deep inside him; could he ever get enough of this girl?

Her thoughts were much the same. Being an inexperienced lover, she only had his actions to learn from. The hunger within him sparked her own as he softly cupped a breast, causing another low groan from his throat. The feeling in the pit of her stomach moved downward, to a place where this particular sensation was unfamiliar. When she thought she would surely die from his ravishing, he suddenly released her and pushed her away. He had to stop abruptly; his lust for her was

Rhiannon

so great it took all the strength he had. But he had proof of one thing—she couldn't resist him.

"There shall be no more talk of not kissing me back. Admit it, Rhiannon—you want me as much as I want you."

His sudden coldness confused her. She watched him stand up and extend his hand. Not wanting to give him any satisfaction, she ignored his hand and stood up on her own.

"The only thing I want is for you to go away." She turned and stomped off down the path.

He watched the stubborn, haughty, impulsive and beautiful girl he was to marry storm away, and this time followed close behind, expecting anything.

"You might as well get used to me, for I am not leaving your side until you are delivered to your betrothed."

She remained silent as she weaved and careened through the myriad of trails until they entered the clearing, where Daemon stood contentedly chewing away on the clumps of grass that spurted up fortuitously through the sandy dirt. Stopping beside the horse, she ended her silent treatment through sheer necessity.

"Did you happen to bring another dress?"

Jarreth couldn't resist; the humor of the situation was suddenly too much for him. "Why, what is wrong with that one?"

She glanced down at the ripped, dirty, tattered dress, and back at him. "Are you not only a bully, but blind?"

"I rather like it, the look fits you." He folded his arms and kept a straight face.

"Jarreth, did you bring another dress or not?"

Allowing himself to chuckle, he reached inside his pack and brought out another dress. He shook it out and handed it to her.

"Your father knows you well. He said one would not be enough."

Her look would have wilted flowers as she grabbed the dress and began walking toward the trees. He instantly grabbed her.

"Where do you think you are going?"

Her amazed and surprised expression was actually comical. She tried to shake his hand off her arm, to no avail.

"Let go! I have to change my dress."

"Sorry, I am not letting you out of my sight. You might climb another tree."

"And ruin another dress? I think not…now let go!"

"Nay. You will change here."

"In front of you?"

He sighed. "Rhiannon, your body is not exactly a mystery to me. 'Tis rather magnificent, you have no reason to be modest."

"You…you scum! You wish to ogle me as I change? You are no better then that man who tried to rape me!"

"The one I killed to save your honor?"

She drew herself up tall. "Fine. Ogle away, but I am turning my back." He watched without a trace of guilt as she turned around and pulled the torn dress up over her head. Suddenly she was standing in front of him in nothing but linen panties. Her slender back, tiny waist, rounded hips, firm thighs—so perfectly formed, so enticing—beckoned him to reach out. He ran a hand down her back and she stiffened. He quickly withdrew his hand.

My God, he wanted this girl, more than anything ever before. Suddenly all the other women he had bedded held no meaning. Rhiannon, his intended wife, was his only desire, his only need. She had no idea. And he couldn't tell her.

She slipped the dress over her head, and once again her fabulous body disappeared from sight. Her task done, she turned and attempted a look of disinterest, not able to ignore the sly smile he displayed.

"Well, did you enjoy that?"

Rhiannon

"Oh, immensely, your betrothed is a fortunate man."

"Why not let him decide that?"

"Trust me, I know his mind like my own."

"Then he must be as horrible as you." She lifted her chin and sniffed indignantly.

He just shook his head and smiled; marriage to her was certainly going to be interesting.

"Come, Rhiannon. We must leave if we are to reach your home before nightfall." She didn't move, just folded her arms and looked away. "Unless you are looking forward to spending a night in the woods—alone with me."

Her eyes widened, and she quickly hoisted herself up on Daemon. Jarreth mounted up behind her, and kicked Daemon into a canter.

They rode for hours without speaking. Jarreth didn't mind her silence, as he still had the closeness of her body. His arm encircled her waist with ease, lightly pulling her into him as the natural rhythm of the horse compounded his agony.

Finally stopping for a meal, he lifted the sulking girl off the horse and they entered a small Inn. She was still not speaking, which he was beginning to find a bit annoying. He liked her voice, her laugh, her stories. After food was brought, she chose to stare at the wall she was pinned next to, refusing to eat. He took a deep breath, and let it out slowly.

"Are you ever going to speak to me again?"

"Nay."

"Ah, but you just did, so your silence is broken. Talk to me, Rhiannon, I enjoy your company."

"I do not enjoy yours."

"Is that why you chose to stay with me that night at the lake?"

"That was before I knew what you are."

"And what am I?"

"You are a knight without honor, who would force a young girl to her certain doom, while kissing her behind his master's back."

"And confusing the hell out of her, 'twould seem."

Her mouth flew open in surprise. "Confused? It seems you are the one who is confused, Jarreth. I am to marry your master. My lips should be forbidden."

"I tasted them first. They shall never be forbidden to me."

"Even after I am married?"

"Especially after you are married."

He was having much sport with his double-talk, but his mood changed when he saw tears fall down her cheeks, careen over her chin, and drop down onto the front of her dress.

"I do not want to be married, Jarreth."

The tears were genuine. Although he had experienced many women's spontaneous tears—indeed some could cry at demand—he knew a true emotion when he saw it. She was terrified; he felt guilty as hell.

As he gently wiped the moisture from her face, he smiled in an attempt to soothe her. "I promise, Rhiannon, it shall be fine."

"How can you say that? You are just a knight, following your master's orders."

"I told you, I know your betrothed very well. I can say with complete honesty, he would do nothing to cause you harm. Indeed, if you accept him, he shall cherish you." His piercing gaze never left her face, studying every inch as he contemplated the effect of his words.

She wiped her nose on the back of her hand and sniffed, an action so cute to Jarreth he almost burst out in laughter.

"I do not want to be cherished by a demon."

"Oh, a demon now, is he? So soon you judge one you have not met?"

"I do not have to; I have heard the stories."

"And they are just that—stories." He felt duty bound to guard his uncle's unearned reputation, leaving him in the precarious position of appearing to be loyal to his master, yet determined to romance his bride. She didn't miss the seemingly contrary response.

"How do you defend a man whose betrothed you take into your arms?"

He smiled, taking a bite of meat pie as she patiently waited for his answer. Pretending to savor the taste, he chewed slowly and avoided eye contact, simply to aggravate her. Her patience wore thin, turning into indignation.

"Well?"

"You are not his bride yet."

"I am also not a trollop to be used at your whim."

He paused in alarm. "Is that what you think?"

"Why else would you kiss me the way you do? You must be aware I am an innocent, yet you kiss me like—like…"

"Like you drive me mad with desire? That I want you for my own?"

It was her turn to pause; she hadn't considered that aspect. "Well, aye, although we both know that is impossible."

The conversation was finally getting very interesting to Jarreth. The truth of her situation, as she knew it, was surfacing. "And why is that?"

"Because I am a rich baron's daughter, and you are a…" She stopped and turned away, embarrassed she had ever opened her mouth.

"A what, Rhiannon? A lowly **knight beneath your standing?**"

"I did not say that."

He stood up, anger and disappointment overcoming him, and tossed his eating dagger on the table, sticking it proficiently in the wood. "You did not have to."

In total bewilderment, she found herself being forced to her feet—even though she had barely eaten anything—and quickly escorted outside. Her words were not intended to hurt, but she could see that obviously they did.

Jarreth felt flushed with equal amounts of frustration and dismay. She wanted love; she made that fact known the first day they met. But did she mean it? Would her comfort and well being overtake her feeling for him, whom she thought only to be a penniless knight who could offer her nothing?

They didn't speak again until they arrived at Yorkshire castle that late afternoon. Jarreth pushed the horse hard; fortunately the animal was in excellent shape and fulfilled the task. When they rode into the courtyard, Rhiannon was off the horse and running into the castle faster than Jarreth could even dismount. He let her go; there was nothing he could do. She was probably heading straight to her father to complain and whine about her plight.

His mood was not much better than the first time he had arrived at the castle. The same unfortunate groom was given a murderous stare as Jarreth threw him the reins, then sauntered across the courtyard to enter the castle that harbored his little bride. His betrothed, who could not give herself to just a man who kissed her with love and longing. His Rhiannon, who had completely captured his heart and soul, and couldn't stand the sight of him.

He heard the racket the second he walked—actually burst—into the door. Wary servants, most concealing smiles, passed Jarreth as he took long strides down the corridor to the commotion emanating from the great hall. As he rounded the turn to enter, an airborne dish barely missed his head, smashing against the wall behind him. The scene inside made him pause with bemusement.

Rhiannon had her poor father running for his life. He attempted to reason with her, yet keep his distance, as she chased him around the lord's table. Picking up dishes—most with food still on them—she threw with amazing aim as she cursed the day her father was born. All the guests had scattered away from the table, looking on with amused or astonished faces.

Rhiannon

"I hate you! How could you send that big, overgrown bully to come get me? I was just fine where I was. And betrothing me to the Dark Count! How could you? Do you hate me so much?"

"Now, sweetheart," the beleaguered father argued.

"Do not 'sweetheart' me!" She picked up another plate and threw it over his head, only because he ducked.

Jarreth leaned against the door and folded his arms. A small smile began to form; he said he wanted a bride with spirit. Well, the good Lord sure answered his prayer. He wondered if he would ever be the recipient of such anger. Fights usually followed with making up, and it was the latter he anticipated.

The baron suddenly saw Jarreth, and beseeched his help.

"Jarreth! Control her! You are her…"

The look from Jarreth stopped him mid-sentence. "Er, rather, she is your lord's intended. Do something!" A goblet hit him in the middle of the back, causing him to emit a loud "Ouch."

Jarreth just smiled. "It does not appear she needs any help."

"Not her, me! Please!" He ducked from another flying piece of dinnerware.

"Oh, very well." Jarreth unfolded his arms and began to walk toward **Rhiannon. All of a sudden her wrath was turned on him. He caught a** flying bowl mid-air as it was hurled at his head.

"You go away! Go back to your evil count and tell him I refuse to marry him." Before she could toss another item he reached out and grabbed her hands. She fought and squirmed, shouting creative obscenities that made her father flinch. Jarreth simply held her as she vented her rage. Finally he could take no more.

"Little girls who throw temper tantrums should be confined to their rooms, would you not agree, Baron?"

"Oh, absolutely!" The poor father showed extreme relief that Jarreth was taking command of the situation.

In one swift move, Jarreth picked Rhiannon up and threw her over his shoulder. "Would you mind pointing the way, Baron?"

Rhiannon pounded on his back, but couldn't kick because he held her legs. "Let me go! Put me down you big swine! Father, stop him! Do something! I will get even with both of you! When I meet the count I shall spit in his face! I hate you!"

Jarreth suddenly dropped the screeching girl, sending her to shocked silence, and grabbed a linen napkin off the table.

"Excuse me, Baron, there is something I must do." Before Rhiannon could gather her wits, he brought the cloth over her mouth and tied it behind her head, sufficiently gagging her voice to a muffed noise. He then picked her back up, threw her over his shoulders, and gave the baron a smug look.

"Where is her room?"

"Upstairs, two doors on the right."

Jarreth marched from the great hall carrying the silenced girl, who was still pounding his back with her fists. He hopped up the stairs two steps at a time, kicked open the door to her room, and plopped her on the bed. She instantly took off her gag and began screaming, calling him every name she could think of. Finally Jarreth had enough.

"If you do not cease your yelling, I shall gag you again."

"Go ahead! I will simply remove it again!"

"Then I shall tie your hands."

"You would not dare!"

He grasped her hands so quickly she jumped. Within a few seconds the napkin was being tied around her wrists.

"All right! I believe you!" Her anger seemed to have subsided into acceptance, at least for the moment.

A thoughtful look crossed his face as he looked down at her, considering his options. He let her go. "Very well, but remember who is in

Rhiannon

control here. I can gag and bound you within seconds, and shall not hesitate to do so if you continue to act like a spoiled child."

"A spoiled child?" Her anger started to return. "Who is a spoiled child?"

"You are. Rhiannon, you must accept the fact that you are betrothed, 'twould be much easier on everyone concerned. You shall remain in your room until you decide you can act like a lady."

Her haughty look returned. "And just who is going to enforce that?"

He gave her a piercing stare so intense it almost made her shudder. "I will."

She drew herself up tall and faced him, showing him no fear. "You are not my master."

"Nay, but I represent the one who is. Until you are safely delivered to him you shall take orders from me. Is that understood?" He secretly liked her brave, defiant manner. An ordinary, meek, complacent female would have never won his heart. He liked spirit, although there was a question as to what degree.

She nodded her answer while pouting, her large eyes flashing hatred mixed with a bit of passion. It was that small bit of passion that caught him. He roughly pulled her to him, a hand on each shoulder, and gazed soberly into her eyes.

"You are not making this easy, Rhiannon." He captured her lips, and she willingly kissed him in return, with hunger they both felt in the pits of their stomachs. He wondered if she would display the same spirit in her lovemaking, and that thought forced him to release her and step away. The bed was too close and convenient. They stared at each other for a moment, each thinking similar thoughts, neither having the courage to speak them aloud.

"I must talk to your father." He backed away to the door, then gave her one last look and exited, shutting the door behind him.

Rhiannon continued to look at the door long after he left. His kisses were making her crazy with a longing she couldn't explain, and was afraid to admit to. She was deathly afraid she loved him. Confusion consumed her every time he was near. Now that he knew who she really was, he should be treating her with the respect she deserved as a noble-bred lady, not throwing her over his shoulder gagged like a common thief. She lay down on her bed, thoughts running rampant through her mind, and discovered she was dead tired. Her eyes fluttered as she fought fatigue, and finally sleep claimed her.

Chapter Six

Jarreth headed downstairs to talk to his future father-in-law. He found the great hall in turmoil when he entered. Servants were everywhere, picking up broken dinnerware and spilled food, while guests milled around, talking about the scene they had just witnessed. Most were appalled at the unruly girl; some admired her fire.

He stepped over a kneeling servant girl and approached the baron, who was seated at a bench looking extremely distressed. When he saw Jarreth he managed a smile, which faded when Jarreth sat beside him and frowned at the ongoing activity. The baron felt an apology for his daughter's tantrum was in order.

"I am sorry, Jarreth, that you had to see this. Rhiannon is usually not this volatile. She has a gracious side to her, also."

"I am well aware of that, and there is no need to apologize. In a way, I am responsible for this unpleasantness." He stretched his long legs out in front of him and crossed his ankles as he watched the servants clean up the mess.

"You? What in heaven's name did you do to cause this?"

"I made Rhiannon see her true self. She is so attracted to me, I dare say she might even be in love with me, but cannot get past the fact that I am a lowly knight simply hired to bring her to her new home." A slight smile crept across his face. "The trip should be interesting."

The harried father shook his head at Jarreth's analysis. "Nay, you are wrong, Viscount. If my Rhiannon loved you 'twould make no difference if you were a woodcutter."

"I pray you are right. I do not mind telling you, Baron, I fully intend on seducing her before we reach my home."

"You would take my daughter's honor?"

"For all intents, she is my wife. All that remains is for us to say our vows before a priest. Her virtue belongs to me."

The baron smiled through a grimace; he wasn't going to argue with this man. "Of course, you are right, I suppose. The papers are signed, you have accepted her." His face grew grim. "You are not going to change your mind, are you? What if she does something else and displeases you?"

Jarreth slapped the baron on the back and let out a chuckle. "Baron, I am so smitten with your spirited daughter, 'tis all I can do to keep my hands off her."

"Good, good. Well, I do not mean *good*, just I am pleased you like her. And can handle her, from what I have seen."

Jarreth snorted a small chuckle. "I would not say that. I had one hell of a time getting her out of a tree, and that was after I rescued her from rapists and a water-filled cave."

The baron nodded as if this was normal behavior for a girl. "Aye, she will keep you busy."

"Busy, you say?" Jarreth gave him an incredulous look. "More like keep me guessing what mischief she is up to next. She is a curious combination of beauty and impishness." He smiled, the kind a young boy would make when enamored with a girl for the first time. "Aye, I can

Rhiannon

handle her." He stood up and stretched his arms. "I grow weary, Baron. Rhiannon and I depart in the morning. We shall need provisions for at least two weeks."

The baron rose to his feet. "Two weeks? It does not take two weeks to reach your home!"

"Nay, it does not. But it might take that long for Rhiannon to fall in love with me."

"Ah, I understand. You are purposely going to take the long way."

"Aye. Good night to you, Baron."

"Good night to you, Viscount."

Jarreth walked down the upstairs hallway and paused before Rhiannon's door. There was no sound from within. Very slowly, he opened her door and peered inside. Rhiannon slept soundly on top of the bed, curled up like a small child, with no covering. Cascades of hair flowed all around her, hiding half her face. Jarreth brushed the hair back so he could gaze at her, fingering a soft curl before letting it drop on her shoulders. He found an extra blanket folded on the chest at the foot of the bed, and covered her gently, so as not to awaken her. Then he softly kissed her on the cheek and backed away.

"Sleep well, my little bride." He smiled at the tender scene, and then left quietly.

Morning came too soon for Rhiannon. Kady, who was scampering about the room making as much noise as possible, rudely awakened her. Rhiannon opened one eye and frowned.

"Kady, what are you doing?"

"Getting you ready for a two week trip. Your father said you are leaving this morning with that awful man."

Rhiannon sat up and yawned. "He is not so terrible, just a bully." She looked curiously at the blanket she didn't remember falling to sleep with, and then shrugged it off as unimportant.

"Not so terrible? He is the Dark Count! Although, I must admit, I pictured him much uglier and older."

"Nay, he is but a hired knight with a mission to bring me to the Dark Count." She stood up and stretched, then realized she ached all over. "Goodness, I am sore. The caves were horrid. If Jarreth had not come…"

"Oh, 'tis *Jarreth* now, is it?" Kady's eyes lit up knowingly as she gazed at Rhiannon's dreamy expression.

Rhiannon quickly straightened her face. "Oh, really, Kady, he is just a lowly knight. I harbor no feelings for him, and he has none for me."

"I would not be too sure. I saw him sneaking out of your room last night."

Rhiannon raised her eyebrows, then glanced down at the mysterious blanket that just took on a new meaning. "Indeed?" She quickly disregarded the situation. "Oh, he was probably just making sure I did not leave, although he need not have worried. I fell asleep the moment I lay down."

"You did not know he was here?"

"Really, Kady, would I forget something like that?"

"Nay, I guess not. Still, he is handsome, in a dark sort of way, do you not think?"

Rhiannon shrugged. "I suppose, if you like that sort of look."

"And you do not?"

"Certainly not. I want a kind, gentle man, not a behemoth who throws me around and yells at me."

Kady giggled. "From what I hear you deserved it. You practically demolished every piece of crockery. 'Tis going to take the potters weeks to replace the ones you broke."

"Good, I hope Father has to pay a pretty price after what he has done to me. But, no matter. I have a plan."

Kady froze; she hated those four words when they came from Rhiannon. "What sort of plan?"

Rhiannon

"Jarreth has no idea how well I ride. I shall escape the first minute his back is turned." She laughed impishly. "He will not know what happened."

"Oh, Rhiannon…are you sure you want to do this?"

"Positive. And this time I am not telling anyone where I am going."

"Well, thank you." Kady gave her an indignant look.

"Kady, I do not even know myself. The truth of the matter is, I only have half a plan."

Kady glowered suspiciously.

"All right, a third of a plan, but I am sure more shall come to me later."

"Rhiannon, you just cannot go off by yourself like that! Stay with the knight; he shall protect you."

"Ha! Protect me? He is taking me to the Dark Count to be married, in-between kissing me himself."

Kady's eyes grew large and her face brightened with a smile. "He kissed you?"

Rhiannon realized she shouldn't have opened her mouth. "Ah…well, aye, once or twice, I forget. No matter, they were awful kisses and I did not enjoy them."

Kady didn't look convinced. "Uh-huh."

"Nay, really, he is too big…and powerful…and strong."

"And you are smitten with him."

Rhiannon frowned as she accepted a dress from Kady. "I am not."

"Are too."

"Kady!"

The servant's imagination lit up her eyes. "Oh, Rhiannon, are you going to run off with him and live in the forest in poverty, moving from place to place like Gypsies, running from the Dark Count?"

"Absolutely not!"

Kady's face fell. "Oh."

"Besides, he is determined I meet this count before I make a decision not to accept him. But I do not plan on meeting him, so I shall be home very quickly."

"And what of this Jarreth?"

Rhiannon hid disappointment through a feigned smile. "What of him? He shall go back to doing whatever 'tis knights do."

"But…he kissed you!"

"He probably has kissed many women, I am not exceptional."

"I hope you are wrong."

Secretly Rhiannon hoped she was, also. It would be nice to think her lips were a little special; she certainly knew his were. Of course, since he was the only one she had ever kissed, she had no one to compare him to. All men kissed the way he did, for all she knew.

"Kady, how many men have you kissed?"

The blurted question made Kady blush, as she wasn't used to discussing the intimacies of her love life. "A few. Why?"

"Do they all kiss the same?"

Kady's blush turned to a giggle. "Oh, heavens, nay! Some are weak, wet…too wet." She made a face. "And some are passionate, strong."

"Well, Jarreth is assuredly passionate."

"And what of you? Does he not stir feelings inside of you?"

"Mostly of murdering him." Rhiannon did not want to indulge her true feelings, and decided a subject change was in order. "Enough of this talk, we must finish this packing. Oh, Kady, I shall need some men's clothing."

Kady stopped what she was doing and gave Rhiannon a wary look. "Why?"

"Just never mind, find a man or boy my size and secure some clothes." She smiled as her eyes flashed. "Jarreth has quite a surprise in store for him if he thinks I am just going to ride into the Dark Count's castle and get trapped into marriage."

Rhiannon

When Jarreth saw Rhiannon coming down the stairs, dressed in fine riding clothes, her hair done fashionably up, he stared with amazement. He hadn't seen her when she wasn't wearing plain or ripped clothing, or dripping wet naked, for that matter. He wondered to himself how long this outfit would last. She smiled sweetly upon seeing him, which made him nervous. What was she up to now? He walked up to the bottom step and held out his arm, and to his surprise she took it. He began escorting her to the great hall for breakfast.

"Good morning, Sir Jarreth," she said lightly and syrupy. He frowned suspiciously and didn't answer. She noticed his frame of mind, and cocked her head up at him. "Oh, come now, surely one can be in a good mood on a beautiful morning like this?"

"I suppose one could, unless he is in the company of a hellcat with an overwhelming penchant for misbehavior."

She smiled pleasantly back. "Very well, be grumpy, my good knight, and I shall increase my joyful mood to counter your foul one."

They entered the hall, where her father and many guests were already seated, chattering away in myriad conversations. The men all stood when Rhiannon approached their table. Many of them had tried to gain her for their own, to no avail. Now upon learning she was leaving to get married, and to the Dark Count of all people, they felt emptiness within them. No longer would they get to gaze upon her great beauty.

The baron was just bursting to introduce Jarreth as who he really was, but had promised to keep up the ruse until they had departed. "Sir Jarreth, and my lovely daughter! Please join us for your last meal before you leave on your great adventure."

Rhiannon still exhibited the sweet smile as she thought to herself what her father could do with his 'great adventure.' Jarreth took the seat next to her, and began loading his plate.

"I suggest you eat hearty, Rhiannon. This could be the last decent meal we have for a long while." He planned on taking her over the hardest territory, the longest way possible, to reach Stanwyck castle.

"Oh, I shall, Sir Jarreth. I would not want to be weak as a kitten when I meet your liege, the Dark Count." She laughed brightly, joined by all the men at the table, except Jarreth. He studied her intently; what did she have in store for him?

The meal went quickly, with Rhiannon monopolizing the attention and Jarreth barely speaking. Finally the inevitable could not be postponed any longer. He stood up and offered Rhiannon his hand.

"Milady, 'tis time to depart. I trust your clothes and personal items have all been packed?"

Rhiannon smiled charmingly back at him. "I would assume so, but I shall check with Kady." With that she gave a short curtsey and left the table.

She headed straight to Kady, who had finished her chore of packing and was just coming to find Rhiannon. When she saw Rhiannon climbing the stairs, she ran down to meet her, handing her a small bundle.

"Here—the men's clothing you requested. There is a pair of hose, a doublet, belt, and boots. Oh, and a hat. You might be able to jam your hair up under it. I wish you would tell me what you are planning to do."

"Thank you, Kady. I am not sure exactly what I plan, but I shall need this disguise."

"For what? Oh, Rhiannon, I fear for you. If anything happens…"

"Nothing is going to happen, calm down."

Kady was not convinced, but just sighed. There was no talking Rhiannon out of anything she had her mind set on. "Very well, your things are all packed and on a sumpter horse. Please take care of yourself. I shall miss you." She held out her hands for a hug, and Rhiannon hugged her in turn.

"I shall miss you, also. And do not worry! I shall be fine."

Rhiannon

Jarreth came around the corner and unintentionally interrupted the good-byes.

"Rhiannon? Are you ready? The horses are saddled and waiting."

"Aye, I am coming." She gave one last *'don't worry'* look to Kady, and smiled bravely. "Well, this is good-bye for now. Walk me to my horse?"

Kady nodded, and followed the two outside, where the baron was waiting, along with many long-time servants that had been with Rhiannon since she was a little girl. Many woman servants sniffed and fought tears, the men just looked serious and morose.

Jarreth helped her mount, and couldn't miss the small bundle of which she refused to let go.

"Would you like me to put that on the sumpter horse?"

"Nay, these things are personal and I want them easily accessible." She half-smiled innocently; Kady held her breath waiting for Jarreth's reaction. He just nodded, and mounted his own horse. If she wanted to carry a small bundle of lip coloring and hairbrushes and other woman-things, he didn't care; she was the one who would have to maneuver with it.

The baron stepped up and held up his hands to his only child. His love for her knew no bounds, and knowing she was to be married to this young, rich viscount pleased him to no end. Of course, he would have preferred if she were aware of it.

"Good-bye, my precious daughter. I shall miss you terribly."

Rhiannon smiled. *Not for long.* "Thank you, father. I shall miss you, also. Do not worry for my safety, I am sure Sir Jarreth will keep me safe." They hugged as close as they could with her sitting on a horse.

With more kisses, good-byes, and tears they were finally on their way. Rhiannon had been assured her father and Kady would be joining her in a few weeks for the wedding that only she and Kady knew would not be taking place. Kady had been sternly instructed to keep her mouth shut.

They followed the main road for a few hours, and then Jarreth strayed off on a narrow trail leading into the forest. Rhiannon reined up and frowned, then looked at Jarreth through narrowed, suspicious eyes.

"Why are we going in there? Is not the main road faster?"

Jarreth raised an eyebrow and smiled crookedly. "Are you in a hurry?"

"Well, actually, nay."

"Good. But to answer your question, this is the shortest route." He watched her as she looked at the main road, then the trail, and then the main road again. She wrinkled up her nose.

"Are you certain?"

"Oh, absolutely." It was all he could do to keep from laughing.

They rode along single file, Rhiannon in back, Jarreth in front leading the sumpter horse. The trail would take them deeper and deeper into the forest where they would have to camp for the night. He couldn't wait to get her alone.

Rhiannon kept close calculations of the direction they went, the position of the sun, and how long they traveled. If she was going to make a break for it, she had to know what direction to go in. Her plan had already expanded from its vague beginning. Since she had to make sure Jarreth couldn't follow her, she had taken the liberty of "borrowing" a set of hobbles from her father's stables. Hobbles were used to incapacitate a horse's front feet when it was necessary to keep it immobile. They looked like thick leather belts attached in the middle that went around each ankle. By the time Jarreth realized his horse was hobbled, she would have a good head start. It was a dirty trick, but so was taking her to marry the Dark Count. Jarreth suddenly broke her thoughts.

"You are being awfully quiet. Would you like to tell me what you are thinking?" He had started to say 'scheming' but decided against it.

"I was thinking of how pleasant this trip would be if I were not being led to my destruction."

Rhiannon

"You are not going to be destroyed. Really, Rhiannon, can we not just enjoy each other's company on this journey?"

"If I were in someone else's company, perhaps. But my present companionship leaves a bit to be desired."

He chuckled. "Sassy today, are we?"

She quickly changed the subject. "When do we eat? I am hungry."

"Already? I told you to eat a hearty breakfast." Then he thought what the hell, he wasn't in any hurry, as the whole purpose of this trip was to get to know her and vice versa. "Oh, very well, I suppose we can stop for a bite to eat." The trail widened at the top of a hill, and Jarreth reined in Daemon. "Will this do?" He watched her look the area over, and then nod.

He dismounted, and before he could offer any help to her, she jumped off her horse like an expert and stretched her legs. "Ah, solid ground. I feel like my rump fell asleep."

Jarreth suppressed a chuckle. He had never known a woman who would have admitted that. "Here, I will unload some food. Why do you not find us somewhere to sit?"

"I do not want to sit. I have been sitting all morning."

"Suit yourself." He ignored her as he opened the food supplies.

Rhiannon looked the area over as she held tightly to her small pack. *Nay, this place wouldn't do.* She would have to wait until that night, so this little delay would have to be lengthened as much as possible. She was still in familiar enough territory that she could find her way back home, where she planned on hiding out disguised as a boy. Kady would bring her food, she could sleep in the stables, and no one would be the wiser. She could hold out for weeks, while Jarreth searched and her father fussed and fumed. A giggle almost left her, she thought herself so clever she sometimes surprised even herself.

"I asked, duck or chicken?"

She bolted out of her thoughts. "Huh?"

Jarreth sighed. "You have not heard a word I said. I asked if you wanted duck or chicken."

"It does not matter, as long as 'tis not charred."

He glowered at her reference to his attempt at cooking the day they first met. At least she remembered; it seemed so long ago. As he looked at her, he realized he was still as enamored with her as he was that first night.

"You remember my bad cooking, perchance you also recall the kiss?"

"Nay, I do not. The wine, remember?"

"Ah, the wine." He brought a lot of wine with them, hoping to relive that scene. Only this time…

"I need to walk a little, to un-stiffen my legs."

He couldn't shake the feeling that she was up to something, but didn't feel he had the right to stop her from a walk. "Very well, do not stray far."

She nodded with a smile, and traipsed off into the woods. When she was safely out of sight, she found a boulder and sat down to think. Being alone with Jarreth all that morning was difficult for her. She wanted to tell him more of her adventures; he seemed to love them so. Instead she had taken a vow of silence, maintaining an almost dour attitude. She closed her eyes tightly and held back tears. Oh, how she wished things could be different for them! It was obvious he had feelings for her, which was confusing. Why was he so determined to take her to be married to another man? Was she misinterpreting his kisses, or the way he held her? She sat up and set her jaw in determination. It would do no good to dwell and become lost in memories of a love that never was. She had to make her escape, that night if at all possible. Satisfied with her little self-talk, she made her way back to Jarreth.

He had been doing his own thinking in her absence, mostly about her quiet mood that whole morning. She was more than quiet, almost depressed. He had to snap her out of that if he was going to win her.

Rhiannon

When he saw her return, he displayed his best smile and motioned to the food he had conveniently set up on a stump.

"Supper awaits, milady."

Rhiannon looked at the duck, bread, cheese, jellies, and goblets of wine. "Very nice." She wanted to smile, but stubbornly withheld it. Sitting on a log, she took a piece of meat and washed it down with a sip of wine. She knew better than to gulp it down this time.

"Did you have a nice walk?"

"Oh, very...thank you."

No matter how hard he thought, he couldn't come up with a good line in which to start a conversation. Rhiannon was purposely being hard to talk to; she nibbled at some bread and gazed away from him. Her silence was finally too much to bear.

"If you are this quiet for the whole journey, it shall be rather boring. Please talk with me."

Rhiannon was rather pleased her silence was disturbing him; it wasn't an easy task for her to keep quiet. "I have nothing to say to you."

Jarreth sighed. "Can you not think of something?"

"Very well. How long have you known the Dark Count?"

"I have known the Earl of Suffolk, Count Stanwyck, practically all my life, since I was five. He took me in when my parents succumbed to the fever."

She looked up with a flash of surprise. "Why did he do that?"

"I had nowhere else to go." That much was true, he was just failing to mention he was the earl's nephew.

"So, he just took you in and made you a knight?"

"Well, not at age five." He laughed, glad they were at least having a conversation. "I was schooled first. The earl thought education was most important."

"You read?" She was even more astonished.

"Three languages. I am also well learned in history and mathematics. But probably nowhere near as well as you." He added that last part to put her at ease; he didn't want her thinking he had been better educated than her.

She sat up, her eyes widening hopefully. "Did you study about mythology and ancient gods?"

"Greek or Roman?"

"Both!"

He sat beside her and swallowed some wine. Her brightened spirit was encouraging. "What do you want to know?"

She chewed profusely in her excitement as she thought about whom she wanted to talk about first. "My tutor was not very knowledgeable in mythology. I only had a small book that I wore out from reading so much. It actually fell apart." She had temporarily forgotten her vow of silence. "I love them all, but my favorite as a child was Daedalus and Icarus."

"Ah, the man who learned to fly, and his hapless son."

"Oh, aye! My book said he fashioned wings from feathers and wax. I was fascinated by the concept of being able to fly. I decided to try it myself."

He smiled as he felt another of her wonderful adventures about to unfold. "Do tell."

"Well, I spent months gathering feathers for my wings. I was not choosy; I found chicken, pheasant, duck, goose, swan, peacock, whatever. I kept them all in a large sack in my chamber. After a while I had quite a collection."

His eyes danced with merriment; this was the Rhiannon he had instantly fallen in love with. "I can imagine."

"Soon I needed two sacks, then three. They were hidden under my bed. I was just about ready to fashion them into wings when my father got a new puppy. I loved it so, 'twas to be a hunter. I thought that much

Rhiannon

too mundane a fate, so I sneaked him up to my chamber as often as possible to play with him." She stopped and scrunched her face the way she only could; it was Jarreth's favorite expression.

"Well, do not stop there! What happened?"

"One day we were playing, and father suddenly needed my presence to entertain a guest. I left the puppy in my room, thinking I would be right back. Unfortunately I was gone longer than I anticipated. The puppy found the feathers."

"Nay!"

"Oh, aye. He was being trained to retrieve birds by being allowed to sniff dead ones for their scent. He found the sacks and dragged them all out, then proceeded to rip the sacks to pieces."

"Good heavens!"

"A maid happened into my room, and found nothing but a huge mess of feathers covering everything. The dog bolted through the open door, dragging one of the sacks with him. I fear 'twas a while before they could catch him, not before he managed to strew feathers throughout the castle. 'Twas quite a mess."

He was chuckling so much he could hardly speak. "Then what happened?"

"Oh, it gets worse. Father and I were entertaining an important guest in the study who just happened to have an unfortunate aversion to a certain thing, causing him to sneeze and break out in a rash."

"Do not say!"

"Aye…feathers. When we heard the commotion, we all came out of the study only to be greeted by the puppy aggressively attacking the sack, feathers flying everywhere. The poor man began sneezing violently. I thought he would sneeze his head off."

"And then?"

"Well, the guest stormed out in a sneezing fit, his eyes swollen shut, and father was most upset. He demanded to know where all the feathers came from. I fear the truth was revealed."

"More needlepoint?" He made a sympathetic face.

"Nay, worse. I had to pick up all the feathers. 'Twas the most terrible in my room; I woke up to feathers up my nose for weeks. I believe there are still feathers in some places. The worst part is I never did get to fashion my wings and fly."

"I think that may have been a blessing. Rhiannon, have you always been this precocious?"

"I suppose—that is father's favorite word for me."

"Promise me you will never change."

Her mood shifted suddenly. "What does it matter? In a few days you shall not be around to see my life."

He reached out to hold her hand, so soft, so small. "A lot can happen in a few days."

"Indeed." She quickly reclaimed her hand. Soon she would flee and he could go to the awful Dark Count empty-handed and get flogged, for all she cared.

The rest of the meal was eaten in silence, the mood broken.

Chapter Seven

They traveled until darkness threatened, exchanging small talk about their pasts. Finally Jarreth found a good spot for a camp. He was thankful for her broken silence. She was such a delight to be with; the time passed quickly.

She had her escape planned perfectly, or so she thought. She had gone over the plan again and again in her mind; now all she needed was the unwitting cooperation of Jarreth. The afternoon was enjoyable, she had to admit. He was exceedingly clever, intelligent, and fun to be with.

Of course, she had no way of knowing he was only like that around her. He hid all traces of his sense of humor from most people, since he was Viscount Stanwyck, and was expected to be dark, moody, and dangerous. Rhiannon brought out his playful side. She was good for him; he knew it. Fortune had smiled upon him the day he found her swimming in that lake.

As he set up camp, Rhiannon carefully placed her little pack so she could reach it quickly. As soon as Jarreth was asleep, she would make her move. She hoped he was a sound sleeper.

With a roaring fire going, Jarreth sat on a log and waited for Rhiannon to sit with him. She seemed nervous. He imagined she was apprehensive about being alone with him at night, so he tried to set her mind at ease.

"Come join me. The fire is burning quite nicely."

Rhiannon looked over at him, sitting without even a suspicion, and tried to remain calm.

"All right." She sat beside him and took a deep breath as she gazed up at the stars. "Are they not beautiful?"

"Aye, you are."

She felt her face turning red, and chose to ignore his ardent stare. "I used to sneak up to the highest tower and look at the stars for hours. A guard found me once, and reported to my father, and that ended that."

"You have caused your father much anxiety."

"Well, if he was not so protective, I could have had a lot more fun."

"Fun? You call your little escapades fun?"

She turned to look at him. "They were not *escapades*. I was simply trying to enjoy life."

"I feel you succeeded."

"Aye, until now."

Her mood swing disheartened him, and he fought for words to lighten her spirit. "Do you have any other stories of your childhood you can tell?"

"It seems I do all the talking. Surely you must have some adventures of your own you can share?"

He frowned and looked away. "Not really. I led a reasonable boring life as a child, and did not cause the count any trouble."

"Oh, that is right…I forgot you were raised by that monster. No wonder you were afraid to step out of line. He would have most likely hanged you."

Rhiannon

He smiled at her impertinence. "Rhiannon, he would not have hanged me. I fear the stories you have heard about the Earl of Suffolk are mostly untrue. He is not a monster."

"Do you deny he hung a servant?"

"Nay, I do not."

"Ha! See! I am right, what kind of master hangs a servant?"

"Rhiannon, that servant raped a young girl, who threw herself off a cliff afterwards. The count himself recovered her battered body. He wept for her." He lowered his head and stared at the ground. "I remember that day vividly, although I was very young. The servant bragged about his prowess. That fact alone made the earl so enraged I thought he would strangle him with his bare hands. Instead he decided to make an example of him. He hung him in the public square, promising the same fate to anyone who caused the death of another."

Rhiannon was very quiet. "I am sorry. I did not know."

"For the most part, Count Stanwyck is a fair and honest man. Aye, he is fearsome to gaze upon because of the many scars he acquired during battle. He does not accept any trouble from his tenents and servants. If that makes him a monster, then so be it."

"Very well, I shall accept the fact that he might not be as bad as they say. But I still do not want to marry him."

He offered her a goblet of wine and she declined; no way was she was going to get tipsy again. They shared some more duck, bread, dried fruit and sweetcake, then Rhiannon made a long, exaggerated yawn as she stretched her arms over her head.

"My, but I am tired. I fear my eyes will not stay open."

Jarreth felt disappointed that she wanted to retire so early. He was hoping for more conversation, perhaps a kiss…

"I shall make ready your bed."

"Oh, I can do that, just get my bedroll off the horse for me."

"Nay, I insist. You sit still." He rose and went to his task.

When his back was turned, Rhiannon let out a deep breath. *Stay calm. He does not know a thing.*

Jarreth watched her from the corner of his eye, as she wrung her hands, pursed her lips, and glanced nervously around. He was positive she was up to something, but what? He brought back her bedroll and a blanket, then found a smooth spot by the fire and began rolling it out.

"Er, that is too close to the fire. Could I have it over there?" She pointed to under a distant tree, closer to the horses.

Jarreth almost smiled. So that was it? She was going to keep her distance from him, to avoid any chance of intimacy? He could handle that. "Of course, Milady. Anything you want."

The area under the tree was rather bumpy, and he set to work smoothing the ground. When he was satisfied no stones would disturb her sleep, he prepared the bedroll and blanket. He turned to find her sitting on the log staring into the fire, and went over to sit beside her.

"Your bed is ready."

She glanced over at the bedroll, and back at him. "Thank you."

Their eyes locked. Rhiannon swallowed with apprehension; he seemed to stare straight into her soul. She suddenly found herself in his arms, being held with such intensity that it was almost frightening. He brought his face down to nuzzle her neck.

"If you only knew what you do to me, Rhiannon."

She forced herself to pull away; being held by this man felt too good and could ruin all her plans. "You must not—I am intended for another."

He had to admire her integrity, or at least her feeble attempt at upholding it. Her reluctance was obvious; she no more wanted to leave his arms than he wanted her to. He took a deep breath to calm his tortured body.

"Very well, Rhiannon, play your little game. But we both know you cannot keep denying our attraction to each other forever."

Rhiannon

She lifted her chin and feigned righteousness. "You are sadly mistaken, my good knight. I am a Lady, a daughter of a rich baron. I could no more be attracted to you than a master to a servant."

"Keep telling yourself that." He stood up and turned his back to hide his amusement. Who was she fooling? Certainly not him, and he doubted not herself. He left to prepare his own bed.

Rhiannon hurried to her bedroll beneath the tree and lay down. Her attempts to calm her throbbing heart were futile—the faster she got away from this impossible situation the better. Jarreth confused her. When he held her she wanted to give herself completely to him. She couldn't let herself do that, as it would ruin her for marriage.

The thought hit her like a bolt of lightning. She sat up and stared at Jarreth as he prepared his bed. Maybe the answer to her dilemma was right in front of her. If she lost her virtue to him, then no one would want her—certainly not a count—and she could live out her life blissfully at home and…

Her good sense stopped her destructive line of reasoning. Good heavens, what could she be thinking? Had this handsome, dark knight so bewitched her that she was now beginning to rationalize a reason to give herself to him? She shook her head to rid herself of such logic. Her plan must be implemented tonight. One more day with Jarreth could be her downfall.

She lay back down and closed her eyes, to appear she was falling asleep. Not prepared to discover she actually was tired, she unsuccessfully willed herself to stay awake. A croaking bullfrog suddenly awakened her. She sat up and glanced at Jarreth's reposing form, seemingly asleep. When he didn't move for quite some time, she reasoned it was safe, and silently rose.

After dressing in the clothes Kady had packed for her, she took the hobbles and headed to the horses. Daeman nickered when she approached, and she patted him on the neck.

"Shhhh, boy," she whispered. "Hold still. Good boy." She buckled the leather strap around one ankle, then the other. The horse was effectively made immobile until the hobbles were removed, which would buy her precious time if Jarreth awoke, which was likely. She then headed to her own horse.

She wouldn't need a saddle, as she was an excellent rider who was just at home riding bareback. Unbeknownst to Jarreth, she was riding a special horse that had a certain "Talent". She hoped she wouldn't have to test that talent.

A sound startled her, and she whirled around in alarm. All was still quiet; Jarreth slept soundly by the fire.

She returned to her task, leading her horse silently away. When she determined she was at a safe distance, she leapt on its back and took off in a full gallop.

Jarreth awoke to the sound of retreating hoof beats. Jumping up, he berated himself for falling asleep. He had lain awake for quite some time, until he was positive Rhiannon was sleeping. How could he have been so stupid? Not bothering to put on his boots, he ran to Daeman and grabbed the lead rope.

"Come on boy—we have an imp to catch." His body was jerked to a halt when the rope became taut from the horse's lack of movement. "What is wrong with you? Come on!"

Daemon simply nickered apologetically.

"This is not the time to be stubborn!" He jerked again on the rope, but the horse stood his ground. Finally Jarreth's gaze dropped to Daemon's feet, and he saw the reason for the horse's disobedience.

"What the…?" Jarreth crouched and stared at the hobbles in stunned silence. He knew Rhiannon was smart and resourceful, but he never thought she would go this far. As he quickly unbuckled the hobbles, he realized that to Rhiannon this wasn't a game—she was serious about escaping marriage. He had completely underestimated her.

Rhiannon

With the hobbles finally removed, Jarreth jumped on Daemon's back and took off after Rhiannon. He could no longer hear her horse. Panic started to build within him; all emotions disappeared, except concern for her safety. A beautiful girl alone in the woods was not safe. He had to find her.

He began to breathe easier when he heard her horse directly ahead. The moonlight gave him fleeting glimpses of the horse's backend, but it was hard to make out details. Daemon's great size would make it easy to overtake the smaller horse. Then he would give a certain young lady a stern lecture.

The winding trail finally hit a straight section, and Jarreth seized the opportunity. He guided Daemon beside the galloping horse and reached over to grab the reins. As he pulled back Daemon to stop, the moon came out from behind a cloud and for the first time Jarreth realized with dismay there was no one on the horse. Rhiannon had somehow disappeared.

His first thought was that she had fallen off. He quickly dispelled that notion; she was too fine a rider. Until that moment he didn't realize how fine. She had effectively played him for the fool and completely given him the slip. He had never felt so foolish and helpless in his life.

"Rhiannon!" He yelled her name in desperation, not really expecting an answer, but harboring hope that she might answer back, laughing at her successful little joke. He yelled again. The only sound was a lone hoot owl returning his cry.

Embarrassed, angry, and worried, Jarreth turned the horses and headed back to the camp, hoping to find Rhiannon on the way.

Rhiannon had bailed off when she heard Daemon closing the distance between them. She knew her horse would not stop as most horses would; he was specially trained to continue running when a rider fell or jumped off. That bought her valuable time as Jarreth chased the riderless mount. She bolted blindly into the forest and ran until she felt her lungs would burst. Too excited to be frightened, she finally collapsed in a heap and desperately sought to catch her breath. It was then she actually noticed how dark, strange, and lonely the forest was. She knew Jarreth would be looking for her as soon as it was light, so she forced herself to keep moving. As the sun began to rise, she figured she must have traveled ten miles—and she was hopelessly lost. Exhaustion overcame her, and she fell asleep under a tree using an exposed root for a pillow.

Jarreth sat and stared blankly into the fire until dawn, thinking only of his future wife being lost, alone, possibly hurt. Wild images filled his fatigued and worry-muddled brain. There were wild animals and many other dangers a helpless young girl could fall prey to. He quickly reminded himself Rhiannon was not a typical girl. Upon his return to the camp, he stumbled upon her riding outfit and surmised she had changed into other clothes, possibly men's garments. He had to admire her ingenuity. The whole escape had been planned in advance. And he hadn't suspected a thing.

The hobbles were a nice touch; she certainly had style. He held them for hours, turning them over and over while he sat by the fire, not wanting to believe something so simple had given her such a lead on him. He made up his mind when he got her back—and that fact was certain—he would never underestimate her again. She needed something to keep her busy. A baby, that was it—she needed a baby to keep her out of trouble. He decided to get her pregnant as soon as possible, a task he highly looked forward to. But first he had to find her.

The sun was almost straight overhead when Rhiannon awoke. Her neck was stiff, her feet were sore, and her whole body ached. But she was free. And hungry.

Rhiannon

She rummaged through her pack and pulled out some dried meat. Her mouth was like cotton, and she realized she had to find water fast. There must be a creek nearby—she hoped.

Knowing exactly what to do, she checked the position of the sun to get her bearings. Unlike most girls, Rhiannon had an excellent sense of direction. She knew she had to travel southeast to reach home. If she just followed her instincts and kept hidden, disguising herself as a boy, she figured she could reach home in a couple of days—if that blasted Jarreth didn't find her first.

Jarreth. She smiled as she imagined the look on his face when he chased her horse and discovered her gone. She could almost hear him cursing her name to the heavens. Well, he deserved it. She wished she could see him try to explain to her father how he had "lost" her, or, explaining the whole episode to the Dark Count. A flash of guilt shot through her; she hoped he didn't kill Jarreth. No matter how pig-headed and arrogant Jarreth was, she certainly didn't wish him dead. Oh well, he was perfectly able to take care of himself; she couldn't sit around and worry about him.

She stood up and brushed herself off, then stuffed her long hair up under the cap. The clothes Kady had gotten for her were a bit big, but that was to her benefit; the bagginess would hide her slightness and womanly attributes. The little pouch attached to her belt was gone; she figured it must have come loose after she bailed off. Otherwise the clothes were perfect. She reasoned she would pass for a respectable young lad.

The sudden smell of cooking caught her attention. Her stomach growled in protest as she pondered her dilemma. Should she follow the smell and find its source? Or, should she go the opposite direction to be on the safe side? Her stomach won the argument; she proceeded in the direction of the wonderful smells.

Jarreth studied the trail for any sign of where Rhiannon might have bailed off. Lack of sleep and a combination of worry and anger clouded his mind; his power of observance was not sharp and he doubted his own judgment. He kept coming back to two areas. One was at a turn, where she could have jumped without him seeing her; the other was just before the straightaway where he caught up to her horse. Neither seemed likely places, but there was nowhere else that looked plausible. He wasn't even sure if she was ever on the horse to start with. At this point he wasn't sure of anything.

He decided the turn where he had first caught sight of her was the better choice. Daemon ate the meager grass alongside the trail while Jarreth painstakingly searched for signs of disturbance. Just when he was about to give up, he spotted something black a few feet into the woods. It turned out to be a small empty pouch with drawstrings usually carried on a belt. The drawstrings were broken. Jarreth studied the object with interest; just because he found it out here didn't mean Rhiannon had dropped it. But it was highly likely. If she dropped it as she ran blindly through the darkness, her path would lead her deep into the forest. He sincerely hoped he was wrong.

From her hiding place behind the brush, Rhiannon observed the small group of people that were responsible for the enticing smells. They didn't look dangerous; in fact they looked like a fairly pleasant group. Children and dogs played while the adults went about their business. Women cooked and chattered to each other; the men chopped wood while laughing at stories an elderly man was telling. They were dressed strangely. Their clothes were of bright colors, and the women wore earrings, necklaces, bracelets and scarves. The men also wore bright colors and jewelry. The children dressed largely in rags and cast-off clothing, and ran barefoot while the adults completed their tasks. Six odd wagons formed a semi-circle around the central fire. Rhiannon could see pots and pans hanging inside one, which she assumed must double as a supply wagon. Suddenly Rhiannon realized she was looking at a small band of Gypsies.

She giggled as she remembered Kady asking if she was going to run off and join Gypsies and wander through the woods hiding from the Dark Count. Well, why not? It must be fate that she stumbled upon this band, why not take advantage of it? She didn't know much about Gypsies, only that her father hired them occasionally to tend sick animals, and she saw a few at fairs, playing music and fortune-telling with strange cards. They had the reputation of being shrewd and tricky, and often indulged in petty thievery. But this small bunch seemed harmless, almost enticing, to her. They were free, and Rhiannon was sure their women weren't forced to marry some old, ugly, mean count.

Once more her stomach growled, and she decided it was now or never. She stood up—after carefully checking that all her hair was securely tucked up under her cap—and boldly walked into the camp.

The children stopped playing, the dogs stopped barking, and the people became silent. Rhiannon instantly regretted her action as all eyes stared at her. Even the horses were looking curiously in her direction.

"I...I am sorry. I did not mean to intrude. 'Tis just that I am so hungry, and I smelled your wonderful food."

The oldest woman appeared to soften, and stepped forward. "What is a young lad like yourself doing alone way out here?" Her accent was thick and unfamiliar.

Rhiannon realized she hadn't made up a story yet, so a little improvisation was in order. "I escaped from my cruel master, who starved and beat me." She tried to look as pathetic as possible.

That did the trick. "Oh, you poor thing!" The woman stepped up and wrapped her arms around Rhiannon, giving her a large hug that almost prevented her breathing. "Armond, get him some food! Move, this boy is skin and bones!" A young boy ran to do his task, while all the others gathered round Rhiannon, smiles on every one.

They all had dark skin, at least darker than Rhiannon's, and black hair. Several of the women were curiously beautiful, with natural darkness outlining their deep brown eyes. There seemed to be no problem with them accepting her as a boy. Now, if she could only keep up the ruse…

"Come sit down, boy. What is your name?" The woman led Rhiannon to a rickety stool by the fire.

Rhiannon sat down and was instantly handed a plate of food. The smell drove her crazy with hunger, and she eagerly began scooping food into her mouth. A name…she hadn't thought about that. Only one name popped into her head.

"Jarreth," she managed to say between mouthfuls of needed nourishment. "My name is Jarreth."

Chapter Eight

The campfire was still smoldering when Jarreth found the abandoned campsite. He walked around the area, using his keen sense of observation to determine the former occupants. There had been six wagons, possibly families, as footprints were of all sizes. It appears there were even dogs, judging by the droppings left behind, which meant the families were moving to a new home. Or, they were always on the move—Gypsies. He quickly surmised Rhiannon would not take a chance with Gypsies, and made no effort to follow the wagons. She must be still hiding in the forest, and he wasn't going to waste his time chasing after Gypsies. He left in the opposite direction.

The Gypsies broke camp soon after Rhiannon arrived, and she was told to ride in the largest wagon, which was essentially the supply wagon, with all the children. They seemed to take a liking to her, and she found herself telling stories to the laughing throng, mostly true ones about herself. She carefully avoided any reference to her being a girl. Always inventive, she made up details where they were lacking, and the stories got more and more elaborate. She finally had to revert to her own childhood stories, with pixies, elves, dragons and damsels, and ended with her favorite, Sir Lancelot and Guinevere. The children seemed to believe every word, and laughed constantly. At least they were a happy bunch.

She had no idea where they were going, and didn't care, as long as it was away from Jarreth. He must be furious with her, and she wasn't anxious to sample his wrath. She had a quiet moment when the children settled down for a nap, and realized her thoughts were of Jarreth. Sadness swept over her when she remembered his kisses, his touch, his presence. Oh well, no matter, she must get on with her life and forget the handsome knight that held her with such intensity while all the time taking her to her doom. She could never forgive him for that. Would the Lord grant her just one prayer, and allow her to forget him?

They stopped for lunch, and Rhiannon was quickly put to work with the men gathering firewood, while the women prepared food. Rhiannon delightfully speculated she had the better end of the deal. The women worked much harder cooking and cleaning up afterwards, while the men just attended to the horses and checked the wagons for damage. Rhiannon was given the chore of checking all the horse's hoofs for packed dirt that might have an imbedded rock and cause a bruise. Grateful for a job she actually liked, Rhiannon took to her task with gusto, when she was interrupted by a gruff voice from behind.

"I see they found you a job you can do. At least you are not useless."

Rhiannon turned around and looked up at the young man who was speaking. He was the younger brother of the chief, and appeared to be always angry. She had caught him staring at her several times, but attributed it to normal curiosity. Now she wasn't so sure. "I am good with horses."

The man frowned, and folded his arms. "I think you should know I was against having you join us. You are not one of us, and are not welcome by me."

Rhiannon

Rhiannon felt her mouth go dry from sudden fear. "I am sorry. I will try not to be a burden."

"You are already that."

Their exchange was cut short by a man's voice behind them. "Ramon! I need help with this harness!"

"Yea, yea, I am coming." Ramon looked down at Rhiannon and gave her a crooked smile. "Remember, I am watching you." He turned and sauntered away.

Rhiannon felt a shiver go down her spine. Perhaps she wasn't so safe after all.

Jarreth spent the rest of the morning painstakingly searching the forest for any sign of Rhiannon, to no avail. She seemed to have disappeared without a trace. Lack of sleep, hunger, and now exasperation overtook him as he stumbled across the abandoned Gypsy campsite once again. He made use of the circle of stones and built a fire, knowing he had to eat something before he collapsed. An unlucky quail became his lunch, and as he sat eating he happened to notice something blowing across the ground. It was a single strand of hair. A long blond strand.

He picked it up and delicately fingered it. Suddenly everything became clear. Of course Rhiannon would join up with Gypsies; was he out of his mind earlier to think she wouldn't? That would be a grand adventure for her, plus the added satisfaction of getting away from him right from under his nose. He felt like kicking himself for not following their trail earlier; now they were hours ahead of him. If he only had himself and Daemon there would be no problem catching up to them, but he had the extra burden of the sumpter horse and Rhiannon's horse. But then again, Gypsies usually weren't in a great hurry and they had slow wagons to contend with. He would most likely be able to find them at the next fair, which were prevalent during the warm summer months, or searching for work at the next manor house or castle. With renewed energy he mounted Daemon and took the lead ropes in hand, then began following the Gypsy caravan.

Rhiannon was relieved when they finally stopped to camp for the evening. She learned they were heading for a grand carnival to be held another day's travel away, where the men would sell copperware and the women would read tarot cards, strange large cards with various pictures that the women used for telling fortunes. The first task was to get a roaring fire going, and Rhiannon was told to help gather firewood with the men and male children. She stayed away from Ramon, who cast her several hateful looks. It was the first time in her life she had experienced someone not liking her, and she wasn't sure how to deal with it. Especially as a boy.

Jarreth rode hard, but his fatigue slowly overtook him. Twice he lost the direction of the wagons; twice he found the trail again. The sumpter horse started to limp at one point, and he had to take the precious time to clean her hoofs and dislodge pebbles. He resented every second he had to allow the horses to rest. His mood grew worse with every passing minute that Rhiannon was getting her way. When darkness engulfed him, he had no choice but to stop for the night, not knowing that the Gypsy camp was just over the next hill.

Rhiannon ate with the children, where she felt most comfortable. Everyone except Ramon was kind to her, to the point of inviting her to dance when they brought out the instruments at nighttime. She learned there were two dances; one was called the *verbunkos*, the other *csardas*. The chief played the cimbalom; others played the violin and the dulcimer. Rhiannon loved the music, as she never got to hear many lively tunes as she grew up. Her father preferred more traditional softer, slower music, which always put her to sleep. This Gypsy music was something she could get used to. After a few fast, whirling dances,

Rhiannon

Rhiannon was ready for bed. She slept in the large wagon with several of the older children. She learned it wasn't the custom for children to get their own sleeping wagon, but the children requested—more like badgered—the adults until the parents finally relented. The children got to stay up late and talk, and the adults got some sleep and much coveted privacy. The arrangement seemed to work well.

The next morning, Rhiannon felt she had just fallen to sleep when she was awakened by a loud voice yelling for everyone to get up. She rubbed her eyes as she watched the children bounce around as they got dressed to prepare for the day. Rather rudely, Ramon stuck his head in the wagon flap and barked for everyone to hurry, as there was a storm threatening and they needed to replenish their water tanks. Rhiannon had to remind herself that he thought she was a boy, but wondered if he would be any less rude even if he knew her true gender. She doubted it.

The older children, Rhiannon included, were ordered to take anything that would hold water and go to the small creek about 100 yards away. They had camped as close as they could to the precious water supply, knowing that the tanks were getting low. The children grabbed all available buckets, pots, pans and large mugs, then proceeded to walk the winding trek through the thick trees to the small creek. Rhiannon, being the oldest 'child', took the lead and kept the younger ones close by. She was actually relieved to be away from the ill-tempered Ramon, and performed her task with vigor, organizing the children with expertise. It was actually turning out to be quite fun. For a short time she forgot about her plight and Jarreth.

At the camp, Ramon and the others were readying the wagons when an ominous sight rode into view. The women clustered together behind or in wagons with their men in front of them, prepared for whatever this threat might be. As the man rode closer, the men clutched various weapons for defense against this unknown rider. The chief stood out to meet the man, ready to take the first fall for his people. Always the skeptic, Ramon guarded the women and small children.

Jarreth knew he must be making quite an impression among the Gypsy band. He had deposited the two extra horses in a grassy meadow just minutes away so he could quicken his journey to the camp. Daemon pranced impatiently, delighted he was not hampered by the other horses for even this short while. To avoid any resistance, Jarreth made sure all his weapons were in plain sight.

The chief watched as the huge man on the even greater horse, both black and threatening just in appearance alone, stopped several feet in front of him. The stranger slowly dismounted, holding no weapons, and smiled at the chief. The chief smiled back in relief. The entire troupe was no match for this man.

"I mean you no harm," Jarreth stated, easing the tension. "I am simply looking for someone."

The Gypsy chief held out his hand and returned the smile. "I am in charge here. If you come in peace, we will help you."

Jarreth nodded. "I am Viscount Jarreth Stanwyck of Suffolk, nephew of Earl Hilton Stanwyck. Perhaps you have heard of him—he is known as the Dark Count." He waited for the usual reaction. He got it.

The chief's smile disappeared quickly, and he took a small step backwards. "Of—of course we have heard of him," he said with a shaky voice. "Who has not? I regret I have not had the pleasure of meeting the count. Our travels have not taken us in that direction." This was totally by choice; they avoided that area like the plague. It was rumored the Dark Count beheaded Gypsies just for the fun of it.

Jarreth was well aware of the untrue rumors, and hoped it would work in his benefit. It was almost humorous watching the reaction he got whenever anyone learned his identity. Faces turned white, people stopped breathing, and children ran and hid. The only one who had ever

Rhiannon

stood up to him was Rhiannon. But, of course, she didn't know who he really was. Somehow he didn't think it would make any difference.

"I am bringing the count's betrothed to him. She is a beautiful girl, about this high, long blonde hair and deep blue eyes. She managed to slip away from me. As you can imagine, she is in no hurry to become the Dark Count's wife." He let go with a low chuckle, which the chief returned.

"No, I imagine not. But, we have not seen her." He turned to his people behind him, who had gradually moved a bit closer when it seemed this intruder would not slaughter them. "Has anyone seen this woman the viscount speaks of?"

Everyone shook their heads, or muttered "No."

Jarreth nodded. "Well, be aware there is a fat reward for her if you find her. I will be spending a few days at the residence of an acquaintance of my uncles, called Newcastle manor, which is close by to the west. If by any chance you find her, bring her there. Her name is Rhiannon, although she might use another name. You will be well compensated for your efforts." He remounted Daemon, and turned to leave. "Oh, by the way…she might be disguised as a lad. She is very clever, and will lie about her plight."

The chief nodded. "I understand."

"Remember—a fat reward!" Jarreth kicked Daemon and rode away. All he could do now was hope the possibility of large compensation would flush Rhiannon out. He couldn't shake the feeling she was at the Gypsy camp, although he hadn't seen her. If he had asked to search the wagons, he would have created unneeded animosity. No, it was better this way. If she were there someone would turn her in; Gypsies weren't known for their loyalty to outsiders. All he had to do was wait at Newcastle manor. The baron of the manor knew his uncle, and Jarreth always had an open-ended invitation to stop and rest there in his travels.

Ramon walked up to his brother as the stranger rode away.

"You simpkin! Why did you not turn her in? We could use the reward!"

"What do you talk about?"

Ramon scoffed at the stupidity of his older brother. "Surely you must know he was talking about the 'lad' you so generously took in? She is worth money! I say we take her to him and collect the reward."

The older chief shook his head in disappointment. "Of course I knew she was a girl; no lad could be that pretty. I knew it the first time I saw her. But for her to take such a chance with strangers, for her to seek help at the risk of her own life, does not that mean anything to you? Does it not matter how frightened she must be?"

"The only thing that matters is she is worth money, that we can use to fix our wagons and buy new clothes! I am sick of dressing in these rags!"

"Ramon, Ramon, have you learned nothing in your lifetime? Have none of the Gypsy traditions taught you anything? You would turn over a frightened young girl to a monster such as the Dark Count?"

By now a small crowd had gathered, as the women came out of their hiding places and began to listen in on the argument between the two brothers.

"I am not afraid of this Dark Count," Ramon was shouting. "If he will give us money for this girl, I say we take it!"

"No, we cannot. 'Tis not the Gypsy way." Ramon whirled around only to face his own mother. Her soft eyes beseeched her youngest son. "Would your father turn in this young girl? If he were still alive, do you think he would be so cold hearted?"

Ramon paused, and then stood up tall. "I say we put it to a vote." At the gasps of the listening crowd, he raised his voice so everyone could hear him. "This is a decision that affects all of us! We could have money to buy many things…shoes, clothes, fine food and wine! Why should my soft-headed brother make that decision for all of us?"

Rhiannon

The people began muttering amongst themselves just as Rhiannon and the children arrived back at the camp. At the sight of Rhiannon, everyone stopped talking and stared at her. Rhiannon put down her bucket and felt a shudder flow through her. "What is it?"

Ramon drew himself up tall, fostering a self-satisfied expression he knew would unnerve her. "It is about you, *Rhiannon*."

Rhiannon took a step backwards. "Wh—what do you mean?"

"I mean this!" Ramon sprung toward her before anyone could grab him and ripped off her cap. Her long hair spilled down, leaving no doubt that it was she. As she desperately tried to gather her wits, Ramon went on with his ranting.

"Have you considered the Dark Count might find out we are harboring her, and come after us with his vast army? He could slaughter us all in minutes, and for what? Some lying little outsider who tricked us into taking her in."

The crowd began muttering again, as their chief vainly tried to maintain order.

"Do not listen to Ramon! He is led by greed, and selfishness!"

Another man spoke up. "But what if he is right? I do not want to mess with the Dark Count."

"Nor I."

"He is right, we will be doomed!"

"But," the chief countered, "If we turn her in *she* is doomed!"

The crowd quieted down to listen to their chief.

"She is destined to marry a monster! Would any of you not run away if that was your fate?"

"Bah!" Ramon interrupted. "She is not one of us. I say we…"

A loud crack of thunder broke his sentence. The chief pointed to the dark clouds overhead. "Unfortunately, we do not have time to listen to your ranting, Ramon. Children! Take all your water and fill the water tanks. Everyone, ready for the storm! Rhiannon, come with me."

Rhiannon followed the chief into his wagon, and sat down on a padded stool as she was instructed. The chief's wife, a petite, pretty woman named Midajah, brought her some hot tea as the chief sat across from her, contemplating her fate. In seconds they heard the pounding of rain pelt the wagon.

"How did you know?" Rhiannon finally asked the chief.

"A man rode into camp just minutes before you came back. He said you are the betrothed of the Dark Count. Is that correct?"

Rhiannon nodded morosely. Jarreth. She should have known he would find her.

"Furthermore, he put a high reward out for you."

"I would not doubt that," she muttered.

"There are some of us who will want to turn you over to him for the reward, but I will not allow that. I have heard of the Dark Count. However did you come to be betrothed to him?"

Rhiannon sighed. "'Tis a long story."

"Did you agree to this match?" Midajah asked.

"Not exactly."

"So," the chief probed, "You do this against your will?"

Rhiannon nodded, as tears welled in her eyes. "The man you talked to, Jarreth, is taking me to him. He will do anything to get me back."

"Yea, we know." He put a reassuring hand on her shoulder. "Do not despair, I will not let that happen. As soon as this storm subsides, we will head in another direction, away from this Dark Count. We will not attend the fair."

Rhiannon sniffed. "Y—you would do that for me?"

"Yea," Midajah answered. "'Tis the Gypsy way to help those in need."

"But I thought…"

"You have heard many untruths about Gypsies. We are not the lying, thieving people you hear about."

Rhiannon

"Thank you," Rhiannon whimpered, then burst into tears. Midajah put her arm around the sobbing girl.

"There, you will be fine. Lie down and rest for a while. Here, let me get the bed ready for you." She led Rhiannon in back of the wagon to the bed, overstuffed with many colorful quilts. She fluffed things up a bit, and then helped Rhiannon climb in. "Just rest, listen to the rain. No harm will come to you here."

Rhiannon closed her eyes and instantly fell asleep.

Outside the rain and wind attacked the earth with all its fury. Jarreth had barely made it back to the grazing horses when he heard the thunder, just in time to take refuge in the trees. It was several hours before the storm let up enough for him to continue on. He inwardly hoped Rhiannon was safe and dry, and then questioned why he should even care. Isn't she the one who ran? Wasn't she the one leading him on a merry chase? Maybe he should hope she was wet and freezing. No, even though he was most angry with her, he still didn't hope for that. He silently cursed the day he fell in love with her, while at the same time thanking the Lord for making her.

Chapter Nine

When the storm subsided, the Gypsy families inspected the damage. The wind had blown several holes in the tarps covering the wagons, and one of the horses had spooked and broke his line. Other than that, they seemed to be no worse for wear. Several men, including Ramon, hiked off to find the wayward horse while the women set to work building a fire to cook a hot meal.

Rhiannon helped when she was asked, but otherwise kept a low profile. She didn't know which of these people had sided with Ramon and were eager to turn her in. Even though she was thankful for the refuge, she realized it could only be short-lived. As she peeled potatoes, she wondered how she got herself into these predicaments. All she ever wanted was to live her life in her castle, single and carefree. Was that too much to ask?

That night at Newcastle Manor, Jarreth sat at the guest table while his host rambled on, delighted with his unexpected visitor. Jarreth stared into his mug of brown, flat ale, feeling almost as stale as it was. Servants bustled about, especially females, anxious to catch the eye of the handsome viscount sitting stone-faced by their lord.

Rhiannon

His thoughts were only of Rhiannon, how most of this mess was his fault for deceiving her. Yet, if she weren't so stubborn and impulsive, she'd realize she cared for him, so she deserved whatever her fate was at the moment. Then again, if she wasn't with the Gypsies, she might be hurt and wet, and needed him. But that was her fault for running away. Nevertheless, he could have been nicer. But damn it! She didn't make it easy…she could drive any man crazy with those blue eyes, beguiling smile, lilting laugh, and lush body.

Suddenly Jarreth became aware the baron was waiting for a response to a comment, and he didn't have the foggiest notion of what the man had been babbling about.

"Forgive me Baron, I fear my mind has wandered. What were you saying?"

"I said, you have not touched your pheasant. Is something wrong? I could have the cook make you something different, or…"

"Nay, 'tis fine, I am simply not very hungry." That was a lie; he was famished, but his stomach was in knots. Even after a warm bath, shave and change of clothes, he still felt exhausted and bedraggled. He doubted if he would be able to sleep, as every time he closed his eyes he saw Rhiannon. Of course he imagined her for the worst—hurt, hungry, cold, frightened, lost. No, he reminded himself, this was Rhiannon. She was most likely completely pleased with herself for escaping him, and had been made queen of the Gypsies by now.

At the Gypsy camp everyone was settling down to entertainment. This evening Rhiannon couldn't seem to bring herself to enjoy the festivities. She hadn't seen Ramon after he and the other men brought back the horse. There had been many work details, so she could only assume he was just busy. Or, so she hoped.

The chief had announced that the band would be changing directions and heading south. That would put Rhiannon closer to her home, but she still had no idea if she should just walk in the door and announce that Jarreth set her free, or hide in the barn as first planned. Either way, she was free of Jarreth, and for some strange reason she had mixed feelings about that.

Suddenly Ramon burst into the circle and pointed to Rhiannon. "I say 'tis time we took a vote! She does not belong here, and we need the reward for her."

The others were quiet as their chief slowly rose to face Ramon. "The matter has been settled, Ramon. She stays until she wishes to leave."

Ramon's face turned flush with rage. "The matter is not settled! I have been talking to our people, and some of us do not agree with you!"

The chief turned and looked at each person one by one. As his eyes met theirs, they lowered their gaze to avoid confrontation.

"It does not appear that anyone agrees with you, Ramon."

"Bah! They are all afraid!" He turned to his fellow Gypsies. "What is wrong with you? Tell him! Tell him what you have told me—that we need the money this lying outsider will bring. Do we care more about her than we do our own women?" He grasped the hand of a pretty women sitting nearby, heavy with child. "Does not Myra's child deserve a new cradle and fresh blankets? As our families grow, do we not deserve more wagons? Are we going to throw away a fat reward for someone who is not even one of us?"

The crowd began mumbling among themselves, then the chief put up his hands to silence them. "She came to us for help. How would you feel if it were one of our women? Would you want her to be turned in for a profit?"

"No one would help one of our women," Ramon shouted.

Rhiannon stood up. "I would."

All eyes turned to her. When she realized that once again she had opened her big mouth, she knew she couldn't stop there. She stepped further into the middle of the circle and bravely stood tall.

Rhiannon

"I am sorry I have caused conflict among you. I never meant to do that."

"She lies!" Ramon seethed. "She disguised herself to trick us!"

"I disguised myself as a boy because 'tis not safe to travel as a girl. I was scared; I still am. I understand you could use the money the Dark Count offers. But my father also has wealth, and would greatly appreciate the return of his only child. And, I can guarantee he would be easier to deal with than the Dark Count." Her voice lowered to almost a whisper. "Please, I need your help. Do not turn me in to my death. The Dark Count will surely kill me after this."

"Do not listen to her, she tricks you," Ramon shouted.

"Be quiet, Ramon," the chief said firmly. "We will not turn her in. Does anyone disagree?"

One by one his people shook their heads.

Ramon was beside himself with anger. "Fools! You are all fools! I wash my hands of all of you." He left the gathering in a rage.

Slowly the crowd returned to normal. Several women came up to Rhiannon, smiled, and gave her a hug. Rhiannon suddenly felt safe again. She was invited to dance, and she happily accepted. The music grew faster and louder as she whirled and danced with the others. Once again she felt alive and free.

The chief and his wife invited Rhiannon to sleep in their wagon, but Rhiannon didn't want to intrude, and besides, she liked sleeping in the supply wagon with the children. Each set of parents kissed their children good night, and soon Rhiannon was alone with non-sleepy, whispering, giggling little voices. Eventually they all fell asleep, or so she assumed, as she dozed off within minutes of lying down.

Someone cut her sleep short by gently but firmly shaking her. At first she thought it was one of the children, but when she finally managed to get her groggy eyes open she discovered the pregnant girl, Myra.

"M-Myra? What is wrong?" she whispered.

Evangelynn Stratton

"Rhiannon, I am frightened for you! Ramon is very drunk, and very angry. He is threatening to gag and bind you, and take you to the man who offered the reward. If he goes against his people's rules, he will be cast out. I do not want that to happen."

Rhiannon rubbed her eyes. "Why not? He does not appear to have many friends."

Myra put a hand on her swollen belly. "The child I carry is his."

Too stunned to reply, Rhiannon just nodded.

"I do not want my baby to be without a father. Ramon has promised to marry me. Please, Rhiannon—you must flee! Get away before the wine takes over his mind and he carries out his threat."

"But—but 'tis the middle of the night!"

"I know; I am sorry. Here, I packed you some food and brought some warm clothes. I know this area well; we come through here often. I believe there is a manor not far from here. Follow the creek downstream until you come to a crossing, and then follow the road west. You can reach the manor by daybreak."

Of course, the Gypsy girl had no idea she was sending Rhiannon straight into the grasp of Jarreth. She was gone gathering firewood the morning he talked to the chief.

Rhiannon wrinkled her nose. "I do not think…"

"Please Rhiannon! He is coming. Even if he does not succeed, everyone will know what he tried to do, and he will be cast out from my people."

Rhiannon sighed. What should she do? Why was it even when she tried to avoid trouble it found her, in fact, it came looking for her? "Myra, I want to help you, but I can not just go traipsing off in the middle of the night. What will your chief think, after I asked for his asylum?"

"He will simply think you changed your mind, and left of your own accord."

After a pause, Rhiannon offered, "I could write a letter."

Rhiannon

"'Twould do no good," Myra answered with a shake of her head. "No one here can read."

"Oh." Rhiannon felt trapped. As she desperately sought a solution, a noise was heard just outside the wagon. Myra jumped back and her eyes widened in fright.

"Ramon! He is here! Rhiannon, you must leave, now. Slip out the back and head for the creek. Hurry! Here are the clothes and food." She thrust the pack into Rhiannon's hands and pointed to the back of the wagon. "This way!"

Since it appeared she had no choice, Rhiannon acceded. She barely had enough time to put on her shoes before Myra opened a flap at the back of the tent. Rhiannon jumped to the ground and looked up at Myra's worried face.

"Will you be all right, Myra?"

"Yea—I can handle Ramon. Now go…and thank you, Rhiannon."

Rhiannon smiled, and silently headed for the creek. She did as Myra instructed and followed it downstream. The moon floated in and out between clouds, giving her essential light for brief interludes. The woods were thick, causing her to deviate from the creek bank to navigate brambles and thorny berry bushes. In a short time her clothes were torn in various places and she was hungry. Too tired to argue with herself, she found a large rock and sat down to eat some of the food Myra had packed for her. She felt somewhat refreshed after a rest, and continued her journey.

Myra spoke of a crossing that turned onto a road. So far she hadn't come to anything remotely resembling a road, so she determined it must be even further up. She swore she'd been walking for hours already, and her feet were beginning to hurt. But she pressed on, determined to find the alleged manor Myra spoke of.

Finally, she just had to rest. Exhausted, lost and a little scared, she bit her lower lip to keep from crying and sat down on the ground. She contemplated taking a small nap when she heard a snort just ahead of her. Her eyes widened when she saw a short black shape walking to the water for a drink. She blinked and squinted in an attempt to identify the creature. The moon suddenly made an appearance, and she saw the animal at the same time it saw her.

It was a wild boar, with four-inch tusks that could do a lot of damage. Rhiannon was too terrified to move. She stared at the boar, and he stared back. *Just go away*, she willed, but the animal pawed the ground and snorted loudly. *Oh Lord, he is going to charge me!* She jumped to her feet and leaped to the nearest climbable tree, thankfully only a few yards away

The boar barely missed her legs as she pulled herself up to the first limb. She swung her body over, and sat on the limb while the boar squealed in rage at having missed his victim.

"Ha!" Rhiannon yelled down at him. "Too fast for you, was I?"

The boar snorted some more, than turned and left. She could hear him grunting nearby, when she heard a rip, and realized he had found her food sack. All she could do was sit and listen to him devour all her food.

"You shandy pig!" she shouted. "Go away! Shoo!"

A snort was her reply.

A few miles away, Jarreth awoke with a start. He had finally managed to drink enough ale to pass out, and had no idea what caused him to wake up. The manor was quiet. He got out of bed and walked to the window, then opened the shutters to stare at the woods past the manor grounds. Except for the usual sounds of night, nothing was amiss. He strained his ears one more time. There…what was that?

"Rhiannon," he whispered, "where are you?" He listened again, and heard nothing. Was he going mad, imaging he heard her yell out? Too weary for answers, he lay back down and fell into a restless sleep.

Rhiannon

At that moment Rhiannon would have been thankful for any kind of sleep. The boar seemed intent on staying around, so she was effectively stuck. And sleeping in a tree wasn't the most intelligent, or easy, thing to do. She was afraid if she dozed off she would fall and become a pig dinner. Not that he hadn't already had dinner, damn his fat little porky hide. *Her* dinner—and breakfast, too. She swore the moment she got home she would order baked ham for her first meal.

The boar finally tired of inactivity, and left. Rhiannon waited at least an hour to make sure he was actually gone, and then carefully jumped down off her perch. The sun was just starting to rise, so at least now she had some light to guide her. The food pack was destroyed. She hoped the manor was close so she didn't starve. Her growling stomach agreed.

She followed the creek for a short distance, and suddenly arrived at the crossing. It was only minutes away from where the boar had attacked her. She muttered a few unrepeatable oaths as she turned west and hoped she found the manor before she dropped dead from exhaustion.

A few early-morning travelers passed her along the way. They all looked suspiciously at her, and she realized she must look quite a sight. Before she knew it, she saw the manor straight ahead. By this time she could have fallen asleep standing up. Her exhaustion overwhelmed her hunger, and she curled up in the stable in a pile of hay.

Jarreth slept late into the morning, and awoke in a sour mood. He was a man of action, and could not just sit around waiting for the Gypsies to bring Rhiannon to him. The strange dream last night—was it a dream? Had he heard something? He had to inspect the woods, just for his own peace of mind.

A loud voice awakened Rhiannon. She blinked, still exhausted, as she realized the voice was addressing her.

"'Ere, lass! What be the meanin' of this? Messin' up my fresh cut 'ay, are ye?"

Rhiannon sat up and rubbed her eyes. She was finally able to focus on an old man who didn't appear thrilled to see her. She assumed he was the Avener in charge of the barn and horses. "I—I am sorry."

"Oh, ye'll be sorry, al'right…the master will be 'appy to deal with ye."

Rhiannon abruptly realized the master of the manor would never believe she was a lady, not the way she looked. She had to make up something, fast.

"Oh, please, kind sir! Do not take me to your master! I meant no harm, and will work for any damage I have caused!" She forced a few tears and sniffed pathetically, trying her best to look like a wounded deer.

The old Scotsman softened, as did everyone when Rhiannon went into an act to get her way.

"Now, now, do not cry. 'Ere, let's take ye to the cook, she'll be fixin' ye a 'ot meal and clean ye up. Come, lass."

She nodded gratefully and followed him to the back of the manor, where several servants were performing their chores. One man chopped wood while a maid hung a fresh wash out to dry. Others plucked feathers off geese; all were cheerful and conversed with each other, paying no heed to Rhiannon as the Avener opened the back door and led her in.

A rotund, happy woman immediately stopped stirring her porridge, and wiped her hands on her apron. "What have we here?" She stared at Rhiannon with a mixture of pity and skepticism.

"A lass I found sleepin' in me 'ay. I don'a know what 'er story is, she 'asn't told me yet."

The cook lost her smile and folded her arms. "Well, child? Would you like to explain how you came to be sleeping in Mr. Mctovish's hay?"

Rhiannon's mind began reeling. A story. She had to come up with a good one.

Rhiannon

"I...I was traveling with my lord and lady, and was sent to fetch water. When I returned, I must have become lost, because I could not find them. I fear outlaws attacked them. I have been wandering for days in the woods. I saw this manor, and just had to rest." She lowered her gaze to the floor and hoped her lie was convincing.

The cook didn't look convinced. "Hmmm. You do not look like a lady's servant to me."

Rhiannon sniffed back another fake tear. "I know I must look a fright, but I can prove I was in the service of my lady. I can read and write; they taught me."

The cook raised her eyebrows. "Indeed?" If this lost waif were truly literate, it would prove she wasn't just another thieving commoner. Hardly any peasants could read, let alone write.

"All right—let us test you." The cook went to a cupboard and took down a book, then opened it in front of Rhiannon. "Read this."

"Very well." Rhiannon took the book and began reading.

"Mead: dissolve four pounds of honey in a gallon of water with half an ounce of ginger." She looked up at the cook in surprise. "This is a recipe book? How delightful! Did you write this?"

"Me? Oh, no, child, I found it when I started working here. It is supposed to have all the master's favorite dishes in it, but it is not much good to me—I cannot read."

Rhiannon kept turning the pages, looking them over with delight. "Ummm, plum pudding. And here is one for raisin stuffing."

The cook's eyes lit up. "Raisin stuffing, you say? Let me see that...I've heard rumors the master does not care for my stuffing." She grabbed the book away from Rhiannon, and then belatedly remembered her reading inability. "Er, do you think you could read this to me, child? I would be much obliged."

Evangelynn Stratton

"Of course," Rhiannon answered, and began reading the ingredients while the cook listened intently. Neither noticed the Avener slip out the door.

He hurried back to the barn, and was surprised to see his master's guest standing in the doorway.

"Mornin' to ye, Viscount Stanwyck! What can I be doin' for ye?"

Jarreth nodded a polite acknowledgment to the old Scotsman. "Kindly fetch my horse. I shall be gone most of the day."

"Right away, sir," the old man answered, and left to get Daemon.

Jarreth paced, not able to fathom his nervousness. He felt like his greatest desire was just out of reach, like the waiting he endured while Daemon was being trained. Every day he watched as the great horse fought the trainers, defiant that his spirit would not be broken. Jarreth finally stepped in and took over the training himself. His passion for the animal won it over; he felt the same way now. Somehow he could sense that Rhiannon was close.

Daemon was brought out, and Jarreth began to ready him. If the dream had any meaning, then Rhiannon was nearby in the woods. He vowed to himself that he would ride all day in an attempt to find her. As he saddled the huge warhorse, he heard laughing coming from the back door of the manor. He stopped and listened intently. Something about that laugh…

He shook his head in disbelief. Was he truly going mad, hearing her in her dreams, and now again in the courtyard? Had Rhiannon so bewitched him, he was now questioning his own sanity? He mounted Daemon and galloped from the courtyard.

Almost immediately afterwards, Rhiannon and the cook exited the back door. Both were laughing, Rhiannon having won the cook over with her unequivocal charm.

"You are a delight, child," the cook was saying. "Now, let me find you some better clothes and clean you up a bit. Then you can start reading

Rhiannon

me that book. Will not the master be surprised when I cook him all his favorite dishes?"

After securing a plain, but clean, servant dress, Rhiannon washed her face and hands, silently wishing for a hot bath. She pulled her hair up in a high bun, and then plopped on a white servant's cap. At least now she blended in with the other servants, that is, at first glance. Close up her flawless skin and rare beauty gave away her nobility.

The cook had a cushy job for her—all she had to do was read the recipes, over and over, until the cook memorized them. The older woman wanted to make everything at once, so excited was she with an 'assistant' who could read. Finally, when they took a lunch break, the cook rolled her eyes in disbelief.

"I have not even asked your name, child. Mine is Martha."

Rhiannon grinned. "Mine is…uh…Gwenivere."

"Gwenivere?" Martha smiled in reply. "What a romantic name."

"Aye, I like it." So did Jarreth, at one time. Why did she find herself thinking of him so often?

Jarreth rode through the woods, circling the manor, unaware of what he expected to find. After hours of futile searching, he finally decided to find the Gypsies. When he arrived at their previous location, there was nothing left but flattened ground. His intuition kept gnawing at him; he just knew Rhiannon had been there. Did she flee, or was she able to convince the Gypsies to take her with them? He could ride for days in vain; they could be anywhere by now. He slammed his fist against a tree and cursed. How could one small girl cause him so much trouble?

He found a nearby creek and filled his canteen, letting Daemon rest while he planned his next move. It would be dark in a few hours, and the fastest way back to the manor was to follow the creek. Along the way he had a chance to think. If he ever found Rhiannon again, he would have to treat her as a prisoner. That might prevent her from escaping, but wouldn't do much in the way of endearing himself to her. He detested his confusion. Before he met Rhiannon, he had been confident and commanding. No one questioned his orders. Now he wasn't sure what the next day would bring.

Dusk was upon him. If he hurried, he could make it back to the manor before nightfall. Suddenly something on the ground caught his eye. He dismounted and inspected the item; it appeared to be a pack that had been ripped apart. There were traces of food and a few items of clothing. Although there was nothing to confirm the pack was Rhiannon's, he felt a rush of apprehension flow through him. If it were hers, did she meet the same fate? He frantically checked the area for blood, and relaxed upon finding none. He mounted and rode back to the manor, reaching it just as the sun set.

After an excellently prepared dinner, which his host said was due to a new cooking assistant, he again turned to ale for comfort. It was apparent the Gypsies weren't going to turn Rhiannon in, or perhaps he had been wrong, and she was never with them in the first place. His mind swirled with possibilities. These woods had bears, outlaws, and Lord knew what other dangers. How long could she last? He finally decided upon a course of action. He had to ride back to Yorkshire and invoke help from her father. Perhaps if a hundred men scoured the woods they would find her, dead or alive. He shuddered at the thought of finding her dead. How could he have let this happen?

His sleep was fitful that night.

Rhiannon, on the other hand, slept rather well on a small bed in the servant quarters. She had already made arrangements to work until she earned enough to buy a horse. Then she would return home and convince her father she was not the marrying type.

She helped Martha prepare a wonderful breakfast, and then was given a small break. The sunny day beckoned her, so she decided to take a short walk.

Rhiannon

Jarreth had already saddled Daemon, and was preparing for his long journey. He had already said his farewells to his host, making arrangements to leave the two extra horses there to expedite his journey. His mood was surly; never in a hundred years could he imagine himself in this position. He wasn't anxious to confront the baron.

Daemon pawed the ground, inpatient to get on the road. Jarreth led him out to the courtyard and tightened the cinch. Just as he started to mount, he remembered his canteen was almost empty. He grabbed it and headed for the well.

Rhiannon came around the corner from her walk, and decided she was thirsty. She said hello to a passing servant, then raised her eyes to the person standing at the well. Her jaw dropped in disbelief when she stared straight into the face of Jarreth.

They both blinked in astonishment, too stunned to move. Rhiannon found her wits first. She took off running across the courtyard as fast as her legs would carry her.

Her reaction may have been quick, but Jarreth was faster. It only took a few running strides for him to catch up to her and grab her. It was like holding a wildcat.

She kicked and clawed, yelling obscenities no lady should even know. Jarreth held her tight, and threw her over his shoulder.

"Not this time, Rhiannon. You will never escape me again."

He marched straight to Daemon as a small crowd of astonished servants gathered. He tossed her across the horse's back and quickly mounted, then looked down at the shocked onlookers.

"I fancy this servant girl, so I am taking her. Tell your master I will send compensation for her later." With that he kicked Daemon and galloped off.

Rhiannon held on for dear life; being belly-down across a running horse was not her idea of graceful horsemanship. Jarreth held her down with one hand, his superior strength effectively pinning her. When they were a respectful distance away, Jarreth reined up Daemon, let go of Rhiannon, and dismounted. Rhiannon fell roughly to the ground and immediately picked herself up. Then she braced herself for the fight of her life.

"Y-you big ox! How dare you kidnap me in broad daylight! Who do you think you are?"

"I am the one taking you to your wedding. Or have you forgotten?"

"I thought I made it clear there is not going to be a wedding."

"The only thing you have made clear is you are a disobedient, spoiled child."

"And you are an overgrown, unbearable bully! What must all those servants think, carrying me away like a sack of rubbish?"

"They are probably thinking I am having my way with you as we speak."

She gasped in horror. "You would not dare!"

"No, I would not. Right now I would rather spank you then bed you."

"You stay away from me!" She backed away and looked desperately around her.

"Oh no, not again, Rhiannon." He grabbed her by her shoulders. "From now on you are my prisoner. I will not tie your hands, unless you give me just cause. Do not run from me again." His tone was adamant.

Not one to back down easily, Rhiannon drew herself up tall and looked him bravely in the eyes. "Or what?"

"Or I shall bind and gag you for the rest of the journey."

She closed her mouth and simmered. How could he treat her, the daughter of a baron, like a common thief?

Jarreth had to fight the smile that threatened to give him away. He was so glad to see her, alive and safe, that his first impulse was to hug her. When he saw her at the well, he couldn't believe his good fortune. Now that he had her back, he would never let her go.

Rhiannon

"Get on the horse," he commanded. "Thanks to your little escapade, we have a great deal of ground to make up."

Rhiannon folded her arms and looked away. "Nay."

"Very well." He picked her up and threw her up on Daemon, none too lightly. She squealed in protest as he got on and wrapped one arm around her. "Hold on; if you fall I will not catch you." He kicked the horse into a canter.

Rhiannon felt his strong arm around her, and despite her predicament felt curiously safe. It was understandable he was extremely displeased with her, but she really didn't fear him. Somehow she knew he would never hurt her. His actions didn't match his gruff words.

In a while he brought Daemon down into a walk. Both remained quiet for a long while, when Jarreth finally decided to break the silence.

"Whatever were you thinking, Rhiannon? You could have been killed. I pictured you being attacked by a bear."

Rhiannon was still, and then she cleared her throat. "Actually, 'twas a boar."

Jarreth abruptly brought Daemon to a halt. "A boar? Were you hurt?"

"No, I climbed a tree while he ravaged my food supply."

Jarreth coughed to hide his amusement. "And where did you get the food supply?"

"From the Gypsies."

"So you *were* with them! Why did they not turn you in?"

She took a deep breath and let it out slowly. "'Tis a long story."

"We have nothing but time."

"I do not want to talk about it." She turned her head away.

Jarreth kicked Daemon back into a walk. "Fine."

They were silent for a short while more, and then Rhiannon murmured something inaudible.

"What did you say?"

"I said, they never would have suspected I was a girl if I had just cut my silly hair."

He brought a hand up and ran his fingers through her long tresses. "Whyever would you want to cut your hair?"

"To look like a boy."

"And why would you want to look like a boy?"

"Because boys have all the fun. I have always wanted to be a boy. If I had just cut my hair like before…"

"Before?"

"Aye, I cut all my hair off when I was ten."

"Because you wanted to be a boy?"

"Aye."

"And you thought cutting your hair would make you one?"

She paused. "Well, 'twas a start."

"I see."

"I probably would not have done it if my father had not made me so angry."

"And what did your terrible, mean, cruel father do this time?"

"Refused to teach me archery."

"And that was reason to cut off your hair?"

"Well, not exactly." She paused. "Besides, he had no reason to punish me. 'Twas not really my fault."

"What was not your fault?"

"'Twas a small wound, and it healed quite nicely. Eventually."

Jarreth stopped the horse again. "Rhiannon, what are you talking about?"

She turned to look at him. "I wanted to learn to shoot, is that so bad? My father would not allow it. We had lots of visiting relatives that summer, and all the boys were learning."

"In self defense, I am sure."

Rhiannon

She ignored his sarcasm. "My favorite cousin from Wales was there, and he agreed to teach me. We sneaked out my window on a rope, and…"

"You crawled down two stories on a rope?"

"Well, of course! We could not just walk out the front door, could we?"

"Nay, of course not."

"Anyway, we found a good hay pile to shoot at, and I was doing very well, when some busybody saw the rope and reported it to my father. He came looking for me, and rather ruined my lesson."

"Ah, he dragged you back to the castle."

"Er, not exactly."

"Then just how did he ruin your lesson?"

She was silent.

"I said, how did he…"

"I heard you."

"Well?"

"'Twas his fault! If he had not startled me, I would not have released my arrow like that."

Jarreth grimaced. "Like what?"

"Sort of…straight up. Of course, my clumsy father picked that moment to trip and fall flat on his face. I had no control over where the arrow landed."

"I am almost afraid to ask, but I must know—where did it land?"

"It came down right over him and struck him in the, um, backside."

Jarreth could no longer contain himself. He began chuckling, and then broke into laughter. "You shot your father in the arse?"

"Good heavens, you should have heard him holler! You would have thought he was mortally wounded."

"I am sure."

"Anyway, he was so angry he confined me to my room while he thought of a proper punishment."

"And that is when you cut off all your hair?"

"Nay."

"Nay?"

"Well, not yet. He decided to send me to a prissy finishing school in London, ran by a bunch of sour-faced biddies, to make a lady out of me."

"How horrible."

"Aye. He had to ask a favor of getting me accepted, for the school did not accept just anyone. They choose only the best; he assured them I was a proper young women of noble rank."

"And of course, you set off right away to dispel that notion."

"They sent a representative to consider my application. When I found out she was coming, I was desperate. There was no way I was going to leave. I borrowed a stableboy's clothes and took a knife and cut off all my hair, right up to the ears. I hid in the courtyard, and when the old biddie's carriage pulled up, I began pelting it with mud. The prudish woman thought I was a rowdy peasant boy, and began hitting me with her fan. I was able to place a substantial-sized mudball right in her face. Oh, you should have heard the language! Father came lumbering out of the castle and tried to calm things down, but the woman insisted he beat the unruly peasant boy. When the truth of my identity became known, she turned tail and headed back to London. Father was so embarrassed he did not set foot in London for years."

Jarreth was laughing so hard he feared he would fall off his horse.

"I am glad you find it so humorous. My father did not."

"I am quite sure."

"Anyway, he could not sit down for weeks, and he blamed everything on me. Somehow the full story of his injury became known. He still claims he hears snickering behind his back when he visits London."

Rhiannon

"I would not doubt that." He pulled her tighter into him and enjoyed her closeness. "'Tis a wonder you ever reached adulthood. Rhiannon, promise me you will never flee from me again."

"I cannot promise that."

"Am I so horrible?"

She leaned into him, and had to admit to herself she had missed him. "Nay, you are not, but I fear the Dark Count is. 'Tis from him I flee, not you."

Jarreth didn't answer. He wanted to tell her the truth, but knew it was not time for that.

"Just remember your promise," she continued. "When I meet him and still do not want to marry him, you promised I would not have to."

"Aye, I remember." He highly anticipated the moment she discovered that he, not his uncle, was her intended.

Chapter Ten

They rode until nearly nightfall, when Jarreth found a good clearing to spend the night. During the ride Rhiannon told him all about her adventures with the Gypsies. He was a bit disturbed when she relayed that one man had been hostile towards her, but she assured him for the most part her experience had been positive.

He built a fire and made them some dinner. Then he spread out his bedroll and motioned to Rhiannon.

"Lie down."

She looked at the single bedroll and back at him. "Where are you going to sleep?"

"Beside you."

Her shocked expression changed to confusion, then indignation. "I think not."

"Come, Rhiannon, do you think I will take the chance of you running again?"

"But…"

"There is no discussion. Do not be so indignant; we have already spent one night together in the caves."

Rhiannon

"That was different."

"How so?"

"Well, we…ah…had no choice. We were stuck there."

"And now you are stuck here. Lie down."

"You are no gentleman!"

"I never professed to be."

She glared daggers at him, and then lay down, rolling over on her side facing away. He promptly lay down beside her and threw an arm around her.

"Is it necessary to manhandle me?"

"Aye. Do not bother trying to get away. I am a light sleeper and will wake the moment you stir."

"But…I toss and turn!"

"Then we shall toss and turn together."

She fell silent, and closed her eyes. She hated to admit she rather enjoyed the feel of his massive body next to hers. In a few minutes, after a long bout of silence, Jarreth could no longer resist the opportunity. He brought his mouth down to her neck and gently kissed it.

"I am still awake."

"Good. Turn and face me, Rhiannon."

"Why?"

"So we can talk."

She rolled over and looked at him. The glowing fire illuminated the area so Jarreth could enjoy her beauty. Her haughty expression was gone, leaving a serene, extremely desirable face to torment him. He stared at her, studying every aspect, every line and curve of her face.

"Well?" she finally asked.

"Well, what?"

"You said you wanted to talk."

"So I did." He fingered a long strand of her hair, curling it around his finger while he thought of words to say. "Rhiannon, what do you want from life?"

She furled her eyebrows and frowned. "What do you mean?"

"If you had a choice; if you could do anything you wanted, what would you do?"

She thought for a few seconds, then her face lit up. "For starters, I would not marry the Dark Count."

Jarreth smiled. "Very well. Then what?"

"Hmmm. No one has ever bothered to ask me. You would most likely ridicule me if I told you."

"I promise I will not."

"All right." She raised herself up on one elbow. "I like to write stories."

Jarreth let that sink in, then smiled widely. "Indeed?"

Her face fell. "You are already laughing."

"Nay, nay, I think 'tis delightful! You tell wonderful stories."

"Do you really think so?"

"Oh, absolutely."

She lay down on her back and stared up at the stars. He stared only at her as she continued.

"I have been writing stories ever since I learned to write. I never told anyone, except Kady. They are all in a box under my bed; there are quite a few of them. There are stories about elves, and fairies, but my favorite ones are about Africa."

"Africa?"

"Aye, about lions and zebras, and every other animal. Africa is full of them, you know. I so want to go there some day. My dream to bind all my stories in a book and present it to the king." Her face fell again. "But 'tis just a dream. My father is determined to marry me off, condemning me to a life of boring drudgery. No man, especially the Dark Count, is going to let me write books."

Rhiannon

Jarreth brushed a wayward lock of hair from her face. "I would."

"Ah, but I am not marrying you. Perhaps you are an exception; most men want their wives to be dumb and pretty. But enough about me. Since you know my impossible dream, I believe 'tis only fair that you tell me about yourself. What do you want, Jarreth?"

He closed his eyes when she said his name. Could she not see he wanted only her? Her child-like lust for life had not yet been tempered with tragedy or hardship. He desperately craved her closeness. Trying to avoid her question, he rose to his knees and pretended to stir up the fire, moving logs around in a useless manner.

"You did not answer me."

"What do you think I want, Rhiannon?"

She laughed, sending shivers throughout him. "Ah, but you are answering a question with a question. That is avoiding the subject."

He quit his pretence with the fire and sat down beside her. "You are right. I shall have to think about it."

"Now you tease me. Are you meaning to say you have no dreams?"

"I did as a child."

"And now?"

He let out a deep sigh. He had never opened his heart to a woman, but for some reason felt totally natural talking to her. "I wish to marry, have children, and live a long life."

She wrinkled her nose and grimaced. "How boring."

His hopes sank at her reaction; he thought he had said what she wanted to hear. Apparently not. "And...I have often thought about raising my own breed of horses. War-horses, like Daemon."

Her face brightened. "That would be good!" She smiled in anticipation for him to continue.

"And...I have always wanted to sail on a ship."

She practically beamed with delight. "Ooh, me too! I want to go to Africa! Where do you want to go?"

He struggled with an answer, since he had only been thinking about a short ride around a small inlet, or something. "Er, France?"

"Or Italy! Would that not be a great adventure? What else?"

"More?"

She nodded enthusiastically.

He racked his brain for hidden desires he had buried long ago. Only one surfaced. "I also like to…" he stopped mid-sentence and lowered his head. "Nay, you would laugh."

"What? I will not laugh, tell me!"

He smiled and shook his head.

"Oh, please?" She brought her hand over and gently took his hand in hers. His heart leaped at her touch. "Please, Jarreth? Tell me?"

He rolled his eyes at this sweet torture. "All right. I…like to draw pictures."

She squeezed his hand and giggled excitingly. "Truly? Are you good?"

"I suppose…that is, I guess maybe I am. 'Tis hard to judge one's own work."

"Show me?"

He couldn't resist her request. "All right." He smoothed a large circle of ground in front of them, and then found a sharp stick. He began drawing, using skilled strokes that began forming an image. Rhiannon watched intently. In a few minutes the picture was done, and she gasped in delighted surprise.

"'Tis a lion!"

It was, indeed. Jarreth had taken her love of Africa and chose the head of a lion for an example of his talent. The strong, noble king of beasts was drawn in profile, its expression proud and regal.

Rhiannon was awed. "He is beautiful. I wish I could cut out this piece of ground and preserve it forever. Thank you Jarreth. You are very talented."

Rhiannon

Jarreth was pleased by her approval, and pondered as to why. It never made any difference before if anyone liked his drawings; in reality he showed them to very few. But here he found himself content to no end that he had pleased her. She was so easy to be with, from that very day at the lake when he first met her. He felt relaxed, like he could tell her anything—except that he loved her.

"Can you draw unicorns?"

"I never have, but I draw horses. I suppose a unicorn is just a horse with a horn."

Rhiannon got to her knees and began smoothing another area of ground. "Here—let me see!" He hesitated, and she gave him a begging look. "Please?"

He gave a crooked smile, and picked up a stick. This woman could ask him to fly, and he would probably make the attempt. He drew a unicorn, again just the head, as Rhiannon watched with anticipation. She loved this one also, and asked for another, this time a bear. Then an eagle. Within a half-hour the whole area around the crackling fire was alive with a plethora of animals.

"You are wonderful! Why do you waste your talent by being a knight? I would think drawing pictures would be preferable to killing people."

He shrugged. "I draw as a pastime. Killing people, as you put it, is my job."

"As is taking reluctant brides to their doom?" She said it half-teasingly, but there was a hint of truth in her tone.

"As I said, that is my job." He turned his face to hide the look of guilt he experienced by lying to her.

"Aye, I suppose 'tis. Pity, though." There was an uncomfortable silence, and then she sighed. "If only…" She stopped and stared at the ground.

He looked anxiously at her. "If only what?"

She turned and faced him. "If only we could have met under different circumstances, as equals instead of like this. If only you were not bound to serve your lord, who would most likely kill you if you disobeyed him."

Jarreth's heart was jumping to his throat. "And what if all that were true?"

Her face grew sad, and he thought he detected moisture in her eyes. Was this it? Was she finally going to admit she loved him? *Please*, his thoughts begged. *Say it, Rhiannon.*

The words didn't come. Instead, her face set into determination. "I am sorry. I was being silly. I realize you are only being nice to me because you have to. Do not worry, you no longer have to humor me."

Her words cut through him like a sword. She thought he was being phony? Everything that had transpired that night was now for naught? He couldn't let that go without an argument.

"You are wrong, Rhiannon."

"Am I? What would you be doing if you were not being paid to bring me to your master? I doubt drawing pictures on the ground for a silly and stupid girl."

"You are not silly and stupid."

"Aye, I am. Silly for having dreams, and stupid for believing in them."

Jarreth ran a finger across her cheek—her soft, flawless skin was warm and inviting. "Never stop believing, Rhiannon."

"And why not? What good will it do for me to love?"

He traced her lips with his finger. "And who do you love?"

"I…I love no one."

"Then what are you looking for in a man?" He took her hand and stroked it softly, sending tingles up her arm.

She cautiously withdrew her hand. "I…am not looking."

He re-captured her hand and gently kissed it. "Do you not want children?"

Rhiannon

She seemed to be having trouble breathing. "I—I have not thought about it."

"I find that hard to believe. All women think about children." He brought his face to hers and gently kissed her cheek.

"S—stop that." She tried to jerk away, but he held her close.

"Stop what? This?" He kissed her on her cheek again, and then cupped her face in his hands. "Or this?" He brought his lips down on hers. This time she did not try to resist him.

Rhiannon was lost in new-felt emotions. Damn this man; why did he make her feel this way? She was helpless in letting him take command of the moment and enjoyed his seduction. The campfire suddenly got warmer. He relinquished her lips and traveled down to her neck and shoulders. Short, jagged gasps escaped her as she tried to regain her composure.

"Are you trying to ravish me?"

"I am not trying, I am doing."

"But…"

"Shush, Rhiannon." He silenced her with another passionate kiss. Taking total command, he guided her to lie down while still kissing her. His self-control had long ago left him. He wanted her badly; in fact, he had never wanted anything more in his life. His passion seemed to feed hers. As he stroked her back, then dropped to her magnificent hips and thighs, he let out a breath he didn't realize he was holding. Her body was so inviting, and he wanted her so much. He cupped a breast, and she moaned in passion as he continued to ravish her lips. He suddenly realized she did not have the will to stop him. If he continued, it would be nothing short of rape, and rape was not his chosen form of seduction. His blasted guilt began to surface, and he argued with himself as to the end result. Finally his traitorous mind won over his body, and he gently pushed her away and rolled over.

She seemed unable to speak. Finally she found her tongue.

"Why did you stop?"

"Because, as you said, you do not love me."

"And that matters?"

"It matters to you."

There was a long pause. "I take back my statement about you not being a gentleman. You have just proven yourself to be one."

"Nay, I am not. Try to get some sleep, Rhiannon. We have a long day ahead of us." He walked over to Daemon to pull himself together, feigning to check the horse's rope.

She nodded, and rolled over, hiding her tears that threatened to give away her emotions. Although she wasn't sure what being in love felt like, she knew the way she felt about Jarreth must be close. Why did he have to be just a lowly knight? Why did she have to be the daughter of a baron? Did it actually make a difference? Aye, damn it all, it did. Her father would never accept her marriage to a poor knight; he would cut her from her inheritance and she would lose everything. Her tears flowed more freely, and she suddenly became aware of Jarreth's hand on her shoulder.

"Why do you cry, Rhiannon?"

She rolled over. "I am scared, Jarreth." She unsuccessfully tried to sniff back a tear, and her lower lip began trembling.

Jarreth was totally helpless. A woman's tears usually didn't faze him, as most the time they were faked in order to get their way. These were genuine, and it tore him apart because he was the one causing it. He never wanted to hurt her, just make her love him. He lay down beside her and gently pulled her to him, holding her like a father would a frightened child.

"It will all be fine, Rhiannon. Hold me."

She did. She clung to him and cried, as he stroked her hair and let her release her fears. He couldn't help wondering if this was a first step in her accepting his love. He felt both guilty and joyous.

Rhiannon

He held her until she cried herself to sleep, then allowed himself to fall asleep also, still holding her close in his arms.

Rhiannon awoke to the sounds of Jarreth cooking breakfast. Apparently he succeeded in killing a rabbit and building a fire while she slept through the early morning. She sat up, and suddenly remembered the previous night, then felt foolish and embarrassed. The last thing she remembered was crying into Jarreth's shoulder. He must think her a total idiot.

He saw that she was awake, and flashed her a wide smile. "Good morning, sleepyhead! I found us some breakfast. I hope you like rabbit."

She rubbed her eyes, and yawned. "I like to pet them more than eat them."

He looked down at the roasting carcass. "This one is past the petting stage, I fear."

"I see that." She rose to her feet and motioned to the forest. "I have to, um…"

"Can I trust you?" He stood up and faced her, noticing her red, puffy eyes from her crying jag. It didn't appear that running was on her mind.

She nodded her answer, and he motioned for her to go. She lumbered off to the trees to take care of her problem.

Jarreth kneeled and tended to the rabbit. He had awakened at dawn, still holding her in his arms, and knew without a doubt he loved her. She didn't stir when he moved away; apparently she was so exhausted she just needed the sleep. He didn't mind—he certainly wasn't in a hurry. Just a few more days and he would win her heart.

Rhiannon finished her business, and headed back to the camp. As she was just about to clear the tress, she was grabbed from behind. A hand went over her mouth, another around her body, and she was pulled backward. She knew instantly it wasn't Jarreth; this person was nowhere as large as he was. She struggled and managed to free her mouth long enough to scream Jarreth's name. The hand again covered her mouth, and she felt the cold edge of a knife against her throat.

"Did you think you could run from a Gypsy? I have been tracking you ever since you left."

Rhiannon's eyes widened when she recognized the voice. It was Ramon. "Let her go."

Ramon jerked Rhiannon tighter into him as he faced Jarreth, who stood in front of them with his sword drawn.

"No! I come to collect the reward for my people!"

"I said, let her go."

"I will kill her first!" He brought the knife closer against her throat, causing her to freeze in terror.

"But then I shall kill you, so her death will be for naught." Jarreth was purposely keeping his voice low and calm, even though seeing Rhiannon in the clutches of a killer was testing his patience. Many other men had made similar mistakes, and paid with their lives. Jarreth figured this man, whoever he was, would be no different.

Ramon was not about to give up his advantage. "Toss me the money, and then I shall let her go—when I am a safe distance away."

"You are not taking her anywhere." Jarreth tightened the grip on his sword, waiting for the break he needed. He got it sooner then he anticipated. Ramon in his nervousness stumbled over a tree root, and for just a second released his grip on Rhiannon. She took the opportunity to flee, giving Jarreth the opening he waited for. He moved in and knocked the knife out of Ramon's hand. Ramon drew his sword and lashed out at Jarreth in a blind rage, and Jarreth knew immediately this man was no fighter. He was, however, quick. He dodged and rolled out of Jarreth's way, until Jarreth finally had enough and swatted his sword away. He then grabbed Ramon and threw him to the ground, then raised his sword for the final plunge into Ramon's heart.

"Jarreth, stop! Do not kill him! Please!"

Rhiannon

Both Ramon and Jarreth looked at her in surprise. Jarreth rightfully sensed that he suddenly had an atypical situation on his hands. When was it not so with this girl? He pulled Ramon to his feet and wrapped a massive arm around his throat, while he argued the point with Rhiannon.

"He tried to kill you. Why should I not kill him?"

"He would not have killed me. Ramon, tell him—tell him you were not going to kill me."

Ramon shook his head as best he could under the circumstances. "I just wanted the money! I would not have hurt her!" The poor man could barely get the words out for lack of breath.

Jarreth frowned. "You know him?"

"Aye, he is the Gypsy I told you about; the one who wanted to turn me in. Please, Jarreth—he has a baby on the way. Do not kill him, I beg you."

Jarreth rolled his eyes in disbelief. "But Rhiannon, he had a knife to your throat!"

"Please Jarreth! He only wanted the money! His people are poor, and need supplies." She stepped forward and put a hand on Ramon's shoulder. "I understand, Ramon. You wanted to be able to support Myra and the baby. She told me all about it."

"Yes," Ramon gasped. "The baby will need clothes and things I cannot give it."

Jarreth let his captive go and threw up his hands. "I give up."

Ramon lowered his head and took a few deep breaths, then fixed his gaze on Rhiannon. "A Gypsy is honorable, if anything. I was wrong about you, Rhiannon. I beg your forgiveness, and I owe you my life."

"I give you back your life, Ramon. Just take care of Myra and your baby."

Jarreth folded his arms and leaned against a tree as he watched this tender scene. Was everyone forgetting that he was the one who spared Ramon's life? "I think it best you leave now. How did you get here?"

Ramon pointed into the woods. "My horse is not far."

"Then go. I let you live only because of Rhiannon. If I see you again, I will kill you."

Ramon nodded. "I understand. I am sorry, 'tis just when you offered a large reward, I knew my people could use it."

"I am afraid the joke is on you, Ramon," Rhiannon said apologetically. "Jarreth does not have any money. He is just a lowly knight hired to bring me to the Dark Count."

Ramon looked confused, and glanced at Jarreth. "But he said…"

"Here." Jarreth cut him off mid-sentence as he reached inside his coat, pulled out a full coin pouch and tossed it to Ramon. "This is full of gold coins. Leave now, before I change my mind."

Rhiannon gave him a shocked look. "But, Jarreth…"

He ignored her, and kept his gaze on Ramon. "I said leave—and do not forget I shall kill you the next time we meet."

Ramon jingled the coin pouch and nodded. "Thank you." He turned his gaze to Rhiannon. "I hope someday I can repay you." He then turned and disappeared into the forest.

Jarreth turned to Rhiannon, who was still stunned at the amount of money he had just turned over.

"Where did you get all that money?" she finally asked. "That must have been your entire life's savings!"

"Nay, the count gave those coins to me to pay for this trip." He quickly changed the subject. "I have never spared a man's life at the request of a woman. Consider yourself privileged."

Rhiannon stepped up to him and lifted a hand to his cheek. "You are bleeding."

Her touch was worth all the blood in his body. "'Tis just a scratch."

"Here, let me look at that—bend down, I cannot see it clearly."

Rhiannon

Jarreth crouched over so she could inspect the laceration. He enjoyed watching her fuss and fret over him as she satisfied herself that he was not mortally wounded.

"By the way, thank you for not killing him. I know bloodlust runs in your veins; it must have been terribly hard for you to spare his life."

"Oh, awfully. I enjoy killing, as you said. Since meeting you I am totally off my quota."

She drew back, clearly appalled, and then saw his smile. "You are teasing me."

He just smiled.

Rhiannon suddenly sniffed the air. "Do you smell something?"

Jarreth paused and sniffed also. He then let out a loud curse. "The rabbit!" He took off running for the camp, with Rhiannon close behind.

Their breakfast was charred beyond repair. Jarreth took the black carcass and tossed it to the ground. "I do not believe it!" He uttered more curses while Rhiannon hid her amusement by covering her mouth. Finally she giggled.

"I am *still* not impressed with knightly cooking!" She broke out in laughter, while Jarreth fumed about the situation. Her laughter was contagious, however, and Jarreth finally saw the humor in the situation. He smiled, and then began laughing. They both laughed together for several minutes, releasing built-up tensions. Jarreth loved it when she laughed; no one ever made him as happy as she did. He highly looked forward to spending the rest of his life with her.

Chapter Eleven

They rode all that day, talking and learning more about each other. Jarreth kept Daemon at a leisurely pace, adding to the relaxed ambience. Rhiannon shared more childhood stories about herself, causing Jarreth to laugh most of the day. He envied her childhood, as his was neither as eventful nor happy.

Later in the day they found a small abandoned cottage that looked promising for that night. A roaring river was close by, as was a nice fenced field for Daemon's needs. A storm seemed threatening, with dark clouds looming overhead. A clap of thunder boomed the storm's advancement just as they unloaded the horse. Jarreth let Daemon go in the field, and joined Rhiannon in the hut. He found her trying to tidy up the dirty little cottage so it would be livable for that night. There was a small bed in one corner, actually just a frame with old straw piled in it, and a table with one chair. A small stove was in another corner, with a hole cut into the roof for the smoke. He watched with amusement as she swept cobwebs out of corners, making faces and grunting comments about icky spiders and bugs.

"I do not think you will find them all," he commented.

Rhiannon

"I can try. 'Tis dark in here. Is there a lantern? Please tell me there is a lantern!"

Jarreth scanned the room. "There is no lantern."

She sat on the bed and grimaced. "I told you not to tell me that."

"Sorry. Although, I believe I have some candles. Let me see." He rummaged through his pack and brought out a thick, short candle. "I believe this still has some life in it. Now, where is the flint?" He found the items necessary to start a fire, and set to work. Another clap of thunder rumbled outside as Rhiannon watched Jarreth try to start a fire in the small stove using a few pieces of left-behind kindling. She spotted a large flagon, and determined she could also be helpful.

"We shall need water. Perhaps if I went to the river and fetched some?"

Jarreth, preoccupied with getting the kindling to ignite, didn't look up to answer. "Fine. Be careful."

"Am I not always?"

He flashed her a sour look and she grinned back, then took the flagon and left.

The river was wider and faster than she thought, with steep embankments of at least twenty feet on both sides. It looked as if a past flood had washed away any trail. A few raindrops began falling, and she knew that if she waited to find a better place to get down she would become drenched. So, the embankment it was.

She gingerly stepped down sideways, like she had done many times at her own home river. Being sure-footed, she never worried much about falling. She was about halfway down when she hit some loose dirt that suddenly gave way. The flagon went flying as she clawed at the bank for anything to grab hold of, but found nothing. The ground beneath her gave way further, and she began sliding into the river.

She screamed for Jarreth, but doubted he could hear her. It was raining harder now, and thunder and lightning filled the sky. She screamed louder when she hit the river and discovered a strong undertow. Although she was a good swimmer, she usually wasn't fully clothed when doing so. The heavy wool gown soaked up the water and weighed her down as she thrashed and tried to get back to shore. Suddenly something wrenched her ankle, and began pulling her underwater. In panic she realized something, possibly a log, had snagged her. For the second time that day she feared for her life.

Unbeknownst to her, Jarreth had heard her first scream and was already on the bank. He reached it just as he saw something pull her under and carry her down the river. His heart filled with terror as he striped off the clothes above his waist and leaped down the embankment. He dove into the river and frantically swam after her.

She surfaced and screamed again as Jarreth fought the river's current, trying to maneuver toward her. The roar of the river was deafening. "Hold on, Rhiannon! I am coming!"

"Jarreth!" she gasped. "I am caught!"

"I know! Hold on, I will try to free you." He dove under water, but could see nothing in the cold, murky water. He surfaced and grabbed hold of the desperate girl who was literally fighting for every breath. "Put your arms around my neck! I will try to hold your head above water."

Rhiannon reached out, but was pulled back down again. "I cannot! Jarreth, please! Do not let me die!" She disappeared under the water.

Her pleas echoed within his mind. Die? He would prefer his own death before he let any harm come to her. He dove again, and this time found the large log that had wedged her foot. He managed to turn it over so her head came back up above water. She gasped in precious air, and this time got her arms around his neck when he again appeared beside her.

"Hold me, Rhiannon!" His greater strength could better fight the current as she clung to him. She was growing weaker from the cold ordeal, and Jarreth knew that if he didn't free her soon she could die.

Rhiannon

"Rhiannon, listen to me! I have to free your foot. I am going to let you go for just a few seconds. Can you be brave just a while longer?"

She produced a small smile and nodded.

"Good girl. All right, on the count of three let go of me. One, two three."

She let go and he dove once more, determined this time to free her. He found her foot and the v-shaped limb that held her ankle. Working blindly, he pulled on her foot, but it wouldn't come loose. His only option was to break the limb. He mustered all his strength, snapped the limb, and in an instant her foot came free.

She had gone limp from weakness by the time he re-surfaced and grabbed her. Fighting the current and holding Rhiannon was strenuous, but he managed to swim to shore and get her on the bank. He then pulled his own exhausted body up and plopped down beside her, throwing an arm around her still form.

"Rhiannon! Wake up!" His heart pounded in fear.

She coughed and sputtered. Relief swept over his face.

"Good girl, Rhiannon. Come on, breathe."

Her eyes flickered. "Jarreth?"

"Aye, I am here."

She produced a slight smile. "You saved me?"

"Of course, silly girl. I will always save you. I am your Lancelot, remember?" He realized he needed to get her warm. He gathered the strength and picked her up, carrying her back to the cottage as rain pelted them. He kicked open the cottage door and laid her down on the straw bed. Her body trembled as she shivered from the intense cold of the river. He knew what he had to do.

"Rhiannon, we have to get you out of those soaking clothes. Come on, sit up."

She was too exhausted to protest as he unbuttoned the gown and brought it up over her head. Her undergarment also had to come off, and then to help preserve her modesty he quickly wrapped their only blanket around her. Her ankle was red and bruised; he wondered if she would be able to walk for a while. He carried her to the chair in front of the stove.

"You should be warmer in a few minutes. Rhiannon, I left my clothes out there. Are you going to be all right while I go get them?"

She nodded, and he vowed to be right back.

The storm had reached its apex by the time he got back with his soaking wet clothes. He was relieved to find her still sitting in the chair, looking a little warmer. She flashed him a smile when he entered, which warmed his soul, if not his body. He knelt in front of her and took her freezing hands in his.

"How do you feel?"

"I am fine."

He picked up her injured ankle and inspected it closely. "Does it hurt badly?"

"Nay." She winced as he let it down.

"Are you sure?"

"Aye."

"Good." He picked up his soggy clothes and stood up. "I have to lay these clothes out to dry." She clutched the blanket tighter around her and he thought he detected a rosy blush cross her cheeks. "I am afraid 'tis a little late for modesty. I have to strip the rest of my clothes off to dry, so you better turn your head." He began pulling off his pants.

Her head whirled in the opposite direction. After a few seconds she cleared her throat. "Jarreth?"

"Aye?"

"Thank you for saving me—again."

"I am getting used to it."

"I am sorry I am such a nuisance. 'Twould appear I need a personal knight to save me from myself."

Rhiannon

"Aye, 'twould appear so." He came up behind her and put a hand on her shoulder. "I am quite naked, so unless you wish to be rather embarrassed, you had better keep your eyes averted."

She swallowed hard and nodded. "How are we going to sleep?"

"Do we have much choice? There is only one blanket and bedroll, and only one bed. We can put the bedroll beneath us, and the blanket above us. Unless you wish to lie naked on the scratchy straw?"

"Nay." She stood up and slowly turned to face him, making sure she kept her gaze above his waist. She found him harboring a huge smile. Her embarrassment turned to indignation. "You are enjoying this!"

"Is it that obvious?"

"Aye."

"Very well, I admit sleeping naked next to you has its attractiveness."

She pursed her lips together and accidentally brought her eyes downward. The sight of his fully erect manhood brought her head shooting back up. He couldn't help it; he was finding the whole situation highly arousing. She stared with wide-open eyes at his amused face and backed up.

"I—I cannot do this, Jarreth."

"What is wrong? Does the sight of my body repulse you?"

"N—nay, I—I just…"

"Or rather is it my body's response to yours that you find distressing?"

"I—'tis just that—I am…"

"Innocent? I know. That is another reason this situation is extremely interesting."

"Jarreth, please stop teasing me!"

He snickered. "All right, Rhiannon, you may have the blanket and the bed. I will take the bedroll and lie on the ground."

"Nay—the floor is wet and dirty. I know! We shall both sleep on the bed, but you will be in the bedroll, and I will keep the blanket wrapped around me!"

Jarreth raised one eyebrow. "And that will make you feel safe?"

"Well, 'tis better than you sleeping on the floor."

"Granted. Very well, you sleep against the wall and I will take the outside." He eyed the small bed. "Regardless, 'tis going to be cozy."

Rhiannon gulped. She was running a gamut of emotions right then; embarrassment for once again having to be rescued; relief that she was still alive; anxiety about the sleeping arrangements.

"Go ahead and get comfortable; I am going to feed the stove for the night." He turned and began tending the fire.

Rhiannon wrapped the blanket tightly around her until she felt like one of the Egyptian mummies she once read about. She purposely lay facing the wall so there would not be another accidental viewing of Jarreth's magnificent body.

And it was magnificent. She had almost forgotten how much so. For just a second she allowed herself to wonder just how it would feel to have his body next to hers. She quickly rid herself of that thought. After all, she was a lady, betrothed to a count, destined to live the rest of her life in luxury. A tear welled in her eye and she brushed it away. It was that second that she realized she would give up everything to stay with Jarreth. It was then she knew she loved him.

She heard him walk over to the bed and in one move he was beside her, actually on top of her. There simply wasn't enough room in the tiny bed. They wiggled and squirmed in an attempt to get comfortable.

"Rhiannon, you are going to have to lay in my arms. Turn around."

"All right." She rolled over and cuddled into his shoulder with his arm cradling her. That was much snugger, but the tightly wrapped blanket kept her body rigid, making it impossible for her to even bend her knees.

"Rhiannon, you are rather stiff."

"I know—'tis this blanket."

"Why not loosen it a bit?"

"Then I shall get cold."

Rhiannon

A clap of thunder boomed as if on cue, and a flash of lightning momentarily lit the room. Rain pelted the thatched roof and blew down the smoke-hole. They lay there listening to the storm, each lost in private thoughts.

"Jarreth?"

"Aye?"

"Will Daemon be all right?"

"Aye, he will be fine. He is used to being outside."

"But he has no shelter."

"There are trees to stand under. Do not worry, he can fend for himself." He smiled at her concern for the horse's plight. Wasn't that just like her, on her way to a marriage she dreaded, almost killed twice in one day, being in a compromising position with him, and worried about a horse. Perhaps that is what he loved most about her.

They lay in silence for a while more.

"Jarreth?"

"Aye."

"What will my wedding night be like?"

He paused, not sure how to answer. "I do not know; I have never been married."

She missed the double meaning in his answer. "I mean, the Dark Count—what will he be like?"

"Again, I am not sure. How do you mean?"

"Will he be…gentle?"

"He is not known for his gentleness."

"Will it…hurt?"

"I have been told a woman's wedding night can be painful." He put a hand under her chin and tilted her head upward. Their eyes locked. "But it does not have to be," he whispered.

They stared at each other with the same longing they experienced the first time they met. He could no longer stand the torture, and brought his lips down to hers in a tender kiss. She gently kissed him back, as hungry for closeness as he was. He deepened the kiss, begging entrance to her inner sweetness with his tongue. To his euphoria her lips parted, allowing him to seduce her mouth with expertise. His hands twisted in her thick mane of hair as the falling rain outside added to the atmosphere of desire. They tasted each other as he pulled them tighter together, unwilling to destroy the bond. Finally pulling away, he gazed upon her stunning face with his potent dark eyes, wanting her desperately.

"There is a way out of your dilemma, Rhiannon. Give yourself to me. Tonight—right now."

She lowered her gaze and was silent. The silence was so long he started to wonder if she had heard him. Finally she raised her eyes again.

"Do you mean forever?"

He was taken back by her question. "Of course I do. What do you think I meant?"

"To perhaps ruin me for any man. That is what would happen, is it not?"

"You would not be ruined for me."

"How many other women have you ruined?"

He paused at her bluntness, wondering how the conversation got so off course. "They were already 'ruined' when I got to them, except for one."

"What happened with that one?"

He cleared his throat nervously. "I was drunk, and that was a long time ago. Please note I am not drunk now."

She fell silent again. He waited patiently while she mulled things around in her confused mind.

"Will not the count be very angry?"

Jarreth had to carefully choose his words. "I believe he would eventually give us his blessing. I have told you, he is a fair man."

Rhiannon

"You would really have me? I am a lot of trouble."

He kissed her forehead. "Aye, that you are, but like you said—you need your own personal knight to protect you."

Again she fell deep in thought. Finally he couldn't stand it any longer; never had seducing someone been so difficult.

"Rhiannon?"

"Aye?"

"What is your answer?"

"I am afraid."

"That is understandable. I promise not to hurt you."

"That was not my meaning. I am afraid I will not please you."

He let out a low chuckle and gave her a little squeeze. "That is not possible. I think the question is, can I please you? Can you give yourself to someone like me, who cannot offer you riches or an easy life?"

Her eyes beseeched his as she lifted a hand and touched his face. "I cannot fathom giving myself to anyone but you."

He let out a large breath he didn't realize he was holding. "Good, because I cannot fathom another man touching you."

They stared at each other with the realization that they had more or less just professed their love for one another. Finally Rhiannon broke the spell.

"So, now what?"

Jarreth loosened the bedroll and stood up, then offered her his hand. She gazed upon his nakedness, lit only by the flickering small candle, without shame. He helped her rise, then slowly unwrapped the blanket and tossed it aside when she stood before him in her naked glory. Her hair fell in wet tangles down her shoulders and back as he looked upon her in longing. Aware of his gaze, her head hung with unease. He tilted it upward and smiled reassuringly.

"You are the most beautiful woman I have ever set eyes on. Do not be ashamed."

He cupped her face, then slid his hands down her shoulders and arms, and gently took her hands. Then he pulled her into him, and their bodies touched in an instant of ecstasy. He stroked her back and kissed her neck, holding her glorious body tight against his own.

The heat of their bodies seemed to warm the whole world as she explored his back, buttocks and thighs. He brought a hand to one of her breasts and cupped it, then gently rolled the nipple between his thumb and forefinger. To his surprise, she giggled.

"That tickles," she said, trying to suppress further outbreaks.

Jarreth withdrew his hand and exhaled loudly. "If you do not relax, we are not going to get very far."

"Sorry." She straightened her face.

He tried the nipple again. It instantly grew rigid with his touch, and she inhaled quickly from the new sensation. "Jarreth?" she whispered, her voice quivering.

"Shhh, love, enjoy the feeling." His other hand slowly dropped to her thighs and made its way up to her most intimate part. When he touched her, she both gasped and jumped at the same time.

"'Tis all right—I promised not to hurt you."

"I know. I just have never been touched there."

"I should hope not. Now, please relax. You are not making this easy." He gently parted her thighs as he attempted to distract her by kissing her neck; she took a breath and held it. His hand found its destination as his mouth covered a breast and suckled it. She jumped again, but this time he didn't release his hold.

Rhiannon felt as if she would die from these new emotions. Parts of her body ached for a release she didn't know how to provide.

"I—I do not think I can do this. I have changed my mind."

"No, you have not. You are just scared. Go ahead, Rhiannon; I will not touch you again until you are ready." He put his hands by his side and waited for what seemed an eternity.

Rhiannon

She finally got up her nerve and gingerly wrapped her arms around him again, kissing his neck, stroking his back, causing his entire body to tremble with pleasure. He arched his back and took deep, quick breaths at her touch. She stopped when she saw his reaction.

"Am I hurting you?" she asked in innocence.

"Mother of God, no—do not stop!"

She didn't. Her hands explored his body with innocence and curiosity, a somewhat arousing combination he had never encountered before now.

He realized if he didn't have her soon, he would release right then and there. That certainly wouldn't be a memorable first-time experience.

"Stop, Rhiannon."

"But you just said…"

"Never mind that. Lay down, Rhiannon."

She quietly obeyed.

He lowered his body down on top of her. "I might be too heavy, but believe me in a few seconds you will not notice."

"You are not too heavy. I feel protected."

He gently pushed her thighs apart as he kissed her willing lips. "I will always protect you. You are mine, now."

His next motion made her gasp. He raised himself up, then down again.

"Relax, love. You are mine."

"I am yours," she whispered, relishing in the sheer size and heat of his body.

A while later they lay still, the only motion the heaving of their labored breaths.

When he finally rolled off to one side, Rhiannon felt like she was losing a part of herself. One arm and leg remained around her as he regained his composure. In the past, women were used only as a release for his lust. He had never felt attachment, certainly not love,

Until tonight.

He reached up and touched her face, almost not believing she was real. She opened her eyes and looked at him.

"I am sorry I fought you for so long."

"Believe me, so am I." He paused and brushed a wayward strand from her face. "Rhiannon, are you sorry for what you just did?"

She gave him a confused look, and shook her head. "How can I be sorry for loving you?"

His eyes closed in a grateful prayer for her words, and he drew her even tighter to him. She loved him. "Even if it means living in poverty?"

"It will not matter if I have you."

"I shall hold you to your words," he teased. Not that he was worried. He dispelled any guilty feelings for taking her innocence; technically she was his the second he signed the agreement. All that remained was the ceremony and the vows.

"What will we do now?" She ran a finger across his chest in a playful gesture.

"We must confront the count, declare our love, and live happily ever after."

"Again you tease. If only it were so easy."

"Sorry." He gave her a quick kiss on the forehead. "We will reach Stanwyck Castle tomorrow."

Her face fell into a look of terror. "So soon?"

"Do not worry, it shall be fine. Trust me."

"I shall hold you to *your* words."

"I promised to protect you. We shall meet with the count, and 'twill all be over." *After I finally tell you the truth.*

"How can you be sure?"

"Did I not say to trust me?"

Rhiannon

She nodded, and closed her eyes as she cuddled against him. He watched as she fell asleep, a slight smile on her serene face. Soon he joined her in a blissful sleep to the sounds of the crackling fire and the soft rain.

Chapter Twelve

Rhiannon awoke to the sounds of muted shuffling. The faint smell of smoldering ashes from the dying fire still lingered in the room as she pulled the thin blanket tighter around her, giving her no comfort from the crisp morning air. She gradually opened her eyes to find Jarreth fully dressed and sprawled in the lone chair, his head resting against one hand as he stared at her. When he saw her open eyes, he smiled.

"Good morning. I trust you slept well."

She yawned and sat up. "How did you move without waking me?"

"Easy—you were dead asleep. Apparently your busy day exhausted you." He stood up and pointed to an aquamanile filled with warm water. "I heated some water so you can wash up. Your clothes are dry. I will saddle Daemon and wait for you outside." He leaned down and kissed her gently on the cheek. "Are there still no regrets?"

"None."

"Good. Do not tarry, I have something to tell you." He smiled and left the hut, leaving her to clean up in privacy.

Rhiannon

After he stepped outside, he took a deep breath of the invigorating air purified by the heavy rains. He squinted from the bright morning sun as he watched a robin tug a worm from the damp ground. A V-shaped squadron of geese flew overhead, announcing their presence with a myriad of awkward honks. For the first time in his life he felt blissful

He had awakened at dawn and lay in bed holding his precious Rhiannon, feeling guilty as hell for not telling her the truth last night. Starting a marriage off with a lie was not very honorable. Now that she had given herself to him willingly, he saw no reason to continue the charade. He would tell her the truth the minute she walked out that door.

Daemon was none the worse for the storm, and was contently chewing away on the lush grass in the field. He looked up and nickered when he saw Jarreth approach. Jarreth gave a whistle, and the horse trotted up to him.

"Hey big fellow, I see you survived the night. Rhiannon will be glad of that." He led the horse to the tack and began to ready him for the day's ride.

Just as he finished, Rhiannon exited the hut with the blanket wrapped around her shoulders. She shivered as she filled her lungs with air, and then flashed Jarreth a small embarrassed smile. "Thank you for the warm water. I *was* rather messy. Now, what did you want to tell me?"

His smile faded. This wasn't going to be easy. "Uh, well, I…you see, um." He cleared his throat, not knowing how to start. "I—the Dark Count—what I mean is,"

"Speaking of the Dark Count, I've been thinking about our predicament," she interrupted, her voice breathy with excitement.

"Our…*predicament*?"

"Aye!" Her voice lowered with a dramatic tone. "This is so like a fairy tale, like Lancelot and Guinevere. A hopeless romance, with no chance of a happy ending. Only, I think I know of a way to make it happy!"

He blinked. "You do?"

"Aye! We simply buy my freedom."

"Buy our freedom?" He folded his arms and leaned against the wall of the hut. "With what, may I ask?"

Her face lit up and her eyes flashed with delight. "I have a confession to make! Wait here!"

"Rhiannon, I…"

His words fell unheard as she scurried away to her little pack she had thus far so protectively guarded. She ran back with her right hand tightly shut around something.

"Hold out your hand," she said with anticipation.

He did, and she dropped five gold coins into it.

"I got them from the cave. You remember the cave?"

He grimaced with the memory. The thought of the filthy pirate attempting to rape her still filled him with rage. "I am not likely to forget it."

"It is the pirate's booty. There is a whole chest of these coins! We can show the count these, and tell him we will bring him the rest for our freedom."

"You are forgetting something."

Her smile disappeared. "What?"

"The count is a very wealthy man. A mere chest of gold coins would most likely not tempt him. Besides, he pays me well. If I wanted to buy our freedom, I have enough for that."

She stepped in close and put her arms around his waist. "Oh, Jarreth, you would do that? You would give all you had for me? That is so…so…"

A lie, he thought.

"Chivalrous! Just like Lancelot." She snuggled close and laid her face against his body. "I will always love you. The fact that you are a poor knight who is willing to give up everything for me just makes it better."

Rhiannon

He stroked her hair as he hugged her in return, and cast his eyes to the sky. She was so caught up in the whole fantasy of a hopeless romance, if he told her the truth now she would probably bean him with the first rock she found. No, better to wait when he had his uncle for reinforcement. She couldn't kill him with a witness standing there.

"We should get going," he said flatly, feeling guiltier by the second.

"Did you say you wanted to tell me something?" Her face glowed up at him in a look of total trust, making him feel even more like a rat.

His face went blank. "Er, ah…"

Daemon shook his head and nickered, and Jarreth abruptly grinned. "Daemon made it excellently through the night. I thought you would like to know."

She laughed and petted the great horse's neck, while Jarreth turned away and rolled his eyes. That was a disaster. He quickly changed the subject.

"There is a town close by where we can get food. I suggest we get started; I am famished."

"Me too." Her smile captured his heart again, and he gave her another passionate kiss before lifting her up on Daemon.

They stopped and ate at an Inn, then continued the last few miles to Stanwyck castle. Even with his reassurance, it was obvious to Jarreth that she was apprehensive. He cursed himself again for not telling her the truth and putting her through this anguish. *No matter*, he told himself, *soon it will be all over and she will be jumping for joy in my arms. I hope.*

He pictured the scenario over and over in his mind, each time the ending getting better. She would cry for joy. No, no, she would scream with delight and throw her arms around him. Or, better still, she would both cry and scream with glee. Aye, it would be a joyous occasion.

If she didn't kill him first.

Evangelynn Stratton

They exited the forest and came to a vantage point on a hill. As Stanwyck Castle loomed before them, Jarreth reined Daemon back and took Rhiannon's hands. "We are almost there. Are you ready?"

She gazed down the valley at the huge castle, nearly twice the size of her own home. Made of dark stone with tall towers surrounded by acres of well-kept gardens, a high stone wall enclosed the entire grounds with wide gates guarding the only entrance. Smoke rose from several chimneys, weaving its way upward to cast a gloomy pallor overhead. Rhiannon gulped. The Dark Count was even more rich and powerful than she had imagined. Visions of him becoming enraged and striking them down, or worse still, locking them in one of those towers until they starved began filling her head. She nodded her reluctant answer to Jarreth.

He rode down the hill and through the gates, at ease and heartened to be finally home, bringing his bride. Servants passed them, tipping their hats in respect. Several greeted him with "Welcome, Milord," causing Jarreth to cringe. Rhiannon didn't miss the curious salutations and questioned him about it.

"They must mistake me for someone else," he lied. That seemed to appease her momentarily, and he hastened to the stable. He helped her dismount while a groom tended to his horse, and quickly escorted her to the castle entrance before someone called him by his title. Immediately a dozen servants appeared, and he had to talk fast.

"This is the lady Rhiannon. See her to her quarters and prepare a bath." He turned to her and put his hands on her shoulders. "I shall see you soon. Do not worry, all shall be fine."

The bewildered girl was led away by the servants as she looked helplessly over her shoulder to Jarreth, leaving him feeling like the biggest cad in history. He hastened down the hallway to get clean and change into fresh clothes.

Rhiannon

Rhiannon was led to a grand room, much bigger than her own at home. Although she had always thought herself raised in splendor, her childhood home couldn't compare with just this guestroom. It was immaculately clean, with fenestral windows—lattice frames covered in linen soaked in resin and tallow. Painted linen, woven tapestries, and fine wool cloths hung from walls and doorways. A huge canopy bed with side curtains stood against one wall and a crackling fire from an impressive fireplace warmed the room. The strong smell of lavender and tansy, used to make the bed smell sweeter and keep away fleas, permeated the air. A large tub was filled with warm water, and she was stripped of her inferior servant clothes. Being accustomed only to Kady's assistance, she blushed as the unfamiliar servants scrubbed her with rose-scented soap, pouring water over her flawless white skin as if to wash away her sin of the former night. Her eyes grew wide when the loveliest gown she had ever seen, made of the finest satin, was brought in. It was a pale blue, with expensive lace trim around the plunging neckline and sleeves. It fit like it was made for her. During all this the servants didn't speak, having no idea exactly who she was, and Rhiannon was too distraught to start a conversation. Her hair was prepared up in a graceful style with ribbons entwined throughout.

Meanwhile, Jarreth had gotten dressed into gentleman's clothes—black hose, white shirt, doublet and long black overjacket. Not surprising, his uncle had been informed of their arrival, and burst into Jarreth's room uninvited and unannounced.

"Jarreth! 'Tis about time! I expected you here days ago!"

Jarreth was pulling on his boots, and looked up at his uncle with a frown. "'Tis good to see you too, uncle."

His sarcasm was lost on the count. "Well? What think you of my choice of a bride this time?"

Jarreth stood up and folded his arms. "I think you got lucky."

"So, you approve of her?" He burst into a wide grin.

Jarreth tried to maintain a straight face, not about to admit his uncle had actually picked the perfect woman. "She shall suffice."

"Suffice?" The count's scarred face fell into disappointment. "That is all you can say?"

Jarreth couldn't contain himself any longer. He slowly smiled, then began to chuckle. "Very well, although I suppose there will be no living with you when I divulge the truth. Quite by accident you matched me with the most beautiful creature in all England. I also fear I am quite in love with her."

"Love?" The count's face expressed total skepticism. "You, Jarreth? I do not believe it!"

"Believe it. And what is even more amazing, she loves me back. There is one small complication, however."

"Complication? What kind of complication?"

Jarreth took a deep breath and let it out slowly. "I do not know how to begin. It comes down to the fact that she thinks she is betrothed to you."

"Me?" The count could not suppress a chortle. "How did the poor girl get that impression?"

"Apparently her personal servant overheard a conversation between the baron and a guest. She misunderstood who the intended groom was."

"And why have you not corrected this wrong assumption?"

"Ah, that is where it sort of gets complicated."

"More complications?"

"Aye. I fully intended on telling her way before this. After last night…"

"What happened last night?" He observed Jarreth's sheepish grin and shook his head. "Never mind, I think I get the idea. So why did you not tell her?"

Rhiannon

"Rhiannon is not your average girl. She is special, in many ways. It has not turned out to be as easy as I anticipated. I thought maybe you could help."

"Me? You want me to do your dirty work for you?"

"Nay, just help. I have a feeling it might be a whit overwhelming for her. She might get quite emotional, break down, cry—you know how women can be."

"Aye, only too well, I fear. Very well, I shall give you moral support. Er, just who *does* she think you are?"

"A hired knight who works for you."

"Ha! That is a good one! So, this beautiful creature thinks she is in love with a lowly knight?" He suddenly frowned. "Is she not frightened beyond belief to meet me?"

"Aye, she is. Do not berate me, uncle; I have done a satisfactory job of that myself."

"All right, I shall not tell you what a slimy louse you are."

Jarreth winced. "Thank you."

"Let us go meet your bride."

Rhiannon sat on the edge of the bed, afraid to disturb the bedding, clean and dressed and ready for…what? Jarreth had seemingly abandoned her. She was in a strange room, in a strange castle, and she was frightened. A rap announced a presence at the door, and she jumped nervously.

"Who—who is it?"

"Are you decent?"

She ran for the door when she heard Jarreth's voice, throwing it open with plans to jump into his arms. She stopped dead when she saw him.

He looked strange, dressed in rich, well-styled clothes, presenting a conflicting image from the man she had grown to love. His black knee-high boots were polished, his black waistcoat flared over his hips, and his hair was combed. Although he had always been roguishly handsome, this new look curiously fit him. She finally found her voice and managed a weak smile.

"The count *must* pay you well."

Jarreth was a bit tongue-tied himself, not having expected her to be quite so ravishing. Her beauty constantly astonished him. He had seen her in just about every circumstance, but never like this. He held his arm up for her to take, smiling at her appreciatively.

"He wanted me to present you to him. Are you ready?"

She slipped her arm through his. "As ready as I shall ever be."

"Come on, then. I shall escort you." He led her down the hall and up a flight of stairs, down another grand hall, and finally stopped in front of huge, embossed double doors.

"He is inside waiting."

Her hands began to tremble, and Jarreth gave her a reassuring smile. "Relax. In a few minutes you shall be pleasantly surprised. He is not what you assume."

She didn't look convinced as he opened the doors and led her inside the massive room. The sheer magnitude and richness, equal only with furnishings she saw when visiting the White Tower, instantly overwhelmed her. A man stood by a window, his back to them. He was as huge as Jarreth, a wee bit taller, and was dressed like Jarreth in nearly identical clothes. Long black hair with streaks of gray flowed over his collar. The heavy, red velvet drapes contrasted against the blackness of his attire. From the back he looked like an older version of Jarreth.

"Earl Stanwyck, I present the Lady Rhiannon."

The Dark Count turned slowly and gazed at her. She felt herself tremble as she kept her eyes lowered, afraid to face the monster she had so grown to fear. When he finally spoke, his words surprised her.

"So, we finally meet. Your father's description did not do you justice. You are devastatingly beautiful."

Rhiannon

She looked at him and lost all sense of protocol. He was indeed scarred, but not frighteningly so, with eyes as black as coal. His nose was straight, his cheekbones high. It was not hard to imagine his youthful good looks, and impossible not to notice his similarity to Jarreth. For some reason she did not fear him; something in his eyes reflected humanity, not cruelty. As her jaw gaped open in wonder, Jarreth gave her a slight jab and she came back to her senses. She quickly gave an elegant courtesy.

"Thank you, Milord. That is kind of you to say."

The count looked at his nephew with frustration that he could have lied to this seemingly innocuous girl. Jarreth shrugged, and tried to look innocent.

Taking her arm, the count stepped forward and led her to a chair, while casting a frown over his shoulder to his nephew. "Jarreth has told me all about you two. I want to put your mind at ease immediately. I am thrilled beyond measure that you two are in love." He motioned her to sit, which she did in stunned silence. Jarreth stood by her chair, and leaned down into one ear.

"Say something," he urged.

"Y-you are?"

The count smiled sincerely at her, then looked up and scowled at Jarreth. "Aye, I am. You see, I fear there is a small detail that Jarreth failed to tell you."

"T-there is?" She glanced up at Jarreth, who was studying the ceiling.

"Aye. You see Rhiannon, when I arranged your marriage with your father, 'twas not with me."

Rhiannon blinked in utter stupefaction. "But Kady heard…"

"Kady heard wrong." Jarreth finally decided to join his uncle in the explanation. "I was always your intended."

Confusing emotions whirled inside her mind, ranging from total relief to complete bafflement. "B—but you said…"

"I know. After I met you at the lake, I found out who you were. That is why I came back to the caves to get you."

She stood up slowly, cast a confused look at Jarreth, and another one at the count. "You arrange marriages for your knights?"

Jarreth cleared his throat, which developed into a cough. The moment of truth had finally arrived. The count cast him a glare, then shook his head.

"Nay, I do not. What my knights do is their business. Since Jarreth seems to have caught something in his throat, I guess 'tis up to me to tell you the truth."

She raised her head bravely and braced herself for the worst. "Tell me what?"

"You see my dear, Jarreth is not a knight; he is my nephew. His father was my younger brother. I have raised him since his father's death. He is a viscount, and my only heir."

They waited for her reaction, Jarreth with a wide grin. Any second now she would leap into his arms, overjoyed that her life had taken such a wonderful turn. Any second now. He waited.

Rhiannon couldn't speak. She stared at the count with a dropped jaw as suddenly everything came together. The lake, the caves, the pirates, the Gypsies, the boar, the river; all the events of the past few weeks replayed in her mind. Her jaw closed, she stood up, and turned to Jarreth. The gates of wrath broke open.

"You are *what*?"

Jarreth's smile faded. "Now, Rhiannon…do not forget 'twas *you* who first lied about your identity."

"B—but that was when I thought I was engaged to *him*!" She pointed to the count, then quickly added, "No offence, Milord."

The count smiled. "None taken."

Rhiannon

Jarreth began grasping at any weak argument he could muster. "You talked about wanting to marry for love, so I gave you the opportunity! You should be thanking me!"

"*Thanking* you?" She folded her arms and glowered. "I almost get raped, gored by a wild pig, my throat cut, drowned in a river, and I should be thanking you?"

"She has a point," the count offered.

"You stay out of this! Rhiannon, you are being unreasonable!"

"Oh, am I? What about all that talk about living in poverty, about being able to offer me nothing but your love?"

Jarreth raised an eyebrow. "Would you rather live in poverty? I can refuse my inheritance."

"Aye! I mean, nay! I mean…you are confusing me!"

"Aye, Jarreth, you are confusing her," the count chimed in.

"Shut up, Uncle! Rhiannon, what would you have had me do?"

"The truth would have been nice."

"But you said yourself you did not want an arranged marriage. Where did that leave me?"

"You could have talked to me! After our meeting at the lake, did you not feel the attraction between us? I felt horrible when you left me at the ocean to go off on a feigned 'mission.'"

"For your information, I was going to break off my betrothal and come back and get you. Does that not mean anything?"

"'Twould have meant more if you had come back and told me the truth! Instead, you chose to lie to me. I have gone through two weeks of torture because of you!" She turned away with bitter tears welling in her eyes.

"So you think it has been easy for me? Chasing after you, worried about whether or not you were with the Gypsies…"

"Gypsies?" the count asked.

Jarreth waved him off. "I could have died myself rescuing you from that river. What reward did I get from that?" He immediately winced. "Um, that did not come out right."

The count grimaced; Jarreth had really stuck his foot in his mouth this time.

She slowly turned and glared at him. "I would say you got your just reward, at least you seemed to think so at the time."

"That was not my meaning!" Jarreth yelled.

"Is that right? Consider my debt paid, *Sir* Jarreth…viscount…whatever you are! You promised me I would not have to marry my betrothed after I met him if I did not want to. Well, I do not want to."

Jarreth lowered his voice to a desperate plea. "Rhiannon, you cannot mean that!"

"How can I marry a man who cannot tell the truth, indeed, seems incapable of it?"

"I did it for you."

"Than you did it for no one. I would not marry you now if you were the only man in England." She quickly turned to the count, who was looking on in great amusement. "'Twas a pleasure to meet you, Milord." With that, she sauntered out the door, leaving Jarreth in dazed dejection.

The count raised his eyebrows, and turned to his beleaguered nephew. "That went well, I think."

Jarreth slumped into a chair and tried to appear unfazed. "She does not mean it, she is simply…overwhelmed."

"Uh-huh."

"She shall think it over, cool down, and come running back into my arms."

"Uh-huh."

"You are not being very encouraging, Uncle!"

"Sorry. It just so happens I agree with her."

"*You* do not think she should marry me?"

Rhiannon

"Nay, of course I do not think that, not after all the trouble you two have been through. I simply agree that 'twas a dirty trick to lie to her."

"Then what do you profess I do?"

"Something I have never seen you do. Apologize."

Jarreth snorted and frowned. "Grovel at her feet? Never!"

"Then be prepared to live a long and lonely life."

A servant at the door cut their conversation short. "Excuse me, Milords, but there is a messenger."

"Not now, Caleb," the count barked.

"But Sire, he says he was sent by the Queen."

Both the count and Jarreth looked up. "The Queen? Well, send him in," the count ordered. The servant bowed, and left to fetch the messenger. Jarreth furled his eyebrows as he pondered this latest development. What would the Queen want with them? The last they heard she was asking to be regent for her young son, Edward V, who was to become king since his father's death.

The messenger was escorted in, and he bowed to the count. "Earl Stanwyck? I have a message from Queen Elizabeth." He handed the parchment to him.

The count went to his desk with Jarreth close behind, and spread out the parchment. He leaned over it and read the message while Jarreth waited impatiently. He knew his uncle hated anyone reading over his shoulder. "Well?" Jarreth finally asked.

"Oh, this is bad," the count said as he shook his head while frowning. "Richard, the duke of Gloucester, has had young Edward V locked in the Tower of London, and is challenging the legitimacy of Elizabeth's marriage to Edward IV. He claims her son has no right to the throne. The duke of Buckingham is putting together a rebellion, and she wants us to join him."

"By the saints," Jarreth sighed. "I grow weary of this war. Now Richard is getting into the act."

"Well, if 'tis any consolation, I have been in contact with Henry Tudor. He is assembling an army in France, and soon will challenge Richard to the throne." He paused with a worried look. "We must be careful. If Richard supporters suspect we are not on the side of the Yorkists, we could fall like many before us." He looked up at the messenger. "My servant will take you to the kitchen for something to eat. Rest as long as you dare, then ride back and tell Elizabeth I shall leave as soon as possible."

"Aye, Milord." The messenger bowed and followed the servant out.

The count let out a deep sigh. "I am getting too old for this."

Jarreth chuckled. "Nonsense, uncle. You are only forty-two."

"You will see how old that is when you reach that age. Well, I guess I better decide how many men to take with me this time. At least with your return, I will not be leaving the castle undefended. This will probably turn out as fruitless as the last time, when an entire army was summoned and never saw action. That was a wasted two weeks. Oh well, anything for our Queen, I suppose. I certainly do not support Richard's claim." He cut himself off when he glanced at Jarreth. "What is that look for?"

Jarreth was rubbing his chin with a strange smile on his face. "I have been thinking, Uncle, you are right. You *are* too old for this type of thing. I believe I should go in your stead."

His uncle leaned back and folded his arms. "All right, Jarreth—what are you up to?"

"Why, nothing uncle."

The count cocked his head and glared at his lovesick nephew. "This would not have anything to do with Rhiannon, would it?"

"You are too smart for me." Jarreth broke into a large grin. "I know she loves me, but she can be very stubborn. I fear she shall stay angry with me for a very long time, unless I can jar her to her senses. I shall go away on this horribly dangerous mission…"

Rhiannon

"Who said anything about it being horribly dangerous?"

"I did. Anyway, she will see that she loves me and will worry the whole time. In two weeks or so when I return, she shall throw herself at my feet." He appeared quite pleased with his genius. "She shall be the one who grovels."

"I seriously doubt that. But if you are volunteering for this mission, I accept. The last thing I want to do is sleep on the ground for two weeks waiting for a battle that never happens."

"After what I have been through, that sounds like heaven."

"After all you have been through, you still play games?"

"Ha! She is the one playing games. Aye, this is a good plan. I shall let her fret for a few weeks, and I shall return triumphant. And Uncle, you must promise not to tell her the true purpose of my mission."

"Jarreth," the count whined.

"Promise Uncle, or do you fancy the cold, hard ground?"

The count uttered a groan. "Very well, I promise."

Jarreth grinned smugly. This time he would beat Rhiannon at her own game.

Chapter Thirteen

After leaving Jarreth and the count, Rhiannon ran back to her room in an intense rage. She threw herself on the bed and broke out in great, heaving sobs. He had lied—everything, the whole thing—had been a great lie. She even doubted that he ever loved her. But one fact remained—she loved him with all her heart.

It had all seemed so romantic; a hopeless love, indeed, a dangerous one, that they would overcome and endure. She was willing to sacrifice everything, even her own life. And it was all a lie! She felt betrayed, violated, and dishonored. Now it seemed so...*arranged*. How utterly common. She sat up, wiped her tears and began thinking.

So she was to be the wife of a viscount and live there in luxury, pampered by servants and waited on hand and foot. It already sounded boring. Yet, she remembered, Jarreth had said he would let her write her stories. Well, that was something, at least. That is, if she could find time in between throwing boorish parties and entertaining stuffy, conceited guests. She wrinkled her nose in disgust.

Her mind flashed back to the previous night and making love during the storm. She had never felt so wild, so free, so fulfilled. Now she

Rhiannon

realized Jarreth was simply taking what belonged to him. The knave! Even though he had told her she would not have to marry him, she knew by law she had no rights in the matter. The agreement was accepted and signed, and in all intents she was already his wife. The only leverage she had was in taking the vows. Right then she was so upset that she was determined to make him wait forever. Her strategy was now to get even. If he could play games, so could she. She was the master of it.

So where to start? First, refuse to marry or speak to him until he begged her for forgiveness. Maybe she could turn her attentions to an unsuspecting man, and drive Jarreth wild with jealousy. She frowned; no, that wouldn't be fair to the man. No use hurting someone else. But that wouldn't rule out invoking someone's help and staging the whole thing. Aye, she would have to make friends here.

She could certainly refuse him to her bed; she doubted if Jarreth would resort to raping her. But that might drive him to seek a willing woman to satisfy his needs. She had always hated the custom of men having a mistress, and she was sure Jarreth could handle quite a few.

The count seemed like a decent fellow, not at all what she had imagined. Maybe he would help? He would know his nephew better than anyone. Perhaps he could tell her what would make Jarreth come crawling to her feet? It was worth a try.

For the next hour or so, she ran scheme after scheme in her vengeful mind until she heard a rapping on her door. Thinking it must surely be Jarreth coming to apologize, she straightened her gown, pinched her cheeks, and fluffed her hair. She wiped all emotion from her face, holding her head regally high as she opened the door.

It was the count. He smiled at her without comment as he observed an unmistakable look of disappointment cross her face.

"I am sorry—were you expecting someone else?"

She immediately regained her composure and turned on her imperious charm. "Do not be silly, Milord, I am both surprised and delighted to see you."

The count had no difficulty seeing how his nephew had fallen so in love with her. He offered her his arm. "I have come to escort you to dinner, if you will grace me with that honor."

She took his arm and flashed him a wide smile. "The honor is all mine."

He began leading her down the hall, and turned at the grand staircase. They strolled down the stairs as the count attempted to engage in polite conversation, carefully avoiding the subject of her marriage to Jarreth.

"I trust your room is satisfactory?"

"Oh, aye, very. Thank you."

"Good, good. Do you like the gown? I had it made from the measurements your father gave me."

"'Tis beautiful."

"You actually have an entire wardrobe. You may choose the clothes you like, and discard any you find unsuitable."

"I am sure they will all be perfect."

"If you need anything, anything at all, you just let the servants know. If we do not have it, we will get it."

"You are too kind. Thank you."

Running out of small talk and still quite a distance from the dinning hall, the count grasped at any benign subject. "That was quite a storm that passed through yesterday, was it not? Did you and Jarreth encounter it?"

She stiffened just a little as she answered. "Aye, you could say that."

"I fear the rivers shall overflow, and flood some of my tenants. I have a terrible flooding problem, you know."

"Nay, I was not aware."

"Oh, aye. One year I lost three huts. I have to keep a watchful eye every summer."

Rhiannon

Rhiannon couldn't help it. She giggled.

"What do you find so amusing?"

"I cannot believe we are so uncomfortable that we have resorted to talking about the weather."

He also saw the humor, and chuckled much like she had heard Jarreth do many times. "That *is* rather pathetic, I suppose. Very well, you pick the subject."

"This castle…'Tis magnificent. Has it always been in your family?"

"Nay, my grandfather won it in a battle. 'Twas built by James of St. George. Have you heard of him?"

She shook her head.

"Nay? Pity, he was quite an engineering genius. He directed a staff of engineers from all over Europe. James believed in keeping the outworks of his castles strong, but concentrated the main defense on a square castle enclosed by two lines of walls with a stout tower at each corner of the inner line."

Rhiannon felt like yawning, but she nodded with interest. "Fascinating."

"Aye, the keep is then rendered superfluous by the elaborate towers and gatehouses which can hold out independently even if the enemy won the inner bailey. My grandfather was extremely fortunate in winning this keep."

"'Twould appear so."

"Of course, there have been many improvements since then."

"Indeed?"

"Aye, the entire west wing was added by my father, including the chapel where you and Jarreth will be mar…" He stopped when he realized what he had said. "Er, what I mean is… Ah! Here we are, the dining hall!" He hustled her into the great room, never being so glad to see this particular room in his whole life.

Wonderful smells emanated from the hall. Beef, pork, poultry, mutton and game were prepared in stews and soups, as well as roasted.

Carvers stood at the end on each table to cut the desired piece. Rhiannon could smell *blankmanger*, a kind of custard consisting of chicken blended with rice in almond milk. It was one of her favorites. Her stomach growled when she realized how much she had missed castle cooking, since Jarreth's cooking left a little to be desired. The scents of spices and sauces also assaulted her senses, such as vinegar, onions, pepper, saffron, ginger, cloves, and cinnamon.

Comfortably seated at the high table, Rhiannon scanned the room for Jarreth, while pretending *not* to be scanning the room for Jarreth. He wasn't there. At least, she didn't think he was there. The room had at least a hundred people in it, most seated at low tables with shared plates, chattering away contently with one another. This certainly didn't look like a household that was scared to death of their lord. At least that was one thing Jarreth told the truth about.

"He is not coming to dinner, if that is what you are wondering," the count said, interrupting her thoughts.

"Oh?" she expressed, and then brought her voice to a non-caring tone. "I was *not* wondering. I do not care where he is."

"Indeed?" He offered her a slab of roast beast, which she declined. "Then 'twill not interest you to know he is leaving."

"Leaving?" she practically hiccuped.

"Aye, he is preparing his guard as we speak. He is going on a mission for the king."

Remembering how Jarreth could invent missions when the need suited him, she raised her eyebrows in doubt. "A real mission, or another made-up one?"

"Oh, I assure you, a real one. Only too real."

She paused, and then with her emotions in check asked, "For how long?"

"Probably several weeks. One never knows how long these skirmishes can take."

Rhiannon

"Skirmishes? He is going to...fight?"

"That is the intent. Richard has seized the throne, and has caused a threat of a rebellion. Jarreth is going to help organize the resistance. Horribly dangerous mission." He felt guilty expanding the truth like he was, but Jarreth had talked him into it. He hoped he wasn't laying it on too thick.

Rhiannon felt like her heart had stopped beating. So soon he could just take off and forget her? Did she mean nothing to him? She fell into a confused silence for the rest of the meal, simply going through the motions of a graceful diner. When she saw Jarreth enter the hall, her hands grew cold and butterflies filled her stomach. He walked straight to her and gazed down with a cold expression.

"Are you finished? I shall like to escort you to your room."

She tried hard to obtain a haughty demeanor. "I suppose that is your right." She stood up and lightly put her arm through his. As he escorted her from the hall, she looked straight ahead and did not speak. All eyes were on the striking couple as they walked past. By now everyone was aware of whom the beautiful newcomer was, and rumors flew around the room in hushed whispers. Women giggled and men nodded their approval. Rhiannon held her head high and ignored everyone; they could all go jump in the moat for all she cared. Finally in the hallway, he stopped and faced her.

"So, you are still determined not to marry me?"

She refused eye contact. "Aye."

"Rhiannon, I know you love me. To carry on like this is childish."

"I suppose you would rather I lie. That should not be hard; I have had several good examples."

"You are simply upset because for once in your life someone outsmarted you, admit it."

"I admit nothing."

"We both know you shall be over this in a few days. Why not accept it, and get on with your life?"

"If I am married, I have no life."

He began to show signs of exasperation. "Rhiannon, you are testing my patience. Do you think I will wait forever?"

"I do not care how long you have to wait."

He roughly grabbed her arm and began walking again. "You are stubborn, but so am I. I can wait as long as you." Taking long strides that she could barely keep up with, he dragged her up the stairs and to her room. He let go of her arm and opened her door.

"Did my uncle happen to mention I would be leaving tomorrow?"

"T—tomorrow?"

He thought that would get her attention. "Aye, and I should be gone at least two weeks. Perhaps that will give you time to calm that overreactive temper." He pushed her into the room and slammed the door.

She stared at the door, stunned and angry. A small statue took the brunt of her anger as she hurled it at the door, shattering it into pieces.

After the maids dressed her for bed, she cried herself to sleep.

Downstairs in the great hall Jarreth drank himself into a stupor, alone in his anger and frustration. Servants tiptoed around him, not wanting to be the recipient of his surly mood. He hadn't planned on losing his temper like that. He was going to talk to her, warm up to her, use reason and logic—all of which he didn't do. But, damn it! She was driving him mad. He wanted her so badly, and he couldn't touch her. It was difficult to not just sweep her up in his arms and carry her off. Why was she being so difficult? A woman had no right to have such pride. Well, he never had to go crawling to any woman before, and he'd be damned if he would start now. He only hoped his absence would make her realize how much she loved him. He knew he already missed her.

Rhiannon

The next morning, Rhiannon was awakened by servants, and dressed for the morning meal. She half expected Jarreth to escort her to the dining hall, but again the count showed up at her door for that honor. She was beginning to like him a lot; despite his fearful appearance he was a gentleman with a sense of humor. In a lot of ways, Jarreth was just like him. Again they engaged in small talk on the way down, and upon arriving found Jarreth waiting by the entrance looking extremely formidable. He was dressed in all black battle gear, and carried a sword across his back and at his side. Daggers were sheathed on the sides of his boots, and more in his studded belt. He was wearing a long black traveling cape. If she didn't know him, she probably would have been a bit taken back. As it was, she simply stared at him without emotion.

"I shall take it from here, uncle. I would like to speak to my *wife*."

Rhiannon glowered at Jarreth as the count obediently relinquished her arm. He bowed to her before he left. "Be gentle with him, dear. He did not have a good night."

Jarreth glared as he walked away. Damn it, why did he have to divulge that? It was none of her business that after he got drunk, he spent most the night bemoaning his fate to his uncle. He finally passed out in a chair, and woke up with a kink in his neck and an incredible headache.

"I am sorry to hear you did not sleep well," she said sweetly. "Perhaps a guilty conscience clouds your mind?"

"I slept wonderfully, do not listen to him. Rhiannon, I am only going to ask you this once."

"What?"

"I wish to take our vows before I leave."

Lifting herself up as tall as she could, she set her jaw in determination. "Nay, I will not."

He had expected as much. "Then I guess there is nothing more for me to say. Good-bye, Rhiannon. I wish we were parting on better terms."

Rhiannon's heart sank to her toes. She expected more of a fight.

Evangelynn Stratton

"You are leaving...right now?"

Her surprised tone gave him reason to smile inwardly. He cocked his head, folded his arms, and raised an eyebrow. "Unless you want me to stay, and will marry me."

Confusion set in her mind; one side screamed yes, the other would not give him the satisfaction. This was exactly what he wanted, she reasoned, and there was no way she would give in.

"Never! Go on your silly mission, and I hope you rot!"

"Ah, loving parting words for me to dwell upon." He took her trembling right hand and brought it to his lips. "Good-bye, my love. I shall dream often of your warm body."

She jerked her hand away and glared at him without comment while he turned and swaggered down the hall with a cocky grin.

"Jarreth!"

He turned in anticipation. Had he succeeded in breaking her down?

His name had just blurted out of her, and as he stood there waiting for her to continue she could think of nothing to say. She wanted to jump in his arms, tell him not to go, and kiss him until he was breathless. Instead she bit her lower lip and fought her tears.

"Be careful."

He smiled. "Do I detect a bit of concern?"

Unable to answer, she stared at the floor and listened to his retreating footsteps echo down the hall. Food was no longer important; she ran up to her room and flung open the shutters on her window. The immense courtyard loomed right below her, and she watched as Jarreth came out the front entrance and mounted Daemon. There seemed to be about one hundred men, all prepared for war like Jarreth. When they were all mounted, Jarreth rode to the front to lead them out the gates. He suddenly raised his head and stared at her. Their gazes locked, and all the longing they held for one another was conveyed over the distance. He smiled, and kicked Daemon into a lope, his men following.

Rhiannon

Jarreth was pleased to see her watching him. She was already sorry; he could sense it. Two weeks away should have her groveling quite nicely when he returned. He departed feeling devilishly clever, like he had gotten the upper hand.

She watched until they were only small specks on the horizon, with tears distorting their image. When she could no longer see them, she rushed to her bed and kneeled, folding her hands and bowing her head in reverence.

"Please, God," she said between sobs. "I have never asked you for anything, but I ask you now. Please keep him safe."

It rained for two days, then the weather cleared the day the Baron of Yorkshire and Kady arrived for the wedding. Rhiannon couldn't contain her joy in having her friend again. She hurried out to the muddy courtyard the moment she heard they had arrived and ran into Kady's arms, practically knocking her over. They told each other how well they looked, how much they missed one other, and vowed never to be parted again. The baron, who stood by feeling rather dejected, loudly cleared his throat to gain his daughter's attention. The happy reunion shortened, Rhiannon turned to face him with a different temperament.

"I am not sure I am speaking to you, father."

"Oh, Rhiannon! Please!" He held out his hands to her. "'Twas not my idea!"

"But you went along with it."

"Rhiannon," Kady interrupted, "do not be angry with your father. He was only trying to do what was best."

The baron nodded enthusiastically. "Aye, listen to Kady!"

"I thought you were on my side," Rhiannon said with a frown to Kady.

"We both are," Kady assured. "Rhiannon, Jarreth knew you wanted to marry for love, and that you would never accept an arranged marriage. He wanted to give you the chance to fall in love with him."

Rhiannon threw her arms up in exasperation. "Did everyone know of his true identity but me?"

"Your father did not tell me until you had left. Oh, Rhiannon, I am so happy for you! A viscount, who will inherit his uncle's entire fortune!"

"He will? Oh, 'tis even worse than I thought." She wrinkled her nose in disgust.

"So!" The baron clasped his hands together and grinned. "When is the wedding?"

"Never."

Both Kady and the baron stared at her in shocked silence until Kady found her tongue.

"Never? Why not?"

"We are not exactly speaking right now."

"But—but why?" her father stammered. "Oh, Rhiannon! You are not being stubborn again, are you?"

"Do you not love him?" Kady asked. "Did his plan work?"

"Aye, and nay." She took Kady's hand. "Come inside, I shall tell you all about it. Father, you must excuse us."

"Of course. Kady, talk some sense into her."

Rhiannon pulled Kady toward the castle as Kady drug her feet, looking up at the dark, ominous towers with gargoyles leering their hideous grins down at her. "I—I do not know...the Dark Count..."

"Oh, the count is wonderful," Rhiannon assured her. "Come! I have much to show you!"

She hurried Kady up to her room, and spent the next two hours telling of her adventures from the moment she left Yorkshire castle. Knowing her mistress well, Kady was not surprised by any of it, and especially liked the part about joining the Gypsies. When Rhiannon told

Rhiannon

her how she lost her temper and told Jarreth she wouldn't marry him, Kady's eyes got wide in disbelief.

"But you did not mean it, right? You made up?"

"Not as yet. 'Tis hard to make up when he is not here."

"Not here? Where is he?"

"It seemed some dumb battle was more important than me. He left two days ago, and shall not be back for at least two weeks."

"Two weeks! That is horrible!"

"Aye, and what is even worse, I could not bring myself to tell him to stay."

"You mean, he would have stayed if you had asked him to? Oh, Rhiannon, your foolish pride will get you into trouble someday."

Rhiannon sighed. "Aye, this time you are right. But he made me so angry! He acted like he had done me a great favor, and it infuriated me."

"Then you do love him?"

"Of course I do. I would not have given myself to him if I did not."

Kady's eyes showed white all around and a huge smile broke across her face. "You did?"

Rhiannon winced; she didn't mean to divulge that, it sort of just slipped out. "Very well, Aye, I did. Before I found out he was a lying skunk."

"Oh Rhiannon! This is true love! Oh, this is so exciting!" She bounced on the bed in glee.

"Really, Kady, calm down, you shall break the bed."

"But this is so wonderful! Have you picked your wedding gown, yet?"

"Well no, I…"

"Oh, then we must. It should be blue to match your eyes."

"Well, actually I am not sure if…"

"Oh, you are right—it should be rose. You look lovely in rose. We brought some of your gowns; perhaps one of them will do."

"But I…"

"Of course, how silly of me, it should be new. I know! We can ask this count of yours if you can pick your own material. You must be absolutely devastating. Your father has invited practically everyone in England to this wedding. Oh, and your nosegay should be fresh. Does the count have any indoor gardens?"

"Er, I think so, but I…"

"Wonderful! Now, this must be planned perfectly down to the last detail."

As Kady rambled on and on about the wedding, Rhiannon slumped on the bed and became lost in her own thoughts. A large, overdone wedding was just not what she had envisioned. It was so much better before, when Jarreth was just a lowly knight, the Dark Count was a murdering villain, and she had hopes of a romantic, daring wedding. They would steal off in the night, knowing at any moment the Dark Count could burst in and fight Jarreth in a duel to the death. They would fight—Jarreth would win of course—and then he would sweep her up in his arms and leap from the window to the awaiting horse. Then they would ride hard, barely escaping the hundreds of men chasing them, and end up lost in a deep forest. But they wouldn't care, because their love was all they needed. That would have been so exciting, so dangerous, so…"

"Rhiannon?"

She snapped back to reality and blinked. "W-what?"

"Oh, Rhiannon! You have not heard a word I have said!"

"Aye, I did. Um, nosegays."

"I said that ten minutes ago." She frowned at her mistress. "You were daydreaming again."

Rhiannon shrugged. "Maybe a little."

"Rhiannon, this is important!"

"I know." She flopped back on the overstuffed bed with her arms over her head and stared at the ceiling. "'Tis just so…*planned.*"

Rhiannon

"Weddings usually are."

"But that is not the way I want it. Why can it not be exciting?" She sat up with a brightened expression. "Africa!"

Kady drew back in horror. "*Africa*?"

"Aye, Africa! I wonder if Jarreth would take me there?"

"Good Lord, I hope not!"

"He might."

"'Twould help if you were speaking to him."

Rhiannon paused. "You have a point. Perhaps I have been going about this whole thing wrong." She scrunched her face as she became deep in thought.

"Oh-oh. I know that look. What are you planning now?"

"I was just thinking. I have been too hard on Jarreth. I have decided to forgive him."

Kady knew only too well that Rhiannon didn't forgive easily. She didn't have to; her beauty and charm, combined with a scheming wit, always got her what she wanted. "All right, what are you up to?"

"Up to? Why, nothing."

"I do not believe you."

"Oh Kady, really—you are much too suspicious." Actually, Kady was right; Rhiannon had decided to switch strategies. She would use her feminine wiles to make Jarreth do whatever she wanted. Fighting with him was so easy; he was the most infuriating man she had ever known. She would have to learn to control her temper and Jarreth, and then maybe life would be more adventurous. Aye, when he returned she would greet him with loving, open arms.

Meanwhile, she must be the epitome of charm and grace and completely win the count over to her side. He seemed to already be leaning in her direction, so it shouldn't be hard.

Chapter Fourteen

For the next few days Rhiannon busied herself as she wormed her way into everyone's heart. She didn't have to try very hard. The servants all loved her, as well as the many guests who arrived daily for the big wedding. She resigned herself to the lavish festival everyone seemed determined to have for Jarreth and her. If she ever felt miserable or overwhelmed, she retired to her room and hid that side of her. Kady was the only one who knew her friend's true feelings.

She and the count became close. They talked often of Jarreth as they engaged in a game of chess, or simply took a walk through his many gardens. His reputation was indeed unearned, as she found him charming, hospitable and gracious.

When three weeks had passed and there was still no word of Jarreth, the count began to mildly worry. This wasn't like his nephew. Since this whole thing was simply a cooling-off period for Rhiannon's benefit, he couldn't understand the delay. Was Jarreth purposely staying away a little longer for assurance of breaking Rhiannon down? If so, it was working. Rhiannon was losing her sparkle. Granted, she brought out her usual charm at the dining table, but retired early and avoided the

Rhiannon

evening's festivities. The castle was packed with guests waiting for Jarreth's return, and everyone was making the most of it.

Kady was starting to worry about her mistress. She seemed to be sinking into a depression, and her appetite was failing. Although Kady was concerned, she inwardly considered it a blessing in disguise. Rhiannon had always thought only of herself, but this time her heart wasn't her own. Perhaps fate had wisely matched her with the one person who could handle her.

One day Rhiannon was discovered in one of the tall towers, staring out a window that had a sweeping view of the front gate and beyond. It became her main occupation, day after day, as she barely ate or slept. The count tried hard to conceal his concern, assuring Rhiannon that sometimes these things took time. A variety of things might have happened, he explained, none serious. Several guests left, thinking the wedding might not be taking place after all. The mood of the castle grew strained.

Halfway into the fifth week, Rhiannon spotted a lone rider heading for the castle. She strained her eyes until she could make out his red and black mantle, the color of Jarreth's guard. The advance harbinger! The count had explained how Jarreth always sent a rider ahead to announce his impending arrival; Rhiannon was positive he was it. For the first time in weeks she felt alive.

She ran down the long winding stairs only to meet Kady coming up. When Kady saw Rhiannon's beaming smile, she knew something had happened to change her frame of mind.

"What is it?" she asked as Rhiannon brushed past her.

"One of Jarreth's men! They are returning!" She bounded down the stairs without further elaboration.

The flustered servant sighed, and started the long decent back down the tower, something she had done so often lately she thought her legs would fall off. "Thank Heavens. Maybe things will get back to normal around here."

Rhiannon made it to the bottom in record time and ran down the long hallway that led to the front entrance. The count was already at the door, having been told by his own lookout about the rider. When he saw her smile, he knew she was also aware of this latest development.

"Come, we shall greet him together. 'Tis about time; I hope there is a good explanation for this long absence."

Rhiannon nodded, too excited to talk, and they entered the courtyard as the rider passed through the front gate. Practically every servant and guest was standing in the courtyard, eager to hear the news of the young lord's victorious return. The mood was festive; people smiled and exchanged pleasantries. Now there would be a wedding.

As the rider drew closer the lighthearted mood faded. Something was wrong. He wore a bloody bandage around his head and another on his left arm. His face was drawn and weary. The usual signs of victory—a satisfied smile, the proud bearing of his lord's flag, the demeanor of a winner—was missing. His horse also showed signs of battle, with several healing gashes on its neck. The man looked as if he could barely ride, leaning to one side as if balance was arduous.

"Good God!" The count rushed to his side and helped the man dismount. A groom took the exhausted horse as the man collapsed on the ground. "Get this man some water!"

Several servants darted for the well. The count kneeled before his man and carefully unwrapped the arm bandage; then winced when he saw the gaping wound. "Prepare a bed for this man," he ordered, and several more servants hastened away.

"More are coming," the man gasped. "We were ambushed on our way back. We did not see them, we…" He moaned in pain, and closed his eyes.

"Take it easy," the count said, casting his gaze in the direction of the well. "Hurry with that water!"

Rhiannon

Her heart pounding through her chest, Rhiannon knelt before the man and put a hand on his shoulder. "Jarreth," she almost whispered, "what of Jarreth?"

The man stared back with brown vacant eyes. "We were outnumbered two to one," he replied. "Lord Jarreth fought the best and killed the most."

A servant arrived with a flask of water, and the injured man took a large gulp. The count waited, and then also asked the pertinent question. "My nephew—where is he?"

The man lowered his gaze, closed his eyes, and slowly shook his head.

"No!" Rhiannon screamed, her voice shaking with disbelief. "No, 'tis not true!"

"I am sorry, Milady. I saw him get struck myself."

She jumped to her feet with a look of panic. "No! Tell him he is wrong! 'Tis not true!" The count stood and grabbed the hysterical girl into his arms as he blinked back his own unmanly tears. He could think of nothing to say to comfort her.

Rhiannon's father and Kady stood by feeling helpless. Finally the count gently released her to her father as she continued to sob uncontrollably. "Take her inside," he said softly. They nodded and led her away, both their arms protectively around her. The count knelt back down to further question the man.

"Tell me everything; I must know."

The man nodded. "It started out like lord Jarreth told us. Several noble families assembled to take a stand against Richard. We were all waiting for the Duke of Buckingham. There was not much to do, so we just camped for three weeks and nothing happened. Lord Jarreth was anxious to get home to his bride, so we took our leave, seeing how it looked like the duke would not show up. Halfway back we accidentally came across a band of Richard Loyalists on their way to put down the rebellion. They jumped us. We were not prepared." He paused and took another drink. "We were better fighters, but there were more of them. We managed to kill most of them, whoever did not flee when it started to get ugly, but there were only twenty-eight of us left alive. Four died later after the skirmish."

The count drew back in stunned disbelief. "Out of a hundred men, you are saying only twenty-four are left? My God." He hung his head and closed his eyes.

"Aye, Milord. The ones left, like me, were greatly impaired, some close to death. There were bodies everywhere after the battle, and townsfolk from the nearest village came to help us. They took us in and tended to our wounds as best they could. They also buried all the bodies."

The count raised his head. "Are you meaning to say my nephew's body is not being brought back?"

"Nay, Milord. I am right sorry about that, but those of us left were too hurt to handle much. I was only able to ride a few days ago. I took the best horse and rode on ahead to prepare you for the others. They are not far behind, and are bringing all the horses and weapons we could round up. Many of the horses are injured, so they have to go slow."

Drawing a deep breath, the count held back his emotions as he absorbed the cruel facts. "You are absolutely positive Jarreth is dead?"

"Aye, Milord. He was shot in the back. I saw him fall, then shortly afterwards I was knocked off my horse. No one saw what happened to him. He was buried with the rest. I am sorry, Milord."

"'Tis not your fault." He motioned to a few on-looking servants to tend to the fallen soldier's wounds, then braced himself to go comfort Rhiannon. "Tell me immediately when the rest arrive."

He found Rhiannon in the parlor, sitting on the large couch where they had so often had tea and conversation. The baron and Kady sat by her, displaying sympathetic looks for her loss. Several servants stood around, all sad, some crying quietly. Rhiannon was remarkably composed, no longer sobbing, simply staring blankly in numbed devastation.

Rhiannon

The count put a hand on her shoulder and attempted to find words to comfort her.

"He died bravely, fighting for the rightful king."

She remained silent. He sat on a stool in front of her and put a hand over his eyes in grief. "God help me; it should have been me."

Rhiannon slowly turned and looked at him with shadowed eyes. "How do you mean?"

"He went in my stead. How could I have been so foolish?" His voice broke as his buried emotions surfaced, and he fought to bury them again.

Huge tears ran down Rhiannon's cheeks and fell off her chin; she didn't seem to have the energy to wipe them. "You only let him leave. I am the one who sent him away."

Kady sniffed back her own tears, and wiped Rhiannon's face with a napkin. "Rhiannon, you mustn't believe that."

"'Tis true," Rhiannon whispered. "We all know it. My stubborn pride killed him, just as sure as if I had ran him through myself."

"Blaming yourself will solve nothing," the count said. "Jarreth was a warrior with a creed to serve his king. He lived by it—and died by it. His death was honorable."

Rhiannon stood up and raised her head bravely. "There is no honor in death, only emptiness."

"Rhiannon," her father began.

"I need to be alone. Please excuse me." She walked from the room and Kady began following behind her. "No, Kady. Not even you."

"But…" Kady started.

"I need to be completely alone. Please understand."

Kady nodded reluctantly, and let her leave.

Rhiannon didn't know where to go; only that she sought solitude. It all seemed like a mirage, a nightmare that would vanish any second with her awaking with the realization that it was all a cruel joke. She wandered aimlessly down hallways, going nowhere, seeking answers. Curiously, she found herself standing in front of the chapel. She stood at the entrance for a few minutes, then slowly opened the door and entered.

The chapel was gaily decorated for her wedding that would never be. Each pew had a large blue and yellow bow on the end made of ribbon the count had imported from France. The altar had several bouquets of fresh flowers, lilacs and roses that had been replaced many times in the wait for Jarreth's return. Their fragrance maddened her; pleasantness had no right to be there along with her misery. The sun shone brightly through the costly stained glass window, casting soft colored hues in shapeless images in the otherwise unlit room. Rhiannon knelt at the altar and bowed her head. Tears began falling again, and she fought them as she began to pray with intolerable loneliness. Her eyes closed as she attempted to shut out the truth with darkness, but it persisted, cruel and brutally real.

"Please God, give me a reason to live. I have lost the only man I shall ever love."

Her presence wasn't lost on the chapel priest, who stood off to one side watching the hopeless girl cry her plea to God. He walked over and knelt beside her, hoping to give her strength. When she detected her solitude had been broken, she raised her head and gazed at him with bleary, pain-racked eyes.

"Why, father? Why did God take him?"

The priest pursed his lips and looked at her solemnly. "Sometimes it is difficult to understand these things, child. But you must believe that God's plan is good, even if it was not what you wanted or expected."

"How can I accept that, when 'tis my fault he left?"

"It was not your fault. If you believe in the divine order, then it was His plan for Jarreth to leave. You could neither make it happen, nor stop it."

Rhiannon

"But why is God punishing me to a life of loneliness, and most of all, why did God punish Jarreth by taking his life?"

He produced a knowing smile and shook his head. "My dear, death is not a punishment, it is a reward. Jarreth is with his heavenly Father."

"And I am alone! I cannot go on living without him."

"Yea, you will find a way."

"I do not even have a body to bury. He is still vividly alive to me."

"It is best to remember him as such."

Her tears began flowing more freely. "I do not feel like living any longer. I want to join Jarreth in Heaven."

"Child, that is not for you to decide." He put a comforting arm around her. "Let us pray for you to gain hope."

So they prayed. The priest quoted scriptures, all the consoling ones he could remember. Rhiannon listened through her pain, not understanding but relying on her faith to pull her life together. She was strong; she would survive—without Jarreth. She had no choice.

She was still in the chapel hours later when she heard the commotion. Excusing herself from the priest, she went into the hallway to see what was happening. A young servant girl rushed by her, carrying rags and sheets. Rhiannon grabbed her arm, effectively stopping her in her tracks.

"What is happening?"

"The rest of the count's men are returning. We are getting bandages and beds ready for them." Without excusing herself she ran down the hallway, leaving Rhiannon standing alone in uncertainty. After a short pause, she decided to follow her. Maybe they could use the help, and she could surely use the distraction.

By the time she arrived outside, the wounded and bedraggled men were just entering the courtyard, more resembling a funeral procession then a homecoming. They were all leading several horses loaded with weapons and belongings of their dead comrades. Each man looked defeated, haggard, and disconsolate. Battle-worn clothes hung on their weary bodies, some in tatters. But it was their eyes that told the real story, a plethora of empty pools with no hope, no joy.

Everyone became busy; the servants helped the men to the servant quarters where the count had ordered a makeshift hospital prepared, grooms took control of the horses. Rhiannon was helping one of the wounded soldiers when she saw the last soldier walk through the gate, slowly leading a lone black horse. Her heart jumped when she recognized the animal.

It was Daemon.

She motioned a servant to attend her soldier as she ran to greet the great horse. Seeing him again, knowing he had been such a part of Jarreth's life lifted the bleakness that consumed her tortured mind. Throwing her arms around the horse's neck, she fell into grief-wracked tears mixed with a small amount of joy. Her face rubbed against his soft fur as she relished in the smell and size of him once again.

"Daemon, oh Daemon!" He nickered softly in reply, recognizing her sadness by her tone. It was then she noticed his wounds. His back right leg was wrapped from the knee to the hock; fresh blood seeped through the bandage to join dried old blood. A gash was discernible across his flank and another on his shoulder. He had visibly lost weight.

"We knew we had to bring 'im back, Milady," the soldier leading him explained in a cockney accent. "E's right hurt, so we 'ad to go slowly and let 'im rest. It looks like the traveling opened up the leg wound. E's going to need a lot o' care."

Rhiannon swallowed the lump in her throat. "Let us get him to his stall. Maybe being in a familiar place shall help him."

The man nodded. "E's in pain with that back leg, we 'ave to go slow."

Rhiannon yelled for a groom to make ready Daemon's stall, and took the horse's lead rope. "Come on, boy," she coaxed. "Just a few more steps and you are home." She led the horse slowly to the stable just as the

Rhiannon

count looked up from the soldier he was helping. The sight of the great horse, Jarreth's proudest possession, moving in halting, deliberate steps brought pain to his heart. He watched the care Rhiannon took with the horse, talking, petting, encouraging him, and knew without a doubt she had loved Jarreth very much. Satisfied that Daemon was receiving the best care, he went back to his task.

Daemon entered his stall and began turning in a circle, then arduously lay down in the straw. Rhiannon watched him with great concern; he seemed to lack the internal fire she was so used to seeing in him. A young groom came up beside her and joined the silent vigilance.

"He does not look well."

Rhiannon turned to him, her face weary, her eyes brimming with sorrow. "He must live, do you understand? He must live!"

The groom just pursed his lips and kept silent.

"He needs water," she decided, "and apples. Jarreth told me he loved apples."

"He needs more than apples, Milady. He is going to need a miracle."

"It just so happens I believe in miracles."

The count entered the barn at that moment, wiping the blood off his hands on a rag. "The men are all receiving care. I believe everyone shall pull through." He paused as he observed the reposing horse. "How is he?"

The lanky groom shook his head, his pessimism written all over his face. "He is hurt badly, milord."

Rhiannon lifted her chin stubbornly. "He shall live."

"I pray you are right," the groom replied, and left to fetch the requested water and apples.

As the count and Rhiannon observed the great horse, her mood went from sorrow to anger. "They should not have made him walk back. 'Twas too far."

"I talked to several of the men. They felt they could not leave him." He sighed deeply. "He meant too much to them, to all of us. He represents Jarreth."

"I am going to stay tonight with him."

"What?" The count's black eyes narrowed in question. "You mean to sleep in a barn?"

"He needs me," she answered quietly.

The count put a hand on her thin shoulder and attempted to smile through his grief. "Rhiannon, saving this horse will not bring Jarreth back."

She seemed not to hear him, just stared at the wounded horse in dismay. Finally she turned to him with pleading eyes. "Please, Milord...spare me this one indulgence."

He nodded in understanding. The horse was all she had left of Jarreth, and she was clinging to the vain hope of saving him. "Very well, Rhiannon—and I think 'tis time you called me uncle."

"All right—uncle. Thank you."

They were both silent for a brief time as they observed the resting horse. Then, almost as an afterthought, the count mumbled a comment to himself.

"What did you say?" Rhiannon asked quickly.

"Huh? Oh, I was just thinking 'twas too bad there are not some Gypsies around."

"Why?"

"Because they are excellent at animal husbandry and care. I have often hired them for sick animals. They almost always save them, they have a knack for that kind of thing."

Her mind began reeling, could it be that one of her self-indulging escapades could actually benefit them? "But there *are* Gypsies close by...within a few days ride."

Rhiannon

"Aye, I remember Jarreth mentioning something about you running off to join some Gypsies. You must tell me that story sometime."

"Later. Uncle, gather some men. I will go with them and bring help for Daemon."

He snorted his opinion of that suggestion, and she suddenly realized he would be harder to manipulate than her father. "But, I know them, and I know about where they are."

"Very well, I will send some men. But do not think you are going gallivanting around the countryside. Draw me a map."

"But…"

"The matter is closed."

She shut her mouth when it was apparent he wouldn't be changing his mind. When he was adamant about something, a person might as well try to walk through a stone wall then argue with him.

"All right, I will try to show you where they last were." Kneeling down, she brushed some straw away on the dirt floor and smoothed a circle for her to draw on. Flashbacks of Jarreth drawing his animals pierced her memory, and she forced herself to concentrate on the matter at hand. She drew everything; the woods, the manor, the river, and put an "X" where she remembered last seeing the Gypsy band. The count nodded as he observed the primitive but effective map.

"I know exactly where that is. Do not worry, my men shall find them."

"They need to ask for a man named Ramon. He sort of owes Jarreth a favor."

"Really?" He raised one bushy eyebrow. "What did Jarreth do for him?"

"He let him live."

The count paused, then nodded. "I see." His voice softened. "I do not mean to be harsh, Rhiannon. I understand your wanting to help

Daemon, but I cannot allow you to be in danger in any way. Need I remind you I have just lost over seventy-five men?"

She closed her eyes and Jarreth's face appeared, torturing her further, grabbing her soul and ripping it to shreds. She took a shuddering breath as she remembered his touch, his scent, his smile. "If I could trade places with him, I would," she whispered.

Feeling like kicking himself for his insensitivity, the count held out her arms to her. "So would I, Rhiannon, so would I." She fell into his grasp and once again poured out her grief.

Kady and the baron chose that moment to join them in the barn. They could do nothing but stand by helplessly while the devastated girl broke their hearts with her sorrow.

"I was selfish and spoiled. Everything was a game to me, now he is gone, and will never know how much I love him."

Kady reached out to her, blinking back her own tears for Rhiannon's pain. "You will make yourself ill. You need to rest, come."

Too weak to argue, Rhiannon fell into Kady's arms. They left the barn as the two men pondered her plight.

"She is strong-willed," the baron said in a convincing tone, more to himself than to anyone. "She will survive."

The count watched the girls leave, and replied with a nod. "Let us hope."

Kady took Rhiannon directly to her room, asking a young servant girl on the way to bring them tea. She was starting to worry about Rhiannon's health. If she became physically ill, Kady doubted if Rhiannon would have the will to fight for her life.

"Here, lie down; that is good. You look green, Rhiannon. When did you last eat?"

Rhiannon closed her eyes against the cool linen pillow as bile began to rise up her throat. "I—I have not been very hungry lately."

Rhiannon

Kady grabbed an empty water basin and put it beside the increasingly sick girl. A suspicion was beginning to form. "Rhiannon, how long have you been feeling ill?"

"A week or two. I will be all…"

She started gagging, and Kady turned her head as the queasy girl made use of the basin.

Although not an expert on the subject, Kady recognized the signs of early pregnancy. "I think I will see why the tea is taking so long." She quickly left the room, leaving Rhiannon with only her nausea for company.

Out in the hallway, Kady closed her eyes and leaned against the wall. Mixed emotions swelled within her. It wouldn't be long before Rhiannon figured out the reason for her 'illness', and soon after everyone else would know. How would this news be accepted? Never in her thoughts did Kady ever think that her beautiful, adventurous mistress would give birth to a bastard child.

The little servant girl appeared with the tea tray, and Kady took it from her and joined Rhiannon again. She was relieved to see Rhiannon sitting up, wiping her face with a cool cloth and looking less green. Kady produced a cheerful smile for her benefit and brought the tea to her.

"Here, sip this, 'twill make you feel better."

Rhiannon complied, but gulped instead of sipped. "Ow, 'tis hot."

Kady watched her finish the cup, knowing it would be up to her to tell Rhiannon about her condition. "Honey, I need to tell you something."

A rap came at the door, and Kady silently cursed the intruder. It turned out to be the count.

"How is she?" he asked when she answered the door.

Kady glanced nervously back at the unsuspecting girl. "She will be all right…for now."

"Good. Rhiannon, the men have your directions and are prepared to leave. Do not worry, they will find this Ramon and bring him back."

Rhiannon stood up and attempted to reorganize her disheveled hair, then wiped her eyes with the back of her hand. "I will stay with Daemon. I need blankets."

Kady suddenly realized her intention, and began shaking her head. "Er, I do not think you should be sleeping in a cold barn."

Rhiannon waved her off. "Nonsense, I shall be fine." She brushed past Kady on her way to the door.

"But," Kady protested behind her, "do you not think…"

"Quiet, Kady. Uncle—I will stay with the horse until Ramon arrives. I promise you, He will live."

"I have no doubt." He managed a thin smile at the determined girl that had so suddenly been thrust into life's harsh reality. "I will have food brought out to you."

"Thank you."

Kady swallowed her objections and followed Rhiannon down the hall. "I shall stay with you, I know a little about horses." Actually, she knew nothing, but wanted a reason to stay with Rhiannon. Someone had to watch after her in her condition.

Chapter Fifteen

The great horse stood in a corner of his stall, his head bowed low, his spirit waning. Moonlight broke through the shuttered barn windows, leaving protracted streaks of faint light against the inky darkness. Unable to sleep, Rhiannon had finally given in to her insomnia and decided to turn her attention to Daemon. Again she offered him an apple; again he turned his head and refused. It had been two days, and she had not left his side. Neither had Kady, who was curled up sleeping in the straw along with a hen and a fresh brood of chicks. Rhiannon, on the other hand, had barely slept at all waiting for help to arrive. All she could do for the ailing animal was change his bandage and give him encouragement. She had finally succeeded in getting him to eat some hay, but not nearly enough to sustain him. He was slowly dying, and she could do nothing to stop it. She knew what the problem was—he was a one-man horse and missed Jarreth; his injuries were secondary. Whether he survived or not would depend on his own inner strength.

Finally collapsing from fatigue, she lay down next to the snoring Kady and closed her eyes. She was instantly queasy. Sitting up, she took deep breaths to calm her fidgety stomach. Being sick was becoming an everyday occurrence to her, and she didn't think it was from anything she was eating. It couldn't be; she could barely keep anything down. Besides being overly tired, she felt fine, physically that is. What could be wrong with her?

Her stomach calmed, she lay back down and willed herself to sleep. Instead her mind decided to replay events, both good and bad, all involving Jarreth. She remembered the first time she saw him, walking toward her at the lake, so commanding, so powerful. Thinking back, she now realized she had instantly fallen in love with him. A small smile formed as she remembered the charred quail—or was it pheasant? No matter, the burnt meal was beyond recognition after Jarreth was done with it. She remembered waking up in the cold, wet caves, being held against his warm body after he saved her from her fall. But she mostly remembered the night he made love to her, completing her as a woman. The nausea unexpectedly hit her once more, and she wearily sat back up. Suddenly a horrifying thought flashed through her mind, and she instinctively brought a hand to her abdomen. She looked down at the peaceful Kady, and frantically began shaking her.

"Kady! Wake up!"

Kady rolled over to one side and muttered something incomprehensible.

"Kady!" Rhiannon shook her again, this time getting some results. Kady opened one drowsy eye and frowned at being so rudely awakened.

"What? Is the horse…?"

"This is not about the horse; 'tis about me."

She could tell by Rhiannon's white face that she was close to tears. Wiping the sleep from her eyes, she sat up and forced her muddled brain to pay attention. "What is wrong, Rhiannon? You look like you have seen a spirit."

Rhiannon

"'Tis worse. I—I think I might be…" She was unable to finish the sentence, the thought becoming more terrifying each passing second.

"With child?" Kady finished for her.

Rhiannon lifted her head in surprise and blinked a few times at her intuitive friend. "H—how did you know?"

"I have known for a few days," Kady answered, her voice raspy from sleeping in the cold barn.

"And you thought to keep this piece of news to yourself?"

Kady repositioned her chubby legs while letting out a wide yawn, and stretched out her arms. "I was going to tell you after the horse felt better…if you did not figure it out yourself, which you did."

"Kady, what am I going to do?"

Kady shrugged. "You are going to have a baby."

Rhiannon slumped back and stared up at the barn ceiling, squirming into the loose straw as if purposely intending to bury herself into unearthly existence. Cracks between boards let in small slivers of moonlight that would be soon giving way to dawn. The reality of the moment should have overwhelmed her, but she found only one thought entering her mind.

"But I am not married. I cannot have a baby."

"Tell that to this child." Kady poked her in the belly.

"I shall be disgraced. My father will disown me. I will be cast out in the streets, forced to beg for food."

Kady let out a giggle and made a face, the kind one would make to a child telling a wild story. "Rhiannon, do you really believe that?"

After a short pause, Rhiannon shook her head. "Nay."

"Neither do I. If anything, the count will be overwhelmed with joy."

"Most likely."

"When are you going to tell him?"

"There is plenty of time for that. Right now I want Daemon to get well." She sat back up and put a protective hand over her stomach.

"Jarreth would be so pleased. He will live on through this child." Her face brightened suddenly as a revelation swept through her mind. "The priest told me I would be given an answer. He was right. This child is going to be my whole life, my whole reason for living."

"Then you better start eating, and getting some sleep," Kady scolded.

Rhiannon nodded in agreement. "Aye, the babe needs food."

"Nay, you need food, the babe will take what it needs from you."

They heard shuffling behind them as Daemon moved forward in his stall and stuck his head over the gate. He seemed to be looking at Rhiannon with a depth of understanding that no animal could possibly feel. Rhiannon went to him and cradled his large head on her shoulder, petting his soft nose lovingly.

"You know, do you not?"

Kady smirked behind her in amusement as Rhiannon continued to talk to the horse as if he understood every word.

"You have to get well, Daemon, so Jarreth's child can grow up and ride you. Jarreth would want that, aye?"

He nickered and moved his head up, then back down. Rhiannon actually laughed, the first time since she had learned of Jarreth's death.

"See? He knows!"

Kady rolled her eyes. "Oh, honestly, Rhiannon."

"Aye, honestly!" She turned back to the horse and actually kissed him, which made Kady stick her tongue out in disgust. "You do understand, I am sure of it." In a flash of brilliance, she grabbed an apple from the pile and held it up in front of him. "I will make you a deal. For every two apples you eat, I shall eat one. That is only fair, since you are so much bigger than I am. Agreed?"

He nickered again as Rhiannon took a bite and began chewing enthusiastically. "Umm, good. Now 'tis your turn." She held the bitten apple up to his mouth, and to her delight he bit into it. He chewed

Rhiannon

profusely, causing foamy dribbles of apple to fall to the ground as Rhiannon cried welcomed tears of joy.

Kady folded her arms and frowned; as far as she was concerned this was ridiculous. "If you really think that animal understands you, you are crazier than I thought."

"Be quiet, Kady—I will have no doubters around him."

Kady sighed deeply. "Oh, all right. Anything that gets you to eat, I will go along with." She reached out and gingerly patted the great horse, which was still slathering foam from the juicy apple. "Nice horsey."

Rhiannon had already picked up another apple and taken a bite; the horse dutifully accepted the one she held for him. Kady decided to join the spontaneous meal and picked up an apple for herself. She had a feeling this was going to be a long pregnancy. In her grief for Jarreth, her mistress had now taken to carrying on an imaginary conversation with a horse. No matter, if it helped her maintain her sanity Kady didn't care if Rhiannon talked to invisible trolls and goblins.

Daemon ate four apples before he refused one, and Rhiannon considered that a great victory. She flopped back in the hay and took a bite from her second apple, insisting she must keep her word to the horse. Kady managed to get back to sleep, and Rhiannon followed close behind. It was bright daylight out before Rhiannon opened her eyes again, awakened by the sounds of galloping horses in the courtyard.

She heard undecipherable words of several men, then the voices floated closer until they were at the barn entrance. Her heart skipped a beat, maybe two, when she recognized one as Ramon.

Poor Kady was again blissfully asleep when she was roughly shaken awake. "Kady, wake up! They are here!"

Never having been much of a morning person, Kady rolled over and put her hands over her ears.

"I said, they are here!" Rhiannon jumped up and attempted to ruffle the straw off her body, and ran to the barn door. Ramon was being showed in by two of the count's men when she threw herself into his arms, hugging him as if he were the only friend she had in the world.

"You came!" she cried between more tears of joy. "You did not refuse me."

Ramon smiled at the almost unrecognizable girl, with straw tangled in her unruly hair, wearing horribly wrinkled clothes that had been slept in for two days, displaying bluish circles under her eyes that revealed her stress level.

"Of course I came. I owe you my life. A Gypsy is honorable, I told you."

"Aye, you did." She managed to restrain her gratefulness and pointed to Daemon's stall. "He got hurt in battle, and has an ugly gash in his back leg." She paused when she took a better look at Ramon. In her excitement, she neglected to notice his darkened eyes and sallow complexion. "You look terrible."

"We rode straight here without resting. I have not slept or eaten in over twenty-four hours. No matter, let me look at the animal."

She led him to the stall as Kady finally dragged her tired body from the straw pile. When she saw the handsome Gypsy she began to pick straw from her hair, displaying a toothy grin as she waited for an introduction. To her disappointment Rhiannon ignored her and went straight to Daemon's enclosure. The horse greeted her with a soft nicker as he stuck his head over the stall. Ramon entered and had Rhiannon hold the horse's halter while he inspected the back leg.

"This is a nasty cut, but someone has kept it well-bandaged, so the damage is minimal." He cast a glance at Rhiannon. "You?"

Rhiannon nodded as Kady loudly cleared her throat behind her.

"Oh, Kady—good! You are up. Please go fetch Ramon some food, lots of it. He has not eaten in a day." She turned her attentions back to the horse while Kady left feeling rather dejected and put-upon, mumbling what she thought of the situation under her breath.

Rhiannon

"I got him to eat some apples last night," Rhiannon explained to Ramon. "He has no appetite. I think he misses his master."

Ramon finished re-bandaging the leg and stood up, inspecting the huge horse for any other threatening injuries. As he looked the animal over, he rambled absent-mindedly, concentrating on the horse's anatomy. "These war horses are usually quite attached to their owners. Hmmm, this cut is deeper than it looks—hand me that wet rag, thank you. Who is his owner? This horse is magnificent; he comes from good stock."

Rhiannon swallowed the lump in her throat as she answered. "His owner is dead. He was the man who spared your life."

Ramon stopped abruptly and stared at her with curious, then understanding eyes. "You loved him?"

She nodded again and felt her damnable tears sting her eyes once again. "Is the horse going to be all right?"

"That depends on the horse." He motioned her from the stall and sat down on the straw, rubbing his weary eyes hard, as if he could wipe them into alertness. "The others are coming, I hope you do not mind."

"The others?" She smiled as a thought occurred to her. "How is Myra?"

Ramon smiled widely; his proud look was inescapable. "I have a son. You should see him! He is strong, and looks like me."

She squeezed his hand in delight. "That is wonderful. I can not wait to see him."

"It will take a couple of days. The wagons move slowly."

Rhiannon fell silent, and then motioned him closer. "Can you keep a secret?"

He drew himself up indignantly, giving her a mock stern look that made her smile. "I am a Gypsy. Of course I can keep a secret."

"Very well. I am with child." She waited for his reaction, not expecting the one she got. He looked at her with a mixture of condolence and anxiety.

"Are you going to need a place to go?"

His question told her volumes about his depth of understanding. Somehow his Gypsy intuition sensed an unmarried girl who carried the child of a dead lover would be scorned by society in any normal circumstance.

"Nay, Ramon, I shall be fine. But thank you for caring."

"You always have a home with us, remember that."

She nodded. "Thank you."

There was an uncomfortable pause, and then he slapped his leg and stood up. "Now. Let me attend to this horse. Until the wagons get here with my supplies, there are some things I will need. There are herbs that will increase his appetite and others I can make into a salve for his wound. His spirit will die if we keep him cooped up in his stall, so he will need to go outside daily."

She listened to him prattle on about his treatment plan, trying to absorb all the facts he was spewing. When she was confident he had concluded, she pointed to the straw and then to him.

"You need to get some rest. I shall go gather what I can, but meanwhile you sleep. You cannot help the horse if you pass out from exhaustion."

He nodded, and then complied as she left the barn for the first time in two days. She'd almost forgotten what fresh air smelled like. She immediately concluded she needed a bath, and quickly. It wasn't ladylike to smell like a horse.

It took a while to gather everything Ramon wanted, but she prevailed. After cleaning up and donning fresh clothes, she introduced the count and her father to Ramon, who looked a bit better after a few hours sleep and a meal. She was surprised and delighted at the respect the count showed to Ramon, who listened intently as the Gypsy outlined a course of action for Daemon. The count also ordered ready part of a fallow field for when the wagons arrived, and assured Ramon his people would be well compensated for their help. Of course, that

Rhiannon

pleased Ramon to no end, and he showed it by flashing Rhiannon a large smile and a wink.

After Ramon informed them he had everything he needed, the count took Rhiannon by the arm and insisted she get some rest. He practically had to drag the protesting girl from the stable, but she was no match for his size. He deposited her in her room and ordered her to bed.

As she drifted into a weary sleep she had a strange dream. She was alone in blackness, when she heard Jarreth call her name. His voice seemed to be all around her, and she couldn't locate the direction to go to him. In a moment she blinked herself awake, then realized it had all been a vivid dream. She fell back into a fitful sleep, her tears her only comfort.

Hours later when she awoke, she found Kady sitting contently in a corner chair, needle and thread in hand, busy with something. When she saw Rhiannon awake, she smiled and held up her handiwork. It was a baby gown, or would be when it was finished.

"What do you think?"

Rhiannon yawned, then made a face as her stomach loudly growled. "I think I am hungry."

"Good! I will have some food brought up."

"Nay, I shall go downstairs and get something." She swung her legs out of bed and rubbed her eyes. "I really *was* tired."

"Well, of course, silly! You will be this way for several more months, then 'twill get better."

"For someone who has never had a baby, you certainly seem to be an expert."

Kady shrugged. "I have helped deliver lots of babies, plus I was the oldest of five children, remember? That is why I took the job at the castle, to help support my family."

"Aye, I remember. I thank the Lord daily that you did. I do not know what I would do without you."

"You would probably get in even more trouble, if that is possible."

"You have been a true friend, Kady. I know I shall breeze through this pregnancy with you helping me." She suddenly grimaced and brought a hand to her stomach. "Augh. Skip the food, I am feeling sick again."

"That, too, will go away in about another month, at least it usually does."

"Usually?" Rhiannon plopped backward on the bed and displayed a hopeless expression. "If this lasts the whole time I fear I shall never eat again."

"While you were sleeping, I had a chance to speak with your Gypsy friend. He told me you told him about the baby. He told me about the fight with Jarreth, and how you saved his life. He says when the wagons get here, the Gypsy women have special teas that help relieve your sickness."

"Thank God." She sat back up. "I have decided not to tell my father, nor the count about the babe yet. When Daemon is healed, then I have to make a decision."

"What kind of decision?"

"Where to have the baby." She glanced around the room, taking in all the rich tapestries and furnishings that she would trade for one minute with Jarreth. "Not here. Even though 'tis most comfortable, 'tis not home."

"Well, you will have it at Yorkshire, of course."

Rhiannon shook her head. "Nay. My condition shall disgrace my father, and I will not do that. I will never be able to return home."

"Then, where?"

"I am thinking. It shall come to me; until then I must help get Daemon well." She walked to the door with Kady following close behind like a puppy.

"Well, wherever you go, I go. I will not leave you, Rhiannon."

Rhiannon

Rhiannon turned and gave her friend a hug. "I know. Now, let us go see if I can get any food in my tummy. My baby needs nourishment."

They left for the kitchen, arm in arm.

Chapter Sixteen

Earl Stanwyck and Baron Harrison sat glumly staring into their respective brandy snifters, each lost in private thoughts. The count grieved deeply for the nephew that was more like a son to him; the baron grieved not so much for Jarreth but for the pain Rhiannon was experiencing. He picked up the sifter and swirled the thick amber liquid around the sides, watching it coat the glass and slowly flow back down to the bottom. Drinking was no longer as enjoyable as it once was. Seeing his precious daughter mourn so heavily the past few weeks weighed down his heart like an anchor. She only thought of the horse, spending more time in the barn than in the castle. He had always strove to protect her, to keep her from the hardships of life that could turn one into a hopeless pawn that simply went through the motions of a useless existence. Her spirit, her unyielding spark that got her into so much trouble now drove her forward and kept her strong. Would she really survive this? How soon should he take her home, and try to forget the whole tragic experience and get on with life? Not until the horse was well, that much was for certain.

Rhiannon

The count, however, was thinking entirely different thoughts. With Jarreth gone, his life had taken on a new perspective. He had grown quite fond of Rhiannon, thinking of her as family. The thought of her leaving, returning to Yorkshire and not being part of his life was unbearable. Jarreth loved her, and would want her to be well cared for. If he offered her to stay with him, what would she do? He sighed and bowed his head; how foolish he was. Of course she would want to return home with her father, leaving him alone without even her smile for comfort.

Rhiannon was coming in from the courtyard where she had been holding Myra's baby, knowing in her heart that her own child would be even more cherished and precious. A part of Jarreth was living inside of her, which was more priceless than all the gold in England. Myra had given her some special Gypsy tea, which helped her dreadful morning sickness and allowed her to eat more. Rhiannon was thankful for the Gypsies; she realized how much she had enjoyed her short stay with them. Their nightly dances and music had livened the place up at nights, keeping her mind off the living hell she felt when she was alone.

As she walked past the study she saw the two men nursing their drinks, their mood evident by their silence. She stood at the door for a while, and when they gave her no notice she cleared her throat in a high pitch. Both men looked up at once.

"'Twould be nice if I could see a smile," she boldly stated. "If I am able to live through this, I am quite confident you two can."

Both men produced smiles for her benefit, the baron being the first to welcome her.

"Sweetheart! We were just…ah…"

"We were just thinking of you," the count interjected. "At least, I was. Come in, dear, maybe 'tis good that you happened by. I have something I wish to discuss with you and your father."

The baron cast him a wary look as Rhiannon took a seat by the count, who stood up and clasped his hands behind his back, then proceeded to pace in front of them. At one point he stopped and addressed Rhiannon.

"How is the horse?"

"Much better. He is eating well and the wound is healing. Ramon says he will make a complete recovery."

"Excellent." He paced some more, then finally stopped and faced them. "I am not good at this." His voice was shaky, as if this was the most arduous thing he had ever had to do. "I am better at giving orders and fighting. But there is something that must be said, so please bear with me." He cast his gaze at Rhiannon. "You have come to mean a great deal to me. As Jarreth's wife—er, that is, almost wife, you are the only family I have."

The baron saw where all this was leading, and decided to make a preemptive strike. "May I remind you she is the only family I have, also!" He jumped to his feet and faced the count bravely, considering he was six inches shorter and not even a fraction as fearsome.

"Please, hear me out! I know Jarreth would want you secure, Rhiannon, so I have been giving this a great deal of thought."

The baron's balding head grew red with fury as he stepped between his daughter and the count. "What ever 'tis, she is not listening. She is coming home with me!"

Pushing him aside, the count took Rhiannon's hand and sat beside her, leaving the baron fuming with rage. He ignored the ranting father until the insults got personal.

"You think to bribe her, to force her affections away from me! Have you no honor? She will not fall for that! My daughter is loyal, and will not…"

"Be quiet, Cedric, or I shall have you removed."

Rhiannon

Veins began protruding in the baron's thick neck, but he shut his mouth. The count turned back to Rhiannon, who was displaying a bewildered look at what seemed to be happening.

"I cannot give you Jarreth back," the count continued. "But I can give you his name. He was to inherit everything, so instead I would like to give it to you."

"Wait a minute," the baron interrupted, his tone changed to skepticism. "Am I understanding you to be offering Rhiannon your hand in marriage?"

The count continued to gaze at Rhiannon, his disfigured face softening as he smiled. "Of course, 'twould be name only. I promise not to touch you."

Rhiannon's father had completely changed his attitude. "You are offering to make her a *countess*?" The glee in his eyes was obvious.

Rhiannon began to speak, but the count, who stood up to confront the irritating baron, cut her off. "What else do you think I am doing? Of course she would be a countess, and would gain my shire when I die."

"But, surely you know she could never love you. 'Twas your nephew she loved, not you."

"Of course, you foolish twit, I know that. Now why do you not be quiet and let the girl answer?"

Rhiannon opened her mouth. "I…"

"Because this is rather sudden, I think! I mean, you are offering her a great deal, and naturally she is going to need time to think about it."

"But…" Rhiannon stammered.

"What is there to think about? She shall have all the wealth she could ever want, and after my death will have great power to attract a worthy husband."

"If I could just…"

"Aye, with that much wealth, she could attract a rich lord, or perhaps a duke!"

"My point exactly. She would never have to worry again."

"Silence!"

The men stopped and looked at her as if they had both forgotten she was even in the room. She stood up and faced them, teary eyed, with a small, grateful smile.

"I am flattered," she said to the count. "And I must say your offer is tempting. But I have to say no." She turned and walked to the window and pulled back the curtains. Ramon was walking Daemon around the courtyard, letting the great horse soak up the warm sunshine while exercising the hurt leg. The horse had made great strides, and she knew that it would soon be time to leave him. She turned back to the two men, who were softly discussing the situation and ways to make her reconsider the count's offer.

"I have held something from you, from both of you. At first 'twas because I feared your reaction, but later because I had to have time to think. Well, I have thought, and 'tis time to tell you."

Her father felt alarm mixed with apprehension; he never knew what his daughter would pull next. "Tell me what, sweetheart?"

She felt unexpected tears begin to form, and realized this was going to be harder than she first thought. "I know you are going to be very disappointed in me, and for that I am sorry."

Her father put a loving hand on her shoulder and smiled the way only a father can. "I could never be disappointed in you, Rhiannon. Maybe wearied, perhaps beleaguered, but never disappointed."

She smiled through her tears at his vain attempt at humor. "I *have* been a trial, have I not? Now I fear I am an even greater one. You see, I carry Jarreth's child."

Both men became still, to the point of unblinking. She bowed her head and stared at the floor, waiting for the inevitable. There was nothing but silence. The men seemed stunned into oblivion, with neither

Rhiannon

word of comfort nor condemnation to offer. She jerked her head back up and became indignant at their lack of reaction.

"Well, say something! Tell me I am a harlot, and cast me out! Send me to a nunnery in disgrace, disown me forever!"

The two men turned to each other with silly grins. "I am going to be a grandfather," the baron gushed.

"And I am going to be a granduncle," the count added, with equal amounts of gushing.

Rhiannon put her hands on her hips and glowered. "And I am going to be a *mother*."

"Oh, aye dear, we know," the count acknowledged, then got a dreamy look as he faded back into his own thoughts. "I should have known Jarreth would find some way to carry on. He always was tenacious."

The baron folded his hands and paced short steps, deep in thought. "Plans, we must make plans. A midwife must be found, only the best."

"Oh, absolutely," the count agreed. "Of course, the babe shall be born here, at Jarreth's home."

"Oh, no," the baron countered. "The babe will be born at Rhiannon's home, where she will be comfortable."

"Are you meaning to say I cannot make her comfortable here?"

"This place is too big! She needs her own home, where everyone knows her."

"Everyone knows her here! This is my nephew's baby, and I will not have her away from me!"

"Excuse me," Rhiannon shouted over the two quarreling men, "but are you not forgetting something? Because of my stupidity, Jarreth and I did not exchange vows. I am an unmarried woman, and in turn will give birth to a bastard. I cannot have this baby here, or at my home, the scandal would irreversibly tarnish both your names. I cannot allow that."

The baron blinked at this cold slap of truth, the count in turn did the same.

"For that reason," Rhiannon continued, "I have decided to have this baby away from everything and everybody, where I will be loved by family and not subjected to taunting laughter and jabbing remarks. Father, I want to go to Aberaeron."

"Aberaeron?" The baron drew back in surprise, then let her words mull around his mind for a few seconds. "In Wales? Aye, your aunt will welcome you, as will your cousin. That is, if you two can stay out of trouble."

"With my growing belly, I do not think I will be able to crawl out of windows." She let out a short laugh of relief, and the tears began falling down her cheeks.

"Oh, sweetheart, do not cry." Her father took her into his arms and she cried against his shoulder, feeling his fatherly love flow through her.

The count had remained quiet until now, thinking over the situation, trying to be logical and not emotional about the whole thing. "It seems my offer might be the only way to save her name. I still say she should marry me."

Rhiannon drew away from her father and wiped her tears, facing the count calmly, but determined. "Nay, I love Jarreth more with my every breath, and even though we did not exchange vows, my heart could not be more dedicated to him. This is his child, our child, whom I shall raise alone and devote my life to."

"Oh, no," the count disagreed. "You shall not be alone. You and the child shall want for nothing."

"Quite," her father agreed with the count. "This child will know all the love of two grandfathers, so to speak. I do not care about scandal. My name is a laughing stock in London anyway, after that bow and arrow incident. What is one more scandal to my name?"

"I am inclined to think that not much will be said around here," the count added. "I will simply put the word out that I will hang anyone who insults your name. That should stop the wagging tongues."

Rhiannon

The baron nodded with enthusiasm. "Aye, listen to the count."

"That is all good and well, but I still want to have the baby at Aberaeron."

"I have no objection to that," the baron said.

The count nodded. "Nor do I. And again I make the offer for you to live here. I shall always consider you Jarreth's wife, with or without the vows."

"And deprive me of my grandchild!" the baron objected. "I think not!"

"Do not fight again," Rhiannon insisted. "I shall give it some thought. Either way, the child will live in disgrace, with no name to give honor to."

No," the count disagreed, "The baby will be a Stanwyck. I can register his name as the son of Jarreth with the official registry in London. He will be recognized as the heir to my fortune."

Rhiannon flashed a sweet smile. "Thank you, but what if the baby is a girl?"

"No matter, then *she* will be his heir. Either way, the babe will be a Stanwyck."

Rhiannon felt tears of joy mix with her pain and embarrassment as she looked upon the man she had feared with such relish. "I once thought you a monster. I could not have been more wrong."

The count actually felt his eyes mist over, quite unmanly for a man of his position and quite unacceptable. But he couldn't resist the urge to take the remorseful girl into his arms and give her a fatherly hug. "Thank you. You could not even begin to understand how much that means to me."

When the hug was over, she drew back and smiled at the two men who did not condemn her as society surely would. "I should go check on the horse. He likes it when I visit him." She left the men standing there with bleary eyes and silly grins.

Evangelynn Stratton

After she was gone, the count looked the baron over curiously. "What bow and arrow incident?"

Ramon was still leading Daemon in the courtyard when Rhiannon approached him. Daemon nickered when he saw her carrying a treat, some fresh carrots she obtained from the cooks. As the horse crunched his snack, Rhiannon petted his neck and wondered how she would ever be able to leave him. But, she told herself, it would only be for a little while, as after the baby was born she would return to Stanwyck castle. Her child would be heir to the count's vast holdings, so it was only fair. She had also vowed never to marry. No man could ever compare to Jarreth, and his child would call no other man father.

Ramon snapped her out of her thoughts. "He is very fond of you. He will miss you greatly; I sense you will be leaving soon."

She again was impressed by his insight, and nodded with pursed lips. "I shall miss him even more. I do not know how to thank you, Ramon. You have done wonders for him."

"Actually, I have done little. I believe it is your will that made him live."

"Nonsense, your people are great healers." She paused briefly. "I shall miss you all."

"A Gypsy never says goodbye, for we know we will see you again. A Gypsy always is moving." He smiled with genuine affection for the girl he once thought his enemy. "Your uncle has offered us all jobs whenever we are in the area. We will see you again."

"He did that?" She was stunned but pleased the count had taken such a liking to the Gypsies. "I am pleased for you, Ramon. I have made plans to go to my aunt's manor in Wales. 'Tis by a seashore, and is peaceful."

"A good place to have a baby."

"I think so. My aunt loves me greatly, and has had three children herself. She will help me through the carrying of this baby."

Rhiannon

Ramon handed her the horse's rope. "Would you like to take him back to his stall?"

"Aye." She took his rope and began walking toward the barn as Ramon walked beside her.

"Myra has grown rather fond of you," he offered.

"And I, her."

He hesitated, trying to find the right words to convey his thoughts. "She has expressed a desire to remain with you until the baby is born, if you want her to."

"That is very sweet of her, but I could not take her away from her people."

He paused again, and she sensed his uneasiness. "What is it, Ramon?"

"Your uncle has offered me a permanent position—a generous position I might add—to stay and care for all his animals."

"But, like you said…a Gypsy is always on the move."

They reached the stall and secured Daemon inside, and then walked back to the courtyard to soak up the warm sunshine. "Still," Ramon continued, "it is a tempting proposal. He has offered me my own cottage, where Myra and the baby would be most comfortable."

"Have you made a decision?"

"Not yet. I am thinking about it."

"What does Myra want?"

He laughed. "Like a good Gypsy woman, she will do whatever I say."

Kady interrupted their exchange by suddenly yelling Rhiannon's name from across the courtyard, waving in an exaggerated manner to get her attention. Rhiannon let out a sigh.

"Oh dear, I had better see what Kady wants." She left Ramon still pondering his dilemma and started walking toward Kady, who was by now running up to meet her. Kady didn't give Rhiannon a chance to speak, just blurted out her sentiments with a wide grin.

"Your father just told me we are going to Aberaeron! How exciting! I love the sunsets over the ocean, and I simply adore your aunt! Of course, we'll have to keep your cousin away from you, or heaven knows what will happen. Oh, this is just wonderful!" When she saw that Rhiannon wasn't sharing her enthusiasm, she dropped her smile and replaced it with a look of concern. "What is wrong, Rhiannon?"

"I will just miss everyone. Walk with me Kady. We need to talk."

Kady fell in step beside her mistress, slightly alarmed by her serious tone. Rhiannon seemed to be heading for the gardens, and didn't offer any conversation until they were out of earshot of any passing servant.

"Kady," she began, "I am going to have the baby at Aberaeron, but then I am returning here."

Kady stopped, cast a quick glance up at the dark, ominous castle, then back at Rhiannon. "Here? Why?" She couldn't believe her mistress would want to spend the rest of her life in a home that contrasted so greatly from the one she grew up in.

"Because 'twas Jarreth's home, and his child is going to inherit all this. The count is giving the child his name. What else can I do?"

"I see your point." She let out a large sigh and puckered her lips into a crooked smile. "Well, I guess I will have to adapt."

"That is what I wish to speak to you about. Kady, you have been a long and loyal friend, but I do not expect you to come hither with me. Your family is in Yorkshire."

Kady was shocked, then hurt. "You no longer want me?"

"Kady, I did not say that. I simply cannot ask you to leave your home. My father can use your services, and you will always have a job there."

"Nay! My place is with you, and your baby! If you are here, then I am here."

"Oh, Kady…are you sure?"

Rhiannon

"Of course I am sure!" Her eyes twinkled with a hint of mischief. "Besides, I have to be there when you teach your child how to climb a tree."

"And what makes you think I will do that?"

Kady simply rolled her eyes.

"Well, all right...maybe a small tree." Rhiannon gave her a hug. "Thank you, Kady. I guess I knew in my heart that you would not leave me."

* *

The young, timid girl gazed down on her mystery patient as she prepared to shave him, a chore she had taken upon herself ever since he had been brought unconscious to the monastery hospital. Sent to a nunnery at the tender age of seven, she had never been close to a man, at least not a man who wasn't old, diseased or dying. This one was young and handsome, with a dark air of intrigue about him. He was the type of man that hid within the forbidden recesses of her mind, where she allowed herself impossible dreams when the mundane tasks of the hospital tore at her heart and ripped another piece of hope from her soul. She had seen too much death for a girl of thirteen.

As she carefully scraped the cumbersome straightedge razor over his face, taking effort not to nick his skin, a nun draped in a traditional flowing black habit walked in to check on his progress. She was middle-aged but looked older, largely due to her stern and sour expression.

"I suppose there has been no change."

The girl silently looked at the frowning woman and slowly shook her head.

"Well, hurry up and get back to the ward. We have other patients, you know." She cast her eyes down at the sleeping stranger, not able to truthfully deny the attraction he held for any normal woman. "Wonder who he is?"

The girl stared at his face, studying its every line in detail. "Does it matter?"

"Suppose not. One thing is for sure; he is no peasant, not with those clothes he was wearing and the gold that was left for his care. Still think Father Jacob was wrong in giving him this room. He should be in the ward, with the others."

The girl felt a flush to her cheeks as she glanced over to the clothes lying over a chair. She didn't need to be reminded that the man wore nothing but a nightshirt underneath the covers. His body, even with his injuries, was still magnificent.

The older nun straightened some things on his modest nightstand, and looked back at her young charge. "Elizabeth, I am concerned. This man seems to hold a fascination for you. Next year you begin taking your vows. Are you going to be ready?"

Elizabeth looked away from her, hiding her look of desperation. "I will."

"I am not so sure." She paused as she went to the window and closed the shutters, effectively darkening the room from the warm, bright sunlight. "I have told you to keep these windows shut. He will get a draft."

Elizabeth swallowed her annoyance and answered in her normal, soft voice. "I thought the sun would be good for him."

"Whatever for?"

The girl shrugged one shoulder and continued to look at the floor. "It makes you feel good. At least, I know it makes me feel good."

The nun sniffed her disapproval and frowned. "Has he muttered that name today—what is it…"

"Rhiannon."

"Aye, that is it. Wonder who she is. Oh well, no matter—she most likely thinks him dead. He almost was when he was brought here. If not

Rhiannon

for God's mercy, we could lose him still." She contorted her face into a scowl, turning her already homely face even more vinegary.

Elizabeth raised her head sharply, with a look of defiance she ordinarily wouldn't allow herself to display. "He will not die!"

"So certain are you?" The nun lifted her head in a demeaning manner, a look Elizabeth had grown quite used to. "So now you know God's will?"

"I—I have been praying." Elizabeth lowered her gaze and resumed her meek demeanor, her only defense among the older, judgmental nuns who always found such fault in her.

"We have all been praying, Elizabeth, for all our patients. Now, I suggest you finish here and get back to the ward. I will see you in evening service."

"Aye, Sister Mary Catherine." She watched as the nun left the room, then turned back to the sleeping man. Brushing a black lock of hair from his forehead, she stroked his face lovingly. "You will not die," she whispered. "I will not let you."

Chapter Seventeen

Rhiannon lie in bed wide-awake, staring at the bottom of the wooden canopy until she had memorized every knothole and pattern in the grain. It seemed as hard and colorless as her life. Tomorrow she left for Aberaeron, along with Kady, her father, and the count. A carriage had been readied for them, although the count decided he would ride along with his guard. It was a long trip, one she wasn't particularly looking forward to, but in her heart she felt it was the right thing to do. Her only reluctance was in leaving Daemon, but Ramon graciously decided to take the count up on his offer and stay until she returned with her newborn. The count was elated she had chosen to live with him at Stanwyck castle, while she faced quite the opposite sentiments from her father, who still harbored hopes of changing her mind. The ever-faithful Kady was looking forward to caring for a baby, and everyone else seemed resigned to the current situation. All except Rhiannon. Her heart ached for Jarreth day by day, minute by minute, second by second. Sometimes the hurt was unbearable, then she would

Rhiannon

remind herself of the new life growing inside her, and that she must be strong for her child—for Jarreth's child.

She tried to relax and let her tears sooth her weary eyes. In a few minutes her mind began to slip into blackness, the dark realm where peaceful rest or intrusive nightmares dominated. Suddenly Jarreth's face vividly appeared and she heard him call her name. She sat up quickly, her heart pounding from the realistic dream, and felt all the pain of the past few weeks return. "Oh Jarreth," she whispered. "Why do I still feel your presence?"

Elizabeth held the stranger's hand tightly as the tormented man said the word over and over, shaking his head as if attempting to jounce the image from his mind. It was the only word he ever said. Elizabeth felt envy for the woman named Rhiannon who so occupied his thoughts, then reminded herself that envy was a sin. But she couldn't help it; the woman must be very special to cause an unconscious man such unease.

In a few minutes he calmed down and fell back into a restless sleep. Elizabeth watched him for a while to make sure he was indeed finished dreaming, then let go of his hand and blew out the candle. It was often like this at night, when the darkness seemed to invade his mind and conjure memories of which he was unable to cope. He was all right now; it was safe for her to go. She left him to return to her humble room that was void of any color or luxury.

Rhiannon opened her eyes at the first sign of daybreak as the sunrise peeked through the shutters, casting a soft red glow throughout the room. She rose and got dressed, then quietly slipped downstairs and out the back door to say goodbye to her Gypsy friends. They always were up at dawn, and were also planning to leave that morning, their supplies full and ready for the impending winter. The chief's wife Midajah already had tea prepared for Rhiannon as she approached the central fire, which was crackling and filling the morning air with the invigorating smell of burning pine.

"My, we are up early this morning," Midajah teased, as she handed Rhiannon a cup of the special anti-morning-sickness tea.

"I could not sleep."

Midajah nodded in understanding. "It is the excitement of your trip, and the new life that is in store for you."

"Aye, I suppose." She paused briefly in thought. "Midajah, I have only talked to one other person about this, my servant Kady. I dreamt I heard Jarreth call out my name last night."

"That is normal under the circumstances. After my father died, my mother claimed she heard him talking to her for years afterwards. Your mind wants to deny his death."

Rhiannon took a sip of her tea as she became detached from the conversation. It tasted hot and sweet; already the day felt hopeful. She stared blankly while she continued to think, causing Midajah to take notice.

"What is it, child?"

Rhiannon stirred back to the present moment. "Midajah, 'tis not the first time it has happened. In reality, it happens almost every night. And it seems so real—as if he is desperate to contact me."

The Gypsy woman narrowed her eyebrows as she gazed upon the beautiful girl that life had seemingly turned on. "Perhaps he is."

"From beyond the grave?" Rhiannon shook her head as she displayed a small smile. "Nay, I think not. I do not believe in ghosts."

"Maybe you should." Midajah turned away and began stirring something in a pot hanging over the fire.

"That is not funny."

"I did not mean it to be."

"Midajah, you are confusing me. If—and I do mean if—I believed in spirits, why would he want to reach me?"

Rhiannon

The Gypsy took a deep breath and let out a sigh. "Perhaps he is a soul in torment, with unfinished business. You told me that you two did not part on good terms. Maybe he wants you to know he loves you." She saw this piece of spectral insight was causing Rhiannon great uncertainty, which was not what she had intended. "Tell you what—the next time it happens, talk back to him. Tell him you love and miss him, and that you know he loves you. Then perhaps he can rest in peace. Or, at least your mind will be at rest."

Rhiannon felt tears coming again and she turned her head, hiding the ravages of grief. "I need to tell him I am sorry. 'Tis my fault this happened. I was selfish and foolish. For that I shall never forgive myself."

"If you cannot forgive yourself, no one else can forgive you. Including Jarreth."

Rhiannon left the Gypsy camp feeling more lonely and bewildered than ever.

As she walked back into the castle, the count was sipping his morning tea. He was dressed in his traveling clothes, much like Jarreth was the last time she saw him. "Ah, Rhiannon! I am glad you are up—I have something to show you before we partake of our journey."

She produced a small smile, still shaken from her strange conversation with Midajah but repressed it to the back of her mind. "Show me? Show me what?"

"Come with me." He began walking down a corridor, and she fell in step beside him as he explained. "I know Jarreth's death has devastated you as much as me, but I might be able to bring a small part of him to life. He never let anyone in this room, and always kept it locked. Ah, here we are." He stopped in front of a door, and fumbled in his pocket for the key. "Where did I put that blasted—aha!" His face exploded in a smile as he produced the key. He stuck it in the lock and turned it. "I do not know if Jarreth ever showed this side of himself to you, but now that he is gone, well, I think he would want you to see these." He opened the door and motioned her inside. When she entered the room her heart skipped a beat at the sight before her.

Jarreth's drawings were everywhere. All the animals he drew for her that one night around the campfire were there, as well as pictures of people and landscapes. Every inch of the walls was covered with his drawings, some large, some small, causing a wallpapered mosaic effect. Some were done in pastel, but most were charcoal renderings, his chosen medium. Rhiannon walked silently around the room, stopping to stare at familiar ones. The lion, bear, eagle, and numerous renderings of Daemon stared back at her as if they were taunting, daring her to reach out to them. She couldn't force her gaze away.

"They are beautiful. I knew he had talent, but I had no inkling of how much."

The count had been watching at the door up to this point, letting her be alone with the last essence of his nephew. "He would come in here and stay for hours. 'Twas years before he finally let me see what he was doing. For some reason he did not feel comfortable letting other people see his drawings. They were personal; a part of him." He wandered to the large table in the center of the room and glanced down at the drawings in progress. His face softened when his gaze fell on a particular one. "This is the last thing he was working on. I think you should see this."

Rhiannon joined him at the table and looked down at the drawing. Mixed feelings of extreme regret and great joy jumped through her as she stared at his final portrait, unfinished for all time.

Her own face stared back at her. She was captured as he first saw her, rising from the lake, naked with her long, wet hair covering her body. He had tried to say he hadn't seen her. If he were here right now, she would hit him for lying to her.

But he wasn't here now. She couldn't help the consequent tears, and let them fall down her cheek as her lower lip began to tremble. "How could I have been such a fool," she cried. "I did not think he loved me,

Rhiannon

yet he drew this by memory. I had no idea he had studied my face so fastidiously."

"I think there was a lot you did not know about him. Would you like to take any of these with you to Wales? It might comfort you to have a fragment of Jarreth with you."

She nodded as a struggle waged itself within her mind. "I would like to take them all, but I shall settle for the lion, one of Daemon, and this one of me. I wish he had drawn a self-portrait, but I suppose that would be too much to ask."

"As a matter of fact, no it wouldn't. I have one, and you are welcome to it."

She looked at him solemnly. "You do not jest, do you? He drew a portrait of himself?"

"Believe me, 'Twas not easy to get him to do it. He only agreed to as a present that I requested for my birthday. 'Tis quite a good likeness, and is hanging in my room. Come, let us take the drawings you want and I shall fetch the portrait for you." He put a hand on her shoulder with understanding of how difficult this was for her, himself not oblivious to the pain of loss. "I wish I could bring him back. I fear this is the best I can do."

She smiled through her anguish. "Thank you."

Rhiannon's portraits were rolled up and packed for the trip. She then headed for her room to dress in her best traveling clothes at Kady's insistence, even though it made no sense to her. No one was going to see her sitting in a carriage, she argued, and besides, she no longer had anyone for which she cared to be attractive. But Kady prevailed, which surprised her. Rhiannon seemed to have lost her fight, her unshakable spark. Could anything bring that spark back?

Before their departure the count insisted on a grand breakfast, where he presented Jarreth's portrait to Rhiannon. "Here," he said with satisfaction, "I took it out of the frame for easy traveling." With shaking hands she carefully unrolled the parchment and stared at it in stony silence. Everyone around the table held their breath as they watched her.

"On my God," she whispered. Jarreth had captured himself as only he could. His expression was haunting, reaching out to her with eyes that saw into her very soul. The realization of the moment set in and she began to panic. She burst into tears and fled the table in an attempt to escape from the pain.

The baron leapt to his feet, but the count stopped him. "No, let her go. Kady, follow her and bring her to the carriage. We will wait for you."

The loyal father lifted his head in indignation. "Why is it fine for Kady to comfort her, and not me?"

"Right now she does not need a doting father to tell her everything will be wonderful. She is closer to her maid-servant than anyone else." He made a knowing smile. "Besides, I think we can both guess where she is going."

Kady followed as Rhiannon ran outside and went straight to the stable, where she threw her arms around Daemon's neck and broke into heaving sobs.

"Oh, Daemon, I am so sorry," she cried. Kady and Ramon stood by helplessly as she poured her heart out to the complacent horse. "Because of me we both lost him."

She soaked her tears into his soft fur, her energy slowly draining from her. "I cannot do this! I do not know how to be a mother!" Daemon nickered in response as Rhiannon fell into a heap by his feet. He lowered his head and nudged her, as if to tell her to get up. When she gave no reaction he nudged her again. Kady started to go to her, but Ramon stopped her.

"Let them be," he said softly. "They have a special bond."

Kady opened her mouth to protest, and then quickly closed it again. Rhiannon had stood back up and now cradled the horse's head on her shoulder.

Rhiannon

"You are right," she was saying. "I did not give up on you, so I cannot give up on myself."

Kady made a face and grunted. "What is she going on about? That horse does not talk; he did not say anything!"

Ramon just smiled. "Who cares? It worked, did it not?"

"I suppose." She shrugged, unconvinced as Rhiannon left the stall, wiping her tears and displaying a brave face.

"'Tis time. Ramon, I leave him in your hands." She paused, then reached into her pocket and handed him a small piece of parchment. "These are directions on how to get to Aberaeron. No one else here knows where we are going, because of my condition. But I want you to know, in case anything happens to Daemon. Promise me you will send for me if—" her voice broke from the strain. "If he gets worse."

Ramon looked at the parchment, then back at her with a slightly embarrassed smile. "I cannot read."

"I know, but you must find someone who can, if need be. I am trusting you, Ramon."

He put the folded parchment in his coat pocket. "Very well, I promise. But nothing will happen to him. His leg is almost healed, and he is gaining strength every day."

The two exchanged a sorrowful look at the prospect of saying goodbye, when Rhiannon pulled him to her and embraced him in a hug. "Thank you Ramon…for everything."

"No, it is I who must thank you. Because of you my people now have supplies, and Myra and I have a home for our son. You are a special girl, Rhiannon. I wish you lots of Gypsy luck."

"I accept. I will need all the luck I can get."

Kady had been patient until then, but knew the party waited for their departure. "Come Rhiannon. We must leave, or you shall have the babe right here in this barn."

Evangelynn Stratton

That got a smile from Rhiannon, and together they walked to the awaiting carriage, which would take them to a safe refuge and a new beginning.

"He is dreaming again." The nun dabbed the unconscious man's face with a cool, wetted cloth. The mysterious patient seemed to be having an especially lucid episode. He muttered undecipherable words and grimaced as if in pain.

"It is almost like he is re-living an event," the other nun stated.

The first nun agreed. "Go fetch Elizabeth, and do not let Sister Mary Catherine see you. She'll chastise the poor girl again. Hurry!" The second nun nodded and left as her sister in Christ continued to dab the distraught stranger's face.

Jarreth fought for his life. One minute he was on his way home, the next he was fending off a large group of attackers. He yelled orders to his men, but the ambush was so sudden no one had time to think, much less react to him. Who were these men, and why were they attacking him? His questions were answered as an enemy plunged a sword into one of Jarreth's men. "Long live King Richard!" he shouted.

Richard loyalists! He had waited for weeks with his men, camped at the secret meeting place with hundreds of others, until restlessness set in from boredom. The duke seemed to have been delayed. The weather began to turn wet and cold, and Jarreth's party was the first to leave. How ironic that they would end up fighting the loyalists unaided because they accidentally happened upon their path.

His men fought well, but it became woefully obvious that they were outnumbered. Jarreth yelled for them to flee, retreat to safety with every man for himself, but his allegiant men stayed by his side. Jarreth watched as his men fell around him, succumbing to the greater manpower of the opposite side. He had killed several when suddenly he felt

Rhiannon

a sharp pain in his back. At the same time Daemon felt Jarreth's weight drop to one side. The experienced warhorse knew his master was in trouble and shifted his own weight to keep Jarreth mounted, but even with this tactic he couldn't stop Jarreth from falling forward, then toppling off.

Jarreth lie on the ground with an arrow piercing his back. The pain was unbearable, and he felt himself blacking out. A man approached with his sword raised to finish him off, but underestimated the devotion of the fallen man's horse. Daemon stepped in front of the man and blocked him, prepared to defend his master to the death.

"Get out of my way, you bloody beast!" The man raised his sword again, but was once more blocked by the huge horse. He tried to sidestep the animal, which in turn got into position to kick. The man didn't have time to think. A hoof connected with the man's midsection as he struck out blindly with his sword. A deep gash was left in the horse's leg. The man fell to the ground, screaming from several broken ribs.

Jarreth raised a hand in an attempt to pull himself up on Daemon, but lacked the strength. He knew it was just a matter of time before another one of the attackers noticed he was still alive and came to strike the final blow. He saw the blood streaming from Daemon's leg, and knew the horse was injured badly in the attempt to defend him. "Daemon," he gasped, but then saw a riderless horse running in panic directly toward him. Daemon stepped in front of him and veered the horse away, taking an errant arrow to his flank for his efforts. He whinnied in pain, which sunk straight to Jarreth's heart.

Jarreth only had enough strength to utter one more order. "Daemon, go! Get away from here!" The horse ignored him, and deflected a wayward sword with his shoulder. Another gash appeared in the great horse's flesh, adding to Jarreth's horror. The devoted animal pranced around his master as the fighting went on around him, his only instinct to defend Jarreth or die in the attempt.

Jarreth felt himself slipping closer to darkness. He made a choice to seize the opportunity of the horse's protection. Using every bit of energy he could muster, he pulled himself forward, aiming for the dubious safety of a clump of shrubs. He heard a squeal behind him, and turned to see Daemon fending off another fear-ridden horse that had lost its rider and guidance. He made it to the bushes just as Daemon was knocked to the ground; a flurry of activity converged upon the very spot Jarreth had just been laying. A loosened rock flew from the ground and struck Jarreth in the head. The blow was more that he could sustain. He collapsed, and waited for death to overtake him.

In the din of the battle he realized that someone was calling his name. He raised his head to see a familiar face kneeling beside him, a face he had not seen for many years. Jarreth blinked, believing the pain was causing hallucinations.

"Peter?" he uttered in disbelief.

"Aye, Jarreth, it is I. Good Lord, I did not know you were here."

"Peter, wha—how…?"

"You are in no condition to talk, my friend. Damn, you have been hit. Let me get this arrow out of your back." He snapped the long shaft off and grimaced as Jarreth winced in agony. "This arrow has barbs, 'tis going to have to be dug out. I have got to get you out of here. Can you stand?"

"I—I do not know. I cannot feel my legs."

Peter smoothed his curly mop of blond hair away from his face and cursed. "Damn! Why the hell did you have to be here? I would have thought you to be on Richard's side." Jarreth closed his eyes and groaned in pain, and Peter could see the life slowly being drained from his old boyhood friend.

Peter and his family were neighboring landowners to Count Stanwyck when the lads were children. Jarreth and Peter had quickly became best friends, hunting and sparing together, until Peter's father lost his land in a gambling debt. The father abandoned his wife and son,

Rhiannon

leaving them destitute. Jarreth begged his uncle to take them into his protection, and the count opened his home to the mother and son. The boys grew closer, almost inseparable until Peter's father returned months later and dragged his family away. Jarreth was only twelve, Peter ten. They never saw each other again, until today. Peter thought he was seeing things when he saw Jarreth being protected by a huge black horse, and then saw Jarreth crawl to the shelter of some bushes. He fought an inward struggle to either help his old companion, or fight for his beliefs. His affection for his boyhood playmate won out. Jarreth had come to his rescue more than once, and he couldn't turn his back on him now.

"Come on, old friend. I will not let you die, we can discuss politics later." He hoisted Jarreth up and supported him against his shoulders. "Good Lord, you grew big, did you not? Well, no matter, so did I. Stay awake just a little while longer, Jarreth." He helped the injured man away from the battle to an awaiting horse and managed to get him belly first across its back. "Hold on tight, Jarreth. I have got to get you help. If anyone sees us, we are both dead. I am supposed to be killing you, not helping you." Peter then mounted another horse and grabbed the reins, leading the horses away as Jarreth scarcely held on for life.

His mind grew numb. Jarreth barely heard Peter talking to someone. He hardly remembered the jingle of coins that were handed over for his care. Peter's voice telling him to live on, to fight for life, was just a dull dream. A woman's voice floated over him with words he couldn't understand…Rhiannon? Where was his precious Rhiannon? He had to get back to her. Rhiannon…Rhiannon.

Elizabeth rubbed the cool cloth over the stranger's face as he muttered the familiar name over and over. "It is all right," she assured him. "Rhiannon is safe, and you are too."

Chapter Eighteen

Rhiannon's party traveled all day and finally stopped at an inn on the outskirts of Cambridge for the night. So far the trip had offered nothing exciting, just endless scenes of trees, roads, and an occasional town. Even though the carriage was expertly built and comfortable, it was still a bumpy and boring ride. By evening Rhiannon was exhausted, her state of pregnancy most likely a factor in her fatigue. The small room she would be sharing with Kady seemed like a mansion.

She had no way of knowing that just ten miles away there was a monastery, one that provided the region with a hospital ran by Augustinian nuns and monks. Lay brothers and sisters, who had renounced the world to serve the unfortunate, helped perform the actual nursing. Some were only children, brought to the hospital often because a mother was widowed or abandoned.

Rhiannon was too tired to even undress; she just plopped down on the straw-stuffed mattress and closed her eyes. Kady had left to bring some food up from the tavern, so for a blissful short time she was alone. Not able to stay awake a second longer, she drifted into sleep.

Rhiannon

She heard Jarreth call her name. His face appeared, racked with pain and torment. She was jolted awake, but this time remembered Midajah's words, and kept her eyes closed.

"Jarreth," she whispered, and then loudly called his name again. "Jarreth!"

"Rhiannon," he uttered louder. Even though she was not dreaming, she could hear his voice clearly in her mind.

"Jarreth! I am sorry! Please forgive me!" Her tears seeped through her tightly closed eyes as she attempted to reach him, however impossible that seemed. "I love you, Jarreth. I always have, and I always will."

She somehow sensed his pain diminish as he answered back. "Rhiannon! I can feel you near! I need you."

Her tears turned to sobs. "I—I need you too, Jarreth. I shall never forget you, ever. Please forgive me."

"Forgive you for what?"

"I—I sent you away. Oh, Jarreth! If I could take your place, I would." She began to cry uncontrollably, and her mind became disconnected. "I am so sorry. Oh God, I am so sorry!"

"No, Rhiannon—do not leave! Rhiannon! Rhiannon!"

His face disappeared and his voice stopped, as sudden as they had appeared. Rhiannon opened her eyes and sat up, still sobbing when Kady walked in the door with a tray of food. She took one look at Rhiannon and stopped dead in her tracks.

"Rhiannon? What happened?"

"Jarreth is gone," the distraught girl answered. "And I feel this time he will not return to my thoughts."

Jarreth opened his eyes with a shock. It was night out, judging by the lack of light coming through the shutters and the candle burning in the corner. He had heard Rhiannon speak to him, as clear as if she had been sitting right there beside him. She said she was sorry. For what? Was he mad? Was he just dreaming? He glanced around the small room, devoid of any pictures or color, and realized he had no idea where he was. In his foggy mind he tried to piece together the events that led him here.

He recalled the ambush. He remembered being shot. Then he remembered Peter, a face from the past that appeared like an angel from nowhere. Everything got a little muddled from there on. All he could think about was Rhiannon; he must have been sleeping, and reached out to her with his mind. How long had it been, a couple of days, a week? No matter, he was awake now and could return to her. He started to sit up when pain shot up his back, preventing him from moving his legs. Centuries later, modern equipment could have told him the arrow damaged the nerves in his spinal cord, and came within a quarter-inch of paralyzing him forever. Right now the only thing he knew is that he couldn't move. He convinced himself not to panic; he could be drugged or perhaps there was another explanation.

The door opened and he watched as a young girl walked in, carrying some clothes and blankets. She was a pleasant-looking girl, with dark blonde hair pulled back in a modest braid. She had a fair complexion with dark eyes; he couldn't make out their exact color in the dim light. As she moved next to his nightstand, her eyes met his and the supplies fell to the floor as her jaw dropped open. Jarreth forced a small smile, the best he could do under the circumstances.

"Hello."

The girl blinked then smiled back. "You're awake!"

"Obviously, since I am talking to you. Where am I?"

She pulled up the lone chair beside the bed and sat down. "You must have a hundred questions. We thought you might die. Well, the others thought so, but I did not. You are in the Holy Mercy Hospital, located outside of Cambridge."

"Cambridge? How did I get here?"

Rhiannon

"A man brought you to a church in a nearby village, and asked the priest to get help for you. He brought you here."

Jarreth nodded as the pieces began fitting together. He now recalled Peter telling him he would be safe at the church. The priest brought him here by wagon, although Jarreth lost consciousness along the way. He struggled to remember more when the girl interrupted his thoughts.

"May I ask your name?"

"Of course, excuse my rudeness. My name is Stanwyck. Viscount Jarreth Stanwyck, of Suffolk."

The girl clasped her hands together and did a short bounce in the chair. "A noble! We thought so, but we could not be sure. Still, you came with a lot of money, so we assumed—"

"Money?" Jarreth hadn't taken any money with him when he went to battle. He was still stinging from the loss to Ramon, which was a gamble, but paid off at the moment.

"Well, aye, more than was needed for just your care, a whole purse full of coins. Brother Jacob is holding it for you. You did not know?"

Jarreth shook his head. Peter must have given his own money to assure proper care would be given to an unconscious, injured man.

The girl rattled on. "The priest was not told who you were, but I knew you were at least a knight. We gave you this room instead of putting you in the ward with the others. As you can imagine, we do not get many nobles at a charity hospital."

"No, I imagine not." He brought a hand up to his face, thinking he must look a fright with God-only-knew how many days' growth of beard. He was surprised to find his face clean-shaven.

The girl didn't miss his expression. "Oh, I have been shaving you. I hope you do not mind. You came here without a beard, so I assumed you would like to stay that way."

Jarreth smiled again. "That was very nice of you, er…what did you say your name was?"

Her face brightened as if a light radiated from within her. "Elizabeth. I was named after the queen."

"Well, thank you, Elizabeth. Do you shave all your patients?"

"Oh, no. Just the special…" She stopped abruptly, and Jarreth detected a slight blush wash across her face. "I mean, you are not like the others. You did not even have any lice."

Jarreth raised an eyebrow. "I should hope not."

"They all do, you know. Most are dirty, poor, and very sick when they arrive here. We do what we can for them, but they mostly die."

"Elizabeth, how long have I been here?"

"Almost four weeks, next Tuesday."

"Four weeks?" He laid his head back on the pillow, stunned at the lost time. "What is the date?"

"October fourteen. Why?"

"The last date I remember is September seventeen." He mentally calculated how long he had been gone from Rhiannon. "She must think me dead," he muttered to himself.

"You mean Rhiannon?"

He turned his head in surprise. "How do you know about her?"

"You have only been calling out her name every day since you arrived. Who is she—your wife?"

He opened his mouth to explain, then just nodded instead.

"The only reason I ask is because you're not wearing a ring."

Jarreth glanced down at his naked left hand, silently cursing his stubbornness. He should have given in, groveled if that's what it took, to get Rhiannon to the altar. "We have not yet taken our vows."

Elizabeth looked confused at first, and then nodded with enlightenment. "Oh, an arranged marriage."

"Well, not exactly."

"Do you love her very much?"

Rhiannon

After hearing he had been calling out Rhiannon's name for almost a month, it would have been useless to deny it. "Aye."

"I knew it. You have had just beastly dreams. I tried to comfort you the only way I knew. I told you Rhiannon was fine, and that you needed to get better so you could go to her."

Jarreth smiled at the young girl's exuberance. "I guess it worked."

"Are you hungry? I could fetch you some food. I have been feeding you broth and puddings; anything you wouldn't choke on. I fear you still have lost weight."

"Elizabeth, I could eat a whole goat."

She jumped to her feet. "I will be back soon. You rest." She paused, and then lowered her voice and most noticeably, her mood. "Sister Mary Catherine will have to be told you are awake. She will most likely have many questions for you."

He could tell by her tone that the subject had changed to unpleasantness. "And who is Sister Mary Catherine?"

"She runs the hospital, along with Brother Jacob. She is in charge of me."

"I see. And what exactly do you do?"

The girl pursed her lips together and lowered her gaze. "Anything she tells me." Before he could comment, she was out the door.

He closed his eyes, exhausted just by the short exchange. Feeling weakness overtake him, he let himself doze while waiting for Elizabeth to return with food.

It was still dark when he opened his eyes. Food piled on a tray sat on his nightstand, and he wasn't shy about tearing into it. He had almost forgotten what food tasted like. He was washing down a hunk of twice-baked bread with some weak juice when the door opened and a sour faced nun with a glare that could freeze magma appeared. He knew instantly this must be Sister Mary Catherine. She raised the wick on the lantern she carried, brightening the room considerably and unfortunately illuminating her homely face in the process. She put the lantern down on the nightstand and glowered at him.

"Well, how is our special guest?" Her sarcastic tone annoyed Jarreth; he instantly disliked her.

"I was not aware I was special," he replied, matching her sarcasm.

"Come, come, Viscount. 'Tis not every day my helpers get to fawn over someone with your breeding. Even asleep, I am afraid you have been quite a novelty."

"I shall try to be inconspicuous for the rest of my stay."

"It is too late for that. Now that you are awake, I fear your presence will only bring further disruption."

He remained stone-faced as she walked to the window and flipped the locking hook on the shutters. "It is windy tonight. Cannot have the shutters being blown open." She turned to face him again. "Elizabeth told me all about you, Viscount. Stanwyck, is it? You wouldn't by chance be related to the Earl of Suffolk?"

Jarreth couldn't tell if the truth would please her or upset her. He hoped for the latter. "As a matter of fact, he is my uncle."

She raised her eyebrows ever so slightly, and he knew the count's reputation had reached even this small hospital. "Indeed? Would you mind telling me how you came to be injured and found your way here?"

"Not at all. I was on a mission at the queen's request, and was ambushed by Richard loyalists. Someone found me, and brought me here."

His lack of details displeased her, but she held her tongue. "The queen, you say? Well, Viscount—this makes you even more an honored guest."

He pulled himself up to a sitting position, ignoring the tremendous pain without so much as a wince. "Sister, I need to send a message to my uncle. I am inclined to believe he thinks me dead." He quickly reassessed his request. "Make that two messages. I need to send another one to my

Rhiannon

betrothed." He could only assume that Rhiannon had returned to her own home after learning of his 'death'.

The nun narrowed her eyebrows and frowned. "Viscount, I do not have spare workers to go traipsing across the countryside sending messages. We are short-handed as it is."

"Then hire someone. The messages must be sent."

She glared at him with disdain, not liking his ordering her like a servant. But then again, she certainly didn't want the infamous Dark Count's nephew at her facility any longer than was necessary. She quickly changed her mind.

"Very well. I will fetch some writing materials and find a messenger. But he will have to leave soon. It appears we are in for an early winter."

Jarreth nodded his approval. "Of course. Thank you." He produced his most charming smile, simply to irk her. "I do have one more question."

"Aye?"

"Could I ask what are the extent of my injuries?"

She took a deep breath and let it out slowly, purposely delaying the answer. "I will not lie to you, Viscount. I have seen other back injuries such as yours. It may take you a long time to recover, if at all. Fortunately, you have the means to hire the best doctors."

"And that bothers you?"

Her eyes flashed ire, and then she quickly composed herself. "And should it not? I deal daily with the people you shun and neglect. Nobles such as you have no conception of what it is like to be hungry or sick, with no one to care for you. At least here they get cleaned up and fed. Some get well, some do not. But they do not die alone in the streets like your kind would leave them."

Jarreth contemplated her words, trying to see the insight past the emotions. Much of what she said was true. The discrepancy between the classes was just a fact that was accepted. He instantly thought of Rhiannon, and what she would do.

"Sister, I believe a purse of coins was given for my care."

She paused and displayed mild surprise, then nodded. "Aye, a sinful amount—enough to run this place for an entire year. Brother Jacob took only what was needed for your care and is holding the rest for your departure. So do not concern yourself about your precious money, Viscount. We may be poor, but we are not thieves."

Her condemning tone almost made him reconsider what he was about to do. His thoughts of Rhiannon again brought him back into focus. "You misinterpreted my meaning, sister. I wish to donate the money to this hospital. I only ask for enough to purchase a horse. I am going to need one when I leave here." He didn't bother mentioning the money was most likely stolen. Being essentially outcasts, Peter and his comrades probably financed their resistance by stealing. It seemed fitting the money should end up benefiting charity.

His words stunned her into silence; her expression, however, didn't change. She simply stared at him. Finally she found her voice.

"Perhaps I misjudged you. Or, perhaps it is guilt that spurs your generosity. Whatever, brother Jacob will most likely accept your offer, after he verifies it with you." She paused, glaring at him as if he were on trial. "Do you realize what that much money will buy us?"

He shrugged, not having the slightest idea since he didn't know how much money was in the purse.

"Let me enlighten you. It will buy new blankets and sheets. It will fill the pantries and medicine cabinets. We will even be able to buy a few new beds. Money you shrug about will ensure the very lives of many people, money you would bet away in a single card game."

"I am not a betting person, Sister."

"Indeed?" She raised her head in a haughty manner. "You may have some redeeming qualities after all." She opened the door to leave, and cast him one last condemning glance. "Although, I doubt it." The door came just short of slamming as she left.

Rhiannon

Jarreth let out a long breath, feeling like he had just been arrested, tried and convicted. All that remained was his execution. Sleep came hard for the rest of the night.

He was extremely relieved when the next morning his door opened and Elizabeth stepped in. She carried a portable lap table with ink, parchment, and a scroll pen, and widely smiled when she plopped everything across his lap.

"These are from Brother Jacob for your messages. He is searching for a courier as we speak. Whatever did you say to Sister Mary Catherine? She is in a very good mood."

Jarreth's mouth formed into a smirk. "How can you tell?"

The girl giggled and quickly covered her mouth with her hand. "You mustn't speak so. Sister Mary Catherine is a very dedicated nun. She has saved many lives." Even as she spoke, her smile was still evident in her voice.

"She certainly does not like the noble class. I have the feeling she would just as soon watch me die."

Elizabeth straightened her face and shook her head. "On no, she is devoted to her calling. I know she sounds harsh, and perhaps she is. But the circumstances here are harsh, also. It tends to harden one's outlook on life."

He drew back, a bit in awe at the wisdom of this small girl. "I see."

"Now that you are awake, we can begin getting your strength back. You need to eat a lot. I will fetch your breakfast while you write your letters."

After her departure he pulled himself up again, and noticed the pain wasn't as sharp as the night before. That was encouraging; perhaps he just needed to move more. Of course, that would be hard without the use of his legs. He forced himself to concentrate and smiled when he succeeded in wiggling a toe. It was a small victory, but a hopeful one. He sat his mind to the task at hand.

Evangelynn Stratton

The first letter to his uncle was easy and simple.

I am alive. Come get me. Holy Mercy Hospital in Cambridge. Hurry. If Rhiannon is with you, bring her. J. S.

Now came the letter to Rhiannon. How to begin?

My Dearest Rhiannon,

Somehow the term of endearment didn't fit; they hadn't exactly parted best friends. He finally settled for just her name.

Rhiannon—I have sent this letter to your home in hopes you are there.

He stopped writing and frowned; that was stupid. Of course she was there if she was reading it. He began again.

Rhiannon—I am not dead.

He stopped again; that was even worse. His chagrined scowl gave him away as Elizabeth entered with his breakfast.

"What is wrong?" she asked.

He gave out a deep sigh. "I seem to be having difficulty with wording my message to Rhiannon. I do not know what to say."

"Just tell her what is in your heart. That is the only thing that counts." She put down his breakfast tray, and left.

The wisdom of the child hit him in his soul, and suddenly the words came easy.

My Gwenivere,

In the past month I have died and awakened. It is not often that a person is given a second chance in life, and I do not plan to waste this precious gift. I was a fool, Rhiannon. I lied to you, then did not understand why you felt violated. I thought leaving would teach you a lesson, but it is I who has been made wiser. I love you, Rhiannon, and I always will. My thoughts have been nowhere but on you; your laugh, your smile haunts me daily. My only hope is that you can find it in your heart to forgive me and still be willing to be my wife.

Rhiannon

The pain from my injuries is nothing compared to the thought of living my life without you. Forgive me, Rhiannon, and I promise never to be a fool again.
  Your Lancelot

He folded the letter carefully and wrote the hospital's address on the outside. Then he gave a silent prayer that the letter reached her and that she would come to him. It was the only thread of hope he had to hold on to.

Chapter Nineteen

"Rhiannon, wake up!" The groggy girl opened one eye and glared at Kady, who was pointing excitingly out the carriage window. "I can see Aberaeron!"

"Aye, Rhiannon," the baron added. "I swear you have done nothing but sleep this entire trip."

Rhiannon raised her head and yawned. The side of her face felt numb from leaning against the carriage's side. Even though it was padded, it still made a lousy pillow. Her eyes were scratchy and her head throbbed, plus she longed for a lingering, hot bath. "What else is there to do?"

"You could at least *try* to enjoy the trip," her father said. "You have missed some beautiful scenery. The fall leaves are very pretty, look at that tree! Is that not a brilliant yellow?"

Rhiannon shifted her weight and gave him a bored look. "If you have seen one yellow tree, you have seen them all." Nevertheless, she gazed out the window and made an attempt to appreciate the myriad of color that nature had to offer. For some reason she was unable to muster much excitement.

Rhiannon

The baron had tried to maintain a positive attitude, despite the circumstances to the contrary. He had watched his daughter sink into a lifeless state, sleeping her life away as if trying to escape reality. He contributed it to her delicate condition. "When you were a child, you used to bring me huge bouquets of leaves," he said cheerfully. "I remember one year there were leaves all over the castle. The servants kept throwing them out, and you would come bawling to me." He laughed at the memory, hoping to lighten the mood.

Rhiannon kept staring blankly out the window. "I was a silly child," she uttered in a flat voice.

Kady and the baron exchanged looks. The weeklong trip had taken its toll on everyone, but Rhiannon seemed to suffer the most. Her enthusiasm for life had abandoned her, and left an indifferent shell that struggled for a reason to exist.

"I do hope your aunt got our message," the baron continued. "I would hate to think we are arriving unannounced."

"You fret too much, father. Aunt Mary will welcome us whether or not she knows we are coming."

He nodded his agreement. "Aye, you are right. Ah, look! The ocean!" He knew his daughter couldn't resist the sea. Aberaeron had always been her favorite place to visit, mostly because of the ocean and the irresistible beaches with its treasures. Her Aunt Mary, who was the baron's sister-in-law, always extended an open invitation to them. As a child, Rhiannon would spend whole summers there, getting into mischief with her cousin Aaron. It was understandable why she chose this location to have her baby.

As the carriage turned the corner and began the assent to Aberaeron, Rhiannon turned her attention to the seashore that she so dearly loved. It reminded her of Jarreth. The caves flashed through her mind, and how he had rescued her from the pirates. She remembered sleeping in his arms, feeling safe, secure. The memories too painful to endure, she averted her gaze and stared at the carriage floor. A man she would never see again had forever changed her life. Her dreams had stopped; she no longer had even nightmares for company. She closed her eyes and prepared to greet her aunt with a brave face.

Brother Jacob, a tall man with laughing eyes and an attitude to match, walked into Jarreth's room and found him sitting up. "Ah, good! I see you are getting stronger!" He smiled at the man who had made friends quickly throughout the hospital. They all wanted to know the handsome viscount who made their mundane life more interesting.

Jarreth grimaced back at the monk, who, along with many others, visited him daily. "I feel weak as a newborn lamb."

"Ah, but I think that will all be changing. I sent for an acquaintance of mine, a doctor who specializes in therapy for injuries such as yours. I felt it was the least I could do after your generous donation."

"That was kind of you, Brother. I am in your debt."

"Quite the contrary, Viscount. It is refreshing to treat someone who might actually recover." His perpetual smiled disappeared for just a second. "Death becomes customary in a place such as this." There was a short hesitation, and then he quickly regained his self-assured manner. "You are making the day-to-day mission here more positive. For that I thank the Lord."

"And I thank Him for the chain of events that brought me here. Otherwise I could be lying dead on a battlefield."

"So we are thankful together. By the way, have you been warm enough at night? I fear the nights have been quite chilly."

"Aye, I have noticed. Elizabeth brought me some extra quilts, so I have been fine, thank you."

"Ah, that Elizabeth. She has a good heart, but she tends to be a mite undisciplined. Though, I am glad to know she is seeing to your needs."

Rhiannon

"She is a very smart girl. I enjoy her company." Actually, he preferred Elizabeth's company the most. She had volunteered to work with him, but had to do it after her regular duties were over, at Sister Mary Catherine's insistence. This made for slow recovery.

The monk nodded, and gazed out the window at the miracle of nature's paintbrush. "The autumn leaves are beautiful, Aye? The trees have turned color quite early this year. All the signs are pointing to a bad winter."

"In that case, I hope the courier hurries."

"Patience, viscount. It has only been a week. David is a trustworthy man; he will deliver your letters as quickly as possible."

"The waiting is unbearable."

Brother Jacob let out a hearty laugh. "This coming from a man who should be dead."

Jarreth clamed up and gave him an embarrassed smile. He had always been a man of action, never depending on anyone but himself. Now he was totally at the mercy of a young courier to deliver the most important letters of his life. He had given the young man explicit instructions and directions; now he could only hope they would be followed.

Lord Walton, the castle steward for Baron Harrison, wrapped his cloak tighter around him as he observed the darkening clouds that were suddenly rolling in. It almost felt cold enough for snow. The baron had sent notice that he wouldn't be returning until the next spring, so it was up to the steward to winterize the castle in his absence. A bother for sure, but such was the responsibilities he agreed to. As he hurried down the pathway he wondered what had caused this sudden development. The baron had never been an "absent lord", that is, he didn't often leave the castle for long periods of time. Something major must have taken place for the baron not to return to his beloved castle. Unfortunately, Lord Walton had not been made privy to that information.

Evangelynn Stratton

He had already gathered the cleaning staff and assigned them duties. The entire castle would be scrubbed from top to bottom, and then locked up for the winter. He wanted to get the task over and done with as quickly as possible so he could return to his own affairs.

Upon entering the lower floor he was pleased to see it almost done; only a few maids remained upstairs in the bedroom chambers. His next step was the kitchen, which would require the most work. The baron would not want to return to a dirty kitchen.

Upstairs a young chambermaid named Emma swept the hallway that led to the bedroom chambers. A plain girl with a childlike mind, she finished her given task and began to leave, when she passed in front of the Lady Rhiannon's door and stopped. Taking a step backward, she looked at it longingly then down the hallway both ways. Upon seeing no one, she slowly opened the door and slipped inside. She leaned back against the closed door, her heart beating with excitement. Alone in the Lady Rhiannon's chamber! She scanned the room, her brain racing with adrenaline. The only difference, she thought, between her and the lady Rhiannon was the accident of birth. Some costume jewelry sat neatly arranged on a dresser, and she gingerly held a necklace up to her throat. Her simplistic mind began to play out a fantasy. A decorative fan also lay on the dresser, and she spread it out and held it up to her face. She batted her eyes to a pretend suitor, and held out a dirty hand for imaginary lips to kiss. Then she spotted some decorative combs, and brought her stringy brown hair up and stuck them in. The resulting tangled mess was not exactly a lady's fashion, but it would have to do.

Her play-acting continued with a curtsey to an invisible lover, when she was snapped back to reality by her plain wool dress. Her eyes darted to the wardrobe. Surely there must be something there suitable for her to wear?

A rose-colored gown embellished with faux pearls caught her eye. Now, this was a gown fit for her standing! Not having the same curves as

Rhiannon

Rhiannon, the dress fit a bit loose in places. The scrawny girl looked for something to help her anatomy, settling for a few rags stuffed in front to help fill out the dress. Without a mirror to reflect her image, the poor girl only could imagine how lovely she must look.

Her dress and hair completed, she now turned to improve her face. Rhiannon shunned most cosmetics; she was fortunate enough to not need much assistance with her beauty. But over the years she had been given presents of lip and cheek rouge plus several small pots of eye color, wearing them only occasionally for special events. Emma knew they must be there someplace. She found them underneath some spare quilts in a chest at the foot of the bed. The unwitting girl smeared some gray eye color on her eyelids, way too much for a subtle appearance. The lip rouge came next, then the cheeks, turning her into more a clown than a lady. Her lips now looked red and swollen, like she had been the loser in a fistfight. Her cheeks appeared painfully sunburned. But in her mind she believed herself devastatingly beautiful, just as much as the lady Rhiannon.

Swirling around to imaginary music, the pathetic girl resembled an actor from a comedy play, where men dressed like women and often looked laughingly horrible. But at that moment Emma had never felt more comely, much too comely to keep cooped up in that room. She imagined herself going to a regal ball, descending a grand staircase and holding out her hand to her partner at the bottom of the stairs. Yes, she must do that. The castle was practically empty, what harm could it cause?

She left the room and waited at the top of the stairs, listening for voices. When she heard none, she went back into her play-acting and began to walk slowly down the stairs. At one point she almost tripped on the long gown, so she lifted the front and continued her descent, her head held royally high. An illusory crowd clapped at the bottom as she stepped down slowly, letting everyone drink in her beauty.

Evangelynn Stratton

Once down the stairs she began to give orders to her many imagined servants. One was told to fetch her wrap, another to hold her fan. Her arm looped through her invisible partner, who was very handsome and adored her greatly, and they began to walk to the grand ballroom. She was so caught up in her fantasy she didn't hear the first knock. The second knock shook her from her daydream.

Someone was at the door. It wouldn't be the other servants or the steward; they certainly would just walk right in. So, she reasoned, it must be a stranger. Someone who didn't know her. Seizing the opportunity, she fluffed her hair and took a deep breath. Then she went to the door and opened it with a dramatic flourish.

A pleasant-looking young man with the telling signs of long hours in the saddle—wrinkled clothes, scuffed boots, baggy eyes—smiled politely and bowed.

"Good afternoon, milady. I wonder if I may speak to Baron Harrison?"

She pulled herself up tall, taking on the airs of regality. "I fear the baron is away at the moment."

"Oh. Then perhaps you might summon the Lady Rhiannon? I have a most urgent message for her."

Emma thought her insides would burst; this was the moment she had been waiting for. "I am the Lady Rhiannon," she stated proudly.

The courier raised his eyebrows, taken aback by the lady's appearance, but who was he to judge? Nobles were a strange lot. He reached into his pocket and brought out the folded letter. "Then this is for you." He handed the message to the girl, who accepted it without opening it, as if it were a fragile object too precious to disturb.

The wary servant, not knowing what to do at this point, simply wanted to get rid of this man. "Thank you," she said, and started to close the door.

The man shoved it back open. "The sender requested a reply."

Rhiannon

Emma frowned. Oh well, it couldn't be too hard to make something up. In the past she had proven herself to be very proficient at lying. She opened the letter and observed the squiggles, as being a peasant she didn't know how to read.

The courier gave her ample time to read the short message before daring to clear his throat. "Milady?"

She jerked her head up, fear starting to rise inside her. If she were caught impersonating a noble, it would not bode well for her. "Tell the sender I will take the matter into consideration." She had heard the baron say that often, and she hoped it fit under the circumstances,

"Is that all?"

"Aye. Now, you must excuse me, I have many things to do." She shoved the door with all her might, and was greatly relieved when this time he didn't resist.

Outside, David the courier scratched his head in confusion. *She would take the matter into consideration?* That wasn't much of a message to take back to the injured viscount, who had espoused her beauty to no end when he gave instructions. The Lady Rhiannon wasn't what he had expected; the viscount certainly had an interesting concept of beauty. No matter, he still had a long ride to Stanwyck Castle, and that was something he was not looking forward to. Even though the viscount **had told him the rumors about the Dark Count were mostly false, that** still meant some were true. But he had promised, and he would not disappoint the viscount, who had promised him a generous stipend for his efforts. He mounted his horse and galloped away.

Inside, Emma felt exhilarated, like every wish she had ever dreamt had just come true in one brief moment. Her heart beat fast and hard, and her breathing was labored. He thought she was a lady! She suddenly realized what she had just done, and knew no one must ever know. The letter was still in her hand, so she stuffed it down the front of her gown for lack of a better place to put it. Getting back upstairs to her proper place was the only thing on her mind as she turned and ran straight into the steward.

He folded his arms and glared at her. "Well, Emma—what have we here? That is an interesting gown you're wearing. Stealing from the Lady Rhiannon, are we?"

"N—no, I...I was just, ah..."

"Well, I am waiting, Emma. Lie yourself out of this one."

A look of panic embellished her face as she began backing up in fear. "I—I was not gonna steal it, really! I just wanted to see what I looked like in it."

"I can tell you that, you look ridiculous. Did I hear you talking to someone?" He looked over her head at the closed door.

"N—no, I mean, 'twas just the gardener asking where you were." It was a terrible lie, but it was the best she could come up with.

"Really? I told him to go home when he finished. No matter, get out of that gown and for God's sake, wash your face. Then get out of my sight. You are fortunate the master is not here. He most likely would punish you more severely. Now, go!"

"Aye, milord." The frightened girl ran for all she was worth up the stairs to take off the gown. After she carefully hung it back up she looked down at the crumpled letter, wondering what to do with it. She had never had a real letter before. Even though it wasn't meant for her, it was special, because someone actually thought she was a lady. She put back on her old wool dress and stuffed the letter in a pocket, then fled the castle as quickly as possible.

The courier entered the gates of Stanwyck castle one week later. He had taken a wrong turn, but some passing Gypsies gave him excellent directions stating they said they had just left the realm of the Dark Count. They seemed sincere, and none of them appeared to have been tortured or otherwise, so maybe it was relatively safe.

Rhiannon

The dark castle loomed before him. He had been instructed to give the letter directly to the Earl Stanwyck. Hoping he didn't blurt out something stupid and end up in the dungeon, he let a groom take his horse as he reluctantly walked up to the front door.

A young female servant, who raised her eyebrows in suspicion, answered his knock. "Aye?" she asked.

He quickly scanned the girl over. She had lush measurements, nice wide hips and an ample bosom, just the way he liked them. "I have an urgent message for the Dark...er, for Earl Stanwyck."

"Not here. Won't be back 'till spring." She looked him over, smiling with approval.

David felt relief, then indecision. What should he do now? He reached inside his coat and brought out the letter.

"This is for the Earl's eyes only, do you understand? He must be given this message as soon as he arrives back."

The girl took the letter and eyed it with curiosity. "I could put it on his desk."

David nodded. "That would be fine." Then in a weak moment of guilt he added, "You wouldn't happen to know where the count is, would you? If he is not far, perhaps I could take the letter to him."

Much to his relief the servant shook her head. "Nope. Didn't tell no one. But that is not unusual—he goes away all the time."

Satisfied his task was finally done, David gave a short bow and started to leave when the servant lightly grasped his arm.

"The Earl always gives his messengers a hot meal and a place to spend the night, if you would be so inclined."

David paused in consternation. He was tired and his horse could unquestionably use the rest. The absent count was not a threat, and the servant certainly had made her intentions known.

"All right, that would be most appreciative." He followed the willing girl to the kitchen.

Evangelynn Stratton

"Ow!" Jarreth yelped as the doctor pressed a point on his back. "Good!"

Not known for his subtlety, Jarreth returned the doctor's self-satisfied smile with a frown. "Pain is good?"

"Oh, very. If you did not feel anything, then I would be worried." The doctor wiped his balding high forehead, a bit weary from the intensive massage he had just given the reluctant patient.

"So when will I be able to walk?"

"Patience, Patience. Your legs have been inactive for a while. They are weak."

At that moment Elizabeth entered the room, obviously having had rushed through her duties by the looks of her disarranged hair and flour-spotted face. She had been making pies and the time slipped away from her. "Am I late?" she asked the doctor.

The doctor smiled at the girl, to whom he had gotten quite close during her training sessions. "Well, is this the young lady I am training to get this impatient man back on his feet? Or is it some reject from the kitchen?" He loved teasing her; she responded by giggling.

"A little of both." She wiped her face on her apron.

Jarreth was still displaying a dissatisfied scowl as the doctor turned his attentions back to him. "Well, young sir, it looks like you shall get your wish. Would you care to stand up?"

Jarreth's expression changed to sudden apprehension. "Right now? Am I ready?"

An amused chuckle erupted from the doctor as he winked at Elizabeth. "A few seconds ago you were ready to walk out of here. You tell me... are you ready?"

Jarreth cast a helpless glance at Elizabeth; she in turn nodded back. It was all the confidence he needed. "Very well, I am ready."

"All right. Elizabeth, grab his arm like this and support his weight against your shoulder. A little higher, dear, like this. Now Viscount, we

Rhiannon

are here only to keep you from falling. The work will have to be done by you."

He acknowledged with a nod, suddenly feeling more afraid than he ever had before in his life. What if he couldn't do it? What if his legs gave way like a blob of jelly and he collapsed into a pathetic heap? It was almost better not knowing, at least that way he wouldn't have to face the truth.

"Viscount, we are waiting."

Jarreth snapped back to the matter at hand. "Aye, sorry." He pushed himself all the way off the edge of the bed and in one slow movement stood up. The cold stone floor shocked the bottom of his bare feet and his legs felt wobbly. But at last he was standing, transforming him from an invalid into some semblance of a man.

Elizabeth laughed; it was a child's laugh of joy that somehow made it all worthwhile. "You did it! I knew you could!" The doctor joined in her cheering.

Jarreth immediately sat back down on the bed. He had a small inner sense of accomplishment, but failed to see how standing up for just two seconds warranted a celebration. He had never felt so weak and helpless in his life. Even though the good doctor assured him that a full recovery was imminent, Jarreth was unhappy with the slow progress. Daily massages had brought feeling back to his legs, mostly as tingling sensations, which was more that he had before the doctor began the therapy. Still, Jarreth grumbled from his lack of immediate restoration. The doctor soon learned to ignore his musings the way Elizabeth did. The treatment Jarreth hated the most was the alternate hot/cold packs on his legs. The cold made him shiver; the hot made him sweat. He complained incessantly until Elizabeth finally called him a big sissy, which finally shut him up. No one had ever dared call him a sissy before.

Elizabeth knew his bad mood was being caused mainly from the lack of word from the courier. Jarreth felt he should have been back days ago. Everyone reminded him that the cold weather probably hindered travel; they had heard that some places further north were already getting snow. That made no difference to Jarreth. He had endured travel through inclement weather and saw no reason why anyone else couldn't do the same.

It was with great relief, therefore, when Elizabeth saw Brother Jacob appear in the doorway with the young courier in tow,

"Well, Viscount! I believe you have been waiting for this!" His voice fell into mock seriousness as he surrendered to the impulse to tease. "Oh, you are busy. We can come back later." He turned, pretending to leave.

Elizabeth thought Jarreth was going to bolt off the bed. "Get back in here!" His voice held the unmistakable timbre of authority. He might as well have been commanding his guard to battle.

Brother Jacob turned, smiling widely, not for a second intimidated by the gruff patient. He had long ago learned the viscount's bark was much worse than his bite. "Oh very well, if you insist. Come, David."

The doctor saw his cue to leave. "I shall check on other patients. Remember Viscount; your recovery will be based on how hard you work. It is ultimately up to you." He left with Brother Jacob close behind him.

Elizabeth started to leave, also thinking he would want privacy, but Jarreth put a hand up to halt her. "No, stay… please." He was surprised at how much he had come to depend on the girl, and was gradually learning the niceties of relationships he never had to deal with before. It was a humbling experience.

David appeared a little nervous, as well he should have, considering his lateness was due to his lingering at Stanwyck Castle an extra three days. Of course, that small detail would not be forthcoming in his report.

"So were the messages delivered as I instructed?" Jarreth asked as he re-positioned himself on the bed. Elizabeth helped him lift his legs and covered him with the many quilts.

Rhiannon

The courier cleared his throat. "Er, not exactly, Sir…Earl Stanwyck is away on some trip and will not be returning until spring. The message was left on his desk."

Jarreth let this news settle in his mind. This development didn't surprise him. The count was undoubtedly disturbed by Jarreth's 'death', and took a retreat to work through his grief. Jarreth could still remember his uncle going away for an entire year after the untimely death of his last wife.

He hesitated before asking the next question. "And what happened at Yorkshire?"

David instantly drew himself up proudly, happy to be able to impart better news. "I delivered the message to the Lady Rhiannon myself."

The moisture left Jarreth's mouth and his heart began beating wildly. "How did she look? Is she not everything I said?"

Unable to shake the vision of the awful-looking girl who had introduced herself as Rhiannon, and not wanting to insult the viscount's taste in women, David simply smiled through his teeth. "Very lovely."

"What did she say? Tell me everything! Was she excited? Is she coming?"

"Calm down, you are not giving him a chance to speak." Elizabeth gave him a little jab in the arm and he closed his mouth.

"Well," David began, "She… ah… read the note, and…"

"And what? Speak up, man!"

"She said she would take the matter into consideration."

Jarreth felt like someone had punched him in the gut. "That is it?"

David nodded. "That is all she said. She did not seem very talkative."

Jarreth plopped back on his pillows, staring at the ceiling as hopelessness engulfed him. "She is still angry with me."

"I find that hard to believe," Elizabeth countered. "I know you said you did not part on good terms, but was the fight that serious?"

"Apparently."

Elizabeth wouldn't accept that; no woman in her right mind could be that cruel. "Are you sure you spoke to the Lady Rhiannon?" she asked David.

"Oh, absolutely. I asked for the baron, and she said he was away, then I asked for the Lady Rhiannon, and she said she was her."

"But," Elizabeth reasoned, "Did she say she was *not* coming?"

That seemed to confuse David. "Well, no, but…"

"Well, there! You see?" The cheery girl swirled around to Jarreth, determined to put a positive spin on the situation. "She was probably overcome with emotion, and did not want to break down in front of a total stranger."

A small ounce of renewed hope began to swell inside Jarreth. Rhiannon might have been stunned, and simply didn't know how to respond. Aye, that had to be it. Perhaps she would come after all.

Elizabeth echoed his thoughts. "She will come, I just know it. And when she does, you want to be able to walk out of here, right?"

Jarreth nodded.

"So, that means you'll have to work very hard to get well."

Another nod.

It was apparent that Jarreth was lost in his thoughts. Elizabeth sighed, and shook her head. If he had no hope, his recovery would be hampered, as much depended on his performing self-exercises. She didn't know if Rhiannon was coming for him or not, but she had to convince him of the possibility. Before she could utter another word, her eyes happened to pass to the window.

"Look! It is snowing!"

David let out a low whistle. "Looks like I just made it back in time."

Jarreth stared at the snow. The big fluffy flakes would soon cover everything, casting a pseudo pure image, immobilizing travel in the process. Would she come now? One thing he would never do is

Rhiannon

underestimate Rhiannon's tenacity. If she wanted to do something, she would find a way. All he could do is wait.

Chapter Twenty

She winter hit hard. Elders instantly proclaimed it the coldest season in memory. It was particularly distressing to Rhiannon, who couldn't take her fresh-air walks in the bitter cold. Being confined to the manor did nothing for her melancholy, which all her loved ones watched with increasing concern. She only seemed to incite joy from her expanding abdomen. By mid-February she, Kady and her Aunt Mary had abased enough baby clothes for ten children. Her Aunt also presented her with an heirloom cradle, the very one Rhiannon's own mother had used. A room was prepared as a nursery, and the count obtained the best mid-wife money could hire. Everyone kept their mood light and happy for Rhiannon's sake, not daring to mention Jarreth and his untimely death. It wasn't necessary; Rhiannon kept her precious three drawings hanging in her sleeping chamber where she spent the most time. Kady would often catch her staring at Jarreth's portrait instead of taking her prescribed daily nap. She told Kady she didn't want to forget his face, as if it were likely.

Rhiannon

Meanwhile, Elizabeth watched Jarreth go through the motions of recovering, falling deeper into a bitter depression with each passing day when it became apparent that Rhiannon was not going to come to him. Although no longer confined to his bed, his heart was still held captive. As his body grew stronger, his mind grew bitter. The bitterness finally gave way to anger, the anger to apathy. Soon not even Elizabeth could do anything to comfort him. She found herself inwardly hating Rhiannon for reducing him to a broken, empty shell. Even after she reminded herself that hating was a sin, she couldn't help her feelings for a woman she had never met.

The last heavy snow struck in March. Jarreth would sit for hours and stare out the window, not caring that he still walked with a slight limp and his legs had not reached their original strength. The white, bleak view from his window seemed to feed his apathy. The final blow came when Elizabeth came to his room, her eyes red and puffy. He immediately knew something was terribly wrong, and his own self-suffering became secondary for one last time.

"I came to say good-bye," she announced.

"Good-bye? Where are you going?"

She wiped a lone tear and tried to force through a smile. "Back to the convent. It is time for me to begin studying for my vows."

He cast a wary glance out the window. "You are leaving in this weather?"

"The convent is just on the other side of town. We can easily walk there."

"We?"

"Aye, there are four of us who were on temporary assignment here. Right now the patient load is down, and we are not needed."

He paused, and then let out a deep sigh. "I need you." He said it almost as if he feared it might be true.

She smiled at the compliment, feeling like she was abandoning her older brother. "No, you will be fine. I can do nothing more for you."

"You do not want to do this." It was a statement rather than a question, one said dryly with a hint of bitterness.

"No, I do not. But Sister Mary Catherine…"

His eyes flashed rage as he cut off her sentence. "I should have known that witch was behind this! She has done everything possible to make my life miserable, not to mention yours."

"You must not speak so!" She quickly looked back at the door, almost expecting the nun to be standing there, taking in every word. She was relieved to see the doorway empty. "Be careful what you say. Sister Mary Catherine is a powerful woman."

"She has no power over me."

"True." She walked to the window and paused as she gazed out, her back to him. "The only one who has power over you is Rhiannon." She turned and braced herself for his reaction.

Jarreth stared at her in silence, his expression cold as he pondered her words. "Do not mention her; Rhiannon is no longer a part of my life. I am better off without her."

"That would probably be true, if you were truly rid of her."

"What is *that* supposed to mean?"

"Only that she will always be a part of your life until you confront her."

He snorted a short laugh. "I never want to see her again." He lowered his gaze to avoid eye contact.

Elizabeth fell silent, for a moment forgetting her own dilemma as she struggled for a way to reach him. Finally she shrugged and let out a deep breath. "You're probably right. It will be much more fun to wallow in self-pity for the rest of your life."

Rhiannon

She saw his shoulders stiffen at her words, but he pretended to remain unfazed. "What are you talking about—I have simply faced the truth."

"You do not know what the truth is. You have given up."

He turned and glared at her, her words cutting to the very depths of his soul. "I have never been a quitter."

"Then fight!" Her voice rose in desperation. "You could be fully recovered if you did something besides sit around and feel sorry for yourself!"

"Do not speak to me so! Friends or not, I am still your superior!"

She felt stinging tears start to fall as she backed up to the door. "Aye, I suppose you are."

He immediately felt like a total fool. "Elizabeth, I did not mean that. 'Tis just…" His voice trailed off as he sought the right words.

"'Tis just that I am telling you what you do not want to hear. You must face her, Jarreth. If you do not, you will never be free."

"You put too high a price on freedom."

"That is not possible. Freedom is priceless."

His voice lowered to almost a whisper, his tone one of acceptance. "Then I guess that is the cross I shall have to bear."

The comment seemed final. Elizabeth stood there for a short time, almost not recognizing this man as the same one who had fought so hard to survive. "I guess we all have our crosses to bear." She left without looking back, leaving him feeling more alone than ever before.

He buried his head in his hands, wanting to cry unmanly tears, but not allowing himself that release. Finally he stood and took his usual place at the window, staring out with a look of defiance. "The hell with her," he muttered. "The hell with them all."

Several weeks passed. To relieve boredom, he offered to chop wood and perform other tasks that allowed him to be alone. Unbeknownst to him, the sporadic activity was making him stronger. He missed his young nurse, but of course wouldn't admit it, not even to himself. His only desire was to leave this place. Bitterness wracked his mind to the point of illogical thinking, as he attempted to put some order back in his life. The messenger had said his uncle would be gone until spring. That gave him a few months to hole up somewhere, be alone and harden his heart to any future temptress. Then he would come back and publicly renounce Rhiannon as his betrothed. This would disgrace her and possibly ruin her chances for any marriage. He would also make it known she was no longer a virgin, and gave of herself willingly. That would further disgrace her reputation. When he was through no man would want anything to do with her, no respectable man, that is. Even as he plotted his revengeful plans, deep down he knew he couldn't do any of it. Oh, he would go away all right—he had a small manor in Lincolnshire he could retreat to—but as for destroying Rhiannon, he could not be that cruel. Although her presence in his life was short, she had given him the greatest joy he had ever known. She had made him laugh—no small feat. Would he ever laugh again?

The days grew warmer and the snow melted. Jarreth knew it was time to leave, and summoned Brother Jacob to make ready a horse. He instantly thought of Daemon. His last memory of his faithful steed, fending off attackers from him while he lay with an arrow in his back, flashed through his mind. He remembered the gash in the animal's leg, as well as the other wounds. It was inconceivable to think the great horse was dead, but he knew it likely. This further fed his stoicism.

Dressing in his own clothes felt strange, but empowering. One by one everyone came by to say good-bye; he remained cordial but detached. As he gave his room—his home for nearly eight months—one last look, he was surprised to see Sister Mary Catherine standing in the hallway. He had not seen her since Elizabeth left; he assumed she accompanied the girls to the convent.

Rhiannon

"I am fortunate to have arrived back in time to say good-bye, Viscount. I know you might not believe me, but I wish you the best of luck."

Jarreth was compelled to ignore her, but had a sudden impulse to tie up one last loose end. "In a way I am glad to see you, Sister. I wonder if you would be so kind to take a message to Elizabeth for me?"

A smile almost broke her sour, tight lips. "I would be glad to if I could…but I am afraid that is impossible."

"Why is that?"

"Elizabeth saw fit to run away soon after she went back. No one has seen her since."

Jarreth furled his eyebrows in disbelief. "Run away? Why?"

"I imagine it had something to do with her punishment."

"Punishment?" He felt his anger start to surface, and he clenched his fists to contain it. "What did she do to warrant punishment?"

"That is really none of your business, Viscount." She started to turn when a massive hand wrapped around her right arm—none too loosely.

"I asked what she did."

She could tell by his ardent tone that she was going nowhere until she answered him. "Very well. Another of the sisters missed evening mass and was punished to total solitude for one week. No one was allowed to speak to or acknowledge her. Elizabeth failed to uphold that order."

"So, she was punished for not punishing someone else?"

She lifted her chin and looked him in the eyes with distaste. "If you want to put it that way, aye. Discipline is most important in a nun's life, Viscount. I would not expect someone like you to understand."

He ignored her off-handed insult and kept a firm grasp on her arm. "And what was Elizabeth's punishment?"

She paused, and he thought he detected a hint of fear in her eyes. "She was to kneel and pray, without food, drink, or rest for a full day and night. It is a common punishment for minor offenses."

The impulse to bring his other hand up, wrap it around her long, scrawny neck and strangle the life out of her was almost overwhelming. He resisted the urge. "That seems a harsh punishment for such a small offense. Why do you hate her so?"

"I do not hate her, Viscount. She is impulsive and undisciplined. She was brought to us because her widowed mother could no longer care for her, and wanted a secure life for her daughter. We offered her a warm and rewarding home for the rest of her life. She was taught to read and write, and how to care for the sick. All we asked for in return was her loyalty and respect. We got neither."

"But she is young."

"Her youth is no excuse. There are girls married with children at her age."

He released her arm as he begrudgingly agreed she had a point, not that he approved of her methods. "What if she changes her mind and returns?"

The nun rubbed her arm, thinking she would surely be bruised from this heathen's violence. "She cannot be welcomed back. She made a decision, a wrong one in my opinion, but a decision nonetheless. Her only future is begging in the streets or becoming a harlot in some brothel. Now, if you will excuse me, Viscount, I have duties to perform."

He watched her go without comment, wondering if her advantageous arrival was planned simply to goad him with the news about Elizabeth. Knowing there was nothing he could do, he left feeling helpless with more animosity than he cared to harbor.

The monastery had a small stable, large enough for several horses and a wagon used to transport supplies. A groom had saddled the horse Brother Jacob had purchased for Jarreth. It was an adequate animal, an unremarkable brown color, but with strong legs and admirable confirmation. It would do until he could get another horse like Daemon. He smirked at that; there would never be another horse like Daemon.

Rhiannon

The young groom held the horse while Jarreth mounted, then handed him the reins. It felt odd to be back in the saddle again, almost foreign. As he made ready to leave, the groom suddenly held up his hand to halt him.

"Oh… I forgot. I was supposed to give this to you." He took a folded piece of parchment from inside his jacket and handed it to Jarreth.

Curious to who would be sending him a note, Jarreth unfolded the paper and read the short message.

My Noble Friend,

I have chosen to be free, I bear my cross no longer. I pray someday that yours will also be lifted. Remember what I said—freedom is priceless.

God be with you.

Elizabeth

He was stunned. She must have sneaked by, risking being seen, and left the message with the groom. He shuddered to imagine where she was now. After putting the note inside his coat, he kicked the horse into a canter and took his leave of the Holy Mercy Hospital.

He rode without thinking, letting his subconscious lead him, ignoring the numbness in his lower back. The doctor had warned that he would experience periodic symptoms of his injury, some painful, some not. Soon the horse needed a rest, and Jarreth found a small meadow alongside the road. He lay on his back in the grass, watching the languid movement of several clouds as they floated across the sky, changing shapes as if taunting him with their unconstrained liberty. He wished he could be like them—free, no worries, letting the wind take him wherever it pleased. But such was not his lot in life. He needed time to think, to sort things out. The small manor was perfect. No one would know where he was, so essentially he could still remain "dead". As dead as he felt.

He traveled most of the day until he came to the major crossroad. The right fork would take him toward Yorkshire; left to Lincolnshire.

Elizabeth's words tormented him, and he cursed his indecision as he took out the note and read it again. She said she was choosing to be free. What was he to choose? Would he ever truly be free until he faced Rhiannon and asked her why she had abandoned him? Did he care? It was time for a fresh dose of honesty. Damn it all, he *did* care. Elizabeth was correct; deep down he always knew she was. He reined the horse to the right.

Several days later, dirty, unshaven and exhausted, he arrived at the gates of Rhiannon's home, wondering what he was doing there and why he was willing to subject himself to her humiliation. She would most likely laugh, thinking it funny that he would still be interested. He decided he couldn't do it; he was foolish to come here. He lowered his head in capitulation and reined the horse to leave.

Something made him look one last time, perhaps the need to bring closure to his breaking heart. He suddenly became aware of the lack of activity around the castle. It was quiet; too quiet. Where was everyone? He slowly rode through the gates, searching in vain for movement. Except for a few stray chickens, the place was deserted. It was almost as if the castle had been abandoned. He left the horse tied to a post and cautiously knocked on the front door. No one answered. He began walking around the perimeter, looking for a live body. His mind began reeling; this was crazy. Was the whole place hit by the plague? There wasn't even a cat to kick.

"May I help you?"

He whirled around to face a tall, homely man with buckteeth and bad skin. For some reason he felt he knew this stranger, even he though he did not recall meeting him before. There was something about his teeth. Ah yes, the gap. He remembered Rhiannon's description of the castle steward—"*large teeth with a gap so wide he could eat corn on the cob through a picket fence.*" He virtually had to choke back a chuckle that threatened to erupt from his throat.

Rhiannon

"I am..." he began.

"I know who you are, Viscount. Why are you here? Is everything all right with the Baron and Rhiannon? Have you come to check the condition of the castle?"

Jarreth paused, his reaction clouded with confusion. "What are you talking about? Is not Rhiannon here?"

"Of course she is not. She left with you, correct?"

"Aye, but did she not come back?"

Lord Walton folded his arms and looked at Jarreth with suspicion. "Why would she come back? Was she not to marry you?"

"Aye, but..." he stopped when he realized they were not getting anywhere with their volley of questions. "Perhaps you should just tell me what has transpired here for the last eight months."

The steward frowned, clearly confused as much as Jarreth. "All right. A few days after you left with the lady Rhiannon, the baron left with his party to attend the wedding. About six weeks later I received a message from the baron stating that he would not be returning until spring, and to secure the castle for the winter. I did so, and make weekly checks to watch for thieves or trespassers, which I am doing today. Now, I would still like to know what you are doing here."

Jarreth waggled a hand as he shook his head. "Wait a minute. Are you meaning to say Rhiannon never came back here?"

"I believe I have made that abundantly clear."

"You are lying." Jarreth's face fell into a grim mask of animosity, causing the surprised steward to take a stumbling step backward.

"N... no, I swear! No one has been here, all winter!"

"You can drop the pretense. I sent a courier to deliver a message to Rhiannon. He said he handed it to her directly."

"But that is impossible!"

Jarreth was so wrought with anger at this point, he would have ran the man through if he had his sword. "Do not lie to me. I realize you are protecting Rhiannon; a few months ago I would have done the same thing. But right now, I need the truth."

"But I *am* telling you the truth! No message was received here! If a courier had come, we would have told him—"

He stopped mid-sentence as his mind suddenly flashed to Emma, standing in the hallway, painted like a harlot wearing Rhiannon's gown. "Unless…" He laughed nervously, dismissing the notion as ludicrous. "No, not even *she* would do such a thing."

Jarreth decided to extend the man's life span by a few minutes. "What? Who?"

"This could be nothing, but there was a small incident. At the time I thought…"

"I grow impatient. Just tell me."

Lord Walton swallowed hard; he certainly didn't want to further incur the viscount's wrath. "Very well. There is a chambermaid, Crazy Emma she is called behind her back, who sometimes tells great lies and has a tendency to pretend quite often. I caught her wearing one of Rhiannon's gowns during the fall cleaning, standing in the entrance hall. I thought I head her talking to someone, but I found her alone. I dismissed her, of course. She will never work here again."

Jarreth let this information mull around in his mind. Could it be possible that the courier thought this Emma person was Rhiannon? If so, the assumption he had lived under for the last five months had been wrong. But he had to be sure; his whole future depended on it.

"Not that I doubt your good word, but I must speak to this Emma. Can you take me to her?"

The steward frowned at this imposition being thrust upon him, but nodded anyway. "I suppose. Her family has a small farm just east of here."

"Show me."

"Right now?"

Rhiannon

"Now." He grabbed the steward's gaunt upper arm and began dragging him back to his horse, taking long, purposeful strides while the steward sputtered his opposition.

"I daresay! There is no need to manhandle me! You are hurting me! Let go, I say!"

Jarreth released the man with a jolt. "Get your horse."

Lord Walton stumbled off to retrieve his horse from the stable, muttering about life's injustices and mean, Dark Counts and their kin.

Chapter Twenty-one

Emma was milking her father's goat when she saw the two men approaching on horseback. Being a bit nearsighted, she squinted to make them out. Her eyes grew wide when she recognized the castle steward. Thinking she must be in further trouble, she abandoned her milking duties and bolted toward the cottage.

"There she is!" the steward yelled as he pointed her out to Jarreth, who kicked his horse into a trot to catch her. He cut her off and jumped off his horse before she got to the house. He grabbed her by the shoulders as gently as possible, knowing that he must be extremely frightening. Even so, the girl trembled with fear and struggled to release his grip.

"I will not hurt you, Emma. Calm down." He looked into her dull eyes and realized he was speaking to no less a child. He softened his voice appropriately. "I just want to ask you a question."

She stopped squirming. "What kinda question?"

By now Lord Walton had dismounted and joined them. "She will not tell you the truth, you know. She lies all the time."

Jarreth looked at him in a flash of rage. "Shut up!" He turned back to the girl, who was pursing her lips and staring down at the ground.

Rhiannon

"Emma, I understand you like to dress up?"

She raised her head and smiled. "Aye, I have a pretty dress. Would you like to see it?"

"Maybe later. Do you remember wearing one of lady Rhiannon's gowns?"

Again she lowered her head and became silent.

"Please, Emma. I am not angry with you; I just need to know something. Did you accept a message that was meant for Rhiannon? 'Tis very important."

Overcome with fear, she shook her head frantically and refused to talk.

"See, I told you! You will not get anything from her." Lord Walton smirked in self-satisfaction that his prediction was right.

Jarreth ignored him. His only other option was killing him, which he highly preferred, but right then was not a convenient time.

"Please, Emma. You are not in trouble; I just have to know. You see, that message was from me."

She raised her head and looked at him without expression. "Really?"

"Really."

Her eyes narrowed. "I did not mean no harm. It is just, he thought I was a lady."

"I understand. Do you still have the message, Emma?"

She nodded.

"Could I see it?"

"It is in the house. I will get it." He followed her to the door and waited outside while she entered. In a few minutes she came out with the folded piece of parchment and handed it to Jarreth.

He unfolded the note with trembling hands; afraid to discover that it was just some other letter she had found lying around somewhere. His heart leapt the moment he saw his words. He closed his eyes and fought the tears that were welling up from relief and joy. Rhiannon had not gotten the message. She had not abandoned him.

"Thank you, Emma." He smiled warmly at the girl, not able to hate her for her transgression. "You have been most helpful."

Lord Walton had been watching this scene with disgust. "This does not mean I am hiring her back, understand? She is still a liar and a thief!"

Jarreth again ignored him—to do otherwise would jeopardize his newly found benevolent mood. "Would you like to keep this, Emma?" He offered the letter to her.

Her simple mind couldn't comprehend his gesture. "I can keep it? You do not mind?"

"Nay, I do not mind. Here." He put the letter in her hand, knowing that it was probably the one bit of escapism in her plain, monotonous life. He walked back to his horse and turned to the steward. "I take my leave of you, Sir. I believe I can say with complete honesty that you are the biggest bastard I have ever met." He kicked the horse and galloped off, leaving Lord Walton sputtering incoherently.

There was nothing else to do but return home to Stanwyck castle; the answer to Rhiannon's disappearance had to lie there. He pushed the poor horse hard, taking every short cut he was aware of, stopping only to eat and sleep out of sheer necessity. The weather cooperated until the last day, when a thunderstorm broke out and drenched him before he reached the castle in the evening. He was a soggy sight as he rode through the gates, finally stopping in front of the stable where a bored, young groom sat observing the downpour from inside the entrance. When he recognized Jarreth his face turned white, as if he was witnessing a ghost riding in from hell itself.

Jarreth quietly tossed him the reins, in no mood for small talk or greetings. He was wet, cold, hungry and exhausted.

Rhiannon

"Lord Jarreth!" the groom said, his eyes wide. "We thought you were…"

Jarreth ignored him, taking long, purposeful steps toward the castle.

"…dead," the young lad finished.

Jarreth entered the castle, thinking only of a hot bath and a warm bed. He needed to sleep so he could think straight. As he rounded a corner he ran smack into Cecil, his uncle's oldest and most trusted servant. The shocked man drew back as his jaw dropped open in total stupefaction.

"Lord Jarreth! How…I mean, what are you—you are dead, that is we were told you were…"

Not realizing he looked as if he might have just crawled from a grave, Jarreth cut him off with an impatient wave of his hand.

"As you can see, they were wrong. I need a bath, and hot food—and make it quick!" He strode off down the hallway, leaving the shocked servant with his mouth agape.

To his weary annoyance, every servant in the castle seemed to come out at once. There were cries of joy, screams of delight, even gasps of horror. As they all fussed and cried, Cecil, having recovered from his shock, appeared from behind to save his young master from the barrage. He expressed Jarreth's gratitude for their concern, but explained the master desperately needed rest. They finally dissipated, some to fetch food, some to start heating the water for his bath. Jarreth acknowledged his thanks with a nod to Cecil, and continued his trek down the hall.

As he passed his uncle's study, the open door made him pause. Not knowing why, he entered and gazed around the room, basking in the familiarity, and finally focused on the desk. He had to smile when he saw his letter lying there, positioned importantly in the middle so the count would see it when he returned. The humor of the situation suddenly hit him. He sat in his uncle's chair, leaned back, and began to laugh.

"A lot of good the letters did," he mused. The laughter made him feel better, considering the circumstances. As if on cue, Cecil happened by the study and saw him sitting there. He hesitated, and then entered just inside the door.

"Your bath is being prepared, Lord Jarreth. Is there anything else I can do for you?"

"Aye, Cecil, there is." He sat back up and waved the letter. "Do you know anything about this?"

Cecil looked the letter over, and shook his head. "No, sire. It must have come by messenger, and was put here for the count upon his return. Why?"

"Because 'tis from me."

"Oh, no!" He brought a hand to his mouth in horror. "I knew not that you sent a message. I am so sorry, sire!"

"'Tis not your fault, Cecil. I told the courier to give it only to the count, so in a way 'tis my fault. I was not thinking he might be absent. Do you know where he is?"

"No, sire. He left last fall with the lady Rhiannon and her father. He said only that they would not be returning until the spring."

"And he did not leave his whereabouts?"

"No, he said 'twould not be necessary."

"Wonderful." He leaned back again and closed his eyes; he was virtually without clues. If his uncle had not confided in Cecil, it was unlikely that anyone knew his plans. "Thank you, Cecil. That will be all."

After a large meal and hot bath Jarreth fell into an exhausted sleep, his last thoughts being of Rhiannon.

Ramon arrived back early the next morning with a wagon full of supplies. Some livestock had taken ill, and Ramon had been treating them with a certain mash of which he ran out. As he unloaded the wagon, he was surprised to find the entire servant staff all abuzz with news of Jarreth's return. At first he didn't believe it, then his thoughts turned to the memory of Jarreth's threat of death the next time they

Rhiannon

met. Surely he wasn't still angry? Uncertain how to handle this latest turn of events, Ramon stayed in the barn out of sight while he thought of a plan. He had to talk with Jarreth, but how to approach him? His gaze fell on Daemon, and he smiled.

Jarreth was eating breakfast when a small figure appeared in the doorway. It was the young groom he had nearly frightened to death the night before. The boy cleared his throat until Jarreth gave him notice.

"Aye, what is it?"

"Your presence is requested in the courtyard, milord."

The boy's attempt to be formal made Jarreth smile. "Is that so? May I ask who is requesting?"

"The Gypsy, sire."

The smile disappeared. "Gypsy? What Gypsy?"

"His name is Ramon, milord."

That got Jarreth to his feet. "Ramon? He is here?" He raised an eyebrow as he tried to think of one reason the Gypsy whose life he spared would be showing up in his courtyard demanding his presence. The only reason he could fathom was the Gypsy wanted more money. Well, this time Rhiannon was not there to save his worthless hide.

"Go tell your Gypsy he would leave immediately if he knew what was good for him. Tell him…"

He stopped when he noticed the boy's confused look. "Never mind, I shall tell him myself." He waved the lad off.

A smile surfaced as he strapped on his sword. He should have killed this man the first time he had met him, when the fool was holding a knife to Rhiannon's throat. If it hadn't been for Rhiannon…He closed his eyes and let out a deep breath, distracted momentarily. *Rhiannon. I have to find her.*

He shook the thought away to get back to the matter at hand, and lumbered down the corridor that led to the courtyard. When he opened the door, no amount of preparation could have minimized the shock of the sight before him.

Daemon stood in the center of the courtyard, his black coat gleaming in the morning sun, pawing the ground in anticipation of his morning exercise. He was well muscled and healthy with no visible signs of injury. His long, thick tail swished nervously as he tossed his great head, impatient to be held in one position. Jarreth blinked. Was he still sleeping, and this was just a dream?

"Daemon," he whispered, then louder repeated, "Daemon?" He took off in a run toward his trusted companion. The great horse recognized him and nickered in response while pulling at the rope Ramon held. Ramon let him go, and Daemon took off in a fast trot to his master. They met half way. Ramon felt his eyes getting misty as he watched the reunion between man and horse. It was hard to tell which one was happier to see the other.

Jarreth wrapped his arms around the great horse's neck and hugged him like a child would a treasured pet. No words were necessary as he buried his head in the horse's silky mane; indeed he was so choked with emotion he doubted he could speak if he had to.

Ramon sighed in relief; he was counting on this reaction. Perhaps now Jarreth wouldn't be so inclined on killing him.

Jarreth finally regained his composure and led the horse back to Ramon. "You did this?" he asked, motioning to Daemon.

Ramon shrugged. "I did a little. It was your Rhiannon who gave him the will to live."

Jarreth laughed; he should have known as much. "He is beautiful. I never expected to see him again."

"I could say the same for you." Ramon folded his arms and gave Jarreth a droll smile.

The grin sobered into seriousness. "She thinks me dead?"

Rhiannon

"Yes, she does. She sent for me to help your horse. He was injured quite badly."

"I know. So was I." Jarreth fought to hold the break in his voice. "This must have been horrible for Rhiannon. I have to find her, but no one knows where she is."

There was a long pause as Ramon carefully considered his next action. Finally he decided he had no choice. "I do."

Jarreth stopped breathing. For a few seconds the world seemed to come to a complete stop. "What did you say?"

"I know where she went. She left me this." He handed Jarreth the carefully written directions that Rhiannon had given him.

Jarreth took the note and read it with a confused grimace. "Wales? What the hell is she doing in Wales?" He glanced up at Ramon. "Do you know why she went there?"

Ramon paused. Telling him Rhiannon's location was one matter; telling him why she went there was another. He didn't feel he had the right to divulge that information. He carefully worded his answer to avoid the question. "Your *death* distressed her greatly. She needed to get away."

Jarreth was grinning as he re-read the note, and took no heed to the evasive answer. "I can find this place. It shall take me a while to get there, but I have Daemon to carry me." The thought of another long trip so soon after days of travel would have ordinarily made him cringe. This time the prize was invaluable; he would travel to the ends of the earth to find Rhiannon. "Have a groom prepare him for travel. I shall leave as soon as I can pack." He bounded off to the castle with renewed hope.

Ramon broke into a smile as he watched the excited viscount. Perhaps it was contemptible not to tell him about Rhiannon's condition, but he would find out soon enough. No need of him worrying the whole trip. Besides, he could still remember what it felt like to have the viscount's huge arm wrapped around his throat. He figured he owed Jarreth one.

Jarreth took two steps at a time as he ran up the stairs to his room. He didn't plan to rest much along the way, so he could pack light. But there one item that was a necessity. He went to his dresser and pulled open the top drawer. Then he took out a small box. He opened it and stared at the brilliant ring, the only thing he had left of his mother. He had planned on presenting it to Rhiannon before their wedding. He let out a captured breath, and stuffed the box into a pocket.

Kady winced as she watched her young mistress, heavy with child, amble down the stairs. Always the mother hen, Kady was terrified something was going to happen to Rhiannon and her unborn child. She had observed maturation in her over the past few months. Rhiannon was no longer the spoiled, carefree spirit Kady had always known. The only thing that mattered now for the expectant mother was her baby. Nothing was done for herself, she ate for the baby, took naps for the baby, and even drank a horrible-tasting concoction the midwife said was nourishing for the baby. She read the bible every day and spent time in prayer, praying for a healthy baby. Kady was sure that this would be the most beautiful baby ever born, at least it had better be after all Rhiannon was going through. When Rhiannon reached the bottom stair, Kady gave her a condescending look, her hands on her hips.

"I told you to wait. You know I do not like you coming down the stairs without me!"

"For heaven's sakes, Kady—I am pregnant, not crippled."

"You are not just pregnant—you are *very* pregnant. Which means you have to execute some precaution."

Rhiannon dismissed her comment with a wave of her hand. "I am fine. Yet, I must admit I will be glad when this baby is out here instead of in *here*." She pointed to her swollen belly. "Are you ready for our walk?"

Rhiannon

Kady made a disapproving face. "I still do not think…"

"Oh, now you are not going to start that again? I told you as soon as the weather turned nice I refused to be confined to this house. Well, the weather is nice and I am going for a walk. The baby needs fresh air."

"Aye, the baby," Kady repeated with a slight sarcastic tone. "All right, if I cannot talk some sense into you, at least bring your wrap. 'Tis still a little chilly, and the seashore is always windy."

"Agreed." Rhiannon paused, then looked at her best friend with teary eyes. "Thank you Kady, for being here for me. I do not think I could have done this without you."

"Oh, balderdash—you would not have had a choice. With or without me, that baby would be born."

Count Stanwyck and the baron entered the room at that point, loudly arguing some political matter until they saw Rhiannon. Their demeanor instantly changed to affection and pleasantness, which they had worked hard at conveying throughout the last few months.

"Sweetheart," the baron said with a large smile. "How is my little girl this fine morning?"

"Not so little, I fear. I grow bigger by the second. I feel like a cow."

The count chimed in with his comments. "Nonsense, me dear, you look radiant."

Rhiannon nodded with a tight smile. She felt as if she was the cause of everyone's anxiety. She was weary of being fussed over, as if she were a valuable commodity that must be protected at all cost. Sometimes she felt smothered by all the advice they all seemed so anxious to bestow. Do this, do not do that; it was an endless cacophony of opinions that all meant well, but served to only depress her even further. Once the baby was born, her life would take on a new meaning. Jarreth's child would be denied nothing. She would live out her life at Stanwyck castle, raising the child as Jarreth's heir. Her own dreams were now dead; she owned Jarreth that.

Evangelynn Stratton

"She insists on taking a walk on the beach," Kady stated, hoping one of the men would be able to talk her out of it.

"Do you think that wise, sweetheart?" the baron asked. "'Tis windy on the beach. You could catch a chill."

To her surprise, the count sided with her. "Oh, let her go, Cedric. For heaven's sake, the child has been cooped up in this house all winter. Just dress warmly, dear," he added, not to be outdone in his concern, "and watch your step on the trail."

"Well, I still think..." her father started.

Rhiannon gave them both a kiss on the cheek. "Thank you, uncle. And you, father, quit worrying. I am fine. Come Kady, before they change their minds and tie me up in the cellar." The girls left the men to their arguing.

Rhiannon was quiet as they slowly descended the gently sloping trail that led to the shore. The sun shone down brightly; she closed her eyes and enjoyed the warmth. Little things that she used to take for granted were now special gifts that were doled out sporadically. The screech of a seagull, the smell of the salty ocean, a seashell washed up on the beach, all were treasured moments that could never be relived. If only she had considered her moments with Jarreth as such. If only she could have been less spoiled, less stubborn. If only...

Back at the manor, the count and the baron exchanged their views on the proper construction of a moat. The baron thought width was of utmost importance; the count considered the depth more significant. Since they rarely agreed on anything, the staff ignored their rather heated discussions and came and went without notice. So it was simply an annoyance when the two men heard a commotion at the door. At first they disregarded the loud exchanges that filtered into their room, but suddenly the count stopped talking and held up his hand to quiet the baron.

Rhiannon

"Did you hear that," he asked. "That voice—it sounds like…" He shook his head with a chagrined grimace. "Now I am hearing things. I could swear that voice is…"

"I said, let me in!"

The loud command could not be mistaken this time. The count jumped to his feet.

"By the saints, could it be?" He took off for the door with the confused baron following. They arrived in the entranceway to find four servants attempting to hold back an angry, very determined Jarreth. He had at least a two-week growth of beard, and by his looks had been riding non-stop for quite some time. The frightened servants thought him a madman as he yelled his insistence to be let in.

"Leave him be! He is my nephew!"

The servants all turned to look at the flabbergasted count. Jarreth looked at his uncle, and produced a crooked smile.

"Hello, Uncle. I am back."

Chapter Twenty-two

The dumbstruck count could not speak at first; he simply stared at Jarreth as if he were witnessing a ghost. Jarreth had to finally jar him back to reality.
"Well, uncle—are you not to welcome me back from the dead?"
The baron had no problem finding his voice. "How is this possible? We were told you were killed!"

Jarreth pushed his way through the confused servants to stand beside his uncle. "The assumption of my death was based on faulty observation. As you can see, I am quite alive. Uncle, you may speak any time."

Still unable to talk, the overcome count pulled Jarreth into a tight hug, constricting back the tears threatening to flow down his face. "I thought you were dead," he eventually managed to say between restrained choking gasps. "I thought you were dead."

Jarreth was a bit bewildered by his uncle's display of emotion, and patted him on the back in a reassuring manner. "'Tis all right, uncle. I understand your shock, but as it turns out I was simply sent to a hospital. I had a slight injury in my back."

Rhiannon

The count drew back, composing himself as best he could. "Injury? Are you all right?"

"No, I am not. I want to see Rhiannon. Where is she?"

The baron stepped up and put a hand on Jarreth's arm. "Er, Rhiannon is not exactly the same as you remember. She has changed a little."

"Tell me nothing," Jarreth demanded. "We have a lot to make up. I want our reunion to be fresh, with no knowledge of the other's pain."

The count cleared his throat. "I have to agree with Cedric—there is something you should know about her."

"I said *nothing*!" Jarreth raised his voice enough to make the on-listening servants jump. "Just tell me where she is!"

"But..." the baron stammered. Jarreth's ardent glare made him stop and shrug. "Very well. She is taking a walk on the beach."

"Show me," Jarreth demanded.

The count took his arm and guided him to the back door as the baron followed. "There is a trail that leads down to the beach between those shrubs—do you see it? Follow that down, and you shall find her. And Jarreth—be gentle. She has been through a lot."

"I am aware of that, uncle. So have I." He rushed off to find the trail, leaving his uncle and the baron shaking their heads. What would his reaction be when he saw her heavy with his child?

Rhiannon and Kady had walked a good distance when a sailing ship caught their attention. Rhiannon was fascinated, of course, and had to stop to watch the ship make its way across the horizon. As she wondered what exciting places it would visit, sadness washed over her with the realization that she would never fulfill her dreams.

Kady happened to turn to see the dark figure approach from behind. When he got closer recognition set in, and she turned white while taking a stumbling, astonished step backward. He put a finger to his lips and motioned for her to leave; she nodded her compliance. Rhiannon was still enthralled with the ship, and took no notice when Kady slipped silently away.

Suddenly Rhiannon detected a presence, one quite familiar but long unfelt. She slowly turned, fearful that her emotions were once again producing impossible sensations. Instead she looked into Jarreth's eyes. Dressed all in black, his long cape whipping behind him, he appeared as a specter sent to haunt her.

He matched her astonishment as he gazed at her face, then down at her bulging belly. Even her loose-fitting gown could not disguise her very pregnant state. Words were not needed; their eyes said everything. He smiled as he absorbed the situation, watching the wind toss her flowing hair about her radiant face. The only sound was the surf lapping up around their feet. Finally Rhiannon reached out to feel his cheek, stopping just short of actually touching him.

"Are you real?" she practically whispered.

He reached out slowly and grasped her hand, erasing the possibility that he was just an image. "As real as our child within you." He gently kissed her hand, and then pulled her to him. "Oh Rhiannon, I have missed you."

She burst into tears as he took her into his arms. "They told me you were dead," she said between sobs. "I—I did not know what to do."

"I am here now, and I will never leave again." He cupped her face lovingly and kissed it all over as she cried out her happiness and pain.

"I am sorry," she sobbed. "I was so stupid."

He silenced her with a kiss. "I was stupid, also. At least we were stupid together."

That got a tiny laugh combined with her tears. "I never wanted you to go. I was too stubborn to give in." She again burst into heaving sobs. "I am so sorry. 'Tis all my fault."

He held her as close as possible, considering her new-gained girth, and tried to calm her as his own tears stung his eyes. "I am sorry, too. It

Rhiannon

was equally my fault. I was bull-headed." His voice lowered to a more serious tone. "Rhiannon, look at me, love."

She lifted her tear-streaked face and gazed into his hurting eyes.

"I caused you pain, Rhiannon. For that I beg your forgiveness."

She managed to smile just a little. "There is nothing to forgive. 'Tis I who should beg your forgiveness."

He kissed her gently as she tried to control herself, causing deep shudders to wrack her body. "We are together, now. That is all that counts. You must calm yourself, or you will become ill."

She simply couldn't stop; the release from her pain had been withheld for so long she needed to cry it out. Her cries were piercing his heart; how could he have ever thought she didn't love him? How did he doubt so deeply? Did a greater fool ever live? At that moment, he doubted it.

A sudden gasp stopped her tears and she grabbed him for support. "I—I think I need to sit down."

She has made herself sick, he thought. "Of course. Here, be careful." He helped her sit in the soft, warm sand, away from the threat of the incoming surf. He sat beside her as she fought to control her shudders. She let out another gasp, and put a hand on her belly.

"The baby", she said with a shaky voice.

Jarreth's eyes widened in terror. "Are you all right?"

After a small pause, she nodded with a brave smile. "Aye, I am fine. I had a sharp pain, but 'tis gone."

He let out a sigh of relief. "See, even our child does not want you to cry." He put his hands on her abdomen and felt the huge hump. "Why did you not tell me?" His tone was more hurt than condemning.

"I did not know until after you had left."

"You have had to bear this alone. I should have been here for you."

"Where *have* you been?" Her eyes beseeched him with newly surfaced pain.

He took her hands in his and kissed them. "I was injured, and taken to a hospital."

"Injured? Are you…?"

"Aye, I am fine," he lied. His back still bothered him, often painful enough to force him to stop what he was doing and rest. He ignored it as much as possible. "Right now my only concern is for you. I think we need to…"

He was cut off by her sudden scream. "Jarreth?" she gasped. "I think the baby is coming."

"*Now*?"

"Aye."

He suddenly felt panic grip him. "Nay, not now! You are on a beach!"

"Tell that to the baby!"

He jumped to his feet and held out his hands. "Can you stand?"

"I think so." She let him pull her up when no sooner she was being lifted in his arms.

"Jarreth! What are you doing? I am too heavy, put me down!"

"Quiet, Rhiannon…our baby is not going to be born on a beach." He began carrying her back to the manor. "I swear, Rhiannon, this could only happen to you. Within minutes of our reunion, you decide to have a baby."

His teasing made her relax a little, and she let herself enjoy being held by the man she so desperately loved. "I do not think 'tis my decision. Augh!"

"Hold on, Rhiannon. We are almost there." He quickened his pace, leaping up the sloping trail into the back yard of the manor. The count, the baron, and Kady were all standing by the door discussing this latest turn of events when they saw them approach. Kady let out a horrified gasp and took off running to meet them.

"What happened? Is she all right?"

"I am not sure… she thinks the baby is coming."

Rhiannon

"*Now?*" Kady exclaimed.

"Now!" Rhiannon yelled.

The baron began wringing his hands and fussing; the count held the door open as Jarreth rushed in.

"We need a midwife," Jarreth barked, then stopped long enough to catch his uncle's gaze. "And a priest."

"A priest?"

"Aye, and hurry! My baby will not be born a bastard!"

The count slowly smiled as he finally caught Jarreth's meaning. "Oh, a priest! Aye, of course… there is one in the nearby vil…"

"Just fetch him!" he hollered, as he carried Rhiannon upstairs with Kady's guidance.

He carefully laid Rhiannon down on the bed while Kady ran off to fetch the midwife. The worthless baron stood in the hallway, still wringing his hands muttering, "Oh my, oh my." Within seconds the midwife entered, took one look at Rhiannon, and ordered Jarreth out of the room.

Jarreth simply raised an eyebrow as he gave the midwife an uncompromising look. "I think not, Madame. I have only just reunited with her, and I am not leaving."

"And just who are you?" she demanded sharply.

"I am the father of the child."

The midwife, set in her ways, put her hands on her hips and gave him an equally haughty look. "I have never delivered a babe with a father present, and I am not going to start now!"

"Then be prepared to physically remove me." He smiled smugly at the small, middle-aged midwife who could no more remove him than fly to the moon.

She began to sputter with indignation. "This is highly irregular! You simply have to leave, you will only be in the way!"

"I will stay on this end. I promise not to compromise the delivery."

Rhiannon held up a hand in an attempt to interrupt the sparring couple. "Excuse me—"

They both ignored her. "Men are useless during a birth—I simply cannot allow this!" the midwife continued.

"I fear you have no choice, Madame."

"*Excuse* me!" Rhiannon said louder, this time catching their attention. "I think something is happening!"

Jarreth jerked his head down to look at her, suddenly remembering the reason he was there. "Oh, Lord...hold on, Rhiannon" He turned back to the slightly embarrassed midwife, who in her entire twenty year practice had never ignored a patient to argue with the father. "Well, do something! Check her, or whatever 'tis you do!"

"Aye, aye...of course." She set to work while Jarreth sat down beside Rhiannon, facing her. "It will be all right. I am staying here with you."

She smiled bravely. "I am scared, Jarreth."

He took her hand and meekly smiled. "So am I."

A contraction hit her and she cried out, squeezing his hand in fright and pain.

"She broke her water," the midwife informed them in a mater-of-fact tone.

Jarreth narrowed his eyebrows. "Is that good?"

The midwife just shook her head and rolled her eyes, disgusted at the stupidity of men. "It means she has not got long. Do not push yet, darling."

The contraction subsided and Rhiannon relaxed, taking deep breaths as Jarreth wiped her brow. He felt extreme guilt that he was equally responsible for this baby, but Rhiannon was the one suffering.

"I am sorry for your pain," he said as he lovingly stroked her cheek. "I wish you could give it all to me."

"'Tis not your fault," she answered. "'Tis part of being a woman."

Rhiannon

He marveled at how much she had matured. Women having babies had always been a part of life, but he had never cared a whit about it. But this was different; this was Rhiannon, this was his baby.

She rested until another contraction came. As she cried in pain, all Jarreth could do was let her squeeze his hand. He had never felt so helpless in all his life, not even when he was lying on the battlefield immobilized with an arrow in his back.

Wondering why his uncle had not yet returned, he glanced at the door. "What is taking so long?" he muttered to himself, but was overheard by the midwife.

"You cannot hurry babies," she said, "although this one seems to be in a rush to come out. You can push now, honey."

Rhiannon bore down, her face straining with the tremendous effort. At that moment the door burst open and the count entered with the priest.

"Finally!" Jarreth barked. "Up here, Father."

The midwife stood up, her eyes wide with this further indignation being thrust upon her. "What are *they* doing here?" she demanded.

"They are also staying," Jarreth informed her.

"Now, really!" the midwife argued. "One man I can put up with, but three are out of the question!"

"Quiet, Madame," Jarreth said with authority. "I need the priest to get married, and my uncle as a witness."

The midwife threw up her hands and muttered a curse.

Rhiannon was resting from a contraction as he looked lovingly into her eyes. "Rhiannon, I asked you this once before, but things did not work out exactly as planned. I want to live my life with you and grow old together. Will you do me the honor of becoming my wife?"

She couldn't help but smile, the impulse to tease was overpowering. "Hmmm. I will have to think about it."

"Well, you better think fast," the midwife chimed in. "The baby is crowning."

Jarreth had no idea what that meant, but could tell by the midwife's urgent tone that he didn't have much time. He gave Rhiannon a stern look. "Rhiannon?" he asked solemnly.

Rhiannon smiled as she enjoyed the moment. "I suppose no other suitor will step up at this point. Oh, very well, if I must. Aye, I shall marry you." A contraction hit, and she screamed with this one.

The befuddled priest opened his book and began reading. "Dearly beloved, we are gathered her today to witness…"

"Push!" the midwife yelled.

"Go to the vows, father!" Jarreth said quickly. "I do not think we have much time!"

The priest nodded, and started turning pages as Rhiannon pushed and screamed.

"Do you…er, I do not believe I know your name." the priest said to Jarreth.

"Jarreth! My name is Jarreth, and hers is Rhiannon! Now, hurry!"

"Do you, Jarreth take this woman…"

"Push harder! The midwife yelled again.

"Aye, I do," Jarreth answered the priest, waving him on. "Hurry!"

The harried priest wiped his sweaty brow and nodded. This was the strangest ceremony he had ever performed, and ever would, he was sure. "Do you Rhiannon, take this man to be your…"

Rhiannon screamed.

"Say aye, Rhiannon! Please!"

"He did not finish the question," she answered through gritted teeth.

Jarreth gave her an incredulous look. "For God's sake, Rhiannon! We do not have time for that! Just say I do!"

"The question!" she said with a strained voice as she pushed.

Rhiannon

The priest decided to take matters in his own hands. If this couple were to be married before the baby was born, he would have to hurry. "Do-you-Rhiannon-take-this-man-to-be-your-lawfully-wedded-husband-if-so-say-I-do."

"I do!" she yelled through a strained voice.

"Push!" the midwife ordered.

The priest turned to Jarreth. "She needs a ring, now."

"Can we not worry about that later?"

"I want a ring!" Rhiannon yelled.

Jarreth let out an exasperated breath and began digging in his pockets. "I swear, Rhiannon, I will get even with you for this." He suddenly smiled and produced his mother's ring, holding it up triumphantly. "Here!" He put it on her finger.

Despite her present occupation, Rhiannon managed to look at the ring with a satisfied smile. "You actually brought one?"

"Of course I did. 'Twas my mothers. Hurry, Father!"

"This is it," the midwife shouted. "Push hard!"

"Then-by-the-power-vested-in-me-I-now-declare-you-man-and-wife!"

No sooner were his words out than the midwife yelled in glee. "Here it comes! It is a boy!"

The cry of the newborn filled the room as Jarreth laid his head on Rhiannon's chest and closed his eyes. "We did it," he said in a slightly amazed tone.

Rhiannon let out a short amused laugh. "*We?*"

The midwife brought the bloody, wrinkled newborn up to them for a quick look. "He needs to be cleaned up, but this is what all the fuss was all about." Despite the unusual birth, she was very pleased with the easy delivery.

Everyone gazed at the baby in wonderment, with silly smiles. Jarreth reached out and stroked the baby's wet hair. "He is beautiful." He looked at his exhausted wife, who was gazing upon the baby in total awe. "Thank you, Rhiannon, for our son."

The count and the priest simply wiped their tears, and headed for the door to joyfully announce the new arrival to the Stanwyck family.

The midwife whisked the baby away as Jarreth gave Rhiannon a gentle kiss. "Only you, Rhiannon. Only you could become a wife and mother in the same minute."

She smiled widely. "More like the same second."

He chortled against her bosom. "I always knew my life would never again be boring the moment I met you, but I certainly never anticipated this."

"I suppose I could make an effort to change."

He raised his head quickly, his smile gone. "Do not dare! I love you for every ounce of mischief within you."

"I believe that is quite a lot."

"Aye, but I love you all the same. Promise you shall never change."

"Only if you promise never to leave me again."

"Agreed." He noticed her heavy eyelids, and almost forgot she just had a baby. "You need to rest. While you sleep, I will tend to Daemon. I left him out front when I arrived."

Her eyes lit up. "You brought him? Ah, of course, Ramon told you where I was."

"Aye, but he left out the tiny detail of your condition, intentionally I believe." He let out a small snicker. "I shall have to talk to him when we return."

"Be nice, Jarreth. He saved Daemon."

"The way he told it, you were responsible more than he. Thank you, my wife." He cast his gaze to the ceiling as if deep in thought. "I like the sound of that. Wife. Aye, I think I can get used to that."

"Good, because now you are stuck with me, and a son."

Rhiannon

"Hmmm. Oh well, I guess if I am stuck, I am stuck." His expression changed to serious. "I love you, Rhiannon. Never forget that. I shall love you until my dying day."

"I have already lived through that day. Please make the next one a long time from now."

"I shall sincerely try."

He gently kissed her on the cheek, and watched her as she fell into an exhausted sleep.

Epilogue

The baron huffed and puffed as he hurried down the pier; he hated being late. The count was close behind, followed by several servants carrying all their luggage.

"This is crazy," the baron said, as he started up the gangplank that led to the ship. "What the heck are we doing, going to Africa? With our luck, we will probably be eaten by a lion our first day."

"Now, now, Cedric," the count answered. "This could be fun. Besides, no one is twisting your arm to go. You can stay if you like."

"And miss seeing my grandchild for an entire year? I think not!" He quickened his steps. "I just hope the ship does not leave without us!"

"That is not likely," the count offered. "I bought it."

Up ahead, Rhiannon motioned to the two servant girls behind her, lugging baggage for the baby. "Hasten your pace!" Rhiannon, of course, held the baby as she hurried up the gangplank. Jarreth was already on the ship, having checked out the quarters he and Rhiannon would be sharing for the trip. Kady and Elizabeth would be close by, as would his uncle and Rhiannon's father.

He smiled as he watched Rhiannon hand his baby son to Elizabeth. After the birth of their son, he and Rhiannon spent hours telling each other everything that had transpired while they were separated. When Rhiannon heard about Elizabeth, she demanded they send out search parties to look for her. It took months, but they found her at Newcastle

Rhiannon

Manor, reading recipes to the castle cook. The cook cursed them quite soundly when they took her away; it seems a rude guest abducted the last assistant the cook had. Elizabeth and Rhiannon became fast friends, and Kady was delighted in having some help keeping the baby busy and clean.

Jarreth was to draw animals; Rhiannon was going to write stories. Then they would put it all in a book and someday present it to the next king's son. Jarreth would deny Rhiannon nothing, and was determined all her dreams would become real to the best of his ability.

When everyone was settling in his or her quarters, Jarreth and Rhiannon stood at the stern as the ship made its way from the harbor into open sea. There was a strong wind to feed the sails, which billowed and relaxed as gusts hit them. He put his arm around her and pulled her close as they watched the town grow smaller and smaller.

"Look," Jarreth pointed out. "From out here you can see the whole town. There is the chapel, see the cross?"

"Aye," Rhiannon said as she scrunched her nose. "Did I ever tell you about the time I almost burnt down my father's new chapel?"

Jarreth raised an eyebrow. "Nay, I must have missed that one."

"Oh, 'tis nothing. Remind me to tell you sometime."

"How about now?" He smiled in anticipation.

"Well, my father had taken me to London, where we attended services in the huge cathedral there. I was enthralled with the altar boys who came out and lit the candles. When I was told that only boys could become altar boys, I decided that was highly unfair and decided to take matters into my own hands."

"Why am I not surprised?"

"Our builders had just completed our new chapel. I went there when 'twas empty, and lined up on the altar all the candles I could find. But I could not find the long lighter thingy to light the candles with."

Jarreth attempted to hide his amusement. "The long lighter thingy?"

"Aye. Anyway, I just used a long candle to light the others with, but the wax kept dripping down on my hand. So, I wrapped a cloth around the bottom of the candle to catch the drips. I had such a grand time, lighting and relighting the candles! In my distraction, I did not notice how fast the candle was burning."

Jarreth was already shaking his head. "Do not tell me…the cloth caught on fire."

"Aye, and in my hurry to keep my hand from also burning, I tossed the lit candle behind the altar. It caught the altar drapes on fire, which caught the altar itself on fire, which caught—"

"I think I get the picture."

"I thought father was going to have a conniption fit when he heard his new chapel was on fire. Luckily, the damage was confined to the altar area."

He gave her a gentle squeeze. "And what was your punishment this time?"

Her face fell into thoughtfulness. "I do not remember. I believe I was still being punished for the apple tree incident."

He looked at her incredulously. "Apple tree incident?"

"Did I not tell you about the apple tree?"

"Nay."

"Well, I still think 'twas an entire over-reaction on father's part."

As she went into her story, Jarreth felt the glow of love rush through him. He had a feeling it would be a long trip, and he wouldn't have it any other way.

*Author's note: Rhiannon's personality is a combination of my two daughters and me. The stories are both made up and exaggerations of my own childhood mishaps, except for the candle-lighting incident at the end, which is based on a true event. The author does not wish to divulge who was involved in that particular event, except that she can still feel her mother's hand on her behind from almost burning down the house. I think it was an entire over-reaction on my mother's part.

Historical note: The Wars of the Roses flared up again as soon as Richard came to the throne. In 1483 he put down a rebellion led by the duke of Buckingham, and had the duke beheaded. In 1485 Henry Tudor landed in Wales with an army he had raised in France. The two armies clashed at Bosworth Field after many of Richard's men had deserted him. Richard fell, and the crown was picked up and placed on Henry's head.

For more stories written in this historic time, read the LADY trilogy, LADY KNIGHT, LADY SEER, and LADY BLUE.

Comments? E-mail the author! *Evangelynn@Knightimes.com*

Watch for the latest by Evangelynn Stratton

Vain Wish

A modern Fantasy

An overweight girl makes a wish, and the next morning finds it fulfilled. But are the consequences worth it? A must read for any woman who has ever struggled with her weight, and wished for a miracle.

Printed in the United States
3874